# LIGHTBRINGER

# LIGHTBRINGER

THE LIGHT THIEF, BOOK 3

DAVID WEBB

First paperback edition June 2020

ISBN 978-1-7343511-3-2 (paperback)

www.jdavidwebb.com

This book is dedicated to Myriah Grabish.

You are the only reason this book released on time,
and I'm forever grateful for all your hard work.

Thank you for reading, helping, and talking me off a ledge.

We must pass through the darkness to reach the light.

— ALBERT PIKE

# PROLOGUE

A man sat in the stadium of the silver coliseum, observing the scene as it unfolded before him.

The criminal waited in the dirt arena below, his hands tied behind him and his head drooping. He stood facing a dozen silver-clad men, each one carrying a loaded gun.

As compelling as the impending punishment was, what was more pressing was the man in black armor who stood near the entrance of the arena, talking to a man in silver.

The observer's eyes narrowed. This was highly irregular. They had already taken the girl. Were they here for the boy now as well?

The Silver Guard officer nodded and marched toward his firing squad, leaving the man in black by the entrance. The observer's suspicions seemed to be confirmed. They were going to take the boy as well.

He placed his head in his hands. After everything had worked out so well, it would all be for nothing.

But the Silver made no move to free the boy. Rather, he pulled his own gun from his holster and checked the ammunition.

The observer's skin tingled. There was still hope.

But what about the soldier? He wouldn't waste his time down here if it were not critical.

The observer got up and made his way through the stands, gently nudging his way past recruits and instructors alike. They barely seemed to realize he was there. All eyes were on the convicted man standing in the center of the arena.

He descended the stairs to the dirt floor. Only an electric fence separated him from the impending execution, a thin barrier that encompassed the combat arena. He skirted the edge of the fence and walked around until reaching the main entrance, and it was then that he recognized the man.

"Jebediah?"

The soldier in black armor turned to him, and a flash of recognition swept across his face. "Good to see you, sir. It's been too long."

"What are you doing here? A soldier of the Director must have better things to do, no?"

Jebediah looked back toward the arena. "I am here on business."

"Business? Of what nature?"

"I'm sorry, sir. That is classified." Jebediah looked intently ahead, his nose twitching as he shifted in place.

The observer frowned. "I trained you, Jebediah. You were a lanky boy when you came to me, and despite your physical limitations, I shaped your mind. I taught you to win with your wits rather than your muscles. I turned you into the best soldier of your class. Without me, you would be here in the Underworld, enforcing curfew and giving citations. You owe me an explanation."

"Why do you care so much?" Jebediah finally turned to the man again. "The Director has the right to demand status updates whenever he wishes."

"Status updates are not classified," the observer quickly retorted. "I ask again, what is your business here, Private?"

Jebediah scowled. "It's sergeant now. And while

I'm grateful for everything you've done for me, I don't answer to you anymore. Now, please return to your seat before I am forced to remove you from the stadium."

The observer took a half-step back.

*I suppose that's what I get for turning him into an order-following drone.*

He opened his mouth to speak again, but a bright reflection caught the corner of his eye. He turned and looked down the entrance tunnel, then froze in place, spotting the assault weapons that the soldiers in the tunnel carried.

"No." The chills that ran down the man's spine were evident in his cracking voice as he uttered his disbelief. "You can't do this."

Jebediah's expression softened. "We have our orders, sir. We were not without hesitation, but in the end, we don't have a choice."

"I refuse to believe that." But even as the observer said it, he was beginning to make peace with the terrible duty the Director's soldiers had come to do. He was already analyzing the situation, preparing for the worst.

He stopped for a moment and turned to face his old pupil, frowning. "What are you waiting for, anyway?"

Jebediah nodded toward the arena.

The observer followed his gaze. The convict was now standing tall, facing thirteen guns pointed at his chest. He seemed to be speaking, but it was too far away for the observer to discern words.

"Why?"

The soldier shrugged. "Director's orders."

"Are you—"

The observer was cut short as multiple explosions sounded, and an intense heat fell on his back as a bright white light blasted through the arena. Jebediah howled in pain, covering his eyes, and as the light died away, the observer turned just in time to see the convicted man stumble backward and fall to the ground.

This was his moment, the observer knew. This was his only chance to stop the imminent massacre.

As the commotion continued, he turned and ran into the center of the arena, pushing past the Silvers that wandered around blindly, grasping at air and shouting for their comrades.

The boy lay in the very middle of the arena, a pool of blood forming below his body. Tiny shards of white light littered the ground surrounding him, a sparkling graveyard that was hauntingly beautiful.

The observer knelt by the boy's side and began his examination. He looked dead, to be sure, but the observer knew it didn't matter either way. He took the boy's hand and squeezed hard, wishing life into his cold flesh.

Shots rang out by the entrance, and the observer spun around to see a sea of black enter the stadium and fire openly at everyone in their path. The Silvers behind him had since fled, leaving him and the boy alone on the dirt.

The purge had begun.

"Come on, come on." The observer grabbed the boy's other hand and squeezed as hard as he could. After several pumps, he let go with his right hand and slapped the boy's face, ignoring the blood that squirted out in protest, shooting from a hole in the boy's jaw.

Suddenly, icy daggers shot through the observer's left wrist. He reflexively attempted to release the boy's hand, but immense pain gripped his muscles and contracted, cramping up his entire left arm and quickly spreading an excruciating cold throughout the rest of his body.

The observer looked down to see jagged red lines form on his left arm, pulsing with light and rippling toward the boy's hand. The pain became unbearable, and with every attempt to release himself, the pain intensified and pulled him closer to the boy's body.

Finally, the sensation ceased, and the observer wrenched his hand away before the process had a chance to begin again. There was no longer any feeling in his left arm, which was now ghostly pale. Even the hairs that rose from his skin and stood straight up were white.

Blood shot up from the boy's mouth like a fountain as he coughed violently, and by the time the observer wiped away the sticky red liquid from his face, the boy was looking back at him with wide eyes.

"What happened?" The boy's voice was just audible over the gunshots around them.

"No time." The observer quickly glanced around him.

Men in black armor swarmed the stadium like a horde of ants, gunning down recruits, instructors, and Silvers mercilessly.

He turned back to the boy. "I need your help, Nicholas."

"Nicholas?" The boy's eyes grew wide. "My name is Nikolai."

"Drop it. I know who you are. We both want the same thing, and we can help each other, but only if you do exactly as I say."

The boy shook his head. "You may think you know me, but I don't know you."

"My name is Caspian. I'm a friend of Aniya's."

At this, the boy's eyes glassed over as he stared off into space. "Aniya."

"We can talk later," Caspian said. "Now, get up."

Caspian stood and extended his right hand toward Nicholas, who grabbed it and started to stand, but as his legs began to bear weight, a pained look flashed across the boy's face and he fell to the ground again, taking Caspian with him.

"I can't," he said, his voice strained.

"You have to." Caspian gestured at the stadium. "They'll

kill us without a second thought. But you . . . you can kill them before they even touch us."

Nicholas shook his head. "That's not how it works." He nodded toward Caspian's left arm. "In case you haven't noticed, I have to be touching someone."

"I don't believe that's true," Caspian said. "Aniya can be quite destructive with her power without having to touch anyone. I believe you can as well."

"How do you know so much?"

"Doesn't matter. What matters is surviving this so we can help Aniya."

Nicholas looked up at the stadium, his eyes growing wider as he witnessed the brutal slaughter. His lip began to tremble, and his mouth slowly dropped open.

With another sharp slap, Caspian brought Nicholas back to reality, ignoring the daggers that raced across his skin. "Nicholas, it's now or never."

Nicholas's eyes cleared, and he turned back to Caspian. "I can't."

"Then we're dead." Caspian shrugged and turned. "Or at least you are. Surely you can't blame me for sticking around and waiting for them to finish off with everyone in the stands."

Caspian took one step before Nicholas spoke.

"Wait."

He turned back again. Nicholas was now kneeling on the dirt, blood soaking his pant legs. His eyes and fists were clenched tight, and his upper body was quivering.

Caspian looked at the stands and tapped his toe nervously. The soldiers in black had nearly finished their deadly search of the stands. Half the squadron was now wandering the seats, checking bodies to make sure they were dead.

It was remarkable that no one had bothered to check the arena yet. Maybe Jebediah had taken mercy on him as his former mentor and given the order to leave him alive.

But Caspian wasn't counting on that.

Nicholas gave a heavy sigh and released the tension in his body as he opened his eyes. "I can't."

"I have no reason to believe that your abilities work any differently than Aniya's, Nicholas." Caspian closed the gap between himself and the boy and grabbed his arms. "You can do this."

"I can't!" Nicholas shouted and slammed his fists into the dirt, sending shockwaves through the ground and a cloud of dirt into the air.

Caspian froze as the arena went quiet. The dirt surrounding them obscured his view, but the complete lack of sound proved that the soldiers were no longer focused on clearing the stands. "If you're going to do something, Nicholas, now's the time."

But Nicholas was staring at the ground, where his fists still lay. His eyes were wide, and he spoke softly, his voice trembling. "What do I do?"

"Think of Aniya, Nicholas. You're going to get her back." Caspian placed a hand on the boy's cheek. "And I'm going to help you."

Without a word, Nicholas slowly closed his eyes. As he leaned into the ground, the veins on his face grew dark red, bulging out and pulsing slowly. A low growl emitted from his throat, and as its volume escalated, so did the pace of his pulsing veins. His growl erupted into a massive shout, and Nicholas slammed his open hands down to the ground.

This time, the ground did not shake. Instead, red jagged lines shot out from Nicholas's palms and spread across the floor of the arena. They glowed orange like the embers of a dying fire, but as they grew brighter and brighter, their power was anything but dying.

The red streaks reached the electric fence, and the instant they touched the metal, lighting shot through every red streak and made its way back into Nicholas, sending his body into convulsions as electricity sparked across his body, his eyes flashing white.

Nicholas reached one hand up and released electricity from his fingertips, sending forked beams of red lightning into the stands. Caspian's eyes grew wide as the dust blew away in a gust of wind, revealing dozens of men in black armor surrounding them in the stands. As Nicholas swept his arm around in a circle, lightning struck each man, conducting electricity through their metal armor. Anyone Nicholas missed was targeted by the red streaks that continued to crawl through the stands. Anyone unfortunate enough to be touched by the streaks was rooted in place, shivering as their energy was sucked away.

Dots of sparkling white light danced over the ground and tumbled toward Nicholas. Caspian looked closer and realized that they were tiny shards of rock, a sort of crystal. These shards floated upward and swirled in front of his chest in a spiral.

Nicholas stood up, releasing his hand from the ground and letting the lightning die out. The only sounds in the air were the screams of the soldiers trapped in their superheated armor, the only smell their burning flesh. With a final shout, Nicholas slapped his hands together. In an instant, the shards floating by his chest snapped together, forming a complete crystal. From it sprang loose a massive flash of white light that shot out in a ring around Nicholas, just barely missing Caspian as he dove to the ground.

The light blasted outward and up into the stands, slicing anything in its path. Screams were cut short as bodies were split in two, the pitiful noise replaced by the thud of metal armor falling to the floor. The electric fence rocked for a brief moment before falling in on itself, snapping in several places and finally crashing to the ground just feet away.

Nicholas collapsed, leaving himself in the same position

Caspian had found him in, though this time, he was still holding on to life.

Caspian knelt by Nicholas's side and placed a hand on his shoulder. "Well done, Nicholas."

"Thanks," he said, wheezing. "That really took it out of me."

"I'm sure." Caspian looked up and down Nicholas's body. His wounds were still gushing blood, his skin retreating to a white color rapidly. Caspian had predicted this, but that wouldn't make it any easier.

"Why am I not healing? That's how this works, right? I hurt them, I get healed?"

Caspian shook his head. "I don't think so, Nicholas. It seems that ability is exclusive to Aniya. Only she can heal you."

"But when you woke me up, I felt better. It worked then. Why isn't it working now?"

"You felt better, yes, because of the energy you stole from me. But look at yourself, Nicholas. You're still injured. Gravely so, I might add. You have a hole in your jaw."

Nicholas raised a hand to his face, and the instant he touched the massive wound, he recoiled. He stumbled backward, looking down at his body and frantically running his hands over himself. "I don't understand. I feel fine. Help me, Caspian. Fix me."

Caspian slowly shook his head again. "I'm afraid I can't."

"You said you'd help me!" Nicholas lunged forward and grabbed Caspian's lapels. His voice was frantic now, his eyes wild.

Caspian slipped away from Nicholas's grasp before he could touch his skin, and he took a long step backward. "I'm sorry, Nicholas."

Tears began to fall down Nicholas's cheek as he fell to his knees. "But Aniya . . . She needs us. She needs me. You said you'd help me."

"And help you I will. The only way I can." Caspian bit his lip. Without another word, he drew his gun and fired a round into Nicholas's forehead.

Nicholas's face froze in confused shock. His outstretched hand slowly receded, and he crashed to the ground, dead.

Caspian placed the gun back at his side and took a deep breath.

"We've got a lot of work to do."

# PART I

# REVIVAL

**1**

---

THREE YEARS LATER

"**G**areth, no!"

Roland reached out toward the doctor, but his old mentor was just out of reach. Instead, he looked at Roland with a sad smile, nodding firmly before turning to mount a mole.

"You don't have to do this!"

Gareth ignored him, kicking the mole and dashing off into the trainyard.

"Don't leave me!"

An explosion rocked the ground, sending Roland flying backward. He fell away from the trainyard and into nothingness.

He fell for several seconds before sitting up abruptly in bed, his eyes flying open.

The abyss was gone, but the dark remained. Not a single torch was lit, not even a candle. But the pitch black had become his home over the past three years, and it no longer bothered him.

His eyes adjusted quickly, and his heart slowed down, a smile creeping over his face as a beautiful twenty-year-old woman appeared by his side. Her faint snores made Roland's smile grow bigger.

Careful not to wake her up, Roland grabbed the spear by his side and stepped over her body and out into the campsite, grabbing a satchel from the ground outside the tent and strapping the spear to his back before continuing on. He would have much preferred a gun, but they had run out of ammunition a long time ago.

The dying embers from the night before cast a tiny glow that was just far enough away that it made no difference in the overwhelming darkness. No matter. Roland had become quite familiar with the path over the years, and he walked toward the border of the campsite with ease.

He grabbed a torch from the oil basket and swiftly struck his pocket flint against a nearby rock, sparking the torch and lighting it ablaze instantly. Roland quickly drew the flaming torch in front of his chest, using his body to shield the campsite behind him from the light.

Roland shoved the flint back in his pocket and continued on the path, leaving the campsite and his sleeping beloved behind.

He stopped briefly and glanced to the right, chills racing over his spine. The Host's campsite was just a half-mile away, too close for comfort.

The Host. Even after three years, what was left of Refuge could only guess as to what they were. Mutated humans? People driven mad by isolation and darkness? No one knew for sure, not even Salvador, who had already lived among them for months.

But as horrific as their appearance and behavior was, they had always seemed apathetic enough toward Refuge, even friendly to people like Tamisra who were not put off by their nature.

Roland squinted through the darkness, studying the Host's campsite. It was dead silent, as always, and the taste of blood permeated the air, even at this distance.

Even the moles seemed reluctant to step anywhere near the silent natives of this Web. Back home on the level above, the moles were more than comfortable to ride all the way into Refuge, content to be tied to posts while the rider went on foot, but here in the level below, the moles were perpetually uneasy. At first, Roland thought it was due to the unfamiliar territory. But he had soon realized that they didn't like the Host any more than he did.

Roland looked away from the Host's campsite, shuddered, and continued along his path.

Unlike Holendast, access to the caves was simple. All blockades had been destroyed years ago, keeping the entries open and free for all citizens, the exception, of course, being the massive train tunnel that spiraled up to the Over-world. That would always remain heavily guarded by the Host, as well as the elevator in the Hub.

And so, Roland entered the tunnels without difficulties. Here, the torch was necessary. There were too many side tunnels and debris to risk traveling in the dark. Only the Host could be so bold. They never seemed to need the light.

It was technically forbidden for anyone to travel this far out alone unless they were part of an authorized hunting party. It was a decision that Corrin and Lieutenant Haskill had come to not long after Refuge's arrival in Level XIX.

The Host felt more than comfortable roaming about as they pleased, but for the people of Refuge, unfamiliar to this Web, it was for their own safety. There were more than moles that lurked in the darkest parts of this level.

Roland agreed with this ruling, but he couldn't bring himself to comply. Someone had to venture into the caves and hunt for food, and he wasn't about to let someone else fight for him.

Not again.

No one else would die for him. This was his duty, regardless of the consequences.

Roland reached a split in the tunnel and paused. To the left was the offshoot he had always chosen, marked by the smear of yellow glowworm juice. Ignoring his dilemma briefly, Roland let his fingers trace the shape of the four-fingered hand. He had left this mark two years ago, when he first decided to go hunting by himself. No artificial light shone down here, and it seemed that without intrusion, the light of a glowworm, even a dead one, lasted much longer than he thought.

Of course, it may have had something to do with the more intense radiation on this level. He once thought that the only difference was the color, yellow rather than the green he had come to know on the level above. But the glimmer seemed richer, more vibrant than the green glowworms from back home.

Roland sighed and looked back up. The choice remained before him. The tunnel opposite his regular path was dark, untouched. It hadn't mattered in the past. He had always managed to find wild moles down the tunnel to his left. There was no reason to ever deviate from his pattern. But in the past few months, it had taken longer to find food. The last time he went hunting, he had been forced to retreat to the camp empty-handed.

He took a deep breath and continued down the dark path to his right. There was no choice, and any time he spent pretending there was would be time wasted, just like if he chose a path that had nothing but more dirt at the end of it.

Before going too far, Roland withdrew a pouch from his satchel and pulled from it a wriggling yellow worm, illuminating the immediate area. After whispering a quick "thank you," he quickly squeezed the worm's head between his thumb and fore-finger, and the worm moved no more. Roland had long since become comfortable with the necessary sacrifice in order to bring light, and he no longer grew squeamish with the small act of violence, only thankful for the light it would provide.

He swiped his thumb on the cave wall to his right, leaving a streak of yellow light on a protruding rock. It would be enough to spot from a distance. No need to waste any more juice than he had to.

Roland continued on for several minutes, occasionally pressing his thumb into the worm's body before making another mark. Minutes stretched into a full hour, and as the time passed, regret sank into Roland's heart as he realized that this path would likely be just as fruitful as his regular route. The moles had simply moved on to a different part of the Web.

His spirits fell further as he spotted a yellow glow in the distance. He had managed to turn himself around, and he was now heading back the way he came. With a heavy heart, Roland marched toward the glow. His stomach growled, which just made him dread the night's inevitable hunger even more.

Roland quietly reminded himself that it could always be worse, but as he approached the marking, the reminder instantly became very real. The marking was on his right. He hadn't gotten turned around; he had merged with the other tunnel, and he was now treading on the same ground he had traveled for the last three years.

With a long sigh, he turned and walked back toward the tunnel entrance, knowing that he was far enough that the journey before him had to be at least another two hours. It was possible that his path had been indirect enough that the way back would be shorter on this path, but if today had taught Roland anything, it was that it wasn't worth getting his hopes up.

He didn't make it five minutes before a quiet rumble perked his ears. The sound was familiar, and what once made his legs tremble now stirred his excitement and made him forget about the pain in his stomach, knowing that he would have a full belly tonight.

Roland slowly stepped forward as the rumble grew louder. His heart raced as he anticipated the coming fight. It was almost impossible to kill a sleeping mole because it slept in such a position that its vulnerable spots were thoroughly covered. He had to be careful to wake up the mole gently but fast enough to kill it before it realized what was going on. If the mole managed to stir fully from its slumber, its fury would far surpass that of one already awake, and it would be far more difficult to kill.

As Roland played out the fight in his mind, he almost didn't realize that the rumbling noise was getting quieter. It scared him at first to think that the mole was waking up already before Roland was in position, but he quickly realized that he had simply passed the sleeping beast.

Confused, he turned around and looked back at the tunnel. He stretched the torch out in front of him and peered into the darkness. There were no side tunnels he could see.

Roland carefully made his way back the way he had come until he found the point in the tunnel where the rumbling was the loudest. In a near-panic, he spun around, trying to pinpoint the sound. It seemed to be coming from all around him.

Suddenly, the sound vanished.

Holding his breath, Roland leaned up against the cave wall and pressed his ear to the rock, listening for the sound again. Finally, the rumble returned, but with it, the cave wall trembled and seemed to push against his hands.

Roland stumbled backward and held the torch in the air.

Sure enough, the large posterior of a mole was barely jutting out of the cave wall, unnoticeable at first glance and barely distinguishable even now that Roland knew it was there. The animal had apparently burrowed into the spot for a quick nap.

Roland winced. Safely waking the mole was now next to impossible. The beasts tended to kick out their limbs as they woke, which meant that a large paw to his face seemed inevitable if he tried to wake the monster now.

But Roland knew it had to be done.

He set the torch on the ground further down the tunnel and pulled the spear from his back. Gently, he wedged the sharpened point under the beast's back right paw, pulling it out gently and slowly slicing the mole's exposed flesh. The thick outer layer was sensitive enough to ensure the mole felt some sensation, yet tough enough that the cut felt like a tickle to the giant animal.

The mole twitched its paw as the rumble escalated into a quiet growl, and Roland doubled back quickly, bracing for the impending blow that never came.

Roland tossed the spear to the side and stepped forward again. Taking a deep breath, he banged his fists on the mole's scaly armor as hard as he could, ignoring the jarring sensation that shot up his bones as his hands rebounded against the metal-like shell.

The vibrations, dulled as they were by the beast's thick skin, were enough to wake it, and the mole slowly extracted itself from its alcove and stepped backward into the tunnel, slowly shaking its large head.

Now was the time to strike. The mole was still tired enough that its movement would be sluggish. Roland took advantage of this and snatched his spear from the cave floor and brandished it, ready to strike. But before he could lunge forward, a sickening smell drifted through the tunnel and nearly made him wretch.

His hesitation was enough that the mole had enough time to shake loose its slumber and stretch to its full size. Roland forgot about the smell as the monstrous creature seemed to grow before him, expanding to a much larger size than he had anticipated.

Roland shook himself and lunged forward with the spear, but it was too late. The roar that came from the creature was deafening, enough to shake the ground and make Roland lose his balance, dropping the spear to the ground.

The beast didn't wait for him to recover, instead charging forward, its open mouth leading the way with teeth the size of Roland's fist.

Roland spun around and took off down the tunnel, snatching up the torch as he ran. He paused briefly to turn around and thrust the torch in the beast's face, but the animal's rage was such that the hypnotic light didn't seem to register in its mind. It seemed to want only one thing, and the promise of food seemed to outweigh the trance-like effect that fire usually had on the animals' minds.

The beast lunged forward and snapped his teeth at Roland's arm, who pulled back his hand quick enough to avoid losing a limb, but not the torch. The caves went dark as the flame disappeared into the mole's mouth, extinguished by the thick saliva that dripped to the ground below.

The mole paused briefly to spit out the oil-covered tip, and Roland took this opportunity to turn and make a mad dash down the tunnel, desperately searching for the next yellow streak to run toward.

It wasn't long before the tunnel began shaking again, and Roland pushed harder in the pitch black. It would be a miracle if he could run for any length of time without tripping over a rock in the darkness. Even if the way was clear, however, the mole was certainly faster. His only hope would be to lose the beast in the winding tunnels as they grew smaller.

Even then, it wouldn't take much effort for the mole to burrow through the tunnel and make a larger path toward its prey.

Roland passed one yellow mark and ran blindly toward where he hoped the next one would be. Unfortunately, he guessed incorrectly and ran straight into the cave wall and bashed his forehead into a protruding rock. Blood poured down his face as he stumbled to the ground. A cold feeling swept over his body, numbing the feeling of the shaking ground as the monster closed in on his body.

## 2
---

The man in the white cloak lingered in the alley behind the outpost.

His bright, spotless outfit would have drawn attention back home, but in the city, it was the perfect camouflage. Everything was white here. The light from the Overworld's sky ceiling reflected the stark color of the city, causing a white glow to permeate the air in a constant, gentle glare.

A chime alerted the man, startling him briefly. He looked up and watched the ticker crawl across the sky ceiling.

Something about the Council's most recent legislation scrolled by in a long string of words, which the man knew seemed innocent enough but would be oppressive in its own unique way.

A notification about the upcoming hydroball tournament, a distraction for the mindless sheep who the man knew mattered nothing to the overlords sitting contently in their Capitol.

More meaningless text scrolled across the screen until a brief notification popped up at the very end, accompanied by a picture of a cloaked figure crouching on a rooftop.

The Vagabond, wanted for his crimes against the Glorious

Bringers of Light, would now fetch a handsome reward of 50,000 credits.

A smile crept across the man's face. The puppet masters finally bothered to spread the word to the neutered public in an attempt to get their help. There was a time that the Council would never have publicly admitted to a problem such as the Vagabond.

Of course, even now, most would see the notification and ignore it. They were trained by now to blindly trust the Lightbringers.

It would have to serve as a small step in the right direction.

The Vagabond pressed himself up against the wall as three men in white armor passed by. After a moment, he let himself breathe again. To their credit, they were making it much harder to roam about the city.

Several minutes passed, and when the Vagabond was sure the officers had moved on, he stepped forward again and approached the walls of the outpost.

He withdrew two small cylindrical objects from his pockets and thought warmly of the woman who had given him such valuable presents. Closing his eyes for a moment, he took a deep breath, and the faint smell of her hair tickled his nose.

The Vagabond opened his eyes and set his sights on the top of the building, which was at least sixty feet in the air. He took the devices and pressed a button on the side, twin spikes snapping out of the tubes and gleaming in the white light.

He gently placed the spikes up against the wall and pressed another button. The spikes jutted forward again and shot out four supporting spikes from the side of each device, embedding themselves into the side of the building.

With a grunt, the Vagabond pulled himself up, placing his feet on the wall to support his weight. He pressed another button on the device in his right hand, and the spikes receded back for a moment until he pulled himself higher and pressed the device up against the wall a few feet beyond his left hand. The device attached itself to the wall, and the Vagabond began his ascent.

As he scaled the wall, he resisted the urge to look down. After three years, the Vagabond still was not comfortable being more than a few feet off the ground. If he had his way, he would have rappelled to the top of the building, and the ascent would have been over in seconds. But if there were anyone on the roof, it would be a short victory before his capture.

And so, he put all of his focus into one step at a time until he reached the very top.

After checking to make sure the coast was clear, the Vagabond pulled himself onto the flat roof of the outpost and reached over, disengaging the spikes and placing the cylinders back in his pocket. He pulled a long rope from his side, walked over to a large antenna in the middle of the roof, and tied the rope securely to the base of the antenna, tugging on it a few times to test his knot.

Nodding in satisfaction, he continued to the access door and pulled on the handle.

Locked.

He didn't expect any differently.

The Vagabond pulled another tube-like device from his pocket and twisted off the cap. He sprayed an invisible liquid over the lock and stepped back, pressing a button.

He smiled as the lock disappeared in a bright white glow.

*That girl has the coolest toys.*

After a few seconds, the light dimmed and vanished, leaving the lock to tumble to the ground, its steel turned an angry red as wisps of smoke drifted away from it.

The Vagabond kicked the burnt metal away and pulled the door open slowly. Silence would be critical from this point on.

He stepped into a stairway and closed the door to the roof,

shutting out all light save from a hole in the door where the lock was.

The dark was no stranger to the Vagabond, and he welcomed the shadows with a sigh of content. It was a welcome change from the bright, unnatural light from the sky ceiling. Even at night, the artificial stars were so bright that it may as well have been evening.

However, here in the dim stairwell, the Vagabond felt comfortable and descended the steps with ease, reaching the bottom without incident.

The Vagabond pressed his ear up against the door and listened for several seconds. The only noise was a faint hum, accompanied by the occasional beep.

But he wasn't taking any chances.

He slowly opened the door, staying low to the ground as he slipped inside. He found himself in a large room, each wall lined with digital displays and large machines with blinking lights. Four men in white outfits sat at the computers, and a man in white armor paced the room, absentmindedly whistling to himself.

The Vagabond crept inside and gently closed the door behind him. He quickly advanced into the room and grabbed the armored man from behind, pulling a knife from his side and slicing the man's neck open with one smooth movement.

He gently lowered the man to the floor and looked back up at the room. No one had heard his attack, and the four men still sat at their computers, occasionally entering a few keystrokes.

In a matter of seconds, the Vagabond repeated his attack on the remaining men, and soon they all lay dead on the floor, small pools of blood forming beneath their bodies. Before doing anything else, he pulled a small metal sphere from his pockets and placed it in front of the main door.

Better safe than sorry.

The Vagabond approached one of the computers and

inserted a data stick into the terminal. He sat at the chair and began the slow process of cloning their datacenter.

As the progress bar inched across the display, he looked back at the room, sighing. Ever since their strategy changed from sabotage to the gathering of intelligence, life had grown quite boring. But the girl was right. They had garnered too much attention from using brute force, and all it had done was annoy the Lightbringers. There was more value in information, and they had managed to collect quite a bit in the last few months.

He turned back to the screen, his boredom driving him to dig into the files he was copying. He clicked on a few documents and perused them briefly, but nothing sparked his interest.

Suddenly, an annoying beep sounded from the data stick he had inserted in the terminal.

The Vagabond held his breath. It was only a matter of time before they caught him. No matter. All part of the plan. If the datamining tool worked as promised, they wouldn't be able to stop him, and whoever was trying to defend his cyberattack would find themselves vulnerable.

He pulled his hood lower over his face, making sure the cameras he knew were in the room would not be able to get a clear look at his face.

Tapping his toes, he anxiously watched the screen as the progress bar stalled, the persistent beeping continued.

Finally, the beeping ceased, and the progress bar started moving again.

The Vagabond finally exhaled. If the girl was right, he would now be able to access the data of whoever had just tried to stop him.

Sure enough, a remote connection formed and opened a new window on the display to his right.

He cracked his knuckles and dove in. His device would automatically collect the data, but the Vagabond was curious.

He perused the files, opening a few and scanning their contents.

Nothing seemed terribly interesting until he opened a communication chain between a councilman and what looked like a security specialist.

The Vagabond's eyes widened as he read the text.

She would want to know about this.

Movement caught his eyes, interrupting him and drawing his attention to a monitor hanging on the wall.

Several men in white armor were lining up by the gate outside, ready to breach.

Keepers.

Without giving the Vagabond a chance to react, they marched through the gate and toward the door.

He looked down at the monitor again. The progress bar was nearly finished. Some of the data would be corrupted if he pulled the disk out early, and he didn't want to risk losing anything vital.

The Vagabond waited for a moment, but knowing it wouldn't matter if they caught him, he stood up quickly and yanked the disk out of the terminal, heading for the access stairwell again as the door burst open behind him. A flash of white light came from behind the Vagabond, and he closed the door to the stairwell behind him as shots fired behind him.

It would take the Lightbringers some time to recover from the flashbang he had placed, but the Vagabond didn't waste any time, taking the stairs two at a time and running up to the door to the roof.

He burst out into the open air and threw himself over the edge of the building, his heart freezing as he grabbed the rope and slammed into the side of the building. His gloved hands absorbed the burn of the rope as he slid down the wall, and he landed roughly on the ground a few seconds later, a painful shock running up his legs.

The Vagabond sprayed the rope using the flash device

again and pressed a button, letting the rope disappear in a burst of white flame.

Taking a deep breath, he walked out of the alley and stepped out into the street behind the outpost, blending in with a small group of people walking down the street, their white clothes providing perfect cover.

He tapped a comms device in his ear and spoke quietly.

"We need to meet. I found the Key."

## 3

Wincing in anticipation for the quick death that bore down on him in the form of a mole, Roland barely heard the piercing shriek that echoed through the tunnel. But the volume and pitch of the cry soon escalated until it forced his mind back to consciousness. He slowly sat up and clutched the sides of his head as the awful noise violated his ears.

The sound of tearing flesh joined the din, and something warm and wet splashed over Roland's face. As it sank between his lips, he turned to the side and threw up what little was left in his stomach, the stench making him choke on his own vomit.

Roland reached into his satchel once again and pulled more glowworms from the pouch. He threw the glowing creatures forward, and they landed briefly on the giant mole before careering into the cave wall, shook loose by the writhing beast.

The mole was barely visible. Its giant body was covered with dozens of humanoid creatures, their white bodies tinted yellow by the glow splattered over the cave walls.

The animal's cries died down as one of the creatures sank its claws into the beast's neck, ripping open a hole. The creature shoved its head into the mole's neck and pulled free its lungs, which hung loosely from the creature's mouth. With a disturbing slurping sound, the mole's innards disappeared into the creature's mouth.

Sounds of tearing and gashing now drowned out the mole's struggle, and soon the beast lay still. The creatures continued to tear apart its body, ripping scaly armor from the beast and digging deep into the animal's side.

Roland grunted and slowly climbed to his feet. "I gotta say, you guys really pulled through. I don't know how you knew I was here, but I'm glad you did."

The creatures froze and looked toward Roland slowly, their bodies still except for their craning necks.

"It was disgusting, sure, but I'm grateful nonetheless." Roland let a smile creep over his face, trying to push past the gut-wrenching sight of intestines hanging from their mouths.

One of the creatures hopped down from the mole's body and stood straight, walking forward slowly. Roland held up a hand and grimaced, blocking out the sight of the creature's naked body.

"What happened to your robes? No offense, but no one wants to see that."

Roland split his fingers just enough to get a good look at the creature's face. The sight was one he never got used to, even after three years. Its wrinkled, snow-white, hairless skin was enough to make him shudder. Roland just hoped it didn't open its mouth.

But, of course, it did, and a gaping red hole appeared in the middle of its white face, exposing a tongue that oozed blood out over the creature's white lips, mixing in with the blood from the mole as it dripped down the creature's bare body.

No words came from the being, only a raspy exhale as its eyes widened and looked Roland over from head to toe.

Roland winced as the stench of blood washed over him, a

pungent smell that never failed to make him question the humanity of the Host. Nothing about them seemed natural, not their smell, not their skin, and certainly not their eyes.

Their eyes.

Roland opened his eyes again and slowly took a step back as he looked into the creature's wide eyes. Rather than the red glow he had come to expect from the irradiated beings, this creature's eyes were pure black. If it were not for the yellow glow around them reflected in the creature's glassy black irises, Roland could have sworn that it had no eyes.

Desolates.

The creature took a step forward to match Roland's backward movement, and its mouth opened wider as the gasp grew louder, escalating into a whining sound that made Roland freeze. Behind it, the rest of the creatures climbed down from the mole and stood behind their leader, their yellow-white bodies trembling in anticipation.

Roland opened his mouth but didn't have time to speak. Their leader reached forward with long, skinny fingers, razor-sharp claws decorating their tips. Shrieks echoed throughout the tunnel as the Desolates lunged forward, each of them reaching for Roland's defenseless body.

Backpedaling, Roland stumbled backward and spun around, grasping at the ground to keep himself from falling. As he pulled himself forward, a thin, sharp claw ripped through his leg. Roland yelped in pain but bit his tongue and forced himself to ignore the pain as he staggered forward, finally managing to regain his balance and take off down the tunnels in a dead run.

The creatures were not as fast as the mole, but they were far more dangerous. Roland knew they didn't need light to see, even in the darkest tunnels. They were also much smaller than the beast that had just chased him, and they could follow him no matter where he went, no matter how far he ran.

His speed was only slightly dampened by the wound in his

leg, but he intentionally ran a little slower than his maximum speed. Because the Desolates were slower than the mole, Roland could afford to go slower now. They were still nearly as fast as Roland's trained body, but as long as he tread carefully and made sure to stay on the path, he knew he could keep a respectable distance between himself and the advancing horde.

The chase continued on for a few more minutes, and it was about the same time that Roland realized he had dropped his spear back by the mole's carcass that a sharp object embedded itself deep in his shoulder, sending him crashing to the ground.

Moaning, Roland wrenched the spear out and tossed it to the side. He knew it was dangerous to open such a deep wound, but it wouldn't matter if the Host caught up to him. He climbed to his feet before immediately toppling back over, the pain and dizziness making it impossible to stand for more than a second.

Pulling his last glowworm from his satchel, Roland glanced back at the oncoming horde, which slowed now and approached him deliberately. They knew he was finished.

The creatures raised their voices in a discordant symphony of hums and gasps, reverberating throughout the tunnel walls in an unsettling chorus that seemed almost ritualistic.

Roland groaned. "Oh, get it over with then. If it means I don't have to listen to this anymore, I'm okay with that."

The leader stepped forward again and knelt next to his body, lifting its hands and raising its voice as it looked to the cave ceiling. Its claws shimmered yellow, and they turned downward as the creature looked back toward Roland, its bleeding tongue hanging loosely from its gaping mouth.

A loud feminine shriek sounded through the tunnel, drowning out the cacophony and causing the leader to look back up sharply.

As Roland recognized the sound, he smiled and glared at

the leader. "Too late. You're scr—"

That was all he got out before a beast leaped over Roland's body and collided with the leader, tackling the creature to the ground and crushing its torso beneath the beast's weight. The animal leaned over and ripped the creature's head clean off its body, tossing it into the group of creatures before letting loose a loud roar.

The creatures seemed unimpressed and rushed forward to attack the giant mole, but immediately halted and cowered in fear as dozens of cloaked figures jumped over Roland's body, running past the mole and into the fray.

The tunnel exploded in noise again as the two sides fought. Shrieks of pain flooded the air, mixed with the roar of the mole and the hiss of the creatures.

Roland looked up at the girl that sat atop the mole. The fierce intruder was spinning a double-sided spear around her body, slicing the throat of one creature to her left before burrowing the weapon deep into another one's chest to her right. A wild grin graced her face as her eyes flashed with every kill.

But as Roland admired the girl, he felt himself shoved back to the ground, face-first. A sloppy wet mouth pressed down onto his shoulder, and he cried out in panic as he felt the intense suction pull at his insides from the exposed wound.

The sucking sensation ceased, and Roland spun around to see a cloaked figure mounting his chest. Glowing red eyes appeared beneath the creature's crimson hood.

Before Roland could retaliate, the creature turned to the side and spat something against the cave wall before hopping off and rejoining the fight. Roland held the glowworms closer to the cave wall and examined the object that the creature had pulled from his shoulder. It was the tip of his spear.

"Thank you," he managed to say, spitting the words out past the blood in his mouth, knowing that the creature could still hear him, even above the din.

Roland simply sat back and let the two groups of creatures continue to fight. Weaponless and severely injured, he would have just gotten in the way.

The fight was soon over. Between sheer numbers and the support of a mole equipped with battle armor, the feral creatures didn't stand a chance. Soon, the tunnel was quiet again, save for the sound of slurping and flesh tearing as the cloaked creatures devoured the bodies of their fallen enemies.

"And thank you," Roland said to the girl as she dismounted the mole and approached his side.

Tamisra examined his shoulder for a moment before standing back up and pulling Roland to his feet, who grimaced in pain as the wound opened just a bit more.

The pain in his shoulder disappeared for a moment as she delivered a swift slap to his face.

"What were you doing out here?"

Roland rubbed his cheek. "I was going for a walk. Nothing like some fresh air in the morning, mixed with nearly getting myself killed. Altogether, a good day."

Another slap on his opposite cheek.

"What were you thinking? Were you trying to get yourself killed?"

"Not really. I didn't think the Desolates spread this far out."

"Even if they didn't, you thought it would be smart to go on a one-man hunting expedition?"

Roland shrugged. "I'm just trying to feed the people I love."

Tamisra narrowed her eyes. "Love? You think that prissy lovebird is your family?" Without waiting for him to respond, she continued. "You have a family. There's not much left of us, but there's still Refuge. That's your family. Salvador, Corrin, me . . ." Her voice faltered, and she blinked rapidly. "You have a family that doesn't need to suffer any more loss."

"My family is stranded hundreds of miles above us,

strapped into a machine and left for dead. *That's* my family." Roland stepped forward as his voice lowered. "The man who died because you failed to do your job? He was my family."

Her mouth dropped open slightly, and her voice shook as she responded. "I know that, Roland. And apparently, I can never apologize enough for it. If you don't move on, that's on you. Neither of us can change what happened. All we can do is make the most of what we have now. And what we have now is a dying civilization to care for, and we can't do that if our best warrior goes off hunting alone."

"Best warrior?" Roland raised an eyebrow.

Tamisra folded her arms. "Well, second best." Her familiar smirk started to appear before she shook her head sharply. "Look, even if you're doing this for Dawn, what do you think you're going to accomplish by coming out here by yourself?"

"I have to take care of her, Tami."

Her eyebrows furrowed at the sound of her nickname, but she made no remark. "Sometimes being a man means coming home and being there for your family, whoever that is."

Roland balled his fists and took a step forward. "Don't you dare put your daddy issues on me, Tamisra. At least I'm trying and not running away from my problems."

Tamisra's eyes widened, and her mouth hung open.

Almost immediately, Roland shook his head and started to speak again, but Tamisra waved her hand.

"Whatever. I didn't come here to argue. My father was looking for you, so I suggest you find him." Tamisra turned and climbed back atop the mole, which was staring at the feasting Host suspiciously. "I have hunting to do."

Without waiting for a response, she kicked the mole and raced down the tunnel, and the Host behind her grudgingly left their food behind and followed her into the darkness.

## 4

"**G**ood evening, ladies and gentlemen."

Todd Lambert, the Director, pushed open the door to the sanctum and strolled inside, spreading his arms wide and smiling at the people waiting inside.

He approached a female scientist, giving a slight bow and taking her hand, kissing it gently.

"Sir."

The Director ignored the interruption and approached a male scientist, shaking his hand firmly, a wide smile on his face.

Finally, he turned to the girl.

"Sir."

His smile shrank by mere millimeters, and he held up a finger, refusing to take his eyes off the beauty before him. The girl was simply gorgeous. She hadn't aged a day. In fact, her face was still frozen in the same pained gasp after three long years. It was the Director's only regret. Perhaps he could have given her something to smile about before sealing her fate.

"Oh, but *mon amie*, forever we are in your debt." The Director bowed deep, speaking in a melodic tone. After a moment, he rose again and let his fingers graze over the epitaph engraved on the podium before him. "Long live the Lightbringers indeed."

"Sir."

The voice was firm now and echoed throughout the sanctum.

The Director spun around and finally responded. "Yes, Mardon, what is it?"

But the man didn't need to say anything. Instead, the Director froze briefly as his eyes fell upon the glowing blue figures standing by a digital readout on the far wall.

"You could have told me they were here." The Director's voice instantly dropped to a low growl.

The scientist who had spoken up raised a finger. "But we did, sir. We——"

"Silence." The Director cleared his throat and glanced toward the ground. "With all due respect, might the Council give me notice before inviting themselves into this humble sanctum?"

One of the glowing figures stepped down onto the main floor, a smirk gracing the man's face. "Why, my dear Director. You didn't predict our arrival?"

The Director waved a hand. "Don't be absurd, Byron. I certainly expected you, but I didn't think you'd be here for another minute and forty-two seconds." He broke eye contact with the man and stared through his body at Mardon, who shrank back slightly from the Director's steely eyes.

Byron shrugged. "Fair enough."

"In any case, I don't have any updates for you. Lucifer is running at optimal levels, same as last month."

"That's not what your readings indicate," Byron said, turning back toward the digital readout where the rest of the glowing figures still stood. "Your energy output has showed a steady decline over the last three months. We said nothing last month because we knew to expect the occasional anomaly.

But three months constitutes a pattern, one that we cannot ignore."

The Director shook his head. "You're reading the wrong graph. The total daily wattage has remained consistent, and nothing—"

"That's not the one I'm speaking of, and you know it. Please do not try to mislead the Council. You know very well the ramifications of such dishonesty."

"Dishonesty?" The Director raised a hand to his chest. "You accuse me of something of which I am quite incapable."

The man scoffed. "We know exactly what you're capable of. The fact that we're standing here before your self-proclaimed masterpiece proves that."

"I assure you, at no point did I lie to Annelise. I didn't have to. The girl is here of her own free will, fully informed of our intentions and purpose."

"Whatever. The stability of the subject is the issue in question here, not your honesty. At the end of the day, we know you wouldn't dare do anything to endanger your relationship with the Council."

The Director looked away briefly. "Her stability, yes. We have noticed irregularities, but nothing to be concerned about."

"Really?" Byron arched his eyebrows. "That's not what Mardon was saying."

"Mardon doesn't know what he's talking about," the Director said, staring at the fidgeting scientist through the blue glow of the hologram between them.

"It seems to me he's perfectly qualified to speak regarding the stability of Project Lucifer." Byron turned toward Mardon, who regained his composure and stood straight. "Would you mind repeating what you told me before the Director's . . . grand entrance?"

Mardon cleared his throat. "J-just that her stability has

always been in question, especially since she's missing the other half of her natural regenerative properties. She—"

Byron didn't let him finish, instead turning back toward the Director. "The other half of her natural regenerative properties. Would you mind elaborating on that, please?"

The Director dared to roll his eyes quickly before responding. "After the Phoenix Mandate, Lucifer was supposed to be able to produce energy and release it safely. However, our asset jumped in with her, splitting the natural cycle of energy and releasing it into two different entities, the girl and the boy. It was all in my report if you bothered to read it."

"We read the report," Byron said, his eyes narrowing. "It didn't matter then because you assured us that your goal would be unimpeded. If this split, as you say, negatively affects your promised results, then we have a problem that you need to fix."

"But it's a non-issue. That's not what's causing her volatility. We accounted for this anomaly, and it actually benefited us. You see, it's not half of anything, despite my ill-informed subordinate's statements. She can produce more energy than we could have hoped for because she doesn't have to worry about releasing it safely. The machine does that for her."

"Then what, pray tell, is the cause of the volatility?"

The Director stepped through the transparent man and joined Mardon at the giant display, ignoring the glowing figures that swarmed around him. He swiped away the graphs cluttering the screen and pointed at an image on the digital readout, a scan of the girl's brain. "Do you see this spot here?"

The glowing, blue man silently ascended the steps behind the Director and leaned in toward the image. "What spot?"

"Here." The Director drew a circle around a small red spot in a sea of glowing yellow. As his finger traced the shape, the image expanded to fill the screen until the red spot was noticeable even to untrained eyes.

Byron frowned. "What is it?"

"We're not sure."

The Director spun around and glared at Mardon. "Your input is neither requested nor welcome. You will remain silent until addressed."

"What does he mean you're not sure?" Byron folded his arms. "Are you losing your foresight, my dear Mr. Lambert?"

"That's impossible, and you know it." The Director continued his death stare at Mardon for another moment before turning back to the image. "It's a foreign substance, one that wasn't on the original scans when the Phoenix Mandate was executed. We didn't see it until she was already in the machine, so it's too late to open up her skull."

"I thought you had contingencies."

"We do. But taking her out of the machine is an unnecessary risk when we can find out what it is while she's still inside."

"And how do you plan on doing that?"

"By analyzing the effect it has on her mind." The Director swiped the image up and made a large opening gesture with his arms. Dozens of images filled the screen, each one a nearduplicate of the girl's brain. "If you look closely, the area surrounding the foreign substance has slowly deteriorated over time, resulting in higher levels of volatility."

Byron peered at the screen for several seconds. "I don't see anything."

"Of course you don't," the Director said, swiping down and erasing the display entirely. "The changes are microscopic at best. It's been three years, and energy levels have not varied. We are at no risk."

"For now." Mardon spoke one more time, ducking quickly as the Director spun around again.

"What's that supposed to mean?" Byron's voice grew everso-slightly louder.

The Director turned back around. "It means—"

"I was asking Mardon."

Fuming, the Director spun around. "Well?"

Mardon spoke slowly. "It means that the variance is at acceptable levels, and they will be for years. But eventually, the decay will spread until her brain can't handle it anymore. One of two things will happen: either she will die . . ."

Byron tapped his toe on the ground. "Or?"

"Or we will."

The glowing holograms surrounding the Director began to murmur loudly.

"Meaning?" Byron prodded.

Mardon gestured toward the girl suspended in the tank. "The energy in her body will lash out in an effort to free itself. But we're not just harnessing her power here; we're amplifying it. The resulting explosion will be not unlike the destruction that leveled the Earth thousands of years ago."

"And you didn't think to consult the Council?" Byron turned back to the Director. "We would have ordered an examination immediately."

"He's being dramatic," the Director said, rolling his eyes again. "It's a moot point. I believe I know the cause of the anomaly. Noah, the president of Level XVIII and self-appointed Chancellor, knew enough of our plans that he likely surmised our end goal and ensured its failure. Kendall advised us that Noah injected the girl with some kind of serum, and I believe it's the very same substance that now troubles us."

"What's the point of knowing the cause if you can't fix it?"

"I never said I intended to fix it." The Director's eyes twinkled. "I plan to exploit it."

Byron placed his hands on his hips. "That shouldn't surprise me, considering your history of manipulation. But exactly how do you intend on doing that?"

The Director raised his wrist to his mouth and spoke into a watch-like device. "Bruno, would you please bring the Lucifer Pistol to the sanctum?"

Ignoring the brutish grunt that came back over the tiny

speaker, the Director lowered his wrist and continued. "Her instability has been a blessing in disguise. Surely you remember that the science team was once appointed with the task of expanding our military's weaponry."

Byron shook his head. "That was centuries ago, before my time. I'm familiar with the initiative, however."

"Well, our primary focus, as you may know, was to develop laser technology. There had been mild success before the Earth's extinction, but nothing to write home about. When the Underworld bore fruit and we reestablished power on the surface, however, the Council's interest was reborn, and so was our work."

"While I'm sure we all appreciate the history lesson, Mr. Lambert, is this going somewhere?"

The Director held up a finger. "Do you know the problem with using lasers as weapons?"

Byron shrugged. "Sure. It cauterizes the wound. Doesn't do any lasting damage unless you hit your target's vitals."

"Well put. We searched for years in an effort to circumvent this caveat, but to no avail. Our report was given, and the project was abandoned."

As the double doors to the sanctum opened, the Director allowed himself to smile again. "I am happy to report that we have actionable results for the first time in five hundred years."

"Even if you did, does it matter? Bullets have proved more than effective in getting the job done."

A large man lumbered across the room and gave a white pistol to the Director.

"Thank you, Bruno." The Director turned the pistol over in his hands. "I suggest withholding further comments until you have witnessed its power."

The giant turned to leave, but the Director placed a hand on his shoulder. "A moment, please, Bruno." He flipped a switch on the side of the gun, and a faint hum emitted from the weapon. "Legend speaks of an angel named Lucifer, a celestial being that fell from the sky after his rebellion. Ancient texts tell us he was one of the most high-ranking angels, and one of the most beautiful and powerful of them all."

Byron rolled his eyes. "Angels? Are you going somewhere with this? Please tell me you don't believe any of this."

"Of course not." The Director smirked. "But the name Lucifer has always stood out to me. It is a Latin word, the same word that inspired the English name for our government. It means Lightbringer. And now the light from our very own Lightbringer is the most beautiful, powerful, and will be our very salvation. But until that time, we must harness it and use it to further our purpose, even if it means turning it into a terrible weapon."

The Director placed the tip of the gun up against Bruno's back. The giant jumped and moved to turn around, but it was too late. With a squeeze of the trigger, a white light shot from the barrel and encompassed Bruno's body in a glow that made everyone but the Director hold their hands in front of their eyes. Even the holograms had to shield their faces in defense against the blinding light.

Just as soon as it came, the light vanished, and with it, Bruno.

Moments passed as the room recovered, and Byron was the first to speak. "Good lord . . ."

The Director nodded to where the large man once stood. "Thank you, Bruno. Faithful 'til the last."

"How is this going to fix our current problem?" Byron asked, still struggling to speak.

"We've been able to successfully harvest the subject's 'dark' energy, as we've come to call it, and extract it safely before using it to power all sorts of prototype weapons. This leaves the rest of the girl's energy to power your microwaves."

The man frowned. "But it's lethal."

"With all due respect, Councilor, I think you and I have

somewhat different expectations when it comes to weaponry. Of course it's lethal."

"Wouldn't it blind whoever uses it?"

The Director shrugged as he spun the pistol around his finger, causing the entire room to cover their eyes again. He flipped the switch back down and tucked the barrel of the gun into his pants. "There are some kinks to work out, sure. But do you really think this isn't worth further development? You really don't want some shiny new toys?"

"I'll never get used to your demeanor," Byron said, shaking his head. "One minute you're quoting Shakespeare, the next you're acting like a child playing cowboy."

"If you can't enjoy your work, what's the point?" The Director flashed a large grin. "So what do you say, Councilor?"

Byron rubbed his chin. "What do you have against regular bullets? Aren't they just as effective and less prone to failure? I mean, imagine if one of those guns backfires. It could be catastrophic."

"Yes, but great victory does not come without sacrifice. Besides, if another human with the girl's powers managed to put up a fight, using their power against them would be the only thing that could harm them. You'll want these weapons, Councilor."

Byron stared at the Director for a long moment. "We'll be in touch."

With that, the glowing blue figures vanished from the sanctum.

"Well, that was abrupt." The Director looked around the room, still grinning. When his gaze fell on Mardon, however, his smile vanished. "Dr. Mardon, please step forward."

The scientist's bravery had disappeared, and when he finally approached the Director, his hands were visibly shaking.

The Director cleared his throat. "I know this can't possibly be the case, but it seems as if you've begun to question my foresight."

"Not at all, sir." Mardon waved his hands in front of him, stepping away slightly as the Director advanced. "You know I would never dare to doubt you."

"My apologies, then. It seemed as if you don't trust my ability to deliver to the Council."

Mardon looked at the floor. "It's not that, sir. It's just . . . The Council, sir. Do you really want to lie to them?"

"You were listening to me. Did I at any point lie to them?"

"No, sir. I just—"

"Then why accuse me of such a thing?"

"Sir, you didn't tell them—"

"I told them exactly what they needed to hear. I certainly didn't want to show them the Lucifer weaponry yet, and thanks to you, we will have to continue on with the next stage of our plans much sooner than I wanted, yet no sooner than I anticipated."

Mardon looked up and raised an eyebrow. "Plans, sir?"

"Yes, Mardon. You see, despite your doubt, I have foreseen all that has happened. I've planned for it. Do you take me for a fool?" After Mardon said nothing, the Director's voice raised. "That question was not rhetorical, doctor. Do you think me a fool?"

Mardon shook his head rapidly.

"As well you shouldn't. I am not a councilman, adviser, or an operative. These pawns are replaceable. You are replaceable. I am the Director. I wrote these events long before you manufactured your first stem cells. And when you undermine me in front of the Council, do you know what I feel?"

"N-nothing?"

"Fair point. But do you know the danger in making me appear incompetent in front of them? We've been given a task with near-complete autonomy, and you know how valuable that is to me."

"But misleading the Council, sir . . . They can shut you down. They have the Key, and they——"

The Director reached out swiftly and clamped down on Mardon's throat. "I know what the Council holds. Your breath should not be wasted on reminding me but begging for your life."

Mardon's mouth moved, but no words came out. Instead, he croaked and slapped his hands on the Director's wrist.

After a moment, the Director released the scientist and pulled the pistol from his pants. As Mardon knelt on the ground and wheezed, the Director flipped the switch again. "I'll prove it to you. You think my foresight has decayed? Now's your chance to prove it. Stand up."

Mardon slowly climbed to his feet and stood, facing the Director and the gun.

"I'm going to fire this weapon, either to your right, your left, or directly at you. You get to try to dodge. If you somehow survive, then you survive. If not, well, it really won't make that much of a difference to me, to be honest."

Mardon stretched his hands forward, his palms open. "Please, sir. Give me another chance."

"What are you panicking for, Mardon? If I cannot predict the future, as you believe, then you have nothing to worry about."

"I believe you. I swear to you, I believe you."

The Director grinned once again and placed his finger on the trigger. "Time to choose."

The gun fired, a ray of pure light shooting across the room and into a computer against the far wall, sending sparks flying as a small explosion echoed throughout the sanctum.

Mardon lay on the ground in the fetal position, a faint whimper emanating from his lips.

"Get up. You look idiotic." The Director flipped the switch and tucked the gun back into his pants.

But Mardon remained on the ground, moaning quietly.

"I said get up."

Eventually, Mardon stood again, but his entire body shivered now.

"What's wrong, Mardon?" The Director tilted his head and stuck out a lip. "You successfully dodged the shot, didn't you? I thought you'd be happy to be alive."

"You-you—"

"I'm sorry, what was that?" The Director held a hand to his ear and beckoned Mardon to speak again, but all that came back was more stutters. "Oh, Mardon. You knew all along, didn't you? You knew that my foresight was flawless. A momentary lapse in your judgment? A desperate grasp for power? Your five minutes of fame? I guess we'll never know."

The Director stepped forward and placed a single finger against Mardon's chest. With a slight push, Mardon toppled back over and sprawled out on the floor. "My foreknowledge is perfect. I knew you would do something this stupid. I knew you would say something. I knew you would seal your own fate."

"You-you promised," Mardon said as he squirmed on the ground in obvious discomfort.

"I promised you that if you survive, then you survive." The Director smirked. "I didn't say I had to shoot you. Poison in your breakfast, activated by the stress of a near-death experience, works just as well."

As Mardon continued to writhe, the Director looked up and addressed the room. "I truly regret this necessary demonstration of my gifts. I do not mean to scare or intimidate. Rather, I hope to inspire you all. You follow a man who will deliver unto you ultimate victory, against which there can be no contest. I have seen every possible future, and I will lead you into the best possible one."

The Director raised his arms and his voice as Mardon began to scream. "Know this and love me, love me and obey.

I give you my word that the sun will shine again, and we will be honored for eternity."

As the echoes of the Director's proclamation died away, so did Mardon's screams, and the room went silent.

The Director let his hands fall to his side as he looked around the room. "Would it have been so hard to cheer right there? Some applause? A small 'yay'?"

The remaining doctors and scientists simply stared back at him.

"Whatever." The Director turned and walked out of the room, pushing the double doors open wide as he exited. "Let the games begin."

## 5

---

The Vagabond looked over the cityscape, studying the thriving civilization before him.

Shimmering white buildings filled the sector, twinkling under the light of the dazzling sun. The buildings gave way only for the most pristine parks, filled with lush greenery and crystal-clear water.

The Vagabond shook his head sadly. A few short years ago, the sight would have taken his breath away. But he was one of the privileged—or unfortunate—few to see what was left of the real sun. Even in its decayed state, the sight was too glorious to forget, and this artificial beauty before him now could not compare. It was beautiful, yes. A perfect representation of the world that might have been thousands of years ago. But unmistakably fake.

It was a fraudulent prosperity, a mere shadow of what must have once been a thriving world. The city was enclosed in a giant, invisible bubble that the Vagabond could still see if he looked closely enough. The brilliant sun seemed three dimensional at first glance, but it followed the flat curvature of the invisible ceiling without derivation, that always-present sky ceiling that loomed above the city, always providing ample light with a cloudless tapestry.

But the flawlessness of the scenery only reminded the Vagabond that it was no more than a program, a constant reminder of the invisible, oppressive thumb under which the population lived.

The Vagabond turned away from the cityscape, letting his long, white cloak swirl around his body loosely.

Almost immediately, a gentle thud sounded behind him, and the Vagabond smiled. Years ago, the sound would have gone unnoticed. But he had grown accustomed to the girl's ways.

After wiping the smile from his face, he turned around slowly and greeted the cloaked figure that had appeared where he had stood mere seconds earlier.

"Good to see you again. It's been too long."

The girl tilted her head toward him, a nearly impercep-tible gesture due to the white hood that hung low over her face. If it weren't for the black trim that decorated the full length of her cloak, the Vagabond would not have noticed the movement. "My apologies. We've been quite busy with your old friend."

"Then I take it that it's almost time?"

"That depends. Did you really find the Key?"

"See for yourself," the Vagabond said, pulling the data stick from his pocket and handing it to her.

The girl pulled a small screen from somewhere within the folds of her cloak and plugged the data stick into it. She studied the screen for a moment before nodding satisfactorily.

"Well done," she said. "After three long years, it's finally time to put an end to the madness."

The Vagabond took the girl's hand. "At long last, this world will see the Lightbringers for who they really are. Assuming Caspian holds up his end of the bargain, that is."

"I wouldn't doubt him if I were you. For some strange

reason, you trust me. And if you can trust me, you can definitely trust him."

"I'd like to think I can trust you by now," the Vagabond said, sliding an arm around her waist, beneath her cloak. He pulled her closer ever so slightly, just enough so that their cloaks came together and formed one amalgam of white fabric.

The girl drew in a sharp breath, the whistle tickling the Vagabond's ear and sending shivers down his spine. "After what I've done?" Her lips were dangerously close to his now, and she let herself stay there for a moment before pulling away. "You really shouldn't."

"I'll decide who I should and shouldn't trust." The Vagabond felt his heart sink slightly as she broke free from his arm. "The information you've given me has proven your worth time and time again. I have few reservations about your loyalties."

The girl opened her mouth but seemed to choke on her words for a moment. Her hesitance caught the Vagabond off guard. She rarely had trouble finding something to say. "Is that all I am to you? A source of information?"

"You know that's not true. I chose my words poorly. The looseness of your lips does not determine your worth in my eyes."

A smile graced the girl's lips as she put a hand to her chest. "I must say, you're far from the boy I knew three years ago. Your tongue has turned silver."

"Look who's talking." The Vagabond pulled her close again by the black trim of her cloak, and he pushed her hood just far back enough to reveal her dazzling hazel eyes. "I believe we've had a significant effect on each other throughout the years."

He leaned in and brought his lips close, but the girl pulled away again, this time more forceful.

"I told you, we can't." The girl shook her head. "Not yet."

The Vagabond sighed. "I know."

"I'm sorry," she said, stepping forward just enough to put a hand on his cheek. "There's too much work to be done, and neither of us can afford any distractions. But when our mission is complete, you'll receive your reward that you've deserved for so long, I promise you that."

"I live for that day," the Vagabond said, taking her hand from his cheek and kissing the back of it gently. "Until then, I will do what I must."

"Good," the girl said, stepping away and withdrawing her hand after a brief pause. "It won't be much longer."

The Vagabond nodded. "I'm going to hold you to that."

"Close your eyes."

He did so. A quick kiss blessed his cheek, and a tiny gust of wind swept across his face. He opened his eyes. The girl had vanished.

The Vagabond stepped forward and looked down at the city again. Soon, their world would change. The veil lifted, the lie revealed.

And the puppet masters? They would pay, every last one of them.

## 6

R oland left the clinic that evening with his wounds poorly bandaged. He could have expertly wrapped any shoulder but his own. The awkward angle made it impossible, and he had to settle for a makeshift job that he performed blindly. Dawn would have to patch it up later.

Trying to ignore the discomfort, Roland continued through the camp toward the largest tent that sat in the middle of the clearing. Few torches remained along the path as most of the remaining citizens of Refuge had begun to retreat to their tents for sleep. Like the tunnels in the Web above, there wasn't any reliable way to keep track of time, but without fail, as soon as the first few tents put out their torches before sleeping, the rest of Refuge would soon follow suit.

But Roland knew the Scourge would be wide awake. He seemed to be the last to go to sleep, the first to wake up. It was dumb luck that he hadn't caught Roland leaving for his regular hunting expeditions. Maybe Salvador was too distracted getting ready for his own deadly excursions.

Corrin stepped out of the tent as Roland approached, shaking his head as their eyes met. "If you continue to bait death, son, you'll soon find it."

Roland smirked. "So I keep being told. You know I can take care of myself."

"So I keep telling myself," Corrin said. "But I was nearly proved wrong today. If it hadn't been for Tamisra, I . . . I've lost so much, Roland. I don't want to lose you, too."

Roland's smirk faded. "You sent her after me, didn't you?"

"It was a mutual decision. How did you know?"

"Something she said. Listen, I'll be more careful. I promise."

Corrin nodded as he stared at a point in the distance. "I won't stop you, but surely you won't blame me if I forbid my lieutenant from helping you."

"Haskill? What do you mean?"

"I'm not stupid, boy." Corrin smiled warmly. "We keep a very strict count of our supplies. Lieutenant Haskill has signed away more than your fair share of food and weapons over the years. It hasn't been enough to make a difference to the rest of us, but it does hurt that you went to him instead of me."

Roland looked away, shifting his balance between his feet. "You would have said no."

"You are very correct." Corrin sighed. "I've seen you fight. I know you're capable. Just don't do anything stupid. At least not any more stupid than what you've already done."

Roland grinned. "You know I can't promise you that."

"I know," Corrin said as he gently placed his hand on Roland's head and walked away toward his own tent.

Roland approached the Scourge's tent, but he paused just outside, wondering if the imminent discussion they seemed to always have would end any differently this time.

"Come in."

The voice interrupted Roland's thoughts. Its deep tone and smooth cadence beckoned him forth, yet an intimidating undertone urged him to stay out at the same time.

Roland took a breath and stepped inside.

The Scourge stood in full battle armor, minus his

helmet, which rested on the hilt of a massive broadsword protruding from the ground by his cot. The man stood tall, a far cry from the shriveled man Roland had met all those years ago. His figure seemed to stretch to fill the tent, and despite his menacing reputation, Roland felt safe in the shadow of the man's frame, cast by a flickering torch in the corner.

"Perfect timing," Salvador said, beckoning forward with a four-fingered glove. "I always find it difficult to reach the straps on the back."

Roland nodded and stepped behind the man, quickly undoing the laces that held the metal armor in place. Within seconds, the breastplate and braces lay on the ground. Roland reached for Salvador's chain mail, but the man waved his hand.

"That is fine for now. I just wanted to get that hunk of metal off me first and foremost."

"Where's your squire?" Roland held back a smirk. "I thought he would have had this off you by now."

Salvador did not refrain from smiling, and it looked like he was stifling a laugh. "I gave Lionel the day off. He single-handedly fought off three Desolates after I got knocked off my mole yesterday. From what I understand, he could have lent you a hand this morning on your daily hunt."

Roland cocked an eyebrow. "Daily? You knew about them?"

"Of course. You are not as subtle as you might think. I have seen you depart in the mornings with a spear and pack. I have no delusions about what you do. A word of advice. If you wish to remain undetected, you may want to ensure you do not return with such obvious wounds." Salvador gestured toward Roland's crude bandage.

"I guess I'm lucky Tami was out there, or I would have come back with a lot worse. That is, if I came back at all."

"I am glad someone is looking out for you, dear boy.

We both know Dawn cannot. She is counting on you, a reliance that I worry is misplaced."

"With all due respect, Salvador, I don't need a lecture from you too. I've already heard enough from your daughter."

Salvador held up a hand. "I was not planning a lecture, at least not today. I have no right to take this matter into my hands with any more than a cursory remark. And with your forgiveness, I will give you one more: I have never seen my daughter happier than when she was with you."

Roland bristled. "If you wanted to see her happy, then you never should have left."

"Your statement proves my point."

"How?"

"She said the exact same thing." Salvador gave a sad smile. "I stand by my decision to leave. I felt that matters were safe in your capable hands. And with the Chancellor defeated, you no longer needed a warrior. You needed someone to rebuild the Web. I could not offer that twenty-one years ago, nor could I offer it three years ago."

Roland sighed as he realized this discussion with the Scourge was going to take the same turn it had dozens of times before. "But you'll do it now, now that it's too late?"

"I have no intention of doing such a thing, Roland. I cannot lead Refuge now, not anymore. They have finally seen me for what I truly am."

"A coward?"

Salvador opened his mouth, but Roland continued. "You didn't have to leave. You just didn't want to feel guilty every time you looked at your daughter again."

Fire flashed in Salvador's eyes, but he took a deep breath and closed his eyes, letting the air out slowly. "I will not have this conversation again, Roland. We have more important matters to discuss."

Roland spoke through his teeth. "Well?"

"Corrin has told me that you are still trying to convince my people to leave this level."

"You make it sound worse than it is," Roland said. "It's not like I'm holding secret meetings to turn your people against you."

Salvador raised his eyebrows. "Are you not? Because it sounds to me like that is exactly what you are doing."

"I'm talking with Corrin and Lieutenant Haskill about it, sure. But I'm just trying to get them to talk to you about it."

"Can you not speak to me about it yourself?"

Roland scoffed. "Like you'll listen."

"Even if I disagree with you, I would prefer that you come to me and speak openly rather than turn my general and lieutenant against me."

"I'm not turning anyone against you. I'm just trying to change things. If we stay down here much longer, we'll die."

Salvador rolled his eyes. "This again."

"Yes, this again. There's no protection from the radiation down here. Give it a few years, and—"

"You take Kendall's words too seriously, boy."

"And you don't?" Roland threw his hands in the air. "I could ignore them like you, but do you really believe he was lying? You haven't noticed a difference in your body after three years of hiding down here? Has your skin always been this pale? You don't wake up in the middle of the night, vomiting blood? You should know the feeling of radiation poisoning better than I after hiding in Refuge for eighteen years. We're dying, Salvador, and you know it."

"And what if we are?" Salvador bellowed, taking one massive step toward Roland. "Better to die slowly and enjoy what days we have left than leave this place and be executed by the Director's armies. Because that is what you want, isn't it? Do not come to me and claim that your reason for leaving is saving our people. You and I both know why you want to leave."

"Fine! Can you really blame me for wanting to save my sister? She's up there, alone."

The Scourge stepped toward Roland again as his nostrils flared. "What exactly do you plan to do about it? Picking a fight with the Director is suicide. If you are in a hurry to get yourself killed, you can do that perfectly well down here. Pick a tunnel and start walking."

Roland didn't back away at the Scourge's terrifying advance. He steeled himself and took a step forward of his own. "We're warriors. We can fight—"

"You're a fool if you think we stand a chance against him," Salvador said, sneering. "You were there when he purged the Underworld. Have you forgotten how you watched your friends and family die horrible deaths? And you want to give him another chance to exterminate us? I think not."

"You think I've forgotten?" Roland placed his palms on the side of his head and squeezed, as if it would block out the images. "I watched Refuge and the Silver Guard fall to an army of black like they were no more than an annoyance. I was forced to watch the Director's men eliminate nearly our entire civilization in minutes. But we were ambushed. We weren't prepared for that."

"And you think we are prepared now? There is no fighting them, Roland. There is no winning."

Roland stomped his foot on the dirt floor. "Then we die with honor. The only alternative is staying down here and letting the radiation rot our bodies and kill us slowly." He lowered his voice and glanced outside. "Or worse. Do you really want to end up like the Host? The Desolates? And what if the radiation doesn't kill us? What if *they* do? The Desolates spread out farther every year. It won't be long before they are at our camp. And what's to stop the remaining Host from turning into the monsters that nearly killed me this morning? Our only defense against the Desolates are creatures that are one step away from being mindless animals themselves."

"So we take that risk," Salvador said. "I know all too well what the Director is capable of. I have known it longer than you have known he even exists. If we go up even one level, we face instant execution. At least down here, we stand a chance."

"For all you know, his armies have left the Underworld. They think we're dead."

"It is not worth the risk. Besides, there is no one left to maintain the machine. For all you know, the radiation is just as bad on the other levels as it is here."

Roland folded his arms. "Then the only safe place left is the Overworld."

"Drop it, Roland. I will not let you lead my people to their deaths."

"They're not your people!" Roland finally burst out, his yell a borderline scream.

Salvador took a half-step back, his mouth dropping open a full inch.

"They stopped being your people when you abandoned them three years ago. Corrin had to try to take care of them, Kendall had to pretend to take care of them, but the only one who consistently fought for your people while you were gone was me. I tried to save them from Kendall, and I failed, but at least I tried. At least I was there. Refuge is not yours anymore."

It was a full minute before Salvador spoke again. And when he did, to Roland's surprise, he did not raise his voice. Instead, he spoke quietly, with a hint of a smile.

"For three years, I have hoped that you would be brave enough to say those words to me. It will take someone of such courage to lead Refuge."

Roland scoffed. "You're not listening. I didn't want to lead Refuge. I did what I had to do because no one else would. Corrin tried when it was already too late. Gareth had my back, but he died. So I did it, even though I knew I would fail.

And fail I did. I didn't want to lead Refuge then, and I don't want to lead them now. I can't fail them again."

"So, if they are not my people and you will not take them, what is it that you want, Roland?"

"I want you to step up and save them. I want you to save us all. I want you to save my sister."

Salvador bowed his head. "You know I cannot do that."

"You're telling me you can live with yourself, knowing that if you stay here, you condemn my sister to death? I know what part you played in her so-called sacrifice. I know Kendall was counting on your cooperation. You led her to her death just as much as Nicholas did, but now you have a chance to save her. Can you live with yourself if you don't help her now?"

"I cannot save her, Roland."

"You mean you won't."

"I mean I cannot. The Director is far more powerful than you could possibly imagine. I must protect my family."

"And I have to save mine," Roland said as he turned to leave.

But Salvador called out again. "What of your family here, Roland? What of Corrin? What of Dawn?"

Roland stopped by the exit, but he didn't turn back around. "When the Director is dead and the Overworld is ours, they will be safe."

An audible scoff came from behind him.

"And to think I trusted you to lead my people."

"I never wanted to lead your people!" Roland spun around. "Talk to your daughter. She'll have the guts to do what she we have to do."

"You know she does not care, Roland. She lost interest in anything fruitful when you left her side."

Roland scoffed. "Then do it yourself. Lead them for whatever years they have left. If you can handle Refuge's blood on your hands when you've sentenced them to a slow death down here, go right on ahead. But as for me, I'm going to do what

I have to do and help my family." He turned and walked toward the exit.

"You cannot help anyone if you are dead, Roland."

"Then I'll die trying."

With that, Roland pushed aside the flap and stormed out.

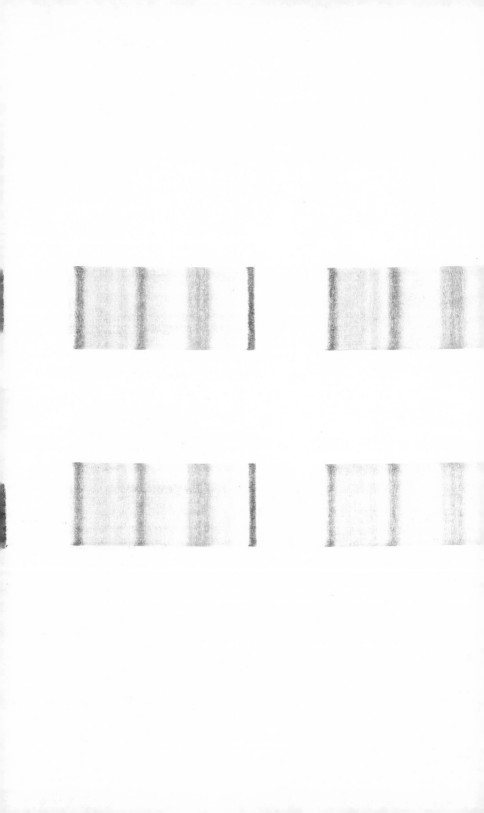

## 7

In the deep dark of the Underworld, a woman in white robes sat alone on the remains of an old stone walkway, surrounded by a chamber of death.

She sat in the midst of a wreckage that would always remind her of her greatest failure. Debris floated around her head, the occasional body drifting by, perfectly preserved by the energizing nature of the chamber.

Despite the horrors that drifted by, the woman's breathing was smooth, deep, yet each breath was separated by the other by minutes. If anyone had happened upon this curious sight, one would swear that she was dead.

But sure enough, as the ceiling of the cave opened above her head, she took a deep breath, perfectly in sync with the wretched creatures that shared her prison in the levels above as a pillar of green light flooded the chamber.

The breath passed away, and the ceiling closed again above her, the cavern going dark again.

This infusion of energy was normally a welcome relief from her perpetual pain. But today, it was a distraction.

Something was calling her name.

She furrowed her brow and dove deep into the dark

recesses of her mind, resuming her focus on the energy that had long since been fused to her very being.

"Yes?" she asked, trusting that the one who had summoned her would hear her words, even though he was miles above her.

"We found it," the voice came back.

The woman smiled. "And Lightbringer?"

"She's ready for you. The serum has broken her mind open."

"Good. Then you know what must be done."

"I do."

The woman opened her eyes without wishing her visitor a farewell.

It was as promised. The words spoken in dreams of deep would finally come to fruition.

Without giving herself too much time to enjoy the moment, the woman closed her eyes and uttered four simple words to her children.

"Bring me the Scourge."

An affirmatory hiss came back in reply, and the woman opened her eyes, deciding to wait for a moment. This next message would be the most draining. Yet it was the most important.

Within minutes, the ceiling opened again, and the Light came rushing down around her. With a deep breath, the woman closed her eyes again.

Wind blew by her face as she dove into the black abyss, falling for several seconds until she was suddenly standing in a room filled with computers and machines.

But the woman ignored everything around her, focused only on the girl in the center of the room.

The prisoner hung limply, suspended by an enormous metal machine, her mouth frozen open in a pained cry. The woman knew it was an accurate outward representation of the girl's inner turmoil. She was trapped in a never-ending torture, a crushing darkness that permitted no joy, no peace. The woman stepped onto the platform and reached through the tank, caressing the girl's face. For a brief moment, she shared in the same pain that overwhelmed the girl.

There was something new, however. A fresh feeling of restlessness that had stirred the woman from her meditative state earlier. And now that she was here with the girl, the feeling was far stronger.

She was almost ready.

The girl showed no signs of life, no visible indication that anything had changed. But it was inherently obvious. Inside the cold void of the girl's mind, there was a spark of light, a heat that was beginning to spread.

With another breath, the woman descended deeper into the void, into the depths of the girl's mind.

There she was. Sitting alone. Weeping.

It was exactly where she had been the last time the dark woman had visited. She was always sitting in the same place, always sobbing.

The woman pitied her. The girl had suffered immensely, and she carried a heavy burden that would only get heavier still.

She had been effectively broken by those who had used her. And her greatest purpose was still to come.

And she would suffer again.

It was the only way.

So it was spoken.

The woman knelt by the girl's side and placed a hand on her shoulder, leaning in and whispering in her ear.

"It's time to wake up."

## 8

R oland winced as the medicinal herbs worked their magic on his shoulder, replacing the stabbing pain with a cold feeling that was terribly uncomfortable. He shuddered under the pressure and took a deep breath.

"Hold still," Dawn's sweet but firm voice came from behind. "I could very easily make this worse."

"I know," Roland said, groaning. "You're doing fine, just keep going."

The pressure on his shoulder increased ever so slightly. "I know I'm doing fine. You taught me well."

Roland bit his lip as a liquid was poured over his shoulder, the burning feeling returning with a vengeance. "You could have let the ginger settle just a little longer."

"Doctors really do make the worst patients," she mumbled.

A brisk kiss brushed Roland's cheek.

"You're lucky I don't mind," she said as she purred softly in his ear.

Roland smiled for a second, then grimaced as the liquid flowed over his shoulder again, this time letting a moan escape his lips.

"Want to tell me what you were doing?"

Roland started to shake his head but then remembered to keep still.

"Not really."

"I thought we talked about this."

"*You* talked about this," Roland mumbled.

His moan escalated as Dawn's hands pressed down tighter on the wound.

"Sorry. Yeah, I talked about it, and you talked about it. That's why I said 'we.'"

"I don't know," Roland said, closing his eyes, trying to block out the pain. "It seemed like a pretty one-sided conversation."

"Can you blame me? I don't want you to get yourself killed."

"Yeah, I get that."

Dawn's voice took on a slightly higher pitch. "Then what do you have against me telling you that?"

"It's not the fact that you said something. It's the words you used. It's almost like Tamisra told you what to say."

"She may have mentioned something. She doesn't want anything to happen to you either, you know."

"I didn't realize you two were talking."

"We're not." A needle jabbed into Roland's shoulder. "At least not like two civilized people should talk. I think she just gave up on talking to you herself and thought I would have better chances of getting through to you."

"Sounds like Tami." Roland winced again as a stitch tightly pulled his skin together.

His opposite shoulder warmed as Dawn's hand gently caressed his skin. "Do you really fault me for wanting you to stay alive?"

Roland reached up to take her hand.

"Hold still."

He rolled his eyes and put his hand back in his lap. "No, I don't blame you. But if I don't go out and find food—"

"Then Salvador will. His hunting party goes out every day. There's always plenty of food for us, you know that. And when Salvador gets too old to carry on, my brother will do it. Lionel's been training every day with the Scourge and will be ready when the time comes. So why are you so intent on going out and looking for a fight? You keep complaining about Salvador's excursions, but you're doing the same thing."

Dawn paused her work and walked around to Roland's front, sitting in front of him and holding his hands. "Refuge needs you, Roland. There's not many of us left, and without a doctor, we won't last much longer. You've been training me well, but you're still the only one skilled enough to handle the more serious things. Ever since Gareth died—"

Without thinking about it, Roland's eyes turned to steel, and his grip on Dawn's hands tightened.

"I'm sorry, Roland. I know he was a father to you. From the brief time I trained with him, I could tell he was a good man, and—"

"A great man." Roland looked down and away from Dawn's pitiful stare as his grip on her hands slipped. "Better than I could ever be. If you think I can take his place, you're wrong. It's too late for that."

"No one ever asked you to. All we can ask of you is to be here for us now. That's all that matters." Dawn squeezed back on his hands. "Forget what happened and just be here now."

Roland didn't pull away, but he nodded slowly as he stared at the ground. He knew she was wrong. He was being asked so much more than she could ever know.

After a moment, Dawn let go of his hands and went back to work on his shoulder. She worked in silence for a few minutes, and when she was done, Roland felt her head rest on his back as her arms wrapped around him.

They sat quietly for a long time, and they would have sat

there until eventually falling asleep if someone had not opened the flap to their tent.

"Roland."

He looked up to see a young man of seventeen poking his head through the flap.

"Yes, Lionel?"

Salvador's squire looked back and forth between Roland and Dawn for a moment. "Hey, sis. Roland."

"What is it?"

Lionel cleared his throat and made a beckoning gesture with his head.

Roland sighed and stood up, Dawn's hands running down his chest as he stood. He turned around and helped her up, smiling faintly at her before turning to leave.

One last squeeze from her hand, and she released him as he left the tent.

Roland followed Lionel away from the tent and was about to ask the reason for the disturbance again, but he cut himself short as he saw the clearing.

Dozens of figures in red cloaks filled the clearing, standing motionless as Salvador paced back and forth in front of the fire, Corrin and Lieutenant Haskill by his side. Tamisra sat at the fire, closer to the Host and seeming ambivalent to the whole ordeal, simply watching the flames. Salvador spotted Roland and Lionel and visibly took a deep breath.

Roland approached Salvador and gestured toward the Host. "What are *they* doing here?"

"Your presence is required," one of them said, hissing through its teeth. "We ask that you accompany us to the center."

"The center?" Roland frowned.

"The Hub," Corrin whispered in Roland's ear.

Salvador folded his arms. "I will go willingly, but you promised my people protection. I have fulfilled my part of the bargain. We are not disturbing anything."

"All of you," the creature said. "She demands it."

Roland stepped forward toward the leader. "Who?"

It smiled thinly, barely revealing its blood-red, toothless gums. "Mother."

Salvador visibly shuddered, a strange sight to Roland.

"Who is Mother?" Lieutenant Haskill frowned.

"Mother is all."

"All what?"

Salvador stepped forward, placing his hand on Roland's shoulder. "We owe her nothing. I rightfully won my place here by defeating your master in combat."

"Master merely guards our border. Master is nothing," the creature said while shaking its head. "Mother is all. You would die without her mercy."

"And I am grateful. But can we not move on in peace?"

"Three years." The creature's tone soured. "Three years we allow you peace. No peace, we taste your flesh. You submit to Mother, peace goes on. That was the deal."

Salvador looked down at the ground for a long moment. When he looked back up, his stone face had softened. "When does she expect us?"

Roland turned to the Scourge, his heart racing. Whatever their mother wanted with Refuge, it couldn't be good. It would mean yet another obstacle standing in the way between him and his sister. "You're really going to give in to their threats, Salvador?"

"We do not have a choice."

Roland lowered his voice to a whisper. "We can fight them."

Salvador's eyebrows raised, and he opened his mouth to speak, but was interrupted.

"Bad idea," a creature's voice whispered in Roland's ear as a drop of something warm and sticky fell on his neck.

"He's right," Corrin muttered. "There are too many of

them. Thousands more than we have ever seen or know about. To fight them would be the end of Refuge."

Roland turned around to face the pale shadow of a man, who still was uncomfortably close to his face. "We'll give you our decision tomorrow."

"This is not your decision, Roland."

Roland spun around to face Salvador. "You made it my decision. You want me to lead Refuge? This is me leading."

"You do not get to choose when you lead them and when you do not," the Scourge said. "Until you decide to carry this burden and are ready for it, I must—"

"We do not care who speaks for your people," the leader hissed. "Mother requires your presence, and you will comply."

Corrin glanced between Salvador and Roland. "I agree with Roland. There's no point in deciding in the heat of the moment. Let's talk about it tonight and give our answer in the morning."

Tamisra stood up from the fire, finally speaking. "I don't know what there is to talk about. They've been gracious enough to allow us to stay as long as they have. The least we can do is see what their mom has to say. Is it really worth making them angry enough to eat us?"

"Says the girl who's pretty much moved in with them," Roland said, rolling his eyes. "Seriously, I see you spend more time with them than with actual people."

Sparks flew as Tamisra stomped in the embers of the fire, not taking her eyes off Roland.

"Enough." Salvador held up a hand and stepped forward to the leader. "We will give you our answer tomorrow."

The creature stared at the Scourge for several seconds before turning and walking away without a word. The rest of the Host followed him, and they soon disappeared into the darkness.

## 9

Caspian stood in the stands, watching the mock fights on the dirt below.

There was nothing ceremonial about the duels, nothing like the celebrated brawls that the President orchestrated when he was the face of Level I. This was simply training, preparation for imminent war.

It hurt his pride just the tiniest bit to watch his lethal, silent assassins reduced to nothing more than foot soldiers. They were the most effective soldiers this level had ever seen, to be sure, but it was brutish work that would have been better left to the Silver Guard back when they were around.

But they had been all but eliminated, wiped out along with the rest of the Underworld. All that was left were the scattered remains of Caspian's own training sector, which held only a few thousand trainees that had managed to overthrow the Director's army.

*Better than the other way around, I suppose,* Caspian mentally noted, trying to find the bright side to these dark circumstances. *If my operatives had been destroyed, I'm not sure the Silver Guard would have been enough.*

Of course, even a few hundred operatives would be wiped out instantly if they faced an army head on.

But what more could he do?

"Sir?"

Caspian smiled, recognizing the voice that came from behind. "Confident enough to leave your squadron without guidance, Omega?"

"They don't need me anymore." The man in black reached Caspian's side and leaned against the railing, letting the silver bands around his wrist show in Caspian's peripheral vision. "There's nothing more I can teach them."

"Can they beat you?"

The assassin smirked. "You know they can't."

"Then perhaps they haven't reached their full potential."

"That's not exactly a fair fight. They're only human, after all."

Caspian turned to Omega. "Even so."

"They'll beat the other squadron leaders in open combat, I can promise you that."

"I believe it. But I didn't summon you to discuss their training. I have a mission for you."

Omega raised his eyebrows. "And here I thought my training would go to waste."

"Never," Caspian said. "I've been saving you all these years for a very important purpose. Your assignment begins today."

"I am at your disposal."

"Good. I trust you've read the dossier on the Vagabond?"

Omega nodded.

"He has located the Key. If it is what I think it is, we can use it against the Director and the Council. We can leverage it to secure our rightful place in the Overworld."

"And you want me to get it?"

"I already have someone on that, but she needs your help."

Omega's eyes narrowed. *"She?* Please don't tell me it's your New Washington operative."

"That's the one."

"I find it hard to believe she needs my help. Surely she didn't ask for me?"

"Even she knows that this mission is one she cannot hope to execute by herself.

Omega smirked. "She really has changed if she's asking for me."

"She knows her limits, perhaps better than you. In any case, she's asked you to remain on standby until summoned."

"Should I gather Omega Squad?"

"No. Her mission is that of stealth, and she's already pushing it as is."

"She has a small army at her disposal. What of the Vagabond's men?"

Caspian scoffed. "They may think they're stealthy, but they're about as subtle as a mole in a market. No, this mission requires a little more tact. Even with herself, the Vagabond, and Lucifer, it will be difficult. I need my best people on this, and that means you."

Omega sucked in air through his teeth. "Lucifer?"

"Yes. Things might get complicated."

"As if they weren't complicated enough. Are you sure you want her? She's dangerous."

Caspian smiled. "That's exactly why I want her. This war will not be easy."

"That's putting it lightly. Even with Lucifer, we'll probably still lose," Omega said quietly.

"With that attitude, Omega, I wouldn't be surprised if we lose." Caspian narrowed his eyes. "I don't raise faithless assassins. I need to rely on you to inspire your squadron, even if it means marching to their deaths."

Omega frowned. "If you wanted someone with faith, you picked the wrong assassin. I'm capable of a great many things, thanks to you, but faith isn't one of them. Again, thanks to you."

"And I have faith that you're wrong. Time will tell." Caspian looked back at the arena. "But if I may be candid with you, I have had many doubts that winning such a war is possible. Even with the Key."

"But . . ." Omega nodded at the ground. "*She* thinks otherwise?"

"She does. And therefore, I deem it worth our efforts."

"And if we lose?"

"Then it won't matter anyway."

"Yes, sir. Do you need anything before I leave for the surface?"

"No, you may go." After a brief pause, Caspian held up a finger. "One more thing, actually."

Omega turned and cocked an eyebrow.

"Be careful with Lucifer. You are right that she is dangerous, and using her is a risk that I don't take lightly."

"Should I be prepared to eliminate her?"

"If necessary."

"Yes, sir."

As Omega's nearly imperceptible footsteps faded away, Caspian turned back to the mock battles.

One of the fighters had drawn blood, but the duo fought on, the wounded dripping blood on the dirt. Caspian sighed and pictured the aftermath of the slaughter three years earlier. The stadium had been covered in blood then, and the tiny spots of red that tainted the dirt now seemed insignificant.

But Caspian bowed his head, knowing that the inevitable war would make the bloodbath he had witnessed look just like these red splotches—mere drops compared to what was to come.

## 10

R oland woke to the sound of screams.

The spear was in his hand even before his eyes fully opened, and he sat up sharply. Dawn was already awake, clutching the blanket in fear and staring at the tent flap, her face cast in an orange glow.

"Stay here," Roland said. He gave her the spear. "If anything comes in here that's not human, just point and thrust." He turned and grabbed a second spear and crawled out of the tent. His breath quickly disappeared, caught by shock and choked by the thick smoke that lingered in the air.

Flames ravaged the sector in hotspots, fueled by the fabric of the tents but unable to proceed due to the dirt ground. Bodies ran through the camp at full speed, first people in clothes carrying weapons, then naked, orange bodies with long claws.

Roland grabbed another spear from a rack outside his tent and took a quick glance at the Host's camp a few hundred yards away. It was in flames as well. The Desolates had completely invaded the sector.

His reflection was cut short as a snarling creature leapt on his back and tackled him, knocking his spear out of his hands.

Knowing he had only seconds, Roland threw his weight to his side and rolled over so now he mounted the drooling creature. He snatched his spear up and buried it deep in the monster's throat, wincing as blood spurted over his face.

As soon as the Desolate stopped gurgling, Roland jumped up and ran toward Salvador's tent at full speed. The Scourge would need help putting his armor on, and he would need it fast. That is, if he hadn't been slaughtered in his sleep already.

Roland shook away the gruesome image and hurtled into Salvador's tent, but he was relieved to find that it was empty already.

An orange creature stepped out of the shadows and lunged toward him, but Roland quickly swiped the spear's tip across the Desolate's throat and pushed it away, leaving it to bleed out on the ground.

He turned away from the tent to face the burning camp and looked around helplessly. The screams sounded from every side, with no way to help everyone at once.

A guttural cry sent tingles down his spine as a smile managed to surface through the panic. The Scourge was indeed awake, and he didn't sound happy.

Roland thrust his spear in the air and opened his mouth to return the shout, but a cold hand clamped down over his mouth.

Red cloaks slowly swept past his body and spread out into the camp, and the hand over Roland's mouth released him as a cloaked, pale figure stepped around him and turned toward Roland, a finger over its bloody lips.

"Shh," it whispered. It backed away and turned to join the rest of the creatures, slowly stepping into the camp and spreading out. Suddenly, they all broke into a dead run, letting their hoods fall against their neck as they simultaneously erupted in a loud shriek.

A monstrous mole burst into the clearing and let loose

with a roar that shook the ground. A man in golden armor sat atop the beast, waving a massive broadsword in the air.

Orange bodies followed the beast, attempting to scale the mole as it ran through the camp. But the mole constantly kicked out, pushing away the creatures, and anything that managed to get any closer met a swift end as Salvador continued to swing his sword.

"My liege!"

Roland turned to the side to see Dawn's brother, Lionel, running toward the clearing, carrying a bundle of arrows. A small torch was strapped to his side, teetering as he struggled underneath the load. With a huff, the young man let the arrows fall to the ground and unhooked a bow hanging from his back.

He nocked one of the arrows to the bowstring and pulled back with some effort. "Sir, the oil!"

Salvador pulled on the reins of the mole, forcing the beast to a halt. He reached down to his side and pulled a sealed jug from one of the saddlebags. After headbutting one of the Desolates off the mole, he threw the jug down on the clamoring creatures, letting the pottery shatter over their heads and leaking its contents out onto the ground. "Now, Lionel!"

The young man touched his arrow to the torch at his side and pulled it back up, letting the now-flaming arrow fly through the air but miss its mark by quite a bit.

"Again, Lionel. Remember your training!" Salvador shouted between swings of his great sword. "Breathe in, then exhale on release. Now, boy, fire again!"

Lionel touched another arrow to his torch, but this one did not light. "No oil," he muttered as he tossed the arrow aside and reached for another.

"Now, Lionel!" Salvador grunted as he swung harder. They were swarming the mole now, climbing aboard the beast from every side.

The Scourge's squire nocked another arrow, but this one

slipped away and fired into the darkness before he could even take aim.

Roland snatched the torch from Lionel's side, tearing the young man's belt open and letting his breeches fall to the ground. Ignoring Lionel's cry of surprise, Roland dashed toward Salvador and tossed the torch into the fray, setting the Desolates aflame.

The fire spread up onto the mole, leaving the Scourge to battle several flaming Desolates. They had reached the warrior and were now clawing at his armor, desperately reaching for an opening through which to sink their razor-sharp claws.

Roland threw his spear at the mass of bodies on top of the mole, wincing as a loud shriek sounded. One of the Desolates fell backward, the spear embedded in its back. As the creature slipped from the mole, Roland grabbed it and yanked the spear out of it. He tossed the creature aside and mounted the mole, which stood still, staring blankly at the fire.

"You took your time, did you not, boy?" Salvador's voice came from beneath a dozen Desolates atop his body, muffled beneath their cries of hunger.

"Sorry about that," Roland said as he jabbed the spear into one of the creatures and pushed it away and off the mole. "No one bothered to wake me up." He kicked another Desolate off the beast and elbowed yet another as it placed a clawed hand on his shoulder.

"Apologies, Roland. I will be sure to wake you before responding to the next invasion." Salvador broke free of the remaining Desolates and pushed them off the mole.

Roland grabbed another creature by the throat and strangled it as he growled in Salvador's ear. "And you still want to stay down here?"

"Later," Salvador simply said as he lobbed the head off another one.

As the last Desolate was clear from the mole, Roland

tossed his spear to the ground, jumped off the mount, and rolled to a standing position, grabbing his spear as he straightened.

Lionel shuffled over, holding his breeches up by a hand. Casting a glare at Roland, he looked up at Salvador and muttered, "Sorry."

Salvador pulled a rope from the saddlebag and tossed it to his squire. "You had the courage to come out here and see to your master. Heart is the first necessity of a battle-worthy warrior, and you showed that. Now, get back inside and secure your clothing. You will not do any good with your trousers around your ankles."

Lionel nodded and trotted away, barely managing to stay upright.

"How bad is it?" Roland asked.

"Not terribly." Salvador surveyed the camp quickly, as much as he could in the pitch black. "Casualties are few, at least from what I have seen. The Host were attacked at the same time, it seems, so their response was delayed, but now that they are here, it seems the fight will be over shortly. What of Dawn?"

"Fine when I left her. She has a weapon, but I should get back to her soon."

Salvador narrowed his eyes. "I am surprised you left her. What happened to caring for your family?"

"I knew I would be needed out here," Roland shot back. "Not many of us fighters are left. If Dawn doesn't make it, then at least I'll have been out here, dying for Refuge."

The Scourge stared at Roland for several seconds before shaking his head. "You should go see to her. Lionel would not be happy to hear that you left his sister alone to fend for herself."

"She's fine."

Tamisra stepped out from the formation of tents, her double-edged spear dripping blood.

"Scared out of her wits, and she nearly impaled me, but she'll be fine."

Roland nodded gratefully. "Thank you for checking on her."

"Don't mention it," Tamisra said without meeting his eyes. "Ever."

Salvador grunted. "We should get back out there."

Tamisra held up a hand. "No need. I just swept the camp with the Host. We're clear. They're already on their way back to their own camp."

"Then we need to talk about what this means for us," Roland said, turning to Salvador. "I told you, the Desolates are spreading out farther, and they're not scared of attacking us in open battle. The Host is not enough protection anymore. We have to leave this level."

Salvador looked like he was about to speak, but as he looked around the burning campsite, his mouth slowly closed. For the first time in three years, it seemed he had no response to Roland's unchanging demand.

"I would hardly call ambushing us in the middle of the night an open battle," a voice came from behind.

Roland turned to see Lieutenant Haskill emerging from the shadows, dual spears dripping blood.

"There is no night to them," Tamisra said, shaking her head. "It's all the same."

"You would know." Roland glared at her.

Salvador stepped in between Roland and Tamisra. "Regardless, you are correct, Roland. At least partially. The Desolates are finally at our front door, and they have shown that they are ready to attack us. They do not answer to Mother and would devour us without hesitation. And if we do not comply with Mother's demands, I doubt we can expect the Host's protection from them. The only way to ensure our safety is to acquiesce."

"The only way to ensure our safety is to leave," Roland growled.

"I will not concede on that point yet."

"Yet?"

Salvador bowed his head. "I do not know what their mother wants. Perhaps they have decided it is time that we owe them for letting us stay here. If I were to agree with your brash wishes to flee to the Overworld, I cannot say that her children will not follow us."

"And if we can leave safely?" Roland asked slowly.

"Then we will revisit this discussion at a later date. For now, I trust you know what we must do."

Roland fumed, clenching his fists as he took a deep breath.

"Fine. Let's go see Mother."

## 11

"It's time to wake up."

The whisper surrounded Aniya's consciousness, echoing, growing until the words turned to a shout.

Aniya opened her eyes, and the voice ceased. But as her eyelids opened fully, she realized that they were actually still closed.

The voice came again, this time more firm. "It's time to wake up."

Frowning, Aniya opened her eyes again, but though she could have sworn she felt motion, her eyes were somehow indeed still closed.

"It's time to wake up!"

The voice came as a shout this time, not even bothering with a whisper. The deafening cry bounced between her ears over and over, and each time Aniya opened her eyes just to find them shut, the voice grew louder.

Aniya thrust open her eyelids again and again, an endless cycle of opening her eyes without them ever closing. They didn't have to close. They were already shut.

Finally, in a cry of agony, Aniya intentionally squeezed her eyes closed and then opened them one more time, this time being granted vision.

Before her in a stadium of dirt stood Nicholas, a warm smile on his face. Instantly, his body was riddled with bullets, and he fell to the ground before her. The dirt vanished beneath his body, and he hung there, suspended in the black nothingness.

Biting her lip until she drew blood, Aniya slammed her eyes closed, just to find them open again, staring at Nicholas's corpse and unable to look anywhere else.

Refusing to subject herself to the pain any longer, Aniya screamed and summoned what light she could from deep within her. The black chamber around her pulsed red, and Nicholas's body disappeared, leaving behind only dancing red sparks.

The sparks slowly approached her, materializing into human form. Aniya winced, preparing to see the sickening sight of her dead lover again, but the form that took shape was not Nicholas.

"Aniya, dear. It's time to wake up."

The Chancellor solidified, his entire body painted in red. Aniya blinked, and when her eyes opened, the man was in his familiar white suit again.

"What are you doing here?" Aniya spat. "Decided to finally show up after all this time? It's been—" Aniya halted. She had no idea how long she had been trapped in this prison. There was no way to tell time, and no one to keep track for her. She hadn't seen the Chancellor or her brother for what felt like years.

"It's not up to me, I'm afraid. I'm no more than a part of your psyche. It's up to you when I show up. Why don't you ask your brother?"

Aniya looked up sharply, ready to fire a witty retort at the man, but she realized that he was right. If her old nemesis was making an appearance after all this time, maybe William could as well. She had tried many times to find her brother in the awful place, but every attempt thus far had proved pointless.

"William?" Aniya spun around, and she nearly fell backward when she saw William standing directly behind her.

Her brother spread his arms and grinned. "It's about time."

"William!" She jumped forward, letting him wrap his arms around her tight. "I didn't think I'd ever see you again."

"Me neither," he said, stroking her hair. "I've been sitting by myself, staring at a black wall, for what feels like forever."

After several minutes, Aniya finally let herself step away. "So you don't know how long we've been here for either?"

"On one hand, it feels like years ago. On the other, it feels like just yesterday."

Aniya nodded. "I know what you mean." After a pause, her nod turned to a shake. "On second thought, no. It doesn't feel like yesterday. It feels like my entire life, times a dozen. And then some."

"Well, I'm here now." William smiled as he stroked her hair.

"Not for long."

Aniya frowned and turned back around to the Chancellor, who stood with folded arms as he looked around the void. "What's that supposed to mean?"

"You know what I mean, Aniya. It's time to wake up."

"Wake up? There is no waking up. Not from this."

The Chancellor shrugged. "Whatever you think, there is no denying the truth. You don't feel it?"

"Feel what?" William stepped around Aniya.

"Oh, my. Nothing's changed, has it? Still hiding behind your emotions, too afraid to face anything real." The Chancellor smiled softly, and Aniya really couldn't tell if it was genuine or in mockery. "As long as you surrender control to the demons in your mind, you'll never be able to be free to embrace your true power."

"Stop speaking in riddles and answer me," Aniya spat. Heat flooded her cheeks, and the Chancellor's suit began to bleed, slowly dying the white fabric crimson. "What am I supposed to be feeling?"

"Life, Aniya. The mere fact that you are talking to us now means that something has changed. William may be a prisoner of your mind, and you may have subjected yourself as a prisoner to yourself, but I am a manifestation of your deepest feelings. You have used me to hide from the pain in your life, and so I see everything. I feel everything. You may have no clue how long it's been, but I have been waiting patiently for three years, forced to watch you hide in a corner, deaf to my cries. I don't know who it's been tougher on, you or me."

Aniya's jaw dropped. "Three years?"

"We can't trust him, Aniya." William touched her arm.

The Chancellor rolled his eyes. "I *am* her, boy. I am merely the image her subconscious has chosen to project, and as such, I have no reason to lie to her, to ourselves."

"Why are we——" Aniya shook her head. No reason to sound as ridiculous as he did. "Why am I waking up?"

He shrugged. "Dunno."

"After your theatrics, ranting about how I'm a dumb child who has no idea what's going on, that's all you have for me?" Aniya fumed. "Dunno?"

The Chancellor smirked. "I don't know why, but I know it's happening, and it's happening fast. Get ready to face the world again, dear Annelise."

With that, the Chancellor vanished.

Aniya spun around, but William was gone as well.

"What the——"

She was cut short as the world around her began to shake. Aniya was forced to the black ground, tumbling as the shaking intensified.

The void looked still as ever, a pure black landscape that appeared motionless. But her body trembled violently, her bones rattling against each other as the quakes continued.

Heat surged through Aniya's hands, and she looked down as the light appeared again, a white glow that quickly grew to shining beacons that pierced through her clenched fists.

The Chancellor was right, and Aniya knew it. The shaking showed no signs of stopping, and Aniya had no idea how long it would take, but he was right.

She was waking up.

## 12

"**D**own."

A week later, in Level XIX, on the bottom floor of the abandoned Citadel, Roland peered over the edge of the elevator shaft, looking down into the depths and seeing nothing but black. "You're kidding."

Lionel appeared by Roland's side and studied the darkness. "You're not going down there, right?"

Roland turned around and faced the red-robed creature, standing by the open elevator shaft with a face void of expression. Standing beside the representative of the Host were Salvador, Corrin, Tamisra, and the lieutenant, all of them looking on dubiously. Behind them, filling the halls of the desolate Citadel, was the entire population of Refuge, crammed into the obelisk and spilling out into the streets of the Hub.

"Down," the creature said again, pointing a clawed finger into the seemingly endless pit.

Lieutenant Haskill shook his head. "How are we supposed to get down there? The instant we call the elevator, the Director will know."

The creature held a torch out into the pit, revealing twin

steel ladders against the cement walls to the left and right, reaching up into darkness and down into the abyss.

"How did you manage to run ladders down here?" Salvador muttered.

"Here long before us," the creature hissed.

Roland stepped forward, letting his toes reach out over the edge. A rush of dizziness swept from his loins to his head, and he wavered slightly. He ignored the pit and turned toward the ladder on the right. "Must have been placed by the Lightbringers in case of emergency. Just gotta hope the elevator doesn't happen to appear out of nowhere while we're on the ladder."

The creature let loose with raspy laughter, a sharp noise that was echoed by the Host down the hallways of the dark Citadel. "Hasn't been down here in ages."

Corrin shrugged. "No reason to stand here thinking about it, I guess."

"You're right," Roland said, nodding. He reached to the right and grabbed the ladder. To his relief, the structure remained firm and did not waver as he placed his weight on it. Taking a deep breath, he stepped out over the pit and placed his feet on the closest rung. "Let's go."

Lionel stepped forward, but Salvador held out a hand and blocked him.

"Stay up here," the Scourge said. "We do not know exactly what is waiting for us down there."

"Yes, sir." Lionel, obviously disappointed, stepped back to Corrin's side.

Salvador nodded and turned to face the others. "Lieutenant, come with me. Corrin, stay here and watch the others. There's more than enough room in the Citadel, so set up camp. I don't know how long we'll be."

"If you don't mind, sir, I'll stay here with Corrin." The lieutenant cleared his throat. "As you pointed out, the Citadel is quite large, and I'm sure Corrin could use my help."

Tamisra stepped forward, pushing past Haskill. "I'll come. I'm curious to know what this Mother is like anyway."

Salvador frowned but allowed her to step in front of him and directly above Roland on the ladder.

"Move," Tamisra's annoyed command came from above.

As Salvador stepped onto the other ladder, Roland descended into the abyss.

"Tell Mother we say hello," they said in one voice, drawing out the last word and letting it turn into a hollow chuckle.

Roland, Tamisra, and Salvador climbed down the ladders for several minutes, taking intermittent rests by tying themselves to the ladder by rope and letting their torsos pull against the restraints as their feet remained on the rungs.

Finally, they reached another opening. Roland could tell that a metal barrier had once stood between the elevator shaft and the dark tunnel ahead, but the opening seemed blown to pieces, metal debris scattered about the immediate area.

As Roland hopped off the ladder, Tamisra looked down at the continuing pit. "I thought you said this was the last level of the Underworld, Father."

"To my knowledge, it is." Salvador dismounted the other ladder and stepped onto the landing. "I have no idea what might be down there."

Roland stepped away from the shaft and into the tunnel. The destroyed blast doors left the path ahead clear. "To be honest, I'm not sure I want to know."

"What happened to your curiosity, dear boy?" Salvador approached Roland from behind and placed a hand on his shoulder. "There was once a day when you would have gone down at least another fifty rungs before resigning yourself to continue on our predetermined path."

Roland shrugged Salvador's hand away and began walking down the tunnel, pulling glowworms from his pack. "I grew up."

The trio continued down the path until they reached the terrasphere that would take them to the reactor chamber. This was no surprise to Roland, but what he didn't expect was that the sphere was lit up with a pulsing yellow light.

"Strange," Tamisra muttered. "I thought the power was out all over the Web."

Roland ran his hand over the sphere, the faint electricity buzzing over his skin. "Maybe this runs off a battery in case of emergency."

"Unlikely," Salvador said. "This level has not had power in a very long time. Any battery would have died by now."

"Does it matter?" Tamisra opened the door to the terrasphere. "You said this takes us to the chamber, right, Roland? Let's just go."

Roland glanced at Salvador before following Tamisra inside.

As soon as they were all inside and closed the door, the sphere took off, traversing the tunnel at breakneck speed, yet providing an impossibly smooth ride that barely registered as motion to Roland. As they journeyed, a green glow began to appear in the tunnel, growing brighter as they continued.

When the sphere finally stopped, they got out and walked for a few paces before reaching a large opening. The sight that awaited them was beautiful and terrible all at the same time.

The reactor chamber lay in chaos. To Roland, it was quite reminiscent of his sister's work three years ago.

All those years ago, he had seen Aniya utterly destroy the reactor chamber in the level above, causing a horrifying earthquake that broke free pillars of enslaved humans, letting them topple over and fall into the abyss below.

The aftermath of this cavern was similar to the state in which Aniya and Roland had left Level XVIII's reactor chamber, yet this one was somehow so much worse.

No pillar seemed to be missing, but every single one of the thousands of pods on the pillars was burst open, some of them leaving a skeleton dangling out of the broken glass, held in place only by the wires that clung to bare bones. Many of the bodies had broken free of the pods, and their remains floated in the air, held up by the anti-gravity shafts.

Green ooze seemed to cover the pillars and rock walls, unmoving yet somehow seeming alive, pulsing with a glow that painted the chamber with light.

The massive hole in the center of the chamber was identical to the one above, and in front of this one sat a cross-legged figure, facing the hole silently.

Roland took a step forward. "Are you—"

A rumble shook the cavern, sending Roland stumbling backward into the arms of Tamisra. As she pushed him away, the shaking grew worse, and Roland fell backward, facing the cave ceiling just in time to watch the steel pull away in a spiral, revealing a gaping hole in the cavern. A hissing sigh seemed to float down from above, and suddenly a beam of green light shot down from the ceiling and blasted into the abyss below.

Roland pulled himself to the edge of the walkway and looked down. The light revealed a massive orb that absorbed the light and flashed a brilliant yellow.

Suddenly, the green light disappeared, and a loud boom resounded from the reactor below, sending a yellow burst of light up from the abyss, accompanied by a shockwave that nearly shook Roland off the edge.

These vibrations were much shorter, and they soon ceased abruptly. The yellow light from the reactor slowly faded, but even when the light disappeared, Roland could see a faint green glow emanating from the orb below.

Roland stood up slowly, his body still shaking. He looked back up to see the ceiling close back up and seal itself.

"That's impossible," Roland said, his voice audibly trembling. "The power is gone."

"The light never dies." A feminine voice echoed throughout the chamber. "It may be crushed into darkness here, and I felt your light snuff out years ago, but it never truly dies."

Roland looked toward the figure sitting in front of the hole. It had not moved, despite the violent commotion just seconds earlier. "Mother?"

"I am not your mother," the voice came back. "Your voice is tainted by the Light, to be sure, but you are not one of my children."

The bald figure finally stood and turned to face them, and by the light of the green glow, Roland looked upon a hauntingly beautiful woman.

Her skin was the same white color as the Host's, but her eyes did not carry the same red glow. Nor were they dark like the Desolates'. They were a brilliant green, just like Aniya's had been right after she first awoke from the tank all those years ago.

She wore a white robe that flowed loosely around her body, which rocked and swayed hypnotically as she approached.

To top it all off, her lips were a bright red that stood out against her pale skin, but they did not bleed like the creatures Roland had come to know. Rather, they seemed to glow, perking up in a soft smile.

"I am pleased to finally meet you," the woman said. "You can call me Neeshika, as you have not yet borne the Light long enough to be of my flock. I understand that this brave fighter is General Salvador, my adopted son who has finally accepted my invitation after all these years."

Salvador bowed his head. "You understand my trepidation, Neeshika. I was not exactly excited about meeting the leader of the Host."

"You are forgiven, dear." The woman turned to Tamisra and stroked her cheek with long fingernails. "And this must be the warrior princess herself, Tamisra. Accounts of your tenacity have ascended to legend, dear one."

For the first time in years, Roland saw a blush creep over Tamisra's face.

Finally, Neeshika turned to Roland. "And the boy with darkness in his heart, Roland Lyons. Your skills indeed rival that of the princess', and like her, they have become your very identity. Just know that the battle will never fill the void in your heart."

As Roland found himself at a loss for words, Tamisra spoke up. "How do you know us so well?"

"My dear, you have few qualms about associating yourself with my children. Did you really not think word would reach me of your exploits?"

"Considering we didn't know about you until just recently," Roland muttered, "I'd say it's understandable for us to be surprised."

Neeshika pouted at Salvador. "After the mercy I gave you, you waited until now to tell them of me? I cannot claim that I do not understand, but I must say, that wounds me deeply."

"Forgive me, Mother," Salvador said. "My first priority was providing for my own children. I did not believe they needed to know of you, let alone make the journey to see you in person. But I feared what the Host would do if we did not answer your summons, let alone what might happen when the Desolates gather their full force against us."

"Yes, dear. My children are restless, I know. The soulless do not like to stay in one place very long, and once they have their hearts set on a new place, they do not care what stands in their way. Even those who still have thoughts of their own are smart and quick enough to adopt change." Neeshika touched Salvador's lips with a white finger. "But that is not the only reason you feel you must leave, yes? You fear what awaits you should you stay."

"I never said I wished to leave," Salvador said.

"No, we don't want to stay here," Roland interjected, stepping forward and ignoring Salvador's glare. "We know we have to leave. My sister is up there, and I don't want to turn into one of your children. No offense."

"Are we not lovely, child? Do you truly dread your fate if it means taking my appearance?" She laughed, and unlike the Host, her mirth was genuine and sent warm tingles down Roland's spine. "You would rather face death at the hands of the Council?"

Roland frowned. "The Council?"

"The hand that guides the Director," Salvador muttered from behind Roland.

Neeshika turned to Salvador. "Yes, you know their influence all too well, do you not, Scourge? You know the pain they can inflict on thousands. You and I learned the hard way. It is because of them that I have resigned myself to this prison."

"Prison?" Roland gestured at the tunnel behind him. "There's ladders in the elevator shaft, you know. It's not like you're stuck here."

Neeshika smiled again, though this one was not reflected in her sparkling green eyes. "Oh, child. My chains are not physical. I am bound here by my guilt. This chamber is an eternal reminder of my greatest failure, the desolate remainder of my pride."

"What are you talking about?" Tamisra shook her head, grimacing. "No offense, Mom, but you're harder to understand than my father."

A light chuckle escaped Neeshika's lips as she pointed at Salvador. "He can explain. He knows better than anyone what it means to fail, why we must never forget the danger of our hubris."

Salvador took a deep breath. "It was long ago, and I have only heard the tale through hearsay, but the story of Level XIX has been told time and time again to encourage those in leadership to never make the same mistake."

After a moment, Neeshika nodded toward Salvador. "Well?"

With a glare, Salvador continued. "It was about two hundred years ago. The president of Level XIX was the first to lead a revolt against the Director, barely a year after being appointed to the position of president. The Council sent their army to quell the rebellion, and after a war that lasted three hours, the President was brought to the reactor chamber and was made to watch as those in servitude each suffered a long and painful death, one at a time. Those who did not participate in the rebellion were left alive to suffer as radiation freely permeated the Web and ravaged their bodies."

Salvador turned to Tamisra. "I told you I came down here to escape my guilt for the lies I told you and the rest of Refuge. To be quite honest, I came here because they understand my guilt. It's all they know. At least I would not be judged here."

"Because no matter how much you have failed," Neeshika said, smiling sadly, "you could not possibly have failed as much as I did." She turned to face the wreckage of the chamber before them. "And so I remain here, prisoner to my guilt and eternally paying atonement for my sins."

Roland frowned. "You mean, you're the president that started the rebellion? I thought he said that was two hundred years ago."

"And it feels like much longer," Neeshika said. "A guilty conscience makes for a hard pillow indeed."

Tamisra smirked. "I bet the rocks don't help much. But how are you still alive?"

"Radiation, it seems, is better than any anti-aging drug the Director has managed to manufacture."

"Are all of you that old?" Roland looked back at the elevator shaft, picturing the Host waiting for them back in the Citadel.

"I cannot imagine them being able to procreate in their current state, so yes. I would say that is a fair assumption."

"So there's only so many of them," Roland said, turning to Salvador. "If we hunt down the remaining Desolates, they'll run out of people eventually."

"Careful, dark one," Neeshika said, her voice taking a sharp edge. "Those are my children you speak of. They have given their humanity to the sickness in their flesh, but they are still my children."

Roland folded his arms. "But they're cannibals. They eat each other and would die out eventually anyway."

"I understand this quandary. Yet so do they. They have learned to go a great deal of time without food, enjoying a feast of flesh only when attacked or as a last resort. The Desolates have no such self-control, and they hunt without reservation. Thus, they present themselves to the Host on a somewhat frequent basis."

Salvador shook his head. "How have you not died out by now?"

"The decline to cannibalism did not happen immediately, child. And even now that their own flesh is all they have taste for, I think you underestimate our numbers. Everyone who did not participate in the rebellion was left alive to live in misery, and there were few who even knew a rebellion existed. Word of my intentions spread far too quickly for me to muster any great number. And so, there is a Web full of my children out there, each of them just trying to survive."

Neeshika paused here and closed her eyes. "A moment, please." She turned and walked to the edge of the pathway and stood before the massive hole.

Several seconds passed before Roland turned to Salvador and opened his mouth, but the shaking resumed again as the ceiling opened. Salvador took Roland's arms and held him upright as the massive beam of green light shot down from above and energized the reactor below. Roland looked over his shoulder to see Neeshika standing before the light, her arms wide.

The light finally ceased, and after one shockwave that roared back up through the cavern, everything was still again, and the ceiling closed back up.

Neeshika turned and approached the trio again. "Now, where were we?"

Roland took a deep breath and finally asked the question that had been nagging him for several minutes. "Why aren't you like them?"

"Like them?" Neeshika asked with a hint of mirth. "You mean vicious, deadly, inhuman?" She bared her teeth, another difference between herself and the Host. "I think I can be plenty vicious if the need arises."

With a sigh, she turned and faced the cavern again. "But no. There is indeed a marked difference when compared to my children. I suspect this is because I face a different hell down here in this cavern. I also do not partake in the flesh of my children. The Light is my sustenance and my only companion. It is why I recognize its traces in every one of you." Neeshika pointed at each of them, pausing for a moment on Roland.

Tamisra scoffed. "You haven't eaten in two hundred years?"

"I have no need," Neeshika said, shrugging with a smile. "Nor have I want. Despite my exile, I am content to live down here alone, to suffer alone."

"If you say so," Tamisra said. "Just wipe that smile off your face when you look at me. You look hungry."

Salvador glared at his daughter. "Quiet, child. You speak of things you do not understand."

"Let it be, Salvador." Neeshika waved a hand. "Her igno-rance is outdone only by her passion, which you will surely need in the coming days. But I regret to say, dear, that neither I nor my people can join you."

He looked back at the woman, surprise written on his face. "Join us with what?"

"It is the question written on your heart. The one your bold, young friend speaks so freely. You must learn to speak your truest self, Salvador, if you hope to survive the wrath of the Council. And angry they will be when he learns of your survival. Angrier still if you manage to rescue poor Aniya."

Roland's heart leapt. "Then you'll help us leave?"

"I did not agree to this," Salvador said as his voice lowered to a growl.

Neeshika frowned. "You would stay here? You would succumb to a darker fate and share in my destiny? It is a heavy path, one I do not wish on you if not necessary."

"We will take it freely," Salvador said. "You know the power of the Director. I refuse to suffer at his hand when at least we stand a chance here."

Neeshika hissed, "You must leave. There is more at stake than the dwindling numbers of the children of Refuge. You must fight for millions more. And if you insist on staying here, know that I can make it rather . . . painful for you."

As Salvador's growl intensified, Roland spoke up again. "How do we get out of here safely? If we call the elevator, the Director will find us instantly. If we take the spiral tunnel, it'll take weeks to get anywhere. We wouldn't survive the journey. Forget climbing the ladder in the shaft. There's thousands of us."

"Fear not, and trust me. You will understand when you go to collect your people."

"Forget it," Salvador said. "It is not safe to leave."

Neeshika laughed again. "Safe? Your road is fraught with danger, child, no matter which path you take. But I can make it less dangerous. I can give you an army."

"An army?" Roland's eyes widened. "The Host can put up a fight, but I don't think they'd stand a chance against the Director. Not with his weapons."

Tamisra scoffed. "They're stronger than you give them credit for."

Neeshika tilted her head softly toward Tamisra. "My children are indeed a force to be reckoned with, but no. Their destiny is sealed, given to another purpose. I offer another army, one that will impress even the Scourge here."

A smile spread across Roland's face. "When can we leave?"

"Immediately," Neeshika said. "They are waiting for you now."

Salvador shook his head and opened his mouth again, but Neeshika stepped forward and placed a finger on his lips.

"You must choose to die here a coward or die protecting the family you claim to love, Aram. But Refuge will leave this level, with or without you. So it has been spoken."

"So you're suggesting we do just that?" Tamisra put her hands on her hips. "We'd be sitting targets for them, waiting for everyone to get up there, wherever there is."

Salvador nodded. "And besides that, the instant we call the elevator, it would alert the Council to our very existence and our position."

"Which is why I do not, in fact, suggest the elevator. I suggest the elevator shaft. Surely you have familiarized yourself with the ladders by now."

Roland shook his head. "That's insane. It's miles to the next level, hundreds to the surface. There's no way we could make it that far."

"I never said it would be easy, dear Roland. You ask for a safe, easy route out of my hellish dominion. I say to you that no such path exists. You can either have safe or easy. The choice is yours. But if you need more reason to do the right thing, I will share with you a secret that the Director himself dare not admit, the reason I have summoned you. There is hope for your people yet. Annelise Lyons is waking up."

Roland's breath caught in his lungs as his eyes widened. "Aniya?"

Neeshika nodded.

"How? I thought the Director had her."

"All will be made clear in time," Neeshika said gently. "She is waking up, but she needs your help. The Council will stop at nothing to enslave her again, and if they manage to do so, they will ensure that this time, she will not wake up."

Roland spun around to face Salvador. "How about now? Could you live with yourself knowing that if you stay here, you condemn my sister to death? I know what part you played in her so-called sacrifice. I know Kendall was counting on your cooperation. You led her to her death just as much as Nicholas did, but now you have a chance to save her. Can you live with yourself if you don't help her now?"

Salvador fell silent and bowed his head.

"Very well," Neeshika said. "Now, go. The Host above have prepared your people for a long journey."

Roland paused. "How do they know? Don't you need to tell them?"

"I already have."

Tamisra scoffed. "How does that work?"

Neeshika gave a final smile. "Best you never know, child."

R oland stepped off the ladder and onto the ground floor of the Citadel with the help of one of the Host. As he looked around, he soon realized that the building was completely empty.

"Where is everyone?" he asked as Tamisra appeared behind him, deftly launching herself out of the elevator shaft and landing on her feet.

The creature only smiled.

Salvador stepped into the hallway and instantly narrowed

his eyes. "Where are my people? What have you done with them?"

Roland pushed past the creature and made his way through the hallway, finding his own way to the front door and bursting it open, stepping onto the front steps and facing the Hub.

His heart stopped as he saw the survivors of the Underworld corralled into the narrow streets of the Hub, surrounded by an army of black.

"No," he whispered as Salvador appeared by his side.

"What is this?" The Scourge roared in anger and spun around, grabbing the creature and hoisting it in the air. "Your mother promised us an army to help us, not destroy us. You've turned us over to the Director!"

"Not quite," a calm voice came from below, and Roland squinted in the shadows as a man in a black suit ascended the steps of the Citadel.

The man stopped in front of Salvador and gently laid a hand on the Scourge's shoulder.

"My name is Caspian Addington, and these are my men. I have come to escort you to Level I and help you destroy the Director."

# PART II

# REAWAKENING

## 13

## ONE WEEK LATER

The sanctum lay quiet in the dead of night.

Not a beep or hum could be heard, despite the high-tech gear that filled the room.

Yet the sanctum was anything but peaceful. A girl in a white bodysuit floated in a tank at the center of the room, attached to a giant machine that sucked the energy from her body. She had been frozen in this position for the last three years, but anyone who had the privilege of witnessing the sight over the years would be alarmed now at the girl's state.

Rather than the green energy that had constantly emanated from her body since she was initially trapped inside, an angry red glow pulsed from within the tank, casting a crimson glow over the room.

And to witness it all was a cloaked figure, standing before the tank and watching the red light grow stronger.

It wasn't long before the girl moved for the first time in three years. It wasn't a gradual awakening, either.

From a completely motionless state, the girl went into convulsions, thrashing wildly, her eyes clamped shut.

Her fists were closed even tighter than her eyes, and from between her fingers intermittently shot thin beams of red light, which shot out of the tank, piercing tiny holes in the glass and leaking drops of water to the floor.

The cloaked figure stood still, not bothering to move.

The light grew brighter still until the girl was barely visible, and the beams of light from her fists grew wider, shooting out bigger holes in the tank and letting water spill out into the sanctum at an alarming rate.

Still, the cloaked figure watched, tapping its toes in ankle-deep water.

Finally, the girl opened her eyes.

## 14

The first thing Aniya saw was a figure standing before her, dressed in a long, white cloak with black trim. Her eyes flew open wide, and she thrust her hands out in front of her, snapping open the metal braces that trapped her arms and letting loose with a massive beam of red light that shattered the tank around her and burned a hole in the wall on the opposite side of the room, the subsequent explosion ringing in her head.

With a gasp, Aniya let her arms fall to her side. She looked back up, but the figure was gone. Her only companion was the ringing in her ears. Sighing, Aniya bowed her head, looking back up sharply as her feet descended to the ground.

As the ringing subsided, Aniya realized that an alarm was sounding, a piercing whine that made her ears hurt. Looking up, she saw a spinning red light on the ceiling that rotated around with every blare of the alarm.

Annoyed, Aniya glared at the light, which promptly exploded in sparks, and the siren died away. The noise still rang out farther away, but it was muffled and not nearly as annoying.

"Aniya."

Startled, Aniya stumbled backward and threw up her hands defensively, sending twin beams of red light into more computers on the wall.

When the beams died away, a cloaked figure slowly appeared where two smoking computers had just been, rising from the ground carefully, hands extended.

"Wait," a female voice came from beneath the hood.

The voice sent shivers through Aniya's body. It was a familiar one, but she couldn't place it.

"You're disoriented," she said. "Still waking up. You need to breathe."

Aniya shook her head violently, unable to get rid of the disgusting feeling in the back of her mind. A heat drew her attention to her feet, and as she looked down, she was only mildly surprised to find that her feet were on fire.

"Breathe, Aniya."

Aniya did, but as she took a deep breath, the flames spread across her body and engulfed her flesh from head to toe. She closed her eyes tight even though the fire was painless.

"Please, you don't—"

These words were enough to send her over the edge, and Aniya felt the heat leave her suddenly, and she opened her eyes in time to see a wave of fire spread throughout the entire room, lighting every piece of equipment in flame and scorching the metal ground.

Everything went silent for a moment, and this time Aniya took a breath with no negative effect.

"Aniya, please, you need to take a moment and pull yourself together. We don't have much time."

Every word hammered sharp pain into Aniya's brain, and at least a dozen beams of red light shot from her body and flew across the room.

"Shut up!" Aniya screamed as she clutched the side of her head.

After a long pause, with the distant siren being the only sound, Aniya took another breath.

"Who are you?"

Another pause.

"I don't think you're ready for that, Aniya."

This time, pure anger surged through her body, and the room lit up in a bright red light as she shouted. "Tell me!"

"Okay, okay! Just calm down before you kill us both."

After another moment, a figure descended from above, falling to the ground before Aniya and landing gracefully. The girl slowly straightened and brushed off her white cloak, the black trim seeming to flash red as it swayed before Aniya.

Finally, the girl pulled her hood away, revealing one of the last people in the world Aniya wanted to see.

With a scream of fury, Aniya pushed her hands forward, releasing a massive burst of light that disappeared down the same hole in the opposite wall that she had burned just moments prior.

But the girl had already vanished, Aniya realized as the light died away. She looked up at the top of the tank, which was still intact and attached to the main machine behind her.

Aniya thrust her hands up and let another beam of light pierce the ceiling of the tank, and out of the corner of her eye, she saw a flash of white. Aniya dragged the beam across the room, following the white fabric, but it quickly vanished again, and Aniya let the light extinguish as a fluorescent light fixture crashed to the ground.

"Please, Aniya. I'm not here to hurt you."

"You tried to have me killed!" Aniya threw a fireball toward the voice, even though she knew it would have already moved.

"I know it's hard to believe, but I'm here to get you out."

"You shot Malcolm and left him for dead!" A volley of lasers this time, landing in quick succession in the shadows toward Aniya's right.

"I woke you up. You would have stayed in there forever if I did nothing, but I woke you up."

"You brought me here to die!" Aniya tucked into a ball and exploded outward, letting a wall of light grow across the room, sending sparks flying whenever the light touched a piece of equipment.

No voice spoke for a long time. The assassin was dead. She couldn't have dodged that last attack, and Aniya knew it.

She breathed in deep and took exactly one step toward the doors before freezing in place at the sound of the girl's voice.

"I know what I did, Aniya, and it's no excuse. But that doesn't matter anymore. I'm here to help now, and I can prove it."

Aniya stared into the darkness, stunned. There was no way the girl could have survived that. There was simply no way.

"Oh, Annelise."

Another voice spoke now, this one from the other end of the room.

Instantly, the assassin was pushed to the back of Aniya's mind. Now, she turned with utter hatred toward the man standing in the double doors toward her left.

"I do wish you had stayed asleep. It's going to be tricky to get you back in there."

Aniya shrieked at a volume that made the room shake, at a pitch that made the remaining glass in the room shatter. Tiny daggers of light shot forth from her mouth and flew like bullets toward the Director, but they fell upon his clothes and fizzled out, sending jagged, red lines over his black shirt.

As her cry declined to a whimper, the Director smirked and rubbed a finger in his ear.

"Ouch. You know, if you really tried, you could be quite the singer. You've got the pipes for it."

Aniya looked down at her hands and back at the Director. "What did you do?"

"Oh, I wouldn't dream of doing anything to you, dear.

You are too precious to risk harming." The Director displayed his arms and the long sleeves that still covered them, dancing with red lines. "I predicted this day would come. As such, I developed a material that would be resistant to your power and give me time to speak with you harmlessly. Now, let's see about getting you back in your tank, shall we?"

Aniya backed away slowly until she collided with the giant machine behind her, her prison for the last three years. As the fog settled over her brain, she slowly slid to the floor. "Good luck with that. I may not be able to kill you with the light, but I think you and I both know that if you touch me, I'll rip your head off."

"That's rude." The Director paused and frowned, shaking a finger at her. "I understand you're mad at me, but that's no reason to make such violent threats against my head. I'm quite proud of this one. Not that you're right, of course. I mean, yes, technically, if you managed to touch me, I'm sure you're agile enough to overpower me. But that's assuming you could touch me. I'll grant you this misinformed assumption because you don't know me well enough, but I am a master of human behavior. I can predict with lethal accuracy your every move, and you wouldn't be able to lay a finger on me."

He continued his approach, placing the syringe behind his back. "I'll even make it harder on myself by giving you a head start. But it won't matter. I'll see your every move coming and have you on the floor in seconds."

Aniya flexed her muscles and prepared to jump up toward the Director, but his eyes flashed blue, and a warm liquid splashed over her face, making her pause.

The Director seemed frozen in place as well, so Aniya took a half second to swipe at her cheek and look down at her fingers to see blood. She looked back up just in time to see the Director's head fall forward and topple to the ground.

"Didn't see that one coming, did you?"

A girl's head appeared where the Director's was, and his

body fell to the side as the girl pushed it away and stepped forward.

Zeta extended a gloved hand toward Aniya, holding a bloody, red sword in her other hand. "Now do you believe me?"

## 15

A niya pushed away the hand, glaring at the assassin. "Not for a second. After everything you've done, you don't deserve my trust."

"You're right," Zeta said. "But you don't have a choice. Reinforcements will get here any second, and you'll need my help to escape."

"I'm sure I can manage." Aniya defiantly stood and stared down the girl.

Zeta shrugged. "You could easily kill me. Do you really think I'd risk standing here if I didn't want to help you?"

Aniya shook her head. "I couldn't hurt you before. I should have killed you, but the light didn't seem to have any effect on you."

"I know. I had to be ready for that." Zeta pulled a string on her white cloak and let it fall to the ground. "As you've seen, the Director has been engineering several safeguards against your powers. He couldn't risk his creation turning against him and ruining everything. This cloak is made from the same material as his clothing."

The assassin stood before Aniya in a form-fitting, white bodysuit, two swords strapped to her back. "Now I have no protection. If you still don't believe me, just aim for my head. You have to trust me, Aniya. I'm here to help you."

Aniya stared at Zeta for several seconds before lowering her hands cautiously. "Explain."

"First we need to get out of here."

"No can do. You owe me an explanation."

Zeta glanced over her shoulder nervously. "They're coming, Aniya."

"Better talk fast."

The assassin took a deep breath and nodded. "Caspian sent me to help you."

"Caspian?" Aniya's mind spun as she pictured the man who had tried to help her back in Level I. She had spent hours with him, training, meditating, trying to gain control of her emotions. "What does he have to do with any of this?"

"Caspian realized that the Director may not have humanity's best interests in mind when he mercilessly destroyed the Underworld. The entire Silver Guard wiped out, just like that, even though they were all on the same side."

Aniya frowned. "I knew he purged the Underworld, but he even killed his own men? Why?"

"Cleaning up loose ends, I guess."

"Then shouldn't Caspian be dead?"

"Caspian is the man who trained me. He trained all the operatives and oversaw the training of the Silver Guard. As you can imagine, he's a smart man and was able to defend himself when the Director's army came for him."

"And why are you working for him and not the Director?"

Zeta smiled. "You need to realize, Aniya, that I'm an operative, a glorified soldier. I do what I'm told to do. Nothing more, nothing less."

"And Caspian's orders override the Director's?"

"They do now." Zeta bowed her head, parting her hair and pointing to a bare, white spot on her scalp. "As a safeguard against corruption, and for the protection of those we belong to, Caspian placed microchips in our brains that would allow him to override all other commands. When he does so, it activates a homing beacon of sorts that brings us back to him. When he executed the override, any loyalty I had to the Director was instantly severed. I now serve Caspian, and him alone."

Aniya processed this information for a moment. "You realize this sounds crazy, right?"

"Fair enough." Zeta gestured toward the Director's dead body. "But I think the evidence speaks for itself."

After another pause, Aniya nodded. "Say you're telling the truth. What now?"

"Now, we go after the Council, the men who unleashed the Director. He was just a puppet, just like Kendall, and if you thought he was bad, wait until you get a load of them. But first, you need to get rid of your excess energy. You'll need to use the machine one last time since Nicholas—"

At the sound of his name, Aniya's hand shot out and clamped down tight around the girl's throat. "Don't you ever say his name again. He's dead because of you. I'm choosing to listen to you now, but when you're done helping me, don't think I won't kill you."

Unable to speak, the girl simply pointed at the machine behind Aniya, mouthing the words, "Use it."

After several seconds, Aniya released the girl and ignored her gasps, turning to the machine. "What do I do?"

"Not sure," the girl said, choking. "You're the one with the magic powers. But I do know that if you don't use it, you'll eventually blow us both up. You're like a time bomb just waiting to go off. So get to it."

Aniya took a deep breath and ascended the platform to the machine. She placed her hands where they had been strapped to the machine and gripped the twin spheres that still crackled with miniature lightning.

Almost immediately, Aniya's entire body seized up,

her eyes forced open by a spasm in her muscles that rendered her helpless against the energy that raced through her body.

Somewhere far away, her name was being shouted, but Aniya could not tear herself away from the machine. It was like she was being magnetically drawn to the device, and a crippling fear sank over her as she realized that she was willingly putting herself back in the prison that had held her for the last three years.

Zeta had tricked her. She was back in the endless torture, and there was nothing she could do about it.

"Aniya," a feminine voice hissed in the darkness. From a veil of red came a Shadow, a dark form that loomed before her menacingly. It took one step forward, and a white face emerged from the darkness, blood dripping from its grinning mouth.

Suddenly, Aniya's vision darkened as another veil dropped over her eyes. She felt herself yanked backward, and she fell away from the machine, jolts of energy spiking her hands as they were ripped away from the twin spheres.

She landed heavily on a soft mass, and Aniya wrenched the cloth away from her body to find herself back in the dark sanctum, wrestling with Zeta's white cloak.

Aniya sat up and spun around to see Zeta moaning, slowly sitting up and rubbing her shoulder. As she looked around the room, she realized that the fires she had caused were extinguished, and the sanctum was even darker than before.

"What happened?"

Zeta retrieved her cloak and stood. "You were in too deep. I had to pull you out before you were too far gone. Good thing I had my cloak, or I would have fried myself."

Aniya glanced back at the machine, which was quickly powering down. She looked down at the floor and muttered, "Thank you."

"Shut up."

When Aniya turned back around, Zeta was standing

frozen, her finger at her lips as she cocked an ear, her eyes growing wide.

"What?" Aniya rolled her eyes.

Zeta glared at her and gave another quiet shush.

After a second, Aniya's ears perked up at the sound of distant footsteps.

Zeta's eyes widened further, and she pulled Aniya away from the machine. "Get over here, quick."

Aniya pulled her arm away but followed as Zeta led her to the corner of the room, motioning behind a smoldering work-station.

"Down here." Zeta pointed underneath the desk.

"Why?" Aniya put her hands on her hips. "I'm more than capable of clearing us a path out of here."

"You and me both, but I'm not going to turn into a nuclear bomb if I get too excited," Zeta said as she shoved Aniya's head down, banging it on the edge of the desk.

Aniya glared back up at Zeta as she rubbed her head. The assassin turned her cloak inside out to reveal a matte black interior.

"And you want me to just sit here and—" Aniya was cut off as Zeta tossed the cloak over her, turning her into a black lump resting on the floor.

"Yes," Zeta's voice came back. "That's exactly what I want you to do."

Aniya grumbled and pulled the cloak back just enough to see, but the assassin had already disappeared.

The footsteps grew louder, and within seconds, a dozen men in black armor poured into the sanctum and spread out throughout the room, their head-mounted flashlights scanning the room rapidly.

One of the men approached the machine and nudged the Director's head, and it rolled to face upward.

"Delta 17 is down. I repeat, Delta 17 is down." The man

spoke into a radio attached to his shoulder. "Better report to the staging area. They'll need—"

But the man vanished, and the only sound that came from his location was his gun falling to the ground.

Aniya squinted in the darkness but saw nothing. The remaining soldiers looked at the machine, but they didn't seem to see anything either.

Another soldier spoke up. "Dispatch, requesting backup at our location. Lucifer is gone, and something weird is going on."

A grunt came from the other side of the room, and Aniya stared but again saw nothing. There were ten left now, unless Zeta had already picked off more that Aniya hadn't noticed.

"There!"

The cry was followed by a hail of gunfire, sending sparks flying from the ceiling. Aniya thought she saw a flash of white, but she couldn't be sure.

Suddenly, Zeta's body fell to the ground in the middle of the room.

"Cease fire!"

The gunfire ceased, and the soldiers slowly approached the assassin's body. She was deathly still, and a pool of blood slowly grew beneath her back. One of the soldiers kicked her, and she flopped over, her arms splayed out.

"Dispatch, show us clear. No backup needed. Target neutralized."

An explosion on the far side of the room shook the ground, and the soldiers looked up and pointed their guns at the sound.

In a flurry of movement, Zeta leapt in the air and pulled a sword from her back, hurtling her body in a spiral as she whipped her sword around her body. The blade cut cleanly through the soldiers' armor, and three men dropped to the ground.

Zeta landed on her feet and instantly went into a series of

ducks and twirls that felled another three soldiers in mere seconds.

The remaining four soldiers finally reacted and turned on Zeta, but she was already halfway across the room, diving behind a table a few feet away from Aniya.

Bullets flew into the wall, too close for comfort. Aniya winced as one of the bullets ripped a hole through the cloak she clutched tightly in her hands.

The soldiers slowly advanced on Zeta's location, two on each side. With their flashlights pointed at her only exits, there was no escaping unseen.

Just before they could reach her location, however, Zeta threw an object to her side, and a cloud of smoke appeared out of nowhere. As the soldiers fired on the smoke, Zeta ran the other way, toward Aniya, and ducked behind another desk.

"Nothing."

Aniya turned back to the commotion, where the gunfire had again stopped. The soldiers were investigating the smoke.

"She must have run the other way. Fan out."

The soldiers spread and advanced toward Aniya and Zeta's location. Aniya turned around, but the assassin had again disappeared.

Aniya looked back to see black armor inches from her face. A soldier's legs slowly crept by her nose, advancing along the path toward where Zeta had just been hiding.

She took a breath and lashed out with an arm, knocking the soldier's legs out from under him. He crashed to the ground, his weapon firing wildly into the ceiling, and Aniya reached out and placed a hand on his face, burning his flesh and letting his screams mix with the sound of gunfire.

The man finally went still, dropping his gun next to Aniya, who turned back toward the center of the room, where Zeta was once again in the middle of it. One of the men was falling to the ground, and another was currently helplessly staring down at his chest, where a sword was embedded. The last surviving soldier seemed to be recovering from shock, and he pulled his weapon up from his side, aiming his gun directly at Zeta's face.

Aniya reached out blindly and grabbed the gun near her. She pulled it around to her front and fired at the man, emptying the clip in his direction.

Zeta rolled to the side as the man was hit by a few of the many bullets Aniya sprayed, and he crumpled to the ground.

"Are you insane?"

The man hadn't even stopped twitching before Zeta spoke.

"Emptying a clip while lying on your side, with a fully automatic rifle?" Zeta pulled the gun away from Aniya, more gently than expected. "I bet your eyes were closed, too. Were you trying to get me killed?"

"You're alive, aren't you?" Aniya grumbled as she stood back up. She tossed the cloak to Zeta. "You're welcome."

Zeta laughed. "Believe me, I didn't need your help."

"Doesn't matter if you needed it." Aniya folded her arms. "You should be just as surprised as I am that I even bothered to help."

"I am," the assassin said as she turned the cloak around so the white side was facing out. "Can't say I would have blamed you if you had just watched. Though considering that's exactly what I asked you to do, I wouldn't have felt too bad."

"Whatever. So what now?"

Zeta grinned. "I'm taking you to see an old friend."

"Who?"

"He goes by many names, but I've become quite fond of the Vagabond."

## 16

A young man ascended the marble staircase at a dead run. He nearly tripped on a step, but he managed to keep his balance and continue upward, now keeping a light hold on the banister, which took on a shine from the sweat of the young man's palms.

His other hand tightly clutched a paper, which was also moist from sweat, nearly blurring the foreboding words freshly printed on its surface.

The man jumped past the last two steps and ran down the ivory hallway, pushing open the massive double doors at the end.

Gasping for air, the man leaned against the doorway for a second before walking into the room, ignoring the many eyes that glared at him.

"What part of 'meeting in process' was not clear?" The man at the Chief Councilor's seat did not rise as the panting intruder approached, only folding his arms and cocking an eyebrow. "I'd like to think you're not foolish enough to barge in without good reason, so as soon as you catch your breath, I expect a full explanation."

The young man simply placed the paper on the table and retreated toward the door, but the leader snapped his fingers.

"Stay. If it's worthy of our time, you'll be needed for a response."

Nodding, the messenger sank into an empty chair at the table, doing his best to avoid eye contact with the other men.

The Chief Councilor picked up the paper, and after grimacing as a drop of sweat trickled down the surface of the damp paper, he gingerly opened the paper and read its contents.

A second later, he slammed his fist into the table and muttered something under his breath.

"What would you like me to say back?" The young man finally asked after a long pause.

The councilor stood and walked away from the table for a moment. When he turned back toward the rest of the room, his face was downcast.

"The Director is dead."

The table stirred as everyone started talking to each other in hushed tones.

One of the men spoke louder than the rest. "How did this happen?"

"It just says that he's dead and the laboratory is all but destroyed." The councilor paused and let the paper fall to the floor. "And Lucifer is gone."

At this, the men at the table raised their voices and let their chatter escalate into a meaningless clamor.

A loud banging sounded from the other side of the table, and the din quieted a little. The men turned to the noise, where a silver-haired, red-faced man was leaning over the table, staring them down.

"We rule by order, gentlemen, not chaos." He stared at them a moment longer before looking up at the other standing man. "Byron, as current Chief Councilor, we defer to your judgment. Do you think it's the Vagabond? It sounds like his doing after his attack on our datacenter. Do you think he's come for the Key?"

But Byron didn't get a chance to respond. A bald man spoke up, his speech rapid as he shook his head. "I don't know what else it could be. It would be just like him to pull something like this. If he gets his hands on the Key, we're as good as finished. There's not much we can do, short of tightening our defenses and preparing the containment field. Whoever Lucifer's working with, they are now capable of great damage, enough to secure the Key and then some. I told you this would happen. I told you all, and you didn't believe me. We authorized the creation of a weapon, one strong enough to destroy us and everything we've worked for."

The silver-haired man lowered his voice. "A weapon in the hands of lesser men. A tool in the hands of the wise."

"It would be like you to sit here and call yourself wise, Deacon." The angry man stood up from his chair. "But you forget that she *is* in the hands of lesser men, for all we know. If the Vagabond indeed has her, he'll destroy us without a second thought."

"Sit down, Soren," Byron said, rolling his eyes. "Panic is the defense of the weak. The Vagabond is nothing more than legend. I do not believe he poses any lasting threat to us."

Soren sat down, folding his arms and muttering. "Tell that to the rebels who walk around in their white cloaks. They believe in him, and that's all that should matter to you."

"I didn't say he wasn't real. I said he was a legend. He's no more than a name. Behind the mask of the Vagabond is a living, breathing man who bleeds just like you and I. Kill their leader, kill the cause. I personally would rather have Lucifer in the hands of the Vagabond than in the hands of the Director."

Deacon frowned. "Careful, Byron. You kill a legend, and he becomes more than a myth. He becomes a symbol, a martyr. But I understand your point. At least the Director doesn't control her at the moment."

"So that's it, then?" Soren threw his hands in the air. "We're just going to roll over, let them do what they want, and then let the army clean up when it's all over? We're supposed to be keeping issues like this out of the public eye. If they storm the Capitol with Lucifer, it's over for us. The entire world will fall. It'll be like the Strangers all over again."

"I don't expect such an overt attack, either from Lucifer or the Vagabond," Byron said. "The Vagabond strikes me as the kind of man who prefers subtlety over a direct attack. His motives may be destructive, but he has more tact than that. I suspect he'll come in through the window rather than banging down the front door. As for Lucifer, she knows nothing of the Overworld and wouldn't know where to begin. If she escaped by herself, I expect her to go to the place she knows best. If she is with the Vagabond, I would suspect they show up here soon. If there's something else happening here we don't know about, all we can do is let it play out. The Director would be the only one able to track her energy signature with any real accuracy."

"So we do nothing," Soren growled.

Byron shook his head. "Not nothing. We have defenses. Let's ready them. Summon the Keepers to the Capitol. Signal the army and have them ready, but don't deploy them yet. I am confident that we can contain the Vagabond, Lucifer, and whoever else wants to show up long enough to take care of the issue and clean up. Does that sound wise to you, Deacon?"

The silver-haired man nodded slowly.

"And what do I tell Communications?"

The men at the table turned to the young messenger, who seemed to have been forgotten.

Byron paused for a moment before responding. "Tell them to dispatch a crew to restore the laboratory and reengage the machine. As soon as we deal with Lucifer, she's going right back in there."

"There's something we're not considering," another man said quietly. "What if this was his plan all along?"

Byron took a deep breath and glanced out the window. "Then may God have mercy on us all."

## 17

"We go on foot from here."

Aniya looked up. She had gotten so lost in her thoughts that she didn't realize that the terrasphere had turned opaque again and had come to a stop. She stood and waited for Zeta to open the door.

"My legs were beginning to cramp up, so I'm not complaining. But why? Isn't your friend waiting on us?"

Zeta nodded. "Yeah, but a transport coming from the edge of the city would raise more eyebrows than I care to explain myself to."

"Fair enough." The door zipped open, and Aniya stepped outside.

The fresh air that fell on her face was the most pleasurable thing she had felt in years. Ignoring the beautiful sight for just a second, Aniya closed her eyes and took a deep breath. She could get used to this, despite living underground or in a laboratory her whole life.

She opened her eyes again and marveled at the sight of massive trees that stretched up higher than she could see. Lush moss covered part of their huge trunks, and large, colorful bugs rested in the shade the tree provided. The only thing that broke her spell of fascination was the gaping black hole behind them and the rails beneath the terrasphere, revealing the edge of the sector and the digital wall.

Zeta pressed a button on the sphere, and the transport receded back into the wall as a door slid down and the digital display corrected itself, blending in perfectly.

If it weren't for this curious sight, Aniya could never have noticed the difference, but the artificial beauty was unmistakably different from the very real atmosphere that surrounded her, and it made the real thing that much less special.

"Come on, we're already behind schedule." Zeta tugged at her wrist, and Aniya turned and followed. She was now dressed in an identical white cloak, this one without the trim that decorated Zeta's outfit.

Aniya frowned and played with the edge of the fabric. "Won't we stand out in these clothes?"

"Not terribly. Everything is white in the city."

"But the cloaks?"

Zeta shrugged. "A bit dated, sure, but it hides our faces, and that's what's important. We don't stick around long enough for anyone to ask questions, so we don't have anything to worry about. Besides, no one knows what they mean, so no one cares."

"What do they mean?"

Zeta's hazel eyes twinkled. "Resistance."

"Surely the Silvers would have something to say about that?"

A laugh came from the assassin, but it was without the spite Aniya had come to expect from the girl. "There are no Silvers up here, Aniya. At least not like the ones you know. Sure, there's the Keepers, the Lightbringer police force, but they never show their faces unless they're needed. And they're nearly never needed."

Aniya frowned. "Why?"

"Because there's no reason for crime. Every need is met

here in the Overworld. Every want is easily gained. Theft is pointless, murder unimaginable. This is the utopia that we've fought so hard to build and maintain."

"What is there to resist, then? You sound like a true believer," Aniya scoffed.

"We *are* believers. But only in the end result. We condemn how it was bought. It was paid for by the blood of your people. It was engineered by murderers, schemers. The Council knows full well the atrocities committed by the Director and his band of so-called presidents. The Council is the governing body that approved it all."

"So you want to wipe out the Council?"

Zeta winced and waved a hand in the air. "We want to persuade the Council to step down from power and allow a new governing body to be established. If they don't see reason, then yes. They must be displaced by force. But the thing is, they have a good thing going. Whether we like their methods or not, they have created a perfect society, one that must be maintained at all costs."

"So if you don't plan on fighting them, what do you need me for?"

"Two things. Leverage, for one. When you stepped into the machine, the Council finally achieved their goal: permanent, self-sustaining energy without the need for the Underworld, which was a black mark on their record. Without you, they find themselves with quite the dilemma. Without you, their power reserves will eventually quickly dry up. The Director severed all connection between the remaining machines in the Underworld and the surface, cutting the Overworld off from any power but you."

"Why not destroy the machines along with the rest of the Underworld?"

Zeta shrugged. "He never said. But I imagine he's using the power for something else. In any case, without power, the Council will be unable to control the Overworld.

The Director made sure that you were the only hope for humanity."

Aniya scoffed. "Sounds kind of stupid not to have any redundancy."

"But it's the ultimate job security. Anyone could manage the presidents of the Underworld. But only the Director knew how you work."

"What happens when the Council is gone? How are we going to have power?"

"We'll be running off the remains of the Underworld for a while—"

Aniya's eyes widened. "You want to keep torturing hundreds of thousands of people still trapped down there?"

"No one wants to, Aniya. But without power, everyone dies. You forget that outside the domes is a wasteland that no one can survive. But don't worry. Caspian says he has a plan."

Aniya knew there wasn't any point in pressing this, so she asked the other most pressing question on her mind.

"You said there were two things you needed me for. What's the second?"

"Our mission is one of stealth, but anything can happen. And if worse comes to worst, you make for a very good weapon."

Aniya held back a smile and followed Zeta to the edge of the forest.

"Welcome," Zeta said, "to New Washington."

They cleared the trees and stepped out onto a ledge that overlooked the city. It was eerily reminiscent of Level I, the training ground for the Underworld's police force. White buildings stretched across the city, casting a white glow all the way to Aniya's vantage point, so much so that it was hard to look at the city directly.

What stood out here were the parks and other decorations splashed throughout the city, just enough to give the utopia a splash of color here and there, keeping the white from completely overwhelming the scenery.

"New Washington?" Aniya finally looked at Zeta. "I never cared for history that much, but I know enough to wonder if that isn't a little presumptuous."

"Understandably so, but it's really not. This has been the capital of civilization ever since we emerged from the Underworld hundreds of years ago. Other major cities were rebuilt around the world: Tokyo, Hong Kong, Los Angeles, and so on, all of them bearing the 'new' title, but this is where the Council decided to make their home, and they oversee the entire world."

"We're standing right above the Underworld, so this city makes sense. But how did they spread so far out? They would have had to run power all the way out there."

Zeta nodded. "And they did. One foot at a time. It didn't happen overnight, and for the longest time, there was just New Washington and the surrounding colonies. Now, we've rebuilt enough that the world's population has reached several million again."

"All powered from the Underworld?"

"It was. And then you took over as the world's primary energy source."

"But I'm not hooked up to the machine anymore. And if the Underworld is disconnected from the surface, how is there any power up here?"

Zeta pointed at the far side of the city, where a large mass of gray buildings stood, standing out from the sea of white. "Each city stores a portion of incoming power and circulates it constantly until it's needed. Sort of like a battery, but on a much larger scale."

Aniya frowned. "But with millions of people to share it, they'll run out quick, right?"

"Between millions of people, regular maintenance, the sky ceilings, and other things, yes. We'll have power for a few more weeks before the city, and the world, starts to shut down."

"And then what?"

"All in good time, Aniya." Zeta hopped down from the ledge, landing on a grassy hill and jogging toward the bottom before Aniya could shout after her.

Aniya sighed. It was hard enough to trust the assassin as it was, and she wasn't making it any easier. Aniya hopped off the ledge and braced herself to land in a run, but she slipped on a wet patch and lost her balance, sending herself headfirst down the hill. She closed her eyes and tensed her muscles, but she never landed.

Instead, Aniya felt her body slowly rise back to a standing position. She opened her eyes to see the grass fly beneath her, and her feet appeared to still be on the ground, but they weren't moving. They appeared to be rooted in place by a column of light that surrounded her ankles.

Aniya looked behind her and saw a trail of sparkling light behind her that perfectly matched her path. Her eyes grew wide, and as she stared at the wonder behind her, she felt herself lose balance again. Aniya looked forward just in time to fall face-first into the grass, slamming her nose into the dirt and tumbling down the remainder of the hill in a painful, awkward roll.

When she finally came to a stop, Aniya looked up, moaning, to see the assassin standing over her, a smile on her face.

"Graceful indeed," Zeta said, reaching down with a hand.

Aniya took the hand and pulled herself back up, wincing as a stabbing pain shot through her shoulder. "Still a little disoriented from the machine, I guess."

"Yeah, I don't blame you," Zeta said, helping Aniya dust off the grass stuck to her cloak. "I wish we had more time to rest, but we need to get going."

"I'm fine," Aniya said. "Good thing these cloaks don't stain."

"Well, they were designed for battle, and if blood doesn't stain them, nothing will." She grabbed Aniya's hand and began walking toward the city. "Now, come on."

Aniya pulled her hand away. "No offense, but I'm not exactly ready to be best friends with you."

"Better get ready fast. We're not going to make it halfway through the city otherwise."

"What?"

Zeta took Aniya's hand again and held on tighter. "Outside of work, all citizens must publicly travel with their mates at all times."

"Seems like a rather strict rule for a utopia."

"But one that people follow willingly. The companionship goes a long way to improve morale."

"Improve it? They'd drive each other crazy."

"I would agree, but the source of most marital conflicts have nothing to do with the marriage itself. They are rooted in money, work, or children. When each citizen has more than enough, unemployment is nonexistent, and children have quality education, most problems cease to exist."

Aniya scoffed. "You sound like someone who's never seen an actual marriage before."

"Caught me," Zeta said, grinning. "But I don't have to see it to know that it works. The people are happy up here. Besides, it serves another purpose, from what I understand. It's another method of deterring crime, since you're less likely to commit a crime if you constantly submit yourself to accountability."

"And it won't seem weird that it's two girls walking together?" Aniya looked down at their joined hands. "What are their thoughts about that stuff up here? You don't expect me to do more than hold your hand, do you?"

"Only if you feel so compelled." Zeta said liltingly, waving her other hand. "We'll be fine. The Council used to care because it messed up their population control, but they gave up on enforcing heterosexual relationships a long time ago. If you care, however, feel free to pull your hood down and no one will ever know."

"I only care that it's you I'm walking with," Aniya muttered.

Zeta smirked but said nothing.

"So the Vagabond is married, then? Wouldn't want to raise any eyebrows, as you put it."

"Oh, no. That's why they call him the Vagabond. That, and he never stays in one place for very long. No, he has to travel using more . . . creative methods. But you'll learn all about that soon enough."

They continued away from the grassy field and into the city, and Aniya soon witnessed the culture for herself.

Just like her and Zeta, the vast majority of the citizens walked in twos. The only people who seemed to walk alone were children or those clearly working, among them individuals carrying covered baskets, others cleaning the pristine roads.

And Zeta was right. Smiles seemed to be in no short supply, laughter echoed through the streets, faint music could be heard in the distance, and couples seemed to occasionally stop for no reason at all other than to kiss their partner.

"It really is perfect, isn't it?" Aniya shook her head in wonder.

"Which is why we have to carry out our mission without ever letting them know that anything is going on," Zeta said, squeezing Aniya's hand. "There are those who believe that it's our duty to expose the Council and change the way the Overworld functions, but they don't understand that happiness like this is hard to come by. You've seen what happens when the people grow tired of the established system. Manufactured happiness is better than no happiness at all, especially when it keeps them from a devastating war."

It was hard to argue. Aniya's parents had been at the forefront of the rebellion back home, and they'd suffered terrible losses. Even after they recovered and managed to live a somewhat happy life, they still faced execution at the hands of a government that was losing control of its people.

But she said nothing, choosing to silently let Zeta guide her through the streets of New Washington. At one point, Zeta quickly turned and pushed Aniya into an alleyway, hiding in the shadows as three men in white armor walked by.

"Keepers," Zeta muttered.

When they were gone, Zeta stepped out of the alley and continued on with Aniya.

After several minutes, they turned down another alley, which looked just as nice and clean as the main streets, only thinner and slightly darker. Zeta paused by a back door and held a finger to her lips. Clearing her throat, she spoke clearly but quietly.

"*Lumen ad mortem.*"

An invisible panel on the door slid aside to reveal a deep carving embedded in a hidden slab of steel. The carving was that of a four-fingered hand.

Zeta seemed to ignore Aniya's gasp and placed her hand into the mark, letting her little finger remain above the carving, and turned the hand counter-clockwise. A clunk sounded, and the door receded sideways into the wall.

"Quickly," Zeta said as she stepped into the dark hallway, finally letting go of Aniya's hand.

Aniya followed, and the door soon shut behind her, leaving them in the shadows. A green glow emanated from her body, enough light to make the way clear.

"See? You're all kinds of useful." Zeta smiled and continued down the hallway, leading Aniya to a dead end. She pushed on the wall, however, and it swung open to reveal a candlelit staircase, leading down into a room that looked to be lit by fire. Loud voices spoke over each other, unintelligible from this distance.

Aniya followed Zeta down the stairs, and they entered a large room filled with barrels and the unmistakable smell of wine.

In the middle of the room was a large table, lined with people in white cloaks, their hoods lowered. Everyone seemed to be shouting, raising their voices to be heard, though no one seemed to be listening.

"Excuse me," Zeta said.

No one seemed to hear her except for Aniya, who raised her eyebrows at the sound of the assassin using some semblance of manners.

"Gentlemen," she said, raising her volume. After no one acknowledged her again, Zeta rolled her eyes and approached a man at the table with his back to the two women, and she leaned over, placing her hands on his shoulders and speaking closely in his ear. The man reached up and caressed Zeta's hand as he listened.

Finally, Zeta returned to Aniya as the man stood.

"Quiet!" The man shouted, and the room went silent.

Zeta nodded toward the man and whispered to Aniya, "The Vagabond."

"We have a guest, one that we've waited on for many years." The Vagabond turned around and smiled widely. "Welcome, Aniya. It's been too long."

Aniya's mouth dropped open as she stared at the man. "Malcolm?"

## 18

"You awake?"

Aniya looked up at Malcolm. She shook her head, muttering, "Barely."

It wasn't that she was tired. Quite the opposite, in fact. After three years of sleep, she felt as if she could stay awake for a week. No, it was dizzying, the meeting she had just sat through. So much talk of revolution, of plans. So much shouting, not enough listening.

Aniya had eventually tuned it all out, instead studying Malcolm and Zeta's behavior. They seemed amicable, even familiar. At very few points during the night did she see them break their gentle physical contact. How could two people change so drastically?

"Are you feeling okay?"

A hand landed on Aniya's shoulder, and she resisted the urge to shrug it off in a shiver at the sound of the assassin's voice.

"I'm fine." Aniya watched the last rebel ascend the staircase, and when she heard the door close, she spun her chair around and faced the duo. "What happened? Last I remember, you tried to kill him," she said, pointing at Zeta.

Zeta laughed. "I promise you, if I had tried to kill him, he would be dead." Her smile vanished as she looked at the floor. "To be honest, I just shot him to hurt you."

"Well, it worked." Aniya clenched her fists. She turned to Malcolm. "And you, what made you trust her after what she did to me? To you? I should hope you would have tried to kill her the second you saw her."

"I did," Malcolm said, pointing to a scar on his cheek. "And that's what I got for it, not that it was a fair fight. I was still nearly dead when she found me in the forest where you left me. I don't know how fruit grows naturally up here, but I'm glad it does. Otherwise I would have been dead for sure."

"So what, she sliced you on the cheek and you made up?"

Malcolm grinned. "Not exactly. It was more like she beat me unconscious, and I woke up chained to a table until she could explain what was going on."

"Sounds romantic."

"Mmm, isn't it?" Zeta circled behind Malcolm, letting her arm glide over his chest and around his neck. "That part didn't come for a couple years. My visits were frequent, as there was always something to report or someone to smuggle in from another city. It took a while, but eventually he couldn't resist me."

Aniya stared at the assassin. "I thought you were trained in Level I. Between the air filtration suppressing your emotions and Caspian turning you into a mindless assassin, how are you even capable of love?"

"Harsh words, Lucifer." Zeta frowned. "Surely it was explained that they don't suppress emotion. They only help you control it. Caspian took this to the next level. He taught me to turn my passion into a thirst to be the best. And now that I am the best, I can focus my passion . . ." Her eyes darted toward Malcolm. "Elsewhere."

"When the job is done, of course," Malcolm said, clearing

his throat as his cheeks reddened. "We have to remind each other occasionally that there will be plenty of time for passion when we complete our mission and the Council is removed."

Aniya shook her head. "I'm not buying it. You killed the mole I rode on without a second thought. You tried to get Nicholas to turn against me and take me to the Director. I've seen your true nature. Caspian may have given you new orders, but I know who you really are."

"You don't have to buy it," Zeta said, shrugging. "I'm offering my help to you both to take out the Council. That's what matters to me. Your approval does not."

"And you?" Aniya folded her arms and looked at Malcolm.

"I have no reason not to believe her. She's given us so much information that we've used to infiltrate Lightbringer outposts and gain even more information. She's supplied us with guns, food, men . . . We'd be fools not to trust her."

Aniya gave a short laugh.

"I understand your hesitation, Aniya."

Zeta placed a hand on her arm, and this time Aniya did not hold back her disgust as she yanked her arm away.

"Then you'll forgive me if I keep an eye on you every step of the way."

"I expect nothing less," Zeta said, backing away.

"Neither do I," Malcolm said. "But it's been three years, Aniya. Things have changed. You'll have to accept that one day. Am I the same man you knew back in the Underworld? The one who sold you out to the Director?"

Aniya shook her head. "At least I don't think so."

"Then give it time. Don't let your bitterness stand in the way of a better world that we can bring to these people." Malcolm pulled a device from his pocket and set it on the table. "In any case, we need to get started."

"Started?" Aniya frowned. "Didn't you just finish with a meeting?"

Malcolm glanced at the stairs in the corner. "Our army has their assignment, but our mission is vital to the success of the resistance. Therefore, only myself and Zeta know anything about it." He looked back at the assassin. "Did you seal the exit?"

Zeta nodded. "We have privacy."

"Good." Malcolm pressed a button on the device, and a holographic image appeared, floating above the table's surface. It was a small, blue object, a glowing rectangle that spun around slowly.

"This is what the Council calls their Key," Zeta said. "A device that stores encryption codes for the Overworld, codes that lock away the Council's secrets, their plans, and even the history of the world."

"History?" Aniya frowned. "What history would they want to hide from the people?"

Malcolm glanced at Zeta. "We don't know. But the Overworld's libraries have very limited access. It's clear that the Council's control of the world is easier when its people are ignorant, but it's been rumored that there is some secret hidden in Earth's past that the Council doesn't want to get out."

"Rumors," Zeta said. "As far as we know, that's all it is. Whether the stories are true or not, the Key is incredibly valuable and will ensure our victory."

Aniya poked a finger through the hologram. "So this is it? It's all we need to do, grab the Key and get out?"

"That's it," Malcolm said.

"Seems too easy."

Zeta gave a short laugh. "Then you don't know the Council. Their security will be near-impossible to beat. No matter how stealthy we are, chances are we'll be forced into a fight that won't be easy."

"Which is why I'm here?" Aniya asked.

"Which is why you're here," Malcolm said. "Trust me,

I know it's a lot to ask after all you've been through, and I argued to Zeta that we could have done it ourselves and just taken you back to the Underworld, but she's confident that we need you."

"Really?" Aniya smirked. "She said that?"

Zeta shrugged. "Even I know when I'm outmatched. It'll take all of us."

"Agreed," Malcolm said. "And we'll have our army just outside in case things go wrong."

"Outside? But don't you have a small army at your disposal? Can't we just storm the Capitol?"

"But you are right when you say small," Zeta said. "It's nothing compared to the Lightbringer army. Better to stick to a more subtle approach. Besides, we can't tell them what we're after."

Malcolm nodded. "They know that we have a mission inside the Capitol, but they don't know what it is we're after. If word gets back to the Council, they'll move the Key instantly."

"Yeah," Zeta said. "We're cutting it close enough as it is. I waited until the last possible second to pull you out, only after Malcolm tracked down the location of the Key."

Aniya narrowed her eyes. "Ignoring the fact that you let me sit in that tank for three years, it never occurred to you that the Key was inside their home base?"

"We knew it had to be," Malcolm said, "but with the location of the Key, I also was able to get access codes into the more secure locations of the Capitol. That was the last piece we needed to pull this off. And trust me, I hated leaving you in there, but if we broke you out any earlier, we would be risking too much. The Council will be on their guard now, and I wouldn't be surprised if they have plans to move the Key already just to be safe."

"What if they already have?" Aniya asked.

Malcolm sighed. "Then at least we'll have tried. This is

our only chance at overthrowing them, Aniya. We're putting everything we've got into this."

"I get it," she said, still staring at the Key. "When do we leave?"

"If you're up for it?" Zeta asked. "Tonight. We've been cautious, but the Lightbringers aren't stupid. When word gets back about the Director's death, if it hasn't already, they'll come for us all. We need to beat them to the punch."

Malcolm shook his head. "She needs to recover. After sitting in that tank for three years—"

"She's been sleeping for three years," Zeta said, rolling her eyes. "I think she's recovered enough."

"Are you speaking for her now?"

Aniya grinned as Zeta visibly struggled for words. "She's right, though. I could use another nap, but I'm honestly sick of sleeping."

"We can wait one more night, Aniya," Malcolm said. "We have to get this right the first time."

Zeta folded her arms. "And we will."

"We're not ready."

"We won't get any more ready than we already are." Zeta turned to Aniya. "You've either been running or imprisoned for three years now. Of course, part of that was my fault, but regardless, it'll be all over soon. Are you ready to just live again?"

Aniya took a deep breath. Living was more than she could say for her parents, for Nicholas, for Roland. For the entire Underworld.

"Oh, I'm ready."

Malcolm sighed and nodded. "Then we leave in three hours. Better get some sleep if you can. It's going to be a long night."

## 19

"It's time to wake up."

A feminine voice echoed throughout Aniya's mind. Despite the feeling of dread that pricked at her mind, the voice carried a smooth, saccharine tone that ironically lulled her into a deeper sleep. And so Aniya let herself drift away farther into the void as she slept, floating aimlessly in the black shores of her mind.

"Aniya."

The void flashed red as another voice spoke. It was just as sweet as the first one, yet it robbed Aniya of the peace that the first voice had brought.

As the voice spoke again, her world shook as she tossed in the waves that were without water.

"Aniya, wake up."

The void turned to a vacuum that sucked Aniya deeper and deeper into the waves, the gust of wind stealing her breath away. Her body shook violently until she finally managed to open her eyes.

Everything went still as Aniya found herself in the wine cellar again, looking up at Zeta's dimly lit face as she gently shook Aniya's shoulder.

"It's time. You awake?"

Aniya moaned as she sat up in bed. Her sleep had been peaceful until the very last second, and it was that abrupt awakening that remained at the forefront of her mind.

"How long did I sleep?"

Zeta stepped away from the bed and lit another candle. "Almost three hours. Hope you had enough sleep."

"It'll have to be. How long until we leave?"

"As soon as you're ready." Zeta tossed a bundle of white clothing on Aniya's lap. "Get dressed."

Aniya picked up the clothing and examined it. It was her white bodysuit from the sanctum, now with the addition of a white cloak, similar to Zeta's but without the black trim.

"Helpful for hiding your face. There's cameras every-where." Zeta leaned up against the doorjamb and picked at her fingernails.

Aniya turned the clothes over in her hand for a second before looking up at the assassin. "Do you mind?"

Zeta smirked and left the room.

A few minutes later, Aniya stepped out of the back room and into the main area of the cellar, only to find that the room was full of people in identical cloaks. Nearly all of them, however, were wearing white armor underneath their cloaks. They looked just like the Keepers Aniya had seen in the city.

"You ready?"

Malcolm's voice appeared by her side, and Aniya turned to see him and Zeta waiting by her door.

Aniya looked back at the room full of people. "What's all this?"

"Backup," Zeta said. "They're standing by in case of emergency. The idea is to use stealth as much as possible, but if all else fails, they'll be standing by."

"Each of them has a squadron of about a hundred men positioned throughout the city along our route," Malcolm said. "One word from us, and they'll come to our defense."

"What if we need them inside the Capitol?"

Malcolm glanced at Zeta, who gave a small smile.

"They have strict instructions not to approach the Capitol," she said. "It can't be breached openly, and to storm it would be suicide."

"Which is why we're not going to be using the front door," Malcolm said, grinning.

Aniya frowned. "They'd be really handy if we run into trouble."

"That's what you're here for." Zeta elbowed her. "Just don't get too excited. Blowing up the Capitol will take care of the Council all right, but I'd like to make it out of this alive. Besides, the longer we can go without alerting them, the better. Ideally, the Keepers will never know we were there."

Malcolm raised a finger. "Just a second." He turned to the group of people and raised his voice. "Remember to follow us closely, but stay behind us and below us at all times. If we need help, we'll call for you, and you can rappel up to our position. Once we're in the Capitol, we will cut our communication and will not contact you until we're out, unless the worst comes to pass and we need to get out a final message. If we're not out of the Capitol in two hours, rendezvous at Staging Point B. If you don't hear from us by tomorrow evening, you know what to do."

The cloaked group spoke no words, but each person raised four fingers in the air in silent acknowledgment.

"Then let's go."

Malcolm led Aniya and Zeta back up the stairs and out of the cellar, followed closely behind by a few dozen cloaked people, each one silent.

As soon as they were out in the alley, Malcolm pulled a gun-shaped device from his belt and fired at the top of the building, then disappeared into darkness as his body flew upward.

Aniya and Zeta followed suit and climbed on top of the roof behind him.

"Are you going to be okay?"

As Aniya adjusted the range on her rappel gun, she turned to see Zeta stroking Malcolm's arm.

Malcolm shook his shoulders briskly. "Yeah, I'm just not exactly looking forward to this. I mean, it's a good plan. I just think the sewers would have been a better idea."

"You'll be fine," Zeta said. "Just don't look down."

Aniya looked over the edge and could barely make out the cloaked figures moving into the alley below. "If it makes you feel better, you can't really see the ground from here unless you look hard."

Malcolm looked up at her with a pained glance.

"Okay," Aniya said. "Noted."

Zeta gave Malcolm a quick peck on the cheek and squeezed his bicep. "Come on, let's go." She turned and ran away from the Capitol, stopping at the far edge of the roof.

Aniya joined her, and she turned to see Malcolm reluctantly jogging to catch up.

As soon as they were all gathered, Zeta almost immediately took off again in a dead run, heading directly for the Capitol. Aniya followed, and she could hear Malcolm's footsteps behind her.

Aniya overtook Zeta and was the first one to reach the edge of the roof, launching herself from the edge and flying through the air. A sinking feeling rushed over her body as she soared through the open air, quickly banished by an odd sense of freedom.

She landed on the next building and seamlessly transitioned into a run. The sound of impact reached her ears followed by footsteps, indicating Malcolm and Zeta were right behind her.

Her confidence building, Aniya picked up speed, throwing herself off the building and toward the next one.

In midair, she turned and glanced down at the ground, barely seeing the group of cloaked figures making their way through the streets below.

She landed awkwardly on the roof of the next building, and she nearly lost her balance. As she waved her arms, desperately trying to stay upright, she decided not to look behind her anymore, only looking on toward the looming Capitol, which they were approaching quickly.

The next building was too high to jump naturally, so Aniya slowed to a jog and pulled the rappel gun from her side. She waited until Malcolm and Zeta caught up, and then she fired her rappel at the next roof. As soon as all three of their hooks latched into the building, the trio activated their rappels and jumped off the roof, letting themselves swing down and land on the white walls of the next building. As their rappels retracted, they ran sideways up the wall before reaching the top, swinging their bodies over the ledge.

Without a word, they holstered their rappel guns and continued their rooftop run.

The next few buildings passed without incident, and it wasn't until Aniya was midair between the sixth and seventh rooftops that she realized that the seventh one was far lower than any of them had estimated. Without any time to fire her rappel, Aniya braced for impact and landed roughly on the cement roof in a spark of light, bashing her shoulder into the ground as she rolled.

She pulled herself out of the way, ignoring the pain for a moment, knowing she shouldn't stay in the same spot and risk Malcolm or Zeta landing on her and injuring them.

Aniya spun around in time to see Malcolm and Zeta flying through the air, surprise written on both of their faces. In fact, it seemed that the jump had taken them so off guard that from this angle, Aniya wasn't sure they had jumped far enough to actually cross the gap.

Without thinking, Aniya thrust her hands in front of her,

sending a thin stream of light that froze in the air, forming a slanted platform of light beneath Malcolm's feet, but not Zeta's.

Malcolm landed on the light and began sliding down toward Aniya's position, but Zeta kept free-falling, already slipping away from Malcolm's position.

Aniya frowned and thrust her hands forward again, but no light came.

Thankfully, Malcolm reached out wildly and managed to grab on to Zeta's hand at the last second, pulling her up and on top of him as they slid onto the next roof safely, tumbling across the concrete as the light faded behind them.

"You okay?" Aniya grunted as she sat up against an exhaust port that jutted out from the roof.

Malcolm nodded as he stood, helping Zeta to her feet.

"Sorry. I meant to catch you both, but I guess I missed. Still don't really have control over this."

Zeta brushed dirt off her pristine cloak, shrugging. "Worked out in the end. Besides, the less light you use, the better."

Aniya nodded. "But I'm going to have to use a bit more." She placed her hand on her shoulder and hoped for the best, trusting that the sentient light inside her would come to her aid. Sure enough, something awoke within her as light trickled from her fingertips, spreading heat over her wound and healing it quickly.

Malcolm grinned and whispered, "So cool."

"Yeah," Aniya said, standing up. "It would be cooler if I could control it."

Zeta waved a hand. "Come on. We need to keep moving."

They continued without incident until they reached the building directly across the street from the Capitol, and they slowed to a halt at the edge of the roof.

Aniya peered over the edge. Hundreds of men in white

armor lined the streets below, slowly marching back and forth, surrounding the Capitol in a living barrier of white.

"Well, you were right," she said as she backed away from the ledge. "There's no way we're getting in by foot." She moved back to the ledge behind them and examined the alley. They had gone too far for their reinforcements to follow. They were officially on their own.

Zeta pulled her rappel gun from her side. "No catching us this time. If they see anything abnormal, it's all over."

"But if you fall and die, I'm pretty sure they'll figure it out." Aniya frowned.

Malcolm shrugged. "So we don't fall."

"Good plan," Aniya muttered.

They fired their rappel guns one more time, this time high and far away into the sky ceiling above the Capitol. After giving the hooks a second to attach themselves to the ceiling, they activated their rappels and jumped away from the roof, swinging directly toward the Capitol as they ascended.

This was the shot that Malcolm had said was one they had to get right the first time. If their aim was off just enough, they would fly directly into the walls of the Capitol or find themselves hanging helplessly over the streets of New Washington. Aniya had asked Malcolm multiple times to check her form to make sure she had the right angle, and he had said each time that she got it, but her heart still froze now as she swung toward the Capitol, knowing that if she'd failed to make the shot just right, they would be caught for sure.

But her aim was perfect. She had copied Malcolm's shot exactly, and she reached the apex of her swing just above their planned entry point, a balcony just below the top of the dome that adorned the tip of the Capitol.

Malcolm and Zeta had also successfully made the jump, and they landed next to her nearly at the same time. They looked at each other and gave a silent nod of congratulations, not daring to speak.

Aniya pressed another button on the rappel gun, which sent a jolt of electricity through her line, remotely detaching the hook that was embedded in the sky ceiling and retracting the line rapidly.

When their rappels were fully retracted, they turned to the window.

Zeta pulled out a small spherical device and placed it on the surface of the window, pressing a button as she stepped away.

A thin rod shot out from the side of the device, and from the tip of this extension emitted a small laser that bore into the window. The rod made one revolution around the sphere before retracting back into the device.

Zeta took the device and pulled it carefully away from the window, taking a circular pane of glass with it, and Malcolm reached through the hole and unlatched the window from the inside.

They pushed the window open slowly and stepped inside, finding themselves in a large room, a massive, circular table resting in the very middle.

Malcolm approached the table and pressed into a device strapped to his wrist, and a large projection appeared on the table, revealing a glowing diagram of the Capitol's interior. He motioned to the large room they now stood in, then traced a line with his finger through the hallway and into another room.

Aniya and Zeta nodded, and the projection disappeared.

They quietly stepped into the hallway and slowly made their way down the path Malcolm had pointed out, approaching a room in the back corner of the second floor.

Before they reached for the handle, Zeta held up a hand and pointed to a console attached to the wall next to the door. Malcolm reached into his pocket, withdrawing a paper with a short string of numbers written on it. He glanced back and forth between the paper and the console as he punched in several numbers, and as soon as the console beeped positively, Zeta thrust open the door, simultaneously drawing her gun.

Aniya stepped inside behind her just in time to see a man in white armor fall to the ground, a bloody hole in his head. He lay in the middle of a room filled with computers and monitors.

Zeta replaced her silenced weapon back in her holster and approached one of the computers, gesturing for Aniya and Malcolm to do the same.

Aniya stepped over to one of the computers and began looking through the system. She was unfamiliar with the layout of the interface, but she knew what she was looking for. Anything that included the words "remote," "vault," and "unlock" would be enough to prompt further investigation.

"Anything?"

Malcolm's unexpected voice came several minutes later, and Aniya turned toward him, her heart skipping a beat. "Not yet," she whispered back. "Are you sure the Key is here?"

"Positive. Hurry up," Zeta's hushed voice came from Malcolm's other side. "The Council knows you've escaped by now. Odds are there will be a patrol coming our way at any second."

Aniya nodded and continued her search.

As it turned out, she was the first to find the command that would remotely unlock the door to the data vault, disabling the biometric security that Malcolm would not be able to hack in person.

Triumphantly, she was about to hit the execute key when a deafening alarm blared throughout the room.

Aniya stood up, panicking, covering her ears.

"What happened?"

But her cry was drowned out by the alarm, as were Malcolm's and Zeta's as they opened their mouths but spoke no intelligible words.

The alarm suddenly shut off, but it was instantly replaced by a beam of light that blasted down through the ceiling, twisting around violently as if it was looking for them.

Sure enough, the light grazed Zeta's hip and latched on instantly, coiling around her body and squeezing tight.

A tendril of light separated itself from the beam and quickly found Malcolm, trapping him and shoving him up against the wall.

Aniya backed away from the light slowly, holding her breath, not knowing if it would help.

Another tendril peeled away from the main beam and began writhing around the room, seeking out any sign of her, and Aniya raised her hands in defense, instantly forming a glowing barrier between herself and the snaking light.

The light eventually found her barrier and shrieked wildly, coiling back in alarm.

Aniya grinned and took a deep breath, knowing her own light would come to her defense and protect them all. She reared back with her right hand and prepared to thrust forward when the snaking light suddenly lashed out, piercing Aniya's barrier effortlessly and latching on to her hands, binding them to her side and wrapping around her body in a death grip.

Black settled over Aniya's vision as feeling was cut off to her extremities, and as the light tightened around her neck, Aniya finally gave in and lost consciousness.

## 20

Aniya woke up to the smell of burnt flesh and the pain of searing heat encircling her wrists and ankles.

Circlets of light wrapped tightly around her extremities, stretching up into the ceiling and down into the floor. Malcolm and Zeta shared her fate, except their bonds bit into their skin, drawing blood that dripped down their bodies.

They hung helplessly in a small room with only one door on the far wall, replete with multiple locks.

Aniya pulled at the ropes of light but found that they offered no slack. She sighed and turned to her fellow prisoners. "You guys okay?"

"No," Malcolm said through his teeth, hissing in pain.

Zeta gave no response, and as Aniya looked over, she was taken aback to see the fierce assassin's lip quivering as a tear trickled down her cheek.

"We'll get through this," Aniya said, doing her best to steady her voice and speak firmly. "As soon as their power runs out, they won't be able to hold us here."

"They probably still have enough power for a couple weeks," Zeta said, shaking her head. "I'm pretty sure we're still in the Capitol, and they have plenty of backup generators."

"So we make it a couple weeks."

"Easy for you to say," Malcolm muttered. "They wouldn't kill you. They need you."

"He's right," Zeta said shakily.

Aniya shook her head. "They would have killed you already. No need to keep you around."

"They can't get information out of us if we're dead," Malcolm said. "As soon as they get what they want, they won't need us anymore."

"Then don't give it to them." Aniya gritted her teeth. "We can take whatever they've got."

"Honestly, Aniya? Caspian trained us to withstand torture, but this?" Zeta looked up at her chains of light. "This is nothing like I've ever seen. You might be able to take it because you're practically made of this stuff, but I don't think Malcolm or I would last very long."

Aniya forced herself to smile through the pain. "And here I thought you were an operative. You don't sound much like the assassin I knew."

"That's because I'm not the assassin you knew." Zeta glanced at Malcolm.

"Well, you'd better tap into your old self before it's too late," Aniya said. "Or you're not going to make it out of here."

"Make it out of here?"

A voice came from the shadows as the door opened and three men walked inside, one with a dark, trimmed beard, one with long silver hair, and the other completely bald. The one with the beard smiled and folded his arms. "My dear Lucifer, I'm not sure what you expect to happen here, but let's not get ahead of ourselves."

"My name is Aniya." She glared at the men and

pulled harder at the light ropes, but they still wouldn't budge. "I assume you're the Council?"

"Forget the Council for a moment," the man said, waving a hand. "My name is Byron. This is Deacon and Soren. We're here to have a conversation."

"Don't expect much," Zeta said, spitting out her words.

Byron approached her and curled his index finger under her chin. "Oh, I expect nothing from you. I know your ilk. Heartless mercenaries, to put it lightly. No, I intend to talk to your friends. You can hang there and watch, for all we care."

"And if we don't speak?"

Byron turned to Malcolm as his smile vanished. "Then this will cease to be a conversation. You see, our own operative vanished a few years ago, leaving all manner of unpleasant work to those unqualified to do so. While we would usually leave such work to a soldier, this is a delicate matter and must be handled by those authorized to discuss such things." He pulled a knife from the folds of his robe and pointed it at Malcolm before handing it to the bald man. "Soren is not an operative, so his attempts to pry information from you would be much more damaging than an exact professional. It could get messy, and I doubt he would be able to keep you alive if he happened to be too violent, which I fully expect, so it is in your best interest to be as forthcoming with us as possible."

Byron's smile returned. "But we needn't go there unless you force us to."

"Might as well have your friend get started," Zeta said. "Why waste your time?"

Byron looked up at the ceiling. "Raise the third pylon to 50%."

A second later, Zeta let loose a piercing scream as the light that held her grew brighter, pulsing rapidly as her cries escalated.

The silver-haired man called Deacon leaned over and whispered something in Byron's ear.

Byron sighed and spoke up. "That's enough."

At Byron's command, the pulsing ceased, and Zeta's howls died down to a quiet whimper.

"Now, please let the adults talk." Byron turned to Aniya and folded his arms. "I must say, I have at times doubted the necessity of your existence. We've been getting along just fine for many years now, just using the Underworld as our main source of power. What possessed the Director to create a being such as you is beyond me. I approved his experiment because at the time, it was nothing more. But when the time came to harvest you, I will admit that I was too curious to pass this opportunity up. I believed he could keep you under control. Unfortunately, I was more right than I realized possible."

Aniya glared at the man. "Do I look like I'm under his control? He can't make me do anything, especially now that he's dead."

Byron smirked. "Is that so? Then what are you doing here?"

"We came to kill you," Malcolm said, puffing out his chest and staring Byron down.

"Ah yes, the Vagabond." Byron turned and brought his face close to Malcolm's. "It's a shame your people follow you so blindly. You have the potential for great leadership, but instead you insist on a more violent path. You're no better than the operative you've managed to turn for your cause. You inspire nothing but bloodthirst, and you live by the sword. We both know what happens to people like you."

Byron stood back up straight and paced in front of the prisoners. "Unfortunately, your anger is misplaced. The Council desires nothing but peace."

"Peace enforced by threat of death?" Aniya frowned.

"But peace nonetheless. To destroy us is to destroy the hard-earned peace that this world thrives on. I think you know that, and so does the man who sent you. No, destroying us will gain you nothing. I believe you're here for something else."

Aniya stared down the smug man. "And what would that be?"

"I do not believe you are this ignorant." Byron glanced at Malcolm and Zeta. "In fact, I refuse to believe all three of you are stupid enough to bring hell upon what's left of this world. You're here to help him, whether you realize it or not."

"What are you talking about?" Malcolm stared at Byron incredulously. "You're making no sense. If you want to accuse us of something, then do it. But I promise you, I don't need any other motivation to come here than to see your head on a stick. You've manipulated this world for thousands of years, hiding the truth. Tell me, do you make people believe that the sun they see is real, or have you just trained them not to care?"

Byron shook his head. "Don't be dramatic, my dear Vagabond. We have created a paradise. A world so perfect that it doesn't matter if every fine detail is natural. You've been around long enough to see that. Lucifer just woke up from her long slumber, so I don't expect her to understand. But I doubt that you're stubborn enough to watch me burn and the rest of the world with me. We both know why you're here. Are you really foolish enough to believe that executing the Council will change the world for you?"

Malcolm didn't respond.

"No, I don't think you are," Byron said, handing Soren the blade. "Unfortunately, I cannot assume to know your purpose, as much as I believe I know what it is. And if I came right out and asked it, I risk exposing our secrets. After all, I don't know what Caspian has done to you. For all I know, he could be listening right now."

Soren took the knife and held it against Malcolm's throat. "What did you come for? Tell us, and we'll make your death quick. I may not be an operative, but I can make your death agonizingly painful if I desire."

Malcolm stared back. After a moment, he chuckled and spit on Soren's face.

"Fine," Soren said, raising the knife in the air and freezing only at the sound of Zeta's voice.

"Stop!"

Byron turned to Zeta and raised an eyebrow. "The assassin speaks. I must say, this is quite unexpected. To break an operative without threat of violence or . . ." He glanced at Malcolm. "No, that's impossible."

"Shut up and leave him alone," Zeta said. "He doesn't know anything, can't you see that?"

"I didn't think it was possible for you to feel anything other than an unrelenting urge to kill. But it's true, isn't it? You've gotten soft. You feel for the boy."

Zeta only glared at Byron, baring her teeth.

"I'm honestly not entirely sure what to do next," Byron said, chuckling. "This is by far the last thing I expected." He turned to Deacon. "Suggestions?"

The silver-haired man stared at Zeta for a long moment. Finally, he spoke firmly. "Pylon three, 70%."

Zeta's chains flashed wildly, and the crackle of electricity was almost instantly drowned out by her desperate wails.

After what seemed like a minute, Deacon raised a hand. "Enough."

The light died down, and all that was left was the awful smell of burning flesh and Zeta's sobs.

Soren approached Zeta and used the knife to lift her chin. "Well?"

Zeta stared back at the man, her tears dripping down onto the blade as she bit her lip.

"Okay, then." Bryon turned to Deacon again. "I would say we don't have another option at the moment. Shall we proceed?"

Deacon nodded. "But we only have three of them. We must choose the order wisely."

"The boy?" Soren grinned at Malcolm. "It's the quickest way to break the assassin."

"Yes, but I think she's strong enough to say nothing even after he dies. I'm not convinced she knows anything anyway."

Byron nodded. "Agreed." He pointed, and Soren turned around and viciously swiped with the blade, ripping Zeta's throat open and spilling her blood on the floor.

"No!" Malcolm's cries rivaled Zeta's as he watched the assassin bleed out, her twitching body shaking loose even more blood until she finally went still. The light ropes unfurled and disappeared into the walls, and Zeta's body fell to the floor.

When her voice finally returned, Aniya glared at Soren, who calmly wiped the blade on Zeta's robes. "You think killing us will get you what you want?"

"I know it will," Byron said. "You're human, at least more than your friend here was. If you won't speak now, you will if it means saving the Vagabond's life. Now that the assassin is dead, you know I mean what I say. So I ask again, what did you come here for?"

"You . . . will . . . die for that," Malcolm interrupted and spoke through his sobs, his anger accentuating his words with a painful groan.

Soren calmly approached Malcolm and pressed the blade against his throat, looking back at Aniya. "Don't make me kill him too."

"Please, no," Aniya said. "Can't you see we don't know what you want to hear? We would have told you. We would have said something before you killed her," she said, glancing toward Zeta's corpse.

Byron shook his head sadly. "Please do not try this, Lucifer. This is a game you cannot win. I will kill him."

Aniya stared down the man for several seconds, defiantly unwilling to yield.

Finally, Byron nodded again, and Soren pulled his arm back to swing his knife at Malcolm's throat.

"Okay!" Aniya screamed, squeezing her eyes shut.

Byron did not offer a triumphant expression at Aniya's defeat. He didn't even smile. "Yes?"

"No, Aniya." Malcolm thrashed against the light, pulling himself closer to Soren's knife. "This is a noble death. Don't rob me of that and betray what I've fought for."

Soren inched the blade closer.

"The Key," Aniya blurted out. As a smirk finally spread across Byron's face, she sighed and let her head droop toward the floor. "We came for the Key."

Instantly, Soren pulled back, flourishing the blade as he turned to Byron. "I told you. We should have moved the Key when we had the chance."

"Silence," Byron said firmly. He turned back to Aniya, pulling her chin up with a finger. "Tell me, dear. Do you know what the Key even does? Do you know what master you truly serve?"

Aniya said nothing.

"Well, at least now we know," Deacon said. "I suggest moving the Key as soon as possible and preparing Lucifer for transport back to the sanctum."

"Agreed," Byron said. "And the Vagabond?"

"Kill him. Forget what I said about turning him into a martyr. Too much is at stake."

Byron nodded.

Soren turned and brandished the knife again, but he paused as the lights flickered. "Was that you?" He asked when the disturbance settled, looking at Aniya.

Aniya only stared back at the bald man, doing her best to keep from trembling as she glared.

"Finish the job," Byron said as he turned toward the door. "I'm not taking any chances. Come to the safe room when you're done."

Byron exited the room, and Soren turned back toward Malcolm.

The lights flickered again before shutting off entirely.

Aniya fell to the floor, free of her bonds. She glared at Soren as she felt strength pour back into her body and a green light began to spread throughout the otherwise dark room. "You should have killed me when you had the—"

Soren's foot landed heavily on her lungs, crushing her windpipe and cutting her off. "Quiet. Deacon, get the power back on. Find out what happened to the emergency generators and get me a report. I'm going to have to subdue Lucifer."

Only silence followed.

"Deacon?"

Through the pain, Aniya looked up at Soren as she grasped at his boot, reaching for words that wouldn't come.

She stopped short as a shadow appeared over Soren's shoulder.

Soren followed her eyes and turned around just as a hand clamped down over his throat. Red streaks raced down his skin as his body began to shake, and the shadow lifted him into the air.

Aniya gasped as her windpipe healed. Her light grew brighter, but it didn't light up any more of the room. Instead, it seemed to funnel itself toward the shadow, swirling around the figure until it finally attached itself to the shadow's arm and pierced itself into Soren's body, mixing in with the red streaks across his body as the councilman began to shake violently.

Finally, Soren went still. The shadow released him, and Soren's body fell next to Aniya, his black eyes staring into hers. His skin was withered and white, wrinkled and leathery. His mouth hung open in a silent scream.

Suddenly, the lights came back on.

Aniya stumbled away from Soren's hideous remains and looked past the man to see Deacon lying against the wall, his body in a similar state. She looked up at the intruder, staring at a man in a black bodysuit, silver rings around his wrists.

Her breath disappeared, even though her lungs were now completely healed. It was impossible, yet here he was, staring back at her. She couldn't even bring herself to say his name, terrified that if she allowed herself to do so, the illusion would vanish and she would be left without him yet again.

The man pulled his sleeve back and looked at a display on his wrist, then back up at her. He let his wrist fall to his side, and Aniya thought she saw her face on the display before it blinked out again.

"Hello, Annelise."

Aniya finally forced herself to speak, but it was no more than a whisper.

"Hello, Nicholas."

# PART III

## RETRIBUTION

## 21

Aniya threw herself into the man's arms, letting her head fall heavily on his chest as she surrendered her weight to him, heaving sobs into his black clothing and clutching at the nape of his neck.

"Nicholas, I thought you were dead!" She buried her face in his shoulder, smearing her own tears over her face. "What happened to you? Where have you been all this time?"

But she felt firm hands grasp her arms and push her backward gently, and she looked up helplessly as she reached for his body, staring back at his dry, empty eyes.

"We don't have time for this, Annelise." His words were cold, monotone, almost an afterthought.

"Time? It's been three years, Nicky."

"He's right," Malcolm said as he stood. "We need to help Zeta and get out of here."

Aniya shook her head. "You don't understand, Malcolm. He was dead. I watched him die." She turned back to Nicholas and placed a hand on his chest, where she had seen a dozen bullets pierce his skin and rob him of life. She whispered, "I watched you die."

"I understand, Aniya, but I don't think you do." Malcolm

looked down at the floor and shifted his weight. "That's not Nicholas."

"What?" Aniya stroked the man's cheek, letting her hand travel up and through his hair. "Who else could it be?" But her hand froze as she reached a part in his hair, her fingertips grazing a rough, jagged line in his scalp.

The man backed away from Aniya's hand. "I know who you think I am, but that's not me. I have his body, but my name is Omega. Caspian sent me to get you."

Aniya blinked. "What do you mean, you have his body? Nicholas, what are you talking about?"

She felt a hand on her arm, but she shrugged it away.

"Aniya, it's not Nicholas," Malcolm said. "Zeta can explain when you wake her up, but she doesn't have much time. We need to get her back and get going."

"No!" Aniya thrust her fists toward the floor, letting a wave of green light flash over the room. She pointed at the man, letting a stream of green light shoot out of her finger and splash over his black clothing. "Who are you?"

The man sighed and looked down at the ground. "I'm a program, what you might call a cybernetic organism. Caspian made me when Nicholas died so that I could take full advantage of his powers, as they were a part of his body. But Nicholas is gone. He died three years ago."

Aniya stepped backward and held her hands to her head. "No, that's not possible."

"It doesn't seem possible, no." Omega gave a soft smile. "But it's not new technology. It's been done before. Caspian had to do extensive surgery just to keep this body alive, but Nicholas's soul had already moved on. This body was an empty shell until Caspian placed a computer in its skull to interface with the brain."

"Aniya, please." Malcolm pulled on her arm again, this time harder. "We're going to lose Zeta if we don't act quickly. I know you've brought people back before, and you can do it again. Nicholas is gone, but it's not too late for her."

"He's right, Annelise. We can talk later with Caspian, but we don't have a lot of time. We have to help Zeta, and the Council's armies are on high alert after your intrusion on the Capitol. Thanks to the disturbance I've caused, they're probably in the building already. We need to leave."

Aniya closed her eyes and tried her best to shut out the world, to retreat to the void in her mind, to find her brother. But all she could think about was how Nicholas was so close, standing right in front of her, but she would never really see him again.

A hand graced her cheek, and as Aniya felt energy leave her body and course into Omega's, a warm peace settled over her. It was the closest she would ever get to enjoying his touch again, and as long as she kept her eyes closed, she could picture her old friend standing in front of her now, the same half-smile on his face as he looked at her with longing.

"Annelise."

But the cold voice of the half-human assassin shattered the illusion, and she opened her eyes to face him again.

His hand dropped back to his side, and as energy surged through her body again, she felt strength return.

"Okay."

Aniya knelt by Zeta's side and placed her hands on the girl's neck, soaking her hands in blood. She took a deep breath and closed her eyes, squeezing her eyes closed as she imagined stitching the gaping wound closed.

But nothing happened. After several seconds, Aniya opened her eyes, hoping that she had healed Zeta and just not felt anything, but the assassin still lay dead on the cold ground, her black eyes staring back up at Aniya.

"It's not working," she said, looking up. "I don't have full control over this. I never have."

"I read the report," Omega said. "Let me help."

The next thing Aniya knew, his hands were on top of hers, and she drew backward with a sharp breath. She took a moment to compose herself and put her hands back, flinching as Omega placed his over hers again.

Almost instantly, a warm trickling sensation crept over her body and funneled down toward her hands. She watched beads of green light race over Omega's hands, just to shoot through his fingertips and back toward her hands, racing over her skin and covering Zeta's neck.

Aniya watched as the assassin's skin pulled itself back together, stitched together with strands of green, glowing thread. As the edges of Zeta's ripped skin met, the seams vanished, leaving a smooth surface of undisturbed flesh.

Malcolm stood nearby, tapping a foot as he watched with a concerned look.

Within seconds, Zeta's neck was completely restored. Almost instantly, the light morphed into a warm, yellow bath that spread over the girl's entire body, pulsing brightly for several seconds before dimming, the lights shooting back into Aniya's body.

Aniya lifted her hands, but Omega didn't let go. Instead, the yellow light redirected itself back into his body, and soon the light changed back to a calm green hue.

Finally, he let go, and Aniya sat back against the steel wall, pulling her hands away and breathing heavily, her energy spent.

Zeta's eyes fluttered open, and with a moan, she sat up. Her eyes met Omega's, and she cursed. "You had to wait until after he cut me open?"

"You told me to wait until after you got inside the Capitol." Omega shrugged. "By the time I was inside, you were already captured. I had to get into the electrical room to find out where you were being held. Besides, you're fine now."

"Spoken like someone who doesn't know what pain feels like," Zeta said as she slowly stood. She turned to Aniya and smiled. "Thank you. I know that couldn't have been easy to do, given our history."

Aniya shrugged. "Don't look at me. I couldn't do it myself. Nich—*he* had to help."

Zeta glanced at Omega. "So I see you're all caught up."

"Not exactly." Aniya stood, unable to bring herself to look at the stranger in Nicholas's body. "But apparently, we don't have time to talk about it further."

Omega nodded. "If we can get back up to the second floor, we can rappel out the way you came."

"But we didn't finish our mission," Aniya said. "We have to get the Key."

"It's impossible to finish it right now," Omega said, shaking his head. "There's an army on the streets outside and in the building with us, and they have ways to defend against you, Aniya. We have all the time in the world to finish the job at a later date, but right now, we need to get out of here."

Malcolm opened the door and peeked outside. "Looks like we're clear."

"That's not good," Omega said. "They know we're here, and they've got to be pretty cautious with the blackout I caused. They should be lining the halls, guns pointed at us."

Zeta looked at Aniya. "Given what you're capable of, I doubt they're willing to come in here after us. It's smarter for them to ambush us when we try to escape. I'll go and draw them out, distract them while you get out of here."

"I can't let you do that," Malcolm said. "It's not safe."

Zeta winked. "You don't give me enough credit. We know enough about the building to know that there are alarms in every section, and I know how to trip them. I can make it look like we're in another part of the building while the rest of you get out of here safely. I'll meet you outside."

"Sounds good." Omega nodded toward Zeta. "Do it. We'll wait for you."

"Wait!" Aniya held up a hand. "You said there's alarms.

You're going to trip them somewhere else, but how do we avoid them ourselves?"

Zeta grinned. "You don't. Wait three minutes, and then start moving. The best we can do is get their attention in one spot and then confuse them. It should give you enough time to get out, but move fast."

"I don't like it," Aniya said. "You're going to get yourself killed just to buy us a few more seconds?"

"If I get killed, then just bring me back again." Zeta smirked. "But I only ended up with my throat slit because I didn't have a weapon in my hand." She leaned over and pried the knife out of Soren's hand. "See if they can touch me now."

Zeta started to leave, but Malcolm grabbed her arm and pulled her close, whispering in her ear just loud enough for Aniya to hear.

"Be careful."

The assassin smiled warmly, kissed Malcolm on the cheek, and disappeared.

## 22

"It's time. Are you ready?"

Aniya looked up from the dead bodies littered on the floor. Omega was staring back at her with those eyes, the eyes that had once looked at her with such passion. They now seemed vacant, dark, void of the light that Nicholas had always been to her.

She nodded once, looking away and at the door, unsure of what to expect on the other side. The halls had seemed empty before, but who knew what would be waiting for them after the three-minute head start they had given Zeta.

"The Vagabond will have to stay between us until we find a weapon for him," Omega said. "We should be able to keep him alive until then."

"Don't worry about me," Malcolm said. "I can take care of myself. Just focus on getting out of here."

Aniya rolled her eyes. "Don't be stupid, Malcolm. They've got guns. Once you have one, I'm sure you'll be fine. But until then, just stay between us."

"No time to argue," Omega said, opening the door slightly and peeking out. "Zeta said three minutes, and it's been four."

Malcolm nodded and took his place behind Omega, following him out into the hallway.

Aniya took one last look at the withered bodies on the floor and left the room, closing the door behind her.

The hallway was empty and silent.

"No alarms," Omega muttered, glancing around. "She's either really far away or they found her first."

Malcolm shook his head. "They didn't find her. We'd hear about it by now."

"Let's go, guys." Aniya pushed gently against Malcolm's back. "I don't know about you, but I don't want to stick around here any longer than I have to."

The trio moved down the hallway, taking it slow as they made their way through the maze-like basement of the Capitol.

Aniya couldn't tell if their trek took so long because the basement was larger than the first floor or they were actually moving that slow, but it was several minutes until they reached the stairway.

But it was just as Omega placed a foot on the bottom step that an alarm rang throughout the building. Aniya froze in place as the ear-piercing noise continued, but when nothing happened after several seconds, she leaned forward and whispered into Malcolm's ear, "Gotta be Zeta."

Malcolm nodded and nudged Omega forward.

They picked up the pace now that the alarm covered the sound of their footsteps, and they reached the first floor of the Capitol shortly, stepping out into the main atrium undisturbed.

Here, they could hear gunfire from the hallways of the first floor, loud enough that although the shots rang out in a hallway deeper in the building, it echoed in the atrium loud enough that it sounded like it was coming from every direction.

"She'll be fine," Malcolm said, tugging on Aniya's sleeve.

"Yeah, I'm not worried," she said, turning back toward the group. "Should we try to go through the front door this time? They know we're here anyway."

Omega shook his head. "All the more reason to get out of here unseen. They're not just going to let you go. They probably have every warm body out there waiting for us."

"Good," Aniya said, feeling warmth spread through her body. "We can end it all here and now."

"It won't be that easy. If they had that prison ready for you, chains of light that you couldn't destroy, you can be sure that they have weapons ready for you. It's not worth finding out the hard way."

"He's right," Malcolm said. "Better to leave the way we came."

Aniya nodded reluctantly and turned back to the stairwell, leading the way to the second floor. It seemed quiet enough, and they proceeded down the hall and back toward their entry point.

But they stopped short as a squadron of armored men suddenly appeared from behind a bend in the hallway, their guns raised as they approached the trio.

Aniya backed away but was stopped by Malcolm's body behind her. She turned around to see another squadron approaching them from behind.

They were surrounded.

"They won't shoot us," Omega said. "They could hit each other, and unless their armor is bulletproof, they can't risk taking out their own men."

Malcolm glanced back and forth. "You think their armor's bulletproof?"

"I don't want to find out." Aniya raised her hands and spoke slowly. "We can explain."

Instantly, the armored men opened fire on the trio from both sides. Aniya pushed Malcolm roughly, letting him fall to the floor, taking Omega with him.

Aniya thrust her arms up and away from her, her palms facing the opposing forces. Light shot out from her fingers and created two large walls of light on either side of her body. The hallway flashed wildly as bullets clashed against her light, sparks flying as the bullets deflected away and back down the hall. Aniya closed her eyes tight as the sound grew louder, each shot echoing against the metal walls.

After several seconds, the gunfire ceased, and Aniya opened her eyes. The armored men still stood, unharmed, pointing their guns at her. She looked down at Omega and Malcolm, frowning.

"That answer your question?"

Without waiting for them to answer, Aniya pushed out with her hands, letting the walls of light shoot away from her and toward the armored men, knowing that touching the light would incinerate them on contact.

But a staggering pain pierced her shoulder, and she fell to the ground, losing control of the light and watching it fizzle out before it could touch her enemies.

Aniya looked down at her shoulder, where a thin hole in her clothing sizzled as glowing fibers calmed down. She looked up to see one of the soldiers pointing a funny-looking gun at her, the tip pulsing with white light.

"What?" Utter shock rendered Aniya defenseless, and all she could do was look back down at the hole in her flesh. She squeezed her eyes closed and willed energy to flow into her shoulder, but all it did was make the pain worse, and she opened her eyes again to see that the wound hadn't healed a bit.

The soldier holding the gun smirked at her and pressed a button on the side. A faint whirring sound came from the gun as the tip started to glow again.

Suddenly, Omega jumped in front of Aniya and slammed his fist into the ground, cracking the cement floor in jagged lines that spread down the hall toward the armored men.

As the ground crumbled beneath their feet, the soldiers froze for a brief second before convulsing wildly, their skin turning white.

Omega stood up and spun around, facing the other group of soldiers and thrusting his palms out. As the lights flickered wildly, red tendrils shot out from his fingertips and wrapped themselves around the men, crimson lines melting into their armor as they began to scream in pain.

Their skin slowly drained of color as they clutched at the ropes of light, desperately clawing at their own armor as they fell to the ground.

Omega closed his palms into fists, and with a red flash of light from the tendrils, the hall went silent and the fluorescent lights stopped flickering.

Ignoring the smell of burnt flesh, Aniya looked back down at her shoulder and placed a hand on her wound, moaning in pain. "What was that?"

Malcolm slowly got up and surveyed Omega's aftermath. "Better question, what was *that*?"

Omega seemed to ignore them both, and he instead knelt by Aniya's side and examined her wound. "Are you okay?"

"Does it look like I'm okay?" Aniya bit her lip and shook her head. "Sorry, I wasn't ready for that. I've never seen a weapon like that before."

"Tell me about it," Omega said. "It looked like the light that you use. They must have harnessed it somehow when you were in the machine."

"If it's my light, how did it hurt me?"

Omega shrugged. "Not a clue. And it's not getting any better?"

Aniya shook her head again.

"Here, let me." Omega placed his hand on her wound and pressed down, and it was all Aniya could do to not cry out in pain.

But slowly, a sliver of white light crept out of the wound

and wrapped itself around Omega's wrist. As soon as it was all the way out of Aniya's shoulder, Omega threw his hand in the air, shooting the sliver of light into the ceiling.

The pain vanished, and the hole quickly began to heal. Aniya exhaled slowly and sat up, shaking dizziness away. "How did you heal me, but I couldn't heal myself?"

"Well, I naturally draw energy from you. My best guess is that whatever that was, I don't think it could be fixed with extra energy. It needed something to pull it out."

Malcolm approached the two and put his hands on their shoulders. "That's great and all, but we can talk about your freakish powers later. We need to get out of here and find Zeta. She's probably waiting for us right now."

Aniya nodded and climbed to her feet. "Let's go."

They made it to the balcony without incident, but Zeta was nowhere to be found.

"We can't wait for her," Omega muttered, glancing back through the now-closed window.

Malcolm folded his arms. "I'm not leaving without her. And if you had any idea how valuable she is, you'd go back in there and pull her out."

"She's replaceable, Vagabond." Omega shrugged indifferently. "Just like you. And I'm not going to risk Lucifer's safety to rescue your girlfriend. Our orders were very clear."

"Then you might as well leave now. And you can't make—"

A hook flew over the balcony and latched on to the railing, narrowly missing Aniya's head. Seconds later, Zeta appeared, running up the side of the Capitol as her rappel retracted. She vaulted over the railing and stood next to Malcolm, breathing heavily.

"They're all over the place," she said between breaths. "Couldn't go through the building."

Malcolm smiled widely for a second before shaking it away, reverting to a stern concentration. "Good thing the

Lightbringers want to keep this under wraps as much as you do, Z. They could have lit up the sky ceiling so it would be easier to track us down, but I guess they didn't want civilians asking any hard questions. I assume we're still leaving the same way we came?"

"We are," Zeta said, taking one last deep breath to recover. "But you shouldn't. They're going to come for us now, especially now that we have this."

She pulled a small, silver stick from her pocket and placed it in Malcolm's hands, and as he looked down, his eyes widened.

"The Key? How?"

Zeta smirked. "You still underestimate me after all these years? But we can talk about how amazing I am later. In the meantime, we've proven ourselves a real threat to the Council, thanks to Omega and Aniya, so I doubt they'll give us time to recover and attack again. They'll hunt us down, which means we need to gather your army and retreat to a secure location. We can't beat them up here, but with your men and Caspian's, we'll be able to defend Level I until we're ready for another attack."

Malcolm nodded. "Understood."

"You remember where the elevator is? It'll be unguarded now that they think everyone underground is dead." Zeta turned toward Omega. "Go with him. He'll need backup."

"No!" Aniya blurted out before she knew what she was saying.

Zeta turned toward her, her eyebrows arched.

Aniya clamped her mouth shut and looked away. She knew it didn't make any sense. It wasn't Nicholas. Omega had made that abundantly clear. But the thought of losing him, never seeing his face again after losing him for three years was unthinkable.

Luckily, Malcolm spoke up before Aniya was forced to answer. "I'll be fine. Staging point B isn't even three miles away. I've been running these streets for years, and they'll need more than a little luck to catch me. Besides, it's better if I go alone."

After a long pause, Zeta bowed her head, blinking rapidly as she pursed her lips. "Fine."

"Hold on to this," Malcolm said as he handed the Key to Aniya. "You'll probably outlive all of us, so you need to make sure this gets to Caspian. I'll see you in Level I."

Aniya squeezed his hand before he could pull away. "Be safe."

Malcolm gave a curt nod and turned, pulling his own rappel gun from his belt. He climbed on top of the railing, fired at an angle to the left of their planned exit, and just like that, he was gone.

## 23

"You are strong, Lightbringer. But are you ready to do what you must?"

Aniya spun around but saw only black. She turned around again, lost in the void, realizing that she had no memory of how she got there.

"Who are you?" Aniya tried to shout, but it came out as a breathy gasp. She cleared her throat and tried again. "Who are you?"

"Your destiny," the voice said gently, in a mix between a purr and a hiss.

Aniya turned again slowly, scanning the black horizon for any sign of the feminine speaker.

But there was nothing. She was seemingly alone in the void. Not even the Chancellor had made an appearance, let alone her brother.

There was only the shadow of the void, and as the voice began to speak again, Aniya sensed the other Shadow, the one that called to her even in her waking hours.

"You have accomplished a great deal, Lightbringer. You have overcome adversity of the highest level. But there is one final task that lies before you, an unthinkable one."

Aniya sat down in the void and began breathing deeply, just like Caspian had taught her. Whatever this voice was, she knew it could be managed, just like the other ghosts that lingered in her mind. Just like her powers.

But as she breathed, the voice only grew richer, sweeter, darker.

"Tell me, child. Are you ready to accept your fate? Are you ready to leave behind the remains of your old life, shed the darkness you have carried so proudly, and become the Light? I think not."

Aniya's heart began racing as a heavy breath tickled her ear.

"What is to give light must endure burning, young one. And you are not done burning. But fear not. I will be with you, Lightbringer."

A hand landed on Aniya's shoulder, and she decided that was enough. Her eyes flew open, and she looked for the Shadow, but instead stared into the cold eyes of her dead boyfriend. They held a blank stare, oddly motionless.

"Are you okay?" Omega asked, his concern sounding forced. "You were shaking."

"I'm fine," Aniya said, shrugging his hand away. His touch felt cold, even through her shirt. She stood up in the elevator and looked at Zeta. "How long was I out?"

"Minutes, if that," the assassin said. "I told you there wasn't any point in taking a nap right now. We're almost to Level I. But you were quite insistent, so I wasn't going to argue."

Aniya brushed off her shirt. "Was I saying anything?"

Omega shook his head.

"We should have Caspian look at you when we get there," Zeta said. "Can't very well fight to Council if you're stressed out like this."

"I said I'm fine," Aniya muttered.

Zeta shared a look with Omega but quickly turned back to the elevator doors.

"She's right," Omega said. "You just got out of the Director's machine. I don't think you're emotionally ready to fight anyone. You barely survived the Capitol, after all. It's not—"

"I don't think you're in a position to lecture me about my emotions," Aniya snapped. "Someone who's not capable of them really shouldn't be giving me advice."

Zeta opened her mouth, but Aniya cut her off.

"You're not much better, so zip it."

Zeta's mouth closed but curled into a smile, which only irritated Aniya further.

She would have snapped at them again, but the elevator finally slowed to a halt. The doors opened, and Aniya's anger immediately vanished as her twin brother looked back at her.

"How . . ." Aniya trailed off as she stared at Roland in wonder.

Roland grinned widely. "Caspian. He brought us up by train."

"But . . . you . . ." Aniya tried but couldn't manage the words. So instead, she leapt forward and threw herself into his arms.

Roland pulled her close, his chest trembling as he stroked the back of her head.

"Welcome home, sis."

## 24

B yron looked around the table. Deacon and Soren's empty seats loomed like a bad omen, and what was left of the Council seemed restless, their uneasiness audible in their concerned grumbling. It was well deserved, Byron decided. It was only an hour since the attack on the Citadel, but that was long enough for the intruders to clear out of New Washington and retreat to the Underworld.

"Enough," Byron said firmly, deciding there was no point in dwelling further on the issue. "I know we're not exactly in a good place right now."

"Good place?" One of the councilmen slammed his palms on the table as his voice pitched up. "Lucifer is gone, and so is the Key. We're in the worst place possible."

Another council member nodded. "Soren was right. We should have moved the Key, at the very least. If this doesn't confirm our worst suspicions, I don't know what will."

"I don't disagree," Byron said. "All signs point to the worst-case scenario, yes. But there's still time. When I spoke to Lucifer, she didn't seem to know what the Key was. I doubt the Vagabond knows either. Maybe not even the assassin."

"I wouldn't count on that," a man to Byron's right said.

"Surely she must know. And to count on her ignorance is foolish."

Byron nodded. "Again, I agree. I'm just saying it's possible. Either way, as of right now, Lucifer is not controlled by the Director. And given her strong will, it will take some time for her to be manipulated into following his orders."

A councilwoman to Byron's right frowned. "Who is even speaking on his behalf? He's gone now, and the computer chamber's supply remains undisturbed."

"It's the Director. He's more than capable of managing things from beyond the proverbial grave. But does it really matter? We know what we're up against now, and thanks to the trackers we embedded in Lucifer while we held her here, we know where they are hiding. I see no other logical next step than a direct assault on their forces in Level I."

The table burst into commotion.

Byron let the chaos continue for a few moments before speaking again.

"Enough."

The table quickly fell silent.

"I know it's a risky move—"

"Risky?" The councilman to Byron's left scoffed. "It's suicide."

Byron glared at the man for a moment before proceeding. "We are more than equipped to deal with a ragtag band of rebels."

"Tell that to Deacon and Soren. You know, I'm wondering if we didn't appoint the wrong High Councilor. At least Soren—"

Byron whipped out the gun strapped to his belt and fired at the councilman. A flash of light erupted from the man's body, and when it faded, the councilman was gone.

As the rest of the table fell deathly silent, Byron tossed the gun on the table.

"Thanks to the Director, we don't have to worry about

Lucifer's powers. These weapons are equipped with the very light that Lucifer provided, which means that her defenses should be quite useless against them. And whatever forces Caspian has managed to rally surely do not come close to our numbers."

No one responded, and most of the councilors stared at the empty space where the dead councilman had sat just seconds earlier. His chair now slowly spun freely.

"The effectiveness of these new weapons was confirmed by the response team that was deployed here in the Capitol after the power outage. Of course, they all died, but our security cameras captured everything. The weapon penetrated Lucifer's shield and caused her great harm. If it had been closer to her heart, she would be dead now. All we have to do next time is not miss."

The councilwoman to Byron's right finally spoke. "But if we kill Lucifer, then we will have lost everything."

"We'll start over. We can install a new Director and have the Underworld back up and running in days. Levels XIX and XVIII are the only ones down. The others are still fully operational and can supply more than enough power in the meantime. The Director's experiment was interesting, but if it causes this much trouble, it's quite frankly not worth it. It's time to clean up our mistakes and get back to what works."

The Council stared at the weapon on the table for several seconds.

"You don't have to like it, but my emergency powers will not expire until the threat at hand is eliminated. This is my choice. We will send our army down to Level I and kill every last one of them."

## 25

"That's quite the story, Annelise."

Aniya sat down and took a breath. She had been talking for the last fifteen minutes, recounting her adventures in the Overworld to old friends and new allies in the meeting room of the Level I Citadel. She looked back at Caspian, who sat at the end of the long table.

"Nothing like yours. I thought the Underworld was gone, that the Director had everyone killed."

Caspian smiled warmly. "The Director was indeed powerful, but he forgot that I have an army of my own down here, and that I trained his."

"You say the Director is dead?" Salvador finally spoke up from the other end of the table. He had remained silent during Aniya's debriefing, whereas others had interjected with clarifying questions. "You watched him die?"

Aniya nodded toward Zeta, who sat by Caspian. "She chopped his head clean off. He's dead."

Salvador frowned but didn't respond.

"And we're supposed to trust her now, just like that?" Tamisra, sitting across the table from Aniya, scoffed and folded her arms.

"Agreed," Roland said from his position at Aniya's left. "After everything she's done, I'd say that's asking a little much."

"But she's quite literally not the same person you remember." Caspian gestured to Zeta, who stood. He turned her around gently, parting her hair on her scalp to reveal a small scar on the back of her head. "Embedded in her brain is a microchip, similar to the one now in Omega's brain, yet more primitive. Each one of my recruits receives the same implant, and it allows me to send and receive simple communication, activate a signal that sends them back to me, or completely override any previous instruction. Zeta was the Director's personal operative, and therefore the most valuable to me."

Caspian released Zeta, who stood by his side quietly. "It is unfortunate that one of her final commands was to kill your chancellor, but it wasn't completely unprecedented. In his final years, Noah was intent on destroying the Council. He contacted me multiple times to try to convince me to join his cause, and I only recently decided to listen. Unfortunately, it was too little too late. All I could do was watch as the Director destroyed the Underworld. But we have more than a fighting chance to continue on and end the Council's rule for good. Between my army, yours, the Vagabond's, and the combined powers of Omega and Lucifer, we can win. It will come at a cost, to be sure, but we can win."

Aniya glanced at Omega at the sound of his name. The robotic assassin hadn't said a word since they had arrived in Level I, and he still sat silently on Caspian's other side, staring blankly at a spot on the wall.

Salvador held up his hands. "Slow down, Caspian. The Lightbringers may have underestimated you three years ago, but they will be ready for a fight now. They must know that you are still alive. If nothing else, they surely know what Annelise is capable of. What makes you think we can win?"

"He just said it," Lieutenant Haskill said gruffly. He paced nearby, staring out the window at the Hub. "We have three armies now."

"Paling in comparison to the Lightbringers, I'm sure," Corrin said, sitting by the Scourge. "Against their numbers and technology, we don't stand a chance."

The lieutenant gestured toward Aniya. "What technology can stand against Aniya's powers? And what about Omega? No, we have the strength to face them head-on, with all our forces combined. It will be a battle to remember."

Salvador rolled his eyes. "Lieutenant, please. Sit. God forbid, if the time comes, you can be the first one out there."

"With pleasure," the lieutenant said as he sat next to Corrin. "I have a bone to pick with them."

"And you'll get your chance," Caspian said.

Aniya finally spoke again. "You're forgetting that they have weapons that can hurt me now. I don't think it will be as easy as you make it sound, Lieutenant."

"No, I doubt it will be," Haskill said, his eyes twinkling. "That just means it'll be even more fulfilling to win."

"What if they never come?" Corrin asked. "They have to know that they could lose a war with us. Are we so sure that they'll try to pick a fight?"

Caspian frowned. "The Council isn't just going to let Annelise go, much less their Key, which has held their civilization together for centuries. They'll come for both of them."

"Let them come," Tamisra said, apparently ignoring a glare from Salvador. "It's time to finally put an end to the Lightbringers."

"Well put, Tamisra." Caspian turned to Zeta. "Any word from the Vagabond?"

Zeta shook her head. "He went dark. I think the Lightbringers are monitoring radio communications."

"You don't think he got himself captured, do you?" Roland lowered his voice. "Malcolm isn't exactly subtle."

"I know he didn't," the assassin shot back. "He's smarter

than that. Our army will come, so you can wipe that smirk off your face."

Caspian held up a hand. "Zeta, please. It's a valid question. We have to make sure he's coming and we're not sitting around, waiting for nothing. Every day we wait gives the Council more opportunity to rally and launch a counter-attack. Surely they've scoured the surface by now, and whether or not they've found the Vagabond, they haven't found Lucifer. It won't take much for them to deduce where she is. We need to be ready for anything, and we need to be ready now." He turned to Salvador. "I know Refuge has suffered greatly in years past, but are they ready to fight?"

But Salvador didn't respond. He instead looked down at his clasped hands, slowly rubbing against each other as beads of sweat trickled over his skin.

Roland narrowed his eyes and stared at the Scourge. "Don't tell me you still refuse to fight. Now that our numbers have tripled? Now that we have ammunition? Allies? Aniya?"

"I agreed to come here on the promise that we would rescue Annelise," Salvador said slowly. He suddenly sprang up from his chair and thrust a hand toward Aniya. "And here she is! She is already safe. There is no need to further provoke a fight that we cannot win. We have been given a miraculous opportunity, can't you see? The Lightbringers have left the Underworld. It belongs to us now. That is all I ever wanted, the only reason why I left Noah's side and started fighting in the first place. Let them have the Overworld. There is no need to subject our people to potential extinction by engaging in a war we are doomed to lose."

"The war is upon us, Salvador, whether we like it or not." Caspian kept his tone even, cool. "The Council will send an army for the Key. We have no choice but to fight."

"You're telling me that within the miles of tunnels and caves of the Underworld, there is nowhere we can hide from them?"

Roland slammed a fist on the table. "No! Enough hiding. We've lived in caves our entire lives while they oppress us from the surface. You told me that all you ever wanted was for Refuge to be free. All your talk about a better future for your people, and you're too afraid to give it to them? Now that we finally have the power to free them once and for all, you want to keep cowering down here?"

"I want to stay alive, boy," Salvador sneered. "And I would hold your tongue if I were you. You have no idea—"

"No," Roland said firmly. "I'm done letting you lead our people in fear. You want me to lead so badly? Well, here you go. Refuge isn't yours to ruin anymore. We're fighting."

The room went silent as Salvador stared at Roland for several seconds, his burning eyes unflinching. "This is treason, boy. Are you sure you want to take this path?"

"It's the only one we have left," Roland said. "You're the only one who wants to keep hiding. I'm just the only one willing to say something."

"Is that so?" Salvador glanced at Corrin and Lieutenant Haskill. "Well? What do you have to say?"

The lieutenant's face was set in stone. "You know how I feel, sir. It's time to give the Lightbringers what they're owed."

Corrin seemed more apologetic. When he finally spoke, he almost sounded sheepish. "If we continue to live the way we always have, what was the point of all the fighting? We've lost so much, all of us. If we give up now, our friends and families have all died in vain."

Salvador's expression softened somewhat as he looked to his daughter. "And what of you, Tami? Are you willing to sacrifice our people at the mere chance of ending the Lightbringers?"

"Whatever it takes," Tamisra said with a firm nod.

Salvador sighed, burying his face in his hands. "Then so be it. I relinquish the name of Salvador and fatherhood of

Refuge." He looked back up at Roland. "Treat them as you would your own children. This is not a responsibility to be taken lightly."

The room fell silent again.

Caspian cleared his throat. "Very well. Please, make yourselves at home here in the Citadel. We have long since cleaned all traces of the Director's purge, and I think you'll find it more than suits your needs. Zeta, Omega, if you would please join me, I need to debrief you in the executive suite."

With that, he stood and left with the two assassins.

When they were out of earshot, Salvador spoke again. "Listen, Roland, there is something you must know. Things are not what they seem, I can assure you. The Director—"

"Save it," Roland said. "You're no less of a hypocrite now than you were back in Level XIX. The only difference is that now I understand what we have to do, that we do have to fight. But you no longer have the balls to do it. You might as well start heading back down the tunnels now because we don't need you here, and I don't know about the rest of Refuge, but I don't even want you here."

He stood up abruptly and exited the meeting room. Tamisra jumped up from her seat and made a move to intercept him, but Roland held up a hand and just kept walking. She watched him leave and then left the room after him.

Aniya turned to Salvador. "What happened to him?"

The Scourge gave a long sigh. "He is not the boy you left behind three years ago, Annelise. He has been through hell. When the Underworld was purged, he was in Holendast, watching his childhood home burn, his friends massacred. He had to watch Gareth give his life so that Roland and the remains of Refuge might escape. He is jaded now, angry, vengeful."

"Do you really trust him to lead Refuge?"

Salvador smiled sadly. "Your brother is a capable man,

Annelise. I trust he will eventually rise to the occasion. In the meantime, my distrust is wisely placed in other people."

"Caspian?" Lieutenant Haskill frowned. "He seems bound and determined to destroy the Council. What greater goal is there?"

"You may one day realize how devious the Lightbringers really are, Misha. Nothing is as it seems with them. The Director, for example, is a heartless genius, an expert of human behavior. He has manipulated your entire life. Who is to say that he is not still orchestrating these events?"

"He's dead, Salvador." Lieutenant Haskill shrugged. "It's over. The only thing that's left is the Council."

"Even if he is really dead, do you really think he hasn't prepared for such a circumstance?" Salvador ran a hand through his hair. "I suspect that we will continue to see his influence long after he is gone."

Corrin frowned. "What do you mean, if he's really dead? Aniya watched Zeta decapitate the man. What more do you want?"

The Scourge took a deep breath. "I did not spend much time with the Director when I served as the Adviser to Level XVIII. But in the conversations I had with him, he made it very clear that as long as he was around, the Underworld would continue to serve its purpose, and the world would continue to thrive. Even as the Uprising began, he was not concerned for his own safety. Even if someone managed to escape the Underworld and track him down, he was always certain of one thing: that he would never be killed. I do not believe we have seen the last of the Director."

"Roland, wait!"

Roland's fists automatically clenched at the sound of Tamisra's voice, and he made no effort to slow down or respond. Her hand landed on his arm, and he instantly jerked it away.

He crashed to the ground as his legs flew out from under him, kicked violently from behind. Before he could recover, Tamisra was on top of him, mounting him with her shins clamping tightly on the sides of his rib cage and her hands squishing his biceps against the cold metal floor.

After thrashing fruitlessly for several seconds, Roland settled and glared at the girl who pinned him to the floor.

"You have five seconds to get off me."

Tamisra smirked. "Or what? You wouldn't hit a girl."

"Don't count on that."

Tamisra pressed harder against his body and leaned in, keeping her head just out of reach. "You're going to lie there and listen to me."

"Not if I can help it." Roland thrust his right knee upward and into the small of her back, and as she released her hold on him for an instant, wincing in pain, he wrenched his arms free and shoved his hands into her chest, sending her rolling off his body.

Without bothering to continue the struggle, Roland got up and continued walking away, only to be tackled again a few seconds later.

This time, Roland was expecting her attack and rolled through the tackle, letting his momentum carry him back atop her body, now mounting her just like she had trapped him.

But before he could secure her to the floor, Tamisra drove her knee between his legs, and Roland's vision went dark as a crushing pain surged through his groin.

He lost his grip on Tamisra's body and let his body roll away, moaning as he stared up at the ceiling and clutched his groin in pain.

Roland didn't even feel Tamisra mount his body again until she slammed his wrists into the floor.

"I said, you're going to lie there and listen to me."

He weakly nodded as he bit his lip.

"Good."

The hold on his body loosened somewhat.

"You are far and away the most emotional man I have ever known." Tamisra leaned back and put her weight on Roland's stomach, making his eyes bulge. "And that includes Malcolm, who nearly killed your sister just to get revenge for his brother, who, by the way, was so sweet it was sick. But you take it to a whole other level. One minute, you're a romantic, and the next, you're throwing a temper tantrum at my father."

"That's not what—"

Tamisra's hand clamped down on his mouth. "Listening."

Roland nodded again.

"My mother and siblings were slaughtered during the Uprising, so Refuge is the only family I have. Not even Salvador was much of a father to me because he had to be a father to thousands. And yet your passion, let's call it, had me convinced that you just cared more about Refuge than I did."

Tamisra snorted. "Which, of course, is ridiculous. It took me longer than I care to admit to realize that you're just trying to prove yourself. To who? Not a clue. I used to think it was to me. Whether that was ever true, that doesn't matter now."

Roland tried to speak again, but her hand grew heavier to where he couldn't even part his lips.

"But as long as you assume leadership of Refuge, you have a responsibility to its people. You have to learn what my father failed to all those years ago. There is more to leadership than carrying a sword or a gun into battle. If we automatically followed the strongest person, we would be answering to your sister. Or worse yet, her dead robot assassin boyfriend, apparently. At least he can't be blinded by emotion. But he's a killer and would lead us to our deaths. You're getting dangerously close to that."

Tamisra's hand had eased up enough for Roland to speak. "I thought you wanted to fight the Lightbringers."

"More than anything. That's why I'm not in charge, Roland. I'm as much of a fighter as Omega or Zeta. If I'm handed that responsibility, bad things would happen. Things like what happened to Gareth. Refuge needs someone with a clear mind, and right now, that's not you. The Roland I met was passionate enough to do anything to save his sister, but at least he had common sense."

"I'm not that person anymore."

"On that we can agree. You've gotten stupider."

Roland glared at Tamisra, who stared back at him with arms folded.

"You want me to become your father, who hid in Refuge for eighteen years doing nothing? Who refused to help us save Aniya until you were captured?"

"My father tried too hard to leave the warrior behind. He became a father instead, his sole purpose to keep Refuge alive. The problem was, he wasn't willing to do what was necessary to truly save them all. And now, he's back to being a warrior. A wiser one now, yes, but a warrior nonetheless. Yet he is still unwilling to do what needs to be done. My father is a great man. He's just not the one that Refuge needs."

Roland sighed and rolled his eyes. "So what do you want from me, Tami?"

"I want you to lead our people. Stop trying to prove your strength to them and do what's best for them. You're just going to get yourself killed, and I don't know what I would do if I had to watch you die. Roland, we're jumping into a war against an enemy we don't fully know with allies we don't really understand. As powerful as your sister is, I don't think it will matter much. If this fight could be won with raw power, she could have finished it on the surface without us. We'll need more than pretty lights to win this war."

"The last time I tried to lead like that, people died," Roland said, fighting back tears. "A lot of people died. Corrin didn't even want to confront Kendall, and you and I had to convince him. If we had just stayed in the caves, maybe we would have stood a fighting chance when the Director's army came for us. Maybe Gareth . . ."

Tamisra's mouth dropped open. "You don't actually blame me for Gareth, do you? All this time, you let me believe that you blame me for his death. You broke up with me and wouldn't talk to me for years, and you're not even mad at me? Roland, I didn't do my job, and Gareth died because of me."

"No. He died because I didn't step up and do what had to be done. And who gave you the job of triggering the payload, anyway? That was my idea."

"Roland, please." Tamisra placed her palms on the floor on either side of Roland's head and leaned in. "It wasn't your fault. None of it was. If you didn't convince Corrin to attack Kendall, we never would have left the caves, and I know you think we could have defended them, but you saw his army. They would have wiped us out. You're the only reason there's any Refuge left at all. And as far as Gareth, that was my fault. You know it was."

Roland bit his lip and looked at the ceiling, avoiding her eyes.

"If you don't blame me, Roland, why did you break up with me?"

After several seconds, Roland pushed her off his body and stood up. He turned to walk again, but Tamisra grabbed him from behind, spun him around, and shoved him up against the wall.

"Why?"

Roland stared at her nose for several seconds before looking into her eyes. "Because you deserve someone stronger, Tami. You deserve someone who will do the right thing. But no matter how hard I try, every time I look at you, I'm reminded of that mistake."

Tears slipped down Tamisra's cheeks as she pushed him harder into the wall. "And Dawn?"

"I used to think it was because life with her is easier than life with you, that it's because I don't feel like half of a man when she tells me she loves me." Roland shook his head. "But what you said makes more sense. She doesn't want a warrior, the person I keep telling myself I have to be. She wants a man, and she keeps telling me that I'm already everything she ever wanted."

Tamisra's eyes widened. "And you think I want something else? You think I want the warrior you're so desperately trying to become? Is that what you're trying to prove, that you deserve me?"

Roland just stared at her.

"I don't want a warrior, Roland, and I don't want a man." Tamisra's voice cracked as her grip tightened. "I just want you."

Stunned, Roland stared back at her as his mind raced. On one hand, Tamisra's pleading face filled his vision, visibly begging for him to be with her again. On the other hand, Roland knew that somewhere in the Citadel, Dawn was waiting for him. Someone who loved him. Someone who never angered him remotely as much as Tamisra could. In fact, Dawn was so drastically different from Tami that a comparison was impossible.

It was in the midst of these hazy thoughts that Roland suddenly realized that Tamisra had let him go. He watched her back away slowly, biting her lip as tears trickled down her cheeks.

Before he could say a word, she ran away, and all that was left was the faint sound of her sobs echoing in the halls.

## 27

"Don't you have anything better to be doing right now?" Dawn tested the power supply on the defibrillator and placed it back on the cart with some effort.

"Like what?" Lionel huffed and threw himself on one of the hundred cots that lined the walls of the barracks, forming a small, makeshift clinic. "If I'm not going to be fighting, it's not like I can train right now. Salvador's in a meeting, so's Roland. I don't have anything else to do, so I might as well bug you."

Dawn grabbed the next defibrillator and hoisted it up on the table. "The least you could do is help. These things are kind of heavy."

Lionel propped himself up on an elbow for a moment and watched his sister. "Nah, I don't know how to work them. Besides, it's more fun watching you."

"Of course," she replied as she tested this next power supply. "Why exactly can't you fight?"

"Salvador's orders."

"Yeah, I got that," Dawn said as she replaced the defibrillator. "But why? You're his squire, after all. Doesn't he want you fighting with him?"

Lionel shrugged as he collapsed back on the cot. "Said it's too dangerous. Which I don't get. We fought monsters down in Level XIX. What's so different about normal men?"

"Well, they do have guns." Dawn began grabbing bottles of chemicals and placing them on the table. "Stands to reason they could be a little more deadly than the Host that had to get up close to do any damage to you."

"And we have armor. Not to mention explosives. And if what Roland told me about Aniya is true, we have a super-weapon on our side."

Dawn twisted the cap off one of the bottles and peered inside to see how much was left. "Then what makes you think they need you?"

"It's not that they need me," Lionel said with a sigh. "But I want to fight for Refuge. It's what I've trained my entire life for. I was too young to fight in the Battle of Holendast, and now that I'm trained and ready, I can't fight in the final battle to destroy the Lightbringers? My training was a complete waste."

"Trained and ready?" Dawn smirked as she looked up at her brother. "I've seen you train. I don't know about ready."

"Close enough. Besides, you wouldn't understand. You get to be part of it all."

Dawn scoffed. "Yeah, as a medic hiding in the barracks. I wouldn't say that I'm exactly a part of it."

"Better than what I get to do, hiding in the Citadel with Caspian as he calls the shots."

"You could always help me."

"Yeah, you said that."

"No, I mean during the battle," Dawn said as she placed the bottles back on the cart. "Caspian doesn't have very many medics or nurses, so I'll need all the help I can get."

Lionel broke out into laughter. "What, you want me to be a nurse?"

"It's better than doing nothing, right? Don't you want to be a part of it?"

"I don't even know how. I would just get in your way."

Dawn smiled. "It's not as hard as it sounds. For most of it, I just need an extra hand. You're not scared of blood, right?"

Lionel snorted.

"Then you'll do just fine. If you really want to help, then you can stay here with me. Surely Salvador wouldn't mind."

After several seconds, Lionel sighed. "Fine. You need someone to watch your back anyway if the Lightbringers manage to break through our defenses."

"That's the spirit!" Dawn tossed him a rag.

"What's this for? I already know how to make a tourniquet."

"My hero. No, I need you to wipe down the cots with rubbing alcohol."

Lionel rolled his eyes. "Great. I already hate this."

"Don't worry. You'll see plenty of blood when the fighting starts."

As Lionel got to work wiping down the canvas beds, Dawn paused and watched him for a moment.

"I'm glad you'll be with me, Lionel," she found herself saying.

He looked back up at her quizzically.

"I'll feel a lot better knowing that you're safe here with me."

Lionel gave a small smile. "Forget about it, sis. I'm here to watch your back. I take care of you, not the other way around, and I won't watch you die. Not if I can help it."

"Gee, thanks." Dawn stuck out a tongue. "You missed a spot there, by the way."

His smile disappeared as he groaned, and Dawn gave a short laugh before returning to work.

## 28

L ate that night, Aniya ran through the dark halls of the Citadel, hoping to trick her mind into sleeping by exhausting her body. Every time she slowed to rest, Nicholas's face appeared, and so she forced herself to ceaselessly run, not giving her a chance to think about those who had fallen.

It was an hour into her run that she felt a slight tug pulling at her body, urging her off-course and down a hallway she had not yet explored.

The hallway led her to a set of clear glass doors, and as Aniya stopped in front of them, she looked outside to see a dark figure sitting on the edge of a balcony outside.

Her heart stopped, and she tried to turn away and keep running, but the magnetic pull compelled her forward, and she found herself opening the doors almost against her will.

Aniya stepped out onto the balcony, closed the doors behind her, and walked up to the dark figure, stopping behind him but unable to speak.

"I can't answer your questions," the assassin said, letting his legs swing gently over the Hub that loomed several hundred feet below. "At least not in the way you want."

"I know," Aniya whispered. "But I'm going to ask them anyway. You understand, don't you?"

Omega nodded, still facing the Hub, his back to her.

"Do you remember anything? I know you're not really him, but can you see his memories?"

A shake of the head.

"Caspian ensured that I would not be able to access that part of his brain. I'm not human, but memories, he said, are a large part of what makes us who we are. The technology that interfaces with what is left of Nicholas is quite advanced and capable of a semblance of human emotion, so Caspian said if I could see Nicholas's memories, it would compromise my ability to act without bias."

Aniya looked at the ground.

"But I read his file. Yours, too."

She held back a laugh. "Great."

Omega finally turned around to face her, his legs gracefully swinging over the railing as he spun. "It sounded like he really cared for you."

"Yeah," was all that Aniya could say, her head still downcast. "And by the time I let myself feel the same, it was too late."

He shrugged. "Maybe not. Maybe none of this would have happened if you had fallen in love with him sooner."

"Would that be so bad? He'd be alive. If none of this had happened, we'd be back in the Hole together, living blissfully unaware of what was happening on the surface."

Omega offered a small smile. "You don't really want that."

"Don't tell me what I want," Aniya said, clenching her fists and meeting his eyes for the first time. "You're more like him than I thought."

"Could you really live with yourself if you could change the past? Going back and living in your bubble, ignoring the fact that you can do something now to change the future?"

"I'd get over it," Aniya spat. "At least we were happy."

"Happiness is overrated." Omega hopped off the railing and approached her, matching every step she took backward away from him. "It's going to get worse before it gets better, you know. You were so willing to sacrifice your life when it meant saving your brother, but you can't sacrifice your happiness to save the world? You're better than that, Annelise."

Aniya slapped his hand away as he reached toward her. "You don't know me."

He continued his advance until she backed up against the glass doors. She pressed herself up against the glass as he stayed a foot away from her.

"I don't have to," he said, his breath close enough to bathe her face in warmth. "You've proven your true character time and time again. When push comes to shove, you do what's right."

Aniya placed her hand on his chest, ready to push him away, but as her hand pressed against something hard, a sharp edge pressing against her flesh, she heard a voice whisper in her ear.

"Save me," it said in an agony-ridden tone. It was Nicholas's voice.

Aniya studied Omega's face. He looked back at her, expressionless. "Nicholas?"

"Aniya," the voice came again. It was so clear to her, so filled with pain that she couldn't help but close her eyes before she could tell if the voice came from Omega or not.

She opened her eyes and pulled her hand away abruptly. Omega was still there, staring back at her with his cold, black eyes.

"Are you still in there, Nicholas?"

Omega looked at the ground. "I told you, Annelise. He's dead. Gone."

"I heard you. I mean, him. I mean—" Aniya shook her head. "He's still there somewhere, I know it."

"I'm sorry, Annelise. I know this is hard. I can only imagine. But—"

Without thinking about it, Aniya lunged forward and kissed Omega, wrapping her arms around his neck and pulling him close. As their lips touched, a chill spread over her body as she felt her energy leave her body, then as it surged through Omega's and back into her, warmth returned, along with it a strength that comforted her and pulled her closer into him.

After several seconds, she backed away, scanning Omega's dark eyes for any sign of Nicholas.

But he simply stared back at her.

Refusing to accept defeat, Aniya grabbed his hands and squeezed tightly. "Nicholas, if you're there, tell me how to save you."

But he shook his head.

"I'm sorry, Annelise."

After another few seconds, she released his hands and threw them to his side, turning away abruptly to hide her tears. She threw the doors open and ran back into the Citadel.

## 29

"Roland."

A soft, feminine voice hissed in the depths of Roland's mind, startling him awake. He looked around his bedroom, but it was seemingly empty.

"Lights," he said with a crack in his voice. He cleared his throat and said again, "Lights."

The room was slowly lit in a white glow, clean light coming from an unseen source. The white bedroom he had been provided in the Citadel was indeed empty.

Roland looked to his right and placed his hand on the empty space. Dawn had insisted on staying in the barracks that night, saying there was too much preparation that needed to be done before the inevitable battle.

He had almost forgotten the voice that had woken him when it spoke again.

"Roland."

He looked around wildly, but to no avail. He was alone in the room still.

"Roland."

Growling, Roland jumped out of bed, dropping to the floor and looking under the mattress.

"Rol—"

With a jerk, Roland started to stand up and banged his head on the bedframe.

"That's it," he spat. "Who are you?"

But this time, the voice didn't answer.

"Come on. You want to talk so bad? Who are you? What do you want?"

Roland's voice echoed against the walls for several seconds.

Finally, as his words died away, he sighed and climbed back in bed, muttering "lights."

The white lights diminished slowly, and Roland was about to close his eyes again when a green glow appeared as the last of the white died away.

Roland peered into the darkness at the thin crack of green light that was coming from underneath his bedroom door.

Without giving a chance for this strange sight to disappear, Roland vaulted out of his bed and raced to the door. He threw it open, but the green light was gone. The hallway was dark ahead of him, with no sign of the light.

Moaning, he turned to retreat back to his room, but out of the corner of his eye, he spotted the light again.

From around the corner of the hallway ahead, the green light reappeared, slowly growing and fully illuminating a path to Roland's right.

Cautiously, Roland walked down the hallway and turned the corner.

Almost instantly, the light raced down the hallway and surrounded the elevator at the end of the hall.

Roland slowly walked down toward the elevator, refusing to take his eyes off the light, lest it vanish again. He knew it didn't matter. He couldn't access the elevator without a keycard, and Caspian was the only person he knew who had one.

But as he drew near, the elevator doors opened unprompted, welcoming him inside.

The instant he stepped into the elevator, the light vanished again, reappearing instantly on one of the buttons on the wall.

Roland pressed it.

The doors closed, and the elevator raced downward, sending Roland's empty stomach into a nauseous fit. He sat down on the floor, holding a hand to his clammy forehead, squeezing his eyes closed and wishing for the trip to be over.

Eventually, the elevator stopped, and the doors opened again.

Roland let his eyes drift open as the nausea passed, and he climbed to his feet and exited the elevator.

He was in a cave, much like the entrance to the reactor chamber in Level XVIII. The green light was still here, and it was gathered around a large sphere several feet away.

Roland approached the sphere and climbed inside, pressing a glowing button on the wall and letting the sphere take off down the cave.

A few minutes later, the sphere stopped again, and the light vanished.

"Well, now what?"

Nothing happened.

Roland groaned, sure that this was either a dream or a hallucination, and climbed out of the sphere. Whatever this was seemed to be a waste of time, distracting him from the sleep he so desperately needed in an actual, comfortable bed, a first for him.

But his curiosity won out over his tired body, and he walked down the tunnel. It wasn't long before the green glow reappeared, growing brighter still as he walked. Soon, he was standing in another reactor chamber, identical to the now-destroyed one in Level XVIII.

However, Level I's chamber was still active, whole.

The massive cavern was filled with tens of thousands of green tanks, each one with a naked man inside, strapped to wires and feeding energy to a reactor far, far below.

A rumble shook the cavern, and Roland spread his hands out to keep his balance. But as the shaking grew worse, Roland sat down on the rock floor just as a loud hiss filled the chamber, giving way to a massive beam of green light flooding the cavern, blasting down into the abyss below as a loud boom came from somewhere in the distance.

The green light disappeared, and Roland slowly climbed to his feet. But he tumbled back to the ground as yellow light burst upward from the void below. As it touched the ceiling of the cavern, a shockwave boomed back down, shaking Roland's bones.

When everything went still, Roland carefully stood again.

"Welcome, child."

The voice that spoke filled the cavern, echoing against the walls and speaking over itself multiple times, resulting in an ominous cacophony.

"Neeshika?" Roland asked, realizing now what being had summoned him here.

"Yes, child."

"I thought you said you weren't my mother," Roland said, annoyed. "Something about not carrying the light."

"You are not my child, no. Not yet."

Roland looked around. "Why did you bring me here? Just to say some creepy, mysterious things? And where are you, anyway? I shouldn't be able to hear you all the way up here."

He hadn't even finished speaking when green light seemed to pull away from the tanks, materializing in a humanoid form on the path ahead of him.

"Yes, my apologies, dear. I'm sure you would be much more comfortable speaking to someone you can see."

Roland stepped forward, peering at the figure. It looked

just like the mysterious Mother he had met in Level XIX, but comprised completely of green light.

"What are you doing here?" Roland shook his head. "No, forget that. How are you here? What is this, magic?"

The being laughed, its light breaking apart from its form slightly and dancing around briefly before settling again.

"No, child. It is Light, the purest form of life itself, free of the shackles of flesh and bone."

Roland rolled his eyes. "Okay, great. Thanks for clearing that up. What do you want?"

The glowing figure stretched out a finger, tapping Roland on the chest.

"Me?"

Neeshika nodded. "The child of light that I have watched over so long, preparing for her ultimate destiny, may yet prove unwilling, or perhaps unable, to fulfill her true purpose."

"Aniya," Roland said slowly.

Another nod.

"She has overcome much, but perhaps we ask too much of her. She may yet fail to become Lightbringer."

"What does this have to do with me?

Neeshika took a deep breath. "I assume you are aware of the details surrounding the source of Annelise's abilities?"

Roland shrugged. "I watched it all happen, if that's what you mean. She also explained a little more when she returned from the surface, but I didn't understand all of it."

"It is indeed complicated, I agree. I suspect the Director intended it to be so. It's certainly harder to interpret his true intentions when he keeps so many secrets. But there is one detail that I want to bring to your attention."

Neeshika floated toward an empty pod, placing her hand on the glass. "When Annelise was placed in the machine the second time, with the intent on destroying the reactor, she should have died. That much energy in one person should have been enough to overload her brain and nervous system, making her heart beat so fast it explodes. Did she tell you how the Director circumvented this?"

"She mentioned that Kendall did something to her before she was even born."

"Correct. And because she was in your mother's womb when her body was prepared for her eventual sacrifice, what the Director arranged was also done to you."

Roland nodded. "It has crossed my mind."

"Then surely you know what this implies."

"I've tried not to think about it," Roland said as he looked away.

"It is a frightening thought, holding all that power. I know Annelise—"

"I'm not scared," Roland snapped. "And neither is she."

"But she is, Roland. Scared beyond words. She's not the girl you knew back in Holendast. The Director made sure of that."

"What do you mean?"

"Everything that has occurred has been the will of a Director who believes he is sovereign. He has orchestrated every second, and whatever has surprised him along the way, he has adapted and embraced it as part of his plan. Annelise came to the Hub broken. Her parents were murdered, she did not know if you were alive or dead, she watched a child die before her eyes, she thought her best friend betrayed her. Her heart broke somewhere along the way, and you cannot fault her for it. The Director's plans worked perfectly. She stepped into the machine willing to die. I would like to think she had the noble aim of sacrifice in mind, but I do believe that she lost the will to live."

Roland balled his fists. "What's your point?"

"My point is that this was all intentional. If the girl you knew as a child had been transformed by the machine into a living weapon, she could not as easily be manipulated. Her headstrong and stubborn will would have been hard to mold. The Director may never have gotten her to agree to his ultimate plan, and she could have destroyed him. But by breaking her, all he had to do was provide guiding hands to push her toward him. That is why I have come to you. And that is why the Chancellor came to you first."

"He never approached me about becoming . . ." Roland looked up toward the Citadel, where he pictured Aniya resting, blissfully unaware. "That."

"Did he not ask you to stop your sister?"

"Sure," Roland said, shrugging. "He wanted me to keep her from wiping out the Citadel."

Neeshika gently shook her head. "He came to you because he knew you would do the right thing and take her place. You would step into the machine instead and take on the responsibility that now falls on Annelise's shoulders. And as I understand it, you tried to do just that."

Roland frowned. "Why me? He didn't even know that Aniya and I were related."

"He knew more than you think. And he was smart enough to see through at least part of the Director's plans. Noah knew that if Aniya stepped into the machine, she would forever belong to the Director. She was broken and needed someone to fix her. Your chancellor saw you for who you were, a strong individual who would do the right thing. He knew that if you were to step into the machine, you would be uncontrollable, just like your sister would have been if not for the Director."

"She's stronger than you give her credit for, Neeshika."

"Yes, I believe it. I have felt the strength of her will. But unfortunately, I have also felt the damage done to her." Neeshika bowed her head as a somber look appeared on her face. "She is angry, Roland. Heartbroken, betrayed, alone. When she was in the machine, the Light latched on to the pain, and the pain to the Light. Her powers are a physical manifestation of the hurt inside. That is why she can't summon the Light when needed, but it comes easily when she is stressed. She is too damaged to harness her power and do what she must."

Roland scoffed. "And you think I'm not? Do you have any idea what I've been through?"

"Yes, child. But you hold a determination that outshines even your sister's. You are ready to do what you must to destroy the Lightbringers."

Roland glanced at the pods again. "So you're asking me to take her place?"

"You are the only other one who can, Roland."

Roland backed away, shaking his head. "No way. Aniya's a ticking bomb and places everyone around her in danger. I don't want that hanging over my head."

"Annelise only suffers this dilemma because of Nicholas. She was meant to take on the full force of the machine's energy and therefore be granted its complete power, generating energy and processing it safely. But when Nicholas joined her in the tank, something happened. The energy split itself into two separate forces, Light and Shadow. As such, Annelise can create energy, but after that, her body does not know what to do. Nicholas is a natural outlet for that energy, a Shadow that can absorb and release it without incident."

"And that didn't ruin the Director's plans?"

Neeshika frowned. "Sadly, no. Since the Director intended Annelise's power to be diverted to an external source for further processing anyway, it made no difference that she could not process it herself. A simple recalculation is all it would take to ready the machine for her. But you could do both parts. You could be Light and Shadow. You could generate energy and handle it safely with no fear of hurting anyone. At least no one you do not intend to hurt."

"So you want to turn me into the weapon my sister was supposed to be?"

"There is no other way."

Roland backed away, holding his hands to his head and

laughing. "There clearly is. Aniya may have a handicap, sure, but she is still perfectly capable of winning this war for you. She has Nicholas. Or Omega. Whatever. He can be there to help her when she needs it. In fact, from what I understand, he's perfectly capable of taking care of himself. We have two weapons already. What makes you think we need a third?"

"They are unreliable, Roland. Both of them. Annelise and her power, as I have explained, are unpredictable. Omega is a computer living in a body. One cannot presume to know how long he will survive in his present state. And if he dies, Annelise will be even harder to predict. Nicholas is the last living link to her innocent youth, a reminder of her only love. I truly believe she might lose whatever control she has and destroy what is left of the rebellion in a tragic disaster."

"Why don't you do it?" Roland glanced down at Neeshika's body, composed completely of green light. "You look like a lightbringer to me if I ever saw one. What's stopping you from saving us?"

Neeshika smiled sadly. "Alas, this is not my true form, child. I am not the Light, though I know it intimately. Thanks to our fellowship, I can take its form, yet I more closely resemble its oldest friend and closest ally. Pure, undefiled Shadow. Yet I hold power not of Light or Shadow. I am merely their mouthpiece."

Roland pressed his hands to his head. "You're not making any sense."

"Nor do I expect to. But you asked. The point is, I cannot take your sister's place."

Roland looked at the empty tank. Three years ago, he had been forced to watch his sister die as she gave her life for him. He had tried to step in and take her place, but that did not end well.

*If I was so willing to do it then, what's stopping me now?* But as much as he tried to sort through his options, all he could see was Tamisra's tear-stained face, begging him to lay aside his hunger to prove himself.

"Well, Roland, what will it be?"

Roland turned to face Neeshika again and gave her his answer.

## 30

T he next morning, Aniya knocked on the large double doors of the executive suite, chills running down her spine. The last time she had stood in front of doors like these, she was being escorted to the Chancellor, who would give Nicholas a death sentence and her the eternal doom of imprisonment in the machine deep below the Citadel.

The doors opened, and Aniya's heart stopped briefly as Omega appeared before her, still using the body of her childhood friend and love.

"Who is it?" A voice came from inside the large room.

Omega turned slightly. "Lucifer."

"Show her in."

Omega nodded and opened the door wider, letting Aniya step inside. The door closed behind her, and she turned to see Omega gone. Her heart sank slightly as she turned back toward the room, where Caspian stood waiting for her by the large window.

"Welcome, Aniya. I suspected you would come to talk to me soon."

Aniya joined him by the window. "It's about Nicholas. Omega now, I guess."

"Yes, I feel like I owe you an explanation."

"Maybe. I think I understand what he is now. I guess I even understand why. When he died, you saw an opportunity to save his body so you could use his power. I don't think I can blame you for that, no matter how I feel."

Caspian smiled softly. "You've come a long way, Aniya. I daresay you would have ripped my head from my shoulders if you had learned of this three years ago."

"I'm not going to lie. I considered it. But you saved him, Caspian. You kept him alive. Even if it's just his body. We just have to find a way to restore his memories."

Caspian shook his head. "I'm afraid that's not possible, Aniya. Nicholas is dead. He's gone. There is no bringing him back. Even if I were to restore his memories, it wouldn't be him. Not really."

"So you can? Bring back his memories, that is?"

"A mild inconvenience, if that," Caspian said. "His memories are intact, but they are blocked by the computer that interfaces with his brain."

Aniya placed a hand on Caspian's arm and tugged longingly, as if she were begging Nicholas himself. "Then give him back his memories. That's all that's standing between a mindless robot and being the man I've known my whole life."

"You don't understand, Aniya. Memories do not make a man. They only give him perspective. There's something more inside each of us that makes us truly human, and when that is removed, we are nothing more than flesh and blood. Some call it spirit, some call it soul, some have called it the purest form of light. Nicholas's light is gone, Aniya, and there's nothing you or I can do to bring it back."

"There has to be," Aniya said, shaking her head and tightening her grip on Caspian's arm. "I saw him, Caspian. I saw Nicholas. I touched him, and he called out to me. Somewhere in Omega's body is the man I love. Help me bring him back."

A tear trickled down her cheek as her voice cracked. "Please, bring him back to me."

Caspian gently removed Aniya's hand and backed away. "I'm sorry, Aniya. Maybe you disabled the inhibiting function of the computer momentarily with your power, and he saw his memories. But these memories are only a ghost of Nicholas, a shell of the man you knew. He's gone, Aniya. He's dead. The sooner you accept that, the sooner you can move on. And it is crucial that you do move on. Your true abilities are governed by your emotions. You may have learned to keep them in check, but if you're not careful, they will rule you, just as they did three years ago."

"I don't care, Caspian. I don't want to control them. I just want him back."

Caspian used his thumb to wipe a tear from Aniya's cheek. "I know, Aniya. But this is not what he would have wanted for you. His last words were begging me to help him save you. If you succumb to your powers, if you let them control you, you will eventually self-destruct. It's only a matter of time. But you can control them, Aniya. I know you can. And that's the only way you'll stay alive. Please, let me fulfill my promise to Nicholas. Let me help you."

Aniya let the tears flow freely now, and she leaned forward and gently placed her head on his chest. For several seconds, she wept. Then, with a wave of realization, she backed away and looked up at Caspian again, frowning.

"You said his last words were asking you to help him. I watched him die. His last words were . . ." With a spark of green light, she slammed her hands against her head, banishing the awful images that came rushing back. "Those weren't his last words."

Caspian looked down at the floor. "I don't know how you watched him die, but he didn't die right away, Aniya. He stayed alive long enough to help me destroy the Director's army."

"How did he die, then? If he stayed alive through all that, couldn't you save his body and soul?"

"No. He would have surely died during the procedure I used to install the computer in his mind. He was so close to death but unable to die, so I . . . I took pity on him. I ended his pain."

Aniya backed away, shaking her head. "You killed him?"

"I put him out of his misery, Aniya," Caspian said as he took a quick step forward. "He would have suffered otherwise. Without you, he had no chance of being truly healed. I don't expect you to understand, but know that at least some form of him is alive now only because of me."

Aniya placed her hands on the sides of her head, staring at the floor.

"Please do not condemn me, Aniya. I did everything I could."

"Yeah, but I didn't." She turned away and pulled at her hair, closing her eyes. "He would be alive if it weren't for me."

Caspian placed a hand on her shoulder, which she instantly shrugged off. "There's no point in blaming yourself. You did the best you could at the time."

Aniya shook her head. "I can't do this right now."

"Please, Aniya. You have to deal with this now while you still have time."

But she backed away, running her fingers through her hair as she stared at the ground. "I can't. I just can't."

"Aniya—"

A sharp siren sounded as the white room suddenly turned red.

Aniya jerked her head up and looked at Caspian, but he had already turned back around to the window. She ran to his side and pressed her hands up against the glass just in time to see a wave of white slowly sweep across the Hub, traveling at a rapid pace toward the Citadel.

"They're here," Caspian said with a sigh of relief.

As Aniya looked up at him in confusion, he continued, "The Lightbringers' army wears black. Their police force wears white, and that's the armor Zeta has been smuggling to Malcolm for the last year."

Aniya nodded. "So that's—"

"Zeta was right. The Vagabond came through," Caspian said, a triumphant smile gracing his face.

But his smile vanished as quickly as it came, and Aniya's spine chilled as a stream of black poured out of the train tunnel on the border of the Hub, spreading quickly across the plains and chasing the wave of white toward the Citadel.

Caspian fumbled for a radio by his side and pressed the button, speaking with a voice that bore a nearly imperceptible tremble. "Vagabond, are you there? Come in, Malcolm."

Silence followed for several seconds before labored breathing finally came back over the radio.

"We . . . must have tripped an alarm by the tunnel. They were on top of us . . . within an hour. Barely escaped. Too many of them."

He was right. By Aniya's estimation, the black army outnumbered the white by at least three times.

Caspian visibly swallowed. He took a breath and spoke into the radio again. "Nothing's changed. We will proceed as discussed. I'll signal my team to surround the Lightbringers. Refuge, report in."

It was mere seconds before Corrin's voice came back.

"Standing by."

"The Vagabond's men will form the front lines, and my Silver Guard right behind. Keep your men in the back. Zeta?"

"Here."

"Take the operatives and gather them in a ring around the Hub. The Lightbringers will be distracted with our forces, and when the time is right, you can lead your teams in a strike from the back and sides. I'll stay in the Citadel with a bird's-eye view and redirect our forces as necessary."

"Roger."

"Omega, I'm sure you're listening. Take your position and be ready to unleash hell. This is what you've trained for."

"Yes, sir."

Caspian placed the radio down and turned back to Aniya.

"Can you do this?"

Aniya gritted her teeth and did not take her eyes off the approaching armies. "It's time to end this."

"No, Aniya." Caspian stepped in front of her and forced her to make eye contact. "Can you do this? Omega will be down there, doing what he must. Can I trust you to do what you must?"

"What I must?" Aniya scoffed and pushed Caspian away. "What I must do is destroy the people who have taken so much from me. What I must do is kill those who threaten to take all that I have left. What I must do is end this now, and when I do, I will find a way to save Nicholas, with or without you."

With a final shove, Aniya spun on her heels and left the room.

"And if you try to stop me, I'll make sure it's without you."

## 31

B y the time Aniya stepped out onto the front steps of the Citadel, Malcolm's white army had already settled into place at the end of the long road that stretched out ahead of Aniya, and Caspian's army of Silvers waited directly behind them. The band of rebels from Refuge were still gathering in the very back, but they were nearly in position as well, also wearing silver armor that Caspian had outfitted them with.

And beyond the sea of silver and white was a massive horde of black that waited in the valley just outside the border of the city, standing unnaturally still.

Aniya ran through the streets of the Hub, reaching the armies and pushing her way to the front.

"Good thing you decided to show up."

She turned to see Roland grinning at her, wearing light armor but carrying a massive automatic rifle. Behind him was Omega, apparently the only person in black that wasn't in the opposing force gathered in the valley just fifty yards away.

"What are you doing here?" Aniya asked, forcing herself to look the assassin in the eye. After holding his gaze for a few seconds, she turned and looked past the Lightbringer army and at the cliffs beyond, where she managed to spot a few moving black dots. "Aren't you supposed to be out there with Zeta?"

"No, he's right here with Zeta."

The other assassin poked her head around Omega's body and stuck a tongue out at Aniya. She was wearing the same white cloak she'd been wearing when rescuing Aniya, covering her body and surely a dozen blades beneath. She stood hand-in-hand with Malcolm, whose otherwise white armor bore a black, four-fingered hand.

"But I heard Caspian say—"

"Caspian's plan is solid, sure," Zeta said, waving a hand. "But my men are quite capable on their own. I wanted to be down here with your robot boyfriend as he sucks the life out of the Lightbringers and I go to town on them with my knives."

"You'll get your chance."

A voice came from behind Aniya, and she turned to see Corrin emerging from the gathered armies, Lieutenant Haskill right behind him.

Malcolm released Zeta's hand and embraced Corrin, holding on to his father for several seconds before letting go.

"Well done, son," Corrin said with moist eyes as he looked at the four-fingered hand on Malcolm's chest. "I do believe you've made quite a name for yourself."

Aniya smiled but looked around doubtfully. "I get the feeling none of us are supposed to be at the front."

"Yet we have the greatest reason to be here," Haskill said, staring down the army of black. "If Caspian thinks we're going to sit in the back, he's got another thing coming."

Malcolm nodded at the lieutenant. "Misha, good to see you again. It's been a while."

"That's Lieutenant to you, boy," Haskill said gruffly before cracking a smile. "But I understand you have an army of your own now. Commendations are in order."

"Save it for later," Omega said. "We have a battle to fight, in case you've forgotten."

Corrin frowned. "Yes, about that." He looked at the waiting black army and back at Lieutenant Haskill. "What do you suppose they're waiting for?"

"I haven't the slightest," Haskill said, rubbing his chin. "Let's find out, shall we?"

Aniya's heart stopped as Lieutenant Haskill turned away from the white and silver armies and walked toward the sea of black, his gun holstered at his side.

"Lieutenant, what are you doing?" Corrin hissed as the lieutenant continued without hesitation. He turned to Roland, who stared at the proceedings, his eyes wide.

Haskill seemed to ignore Corrin and approached the black army, stopping just feet away. He pulled a small, silver stick from his back pocket and held it high above his head. "You have been informed correctly. I have the Key now, and I will from this point on be taking complete control of the Council's resources, including you."

Aniya's body froze as her mouth dropped open.

The lieutenant turned and addressed the white and silver armies. "I regret to inform you that my time with you has come to an end. I have enjoyed my time in this identity and body, but I have more important matters to attend to."

"Lieutenant, explain yourself!" Roland demanded as he stomped the ground.

Haskill's gaze turned to Aniya as his mouth slowly twisted to a smile. "Thank you, my dear. I couldn't have done it without you. You prove to still be just as useful as I predicted all those years ago."

Aniya finally regained the breath to speak. "The Director."

Lieutenant Haskill nodded. "You're more perceptive than I give you credit for, though it doesn't do you any good to see through me only now. It's too late to make a difference, I'm afraid."

"How?" Roland turned to the Citadel, where Caspian would be looking on. "Are you getting any of this?"

"Don't bother," the Director said, waving a hand. "I disabled your communications already."

Aniya took a breath and stepped forward, standing between the two armies. "Zeta killed you. I watched her."

The Director made a clucking noise and jutted out his bottom lip. "My dear, you should know better than to trust your own eyes after everything you've seen, or at least everything you think you've seen."

"So who did Zeta kill?" Aniya glanced at the assassin, who looked on with an unreadable expression. "Just some poor guy you hired to take your place? He's pretended to be you for three years?"

"Oh, that was me," the Director said. "Zeta indeed killed the Director. At least a version of me. I believe you are now aware of the concept of cybernetic organisms?"

Aniya glanced at Omega. "Yeah, so what?"

The Director grinned as he said no words, only gesturing toward his body.

Malcolm's eyes widened. "You mean . . ."

"Yes, Vagabond. I am no more human than the machine that wears Nicholas's body. Though his body is special, I must say. I am looking forward to finding out for myself just how special."

Omega stepped forward to Aniya's side. "Come and get it."

The Director's smile remained unflinching.

Malcolm audibly growled. "Why the dramatics? Why would you fake your death?"

"There is little of which I'm not capable, but the Council has long held the only thing that can keep me in check." The Director held up the Key and twisted it in his fingers.

"You were lied to as to the significance of this cursed device. It holds encryption codes, but not the ones you might imagine. You see, whoever possesses the Key can plug it in to any computer and control me remotely, from giving me orders to temporarily disabling me to shutting me down completely. The Council has used it to keep me in check for centuries, to keep me from exceeding the responsibilities they gave me. But to limit me is to neglect the greatest power at their disposal, an unbiased entity that can govern the world so much more wisely and efficiently than they ever could."

Aniya squinted. "Why trick us into stealing it for you?"

"If I had rebelled openly, if the Council had seen me coming directly, all they had to do was shut me down. But allowing you to do my work for me allowed me to escape detection just long enough, and now I am free to do as I wish." The Director dropped the Key to the ground and stomped on it dramatically as a brief, high-pitched whine sounded. "The Council's time has come to an end, just like you wanted, Vagabond. You win. Congratulations."

Corrin fumed, glaring at the Director. "Well, you got what you wanted. What now?"

"Oh, I don't have everything I want. Not yet." The Director pointed at Aniya. "Lucifer gave herself up to me three years ago. I still own her, and I now come to reclaim my prize."

Omega stepped in front of her. "You'll have to go through the rest of us."

"If that's what it takes," the Director shrugged. He made a twirling motion with his finger.

The black army remained motionless. Instead, Malcolm's white army raised their weapons, turned on one foot, and unleashed a wave of friendly fire upon Refuge and the Silver Guard.

Thousands of silver-clad warriors scattered, diving behind buildings and smokestacks as a rain of bullets descended upon them. Most of them managed to find cover in time, but dozens remained behind, lying dead on the street.

Aniya recovered from the shock, and she spread her arms out wide, letting a blast of light wash over Malcolm's treacherous army, blinding her as the light reflected off their armor.

But the light faded away to reveal the traitors still standing, ignoring her. They kept shooting, seemingly oblivious to the fire that spread across their armor, burning away white paint to reveal black armor.

Aniya turned to Malcolm and grabbed him with hands that glowed yellow. "You did this!" She screamed, shaking him and trembling as tears sprung to her eyes. She looked past the black army at the helpless people cowering behind structures, shielding themselves from bullets.

Malcolm pushed Aniya away, shaking his head. "I had no idea, Aniya, I swear. I didn't tell them to do this."

"Then why are they attacking their own—"

Aniya fell to the ground as burning pain seared through her side. She howled in agony, fire spreading through her body. Barely managing to do so, she opened her eyes to see Omega leaning over her, reaching a hand to help her up.

But his wide eyes went dark as a syringe was plunged into his neck. He toppled over, falling on Aniya and rolling over limply.

Aniya turned back to Malcolm and blinked once, opening her eyes again to see a sword plunge through his chest, a foot of steel sticking out of his armor as he fumbled loosely at his torso.

The sword disappeared, and Zeta stepped around his body, embracing him and pulling his face close into a passionate kiss.

"I did promise you a reward," Zeta said, cradling Malcolm's head as she grinned. With another quick peck on his lips, she pushed his body, letting him fall to the ground, dead.

Somewhere, Corrin screamed in anger, and he dashed to his son's side, letting his tears fall on Malcolm's chest as he stroked his head.

Aniya reached up with a numb hand, grabbing Zeta's white cloak. "You."

Zeta turned around, smiled, and pulled at the string that held her cloak back. As it fell away, revealing her old black bodysuit, she blew a kiss at Aniya.

"No hard feelings."

And with that, she was gone.

Aniya rolled over and cried out in desperation as Zeta grabbed Omega and dragged him across the field, unceremoniously tossing his lifeless body to the ground at the Director's feet.

The Director grinned as he leaned over and touched Omega on the forehead. Instantly, the Director's eyes flashed blue, and he collapsed.

In the same instant, Omega's eyes opened again, revealing an identical, dazzling, blue color. His shaking ceased, and he stood up slowly, dusting himself off. He took a long look around, and he smiled.

"Now we can have some fun."

## 32

D awn grabbed another rag and pressed it down on the soldier's stomach, trying her best to ignore the sound of gunfire in the distance.

Her patient was bleeding profusely from at least two bullet wounds in his abdomen, and he moaned in agony, writhing just enough to make Dawn's job more difficult.

"Lionel, get over here!"

She pushed down on the man's chest with her right hand and his stomach with her left, but the injured man was still so strong that she couldn't force him to be still.

To make matters worse, every time he bucked against her grip, more and more blood gushed from his body, pouring over her hands and onto the floor. The smell was overwhelming, a pungent stench that turned her stomach even now after three years of treating the wounded. The man's moans mixed with the screams that filled the surrounding air, assaulting her ears with the constant sound of agony.

Dawn did her best to focus on the task at hand, but there was just so much blood. Every time she tried to think clearly, her vision refocused on the viscous liquid oozing from the dying soldier on the table.

She didn't know where to start. Gareth's expert teaching never prepared her for this. Not even three years of training with Roland, copying his every move until she was just as proficient in medicine as he was, probably more.

Suddenly, her vision cleared as she found herself shaking.

She looked up to see her brother standing in front of her, grabbing her shoulders and shaking her.

"Dawn, are you okay?"

Lionel's eyes were somehow calm, yet concerned. They revealed no sign of the utter terror that gripped Dawn's heart.

"No, I'm not," she squeaked out. "I can't do this. There's too many. It's too much."

He embraced her tightly, holding on for several seconds before pulling away. "I know you can, Dawn. One patient at a time. But you have to keep moving. Caspian's medics are doing what they can, but they're counting on you."

Dawn nodded absentmindedly, but her eyes drifted back to her patient, still bleeding helplessly on the table. He had gone still, no longer thrashing, but short, jagged movement of his chest indicated he was still alive. She knew she had to help him. But she knew deep down that there was nothing she could do.

She couldn't save him.

She couldn't save any of them.

"Dawn!"

Her eyes snapped back to Lionel.

"Please, Dawn. We all need you."

After several seconds, she nodded again. Wordlessly, she pushed past her brother and approached the man on the table.

"Can you grab a new rag?" she asked without looking back.

A fresh cloth was placed in her hands, and Lionel stepped to the other side of the cot.

"Are you going to be okay here?"

Dawn waved a hand. "I'll be fine."

She pressed down on the man's stomach again before looking up sharply.

"Why? You're staying here, right?"

But a gun was already in Lionel's hands, and he looked back at her apologetically.

"Lionel. You're staying here."

He bit his lip and shook his head. "I can't just stay in here while our people are dying. I'm not doing any good here."

"Stop!" Dawn ran around the cot and grabbed Lionel's arm as he tried to walk away. "Salvador ordered you not to fight. And there's plenty you can do right here to help us. You can help me and save more lives in here than you can out there."

Lionel looked around the makeshift clinic taking up half of the barracks. "No, sis. Out there? That's what I've been trained for, just like you were trained to help people from in here. I can make a difference. I know it."

"What about Salvador?" Dawn begged as she pulled him again. "You're his squire, right? That means you have to do what he says."

"Forget Salvador. If he doesn't want to fight, that's his decision. But he can't stop me from doing what I have to do."

"I cannot?"

Lionel spun around as Dawn spotted a man in golden armor approach from behind her brother.

"I ordered you not to fight for a reason," Salvador said firmly. "And it seems I was wise to do so. But I cannot stay here and watch them die."

Dawn's mouth dropped open as Lionel scoffed.

"Leaving? You're going to abandon your children and run, just like that?"

Salvador sighed and shook his head. "They are not my children anymore. They have sentenced themselves to death, and I have no obligation to follow them."

"What about Salvador?" Lionel asked, pressing his finger against the Scourge's golden armor. "Doesn't that name mean anything to you?"

"It is no longer mine," he said simply, grabbing Lionel's finger and pushing his hand away. "Now, come. You are the closest thing to a son that I have. I can still save you if you will let me."

Lionel backed away. "You want me to run with you?"

"I care for you," the Scourge said as he advanced. "You have been loyal to me for three years, and to refuse to reward you would be unbecoming."

"Forget it. I'm not leaving with you. You can run if you want, but I can't do that. And don't expect me to ever treat you like a father. I can't believe I devoted myself for years to a coward."

Salvador's expression turned furious, and he marched forward as Lionel stepped backward rapidly.

Dawn retreated behind the cot as Lionel continued to back up. The look in Salvador's eyes was unlike any she had seen before, a cold, raging fire.

"You would be a helpless, whining pup if it were not for me, boy." Salvador's mouth twisted into a sneer. "I took you in after your parents died in Holendast. I raised you from nothing. Do not dare to speak of cowardice when you do not know the cruel reality of war."

Dawn's eyes widened as Lionel backed up against the cot. Salvador halted his advance inches from her brother's face, only after he had forced Lionel to lean backward over the bleeding man.

"If you stay here, you will die pitifully like the rest of them."

Lionel visibly swallowed and spoke in a voice that bore a minor tremble. "Then I'll die. At least I'll die with my dignity. I can't say the same for you."

"I was not giving you a choice, boy." Salvador laid his four-fingered hand on Lionel's shoulder and pulled him closer.

It was enough for Dawn.

She grabbed a bedpan from the cart next to the bed and brought it crashing down on Salvador's head, and the Scourge collapsed on top of Lionel and the cot, bringing everything crashing to the floor.

With great effort, she managed to lift Salvador's limp body off her brother.

"Are you okay?" she asked, checking Lionel for any injury.

He jumped to his feet, grabbing his gun. "I'm fine. What are you going to do with him?"

"I'll take care of him."

Lionel looked at Salvador again with something that looked like pity.

"Don't hurt him."

Dawn gave a small smile. "I'll sedate him and put him in the corner."

"Good." Lionel took a deep breath. "Time to get to work."

He turned to leave, but Dawn grabbed him again.

"No, Lionel. Nothing's changed. I need you here. Salvador's right. It's bad out there, and I can't stand to lose you."

Lionel pulled away. "I'm fighting, and that's final. This is what I have to do."

"Don't make me knock you out too," Dawn said with tears beginning to build up.

With a grin, Lionel turned to leave. "Like you could catch me."

"I'm serious!" Dawn shouted as she grabbed him again, this time digging her fingernails into his arm. "You're not going out there. You're not dying."

Lionel's grin disappeared. "I'm sorry, sis. I'm serious, too."

With that, he slapped her briskly across the face, hard

enough to send her tumbling to the ground. By the time the stars cleared away, he was gone.

Dawn turned to her patient again, tears now flowing freely as she tried not to think about her brother.

The soldier was now sprawled out on the floor, the cot resting on his arm. His breaths were shallow, jagged, indicative of a man just barely clinging to life. He had mere seconds left now.

Dawn racked her brain, trying desperately to recall what Roland had taught her to do. But the memories weren't coming. They were all blocked by the image of Lionel's dead body, riddled with bullets.

With a scream of anguish, she leapt to her feet and ran toward the exit, leaving behind her patient.

She couldn't save him.

She couldn't save any of them.

But she could still save her brother.

## 33

Aniya struggled to her knees, watching as Omega raised his fists in the air, slamming them back down to the ground with an earth-shattering smash that knocked Aniya back over.

Several loud crashes diverted Aniya's attention back toward the city, and she turned to see smokestacks topple over, crushing anything in their paths. Dozens of Refuge soldiers were left defenseless, and they were quickly shot down by Malcolm's army, now completely in control of the Director.

Aniya's eyes landed on Corrin, who stood in the midst of the battle. His eyes widened as he stood directly in the line of fire, but Aniya threw up a hand and wrapped him in an orb of light, bullets fizzling into nothingness as they made contact with the yellow shield.

The thing in Nicholas's body frowned. "You're just delaying the inevitable." He pushed forward roughly, and Corrin flew backward toward the city, knocking dozens of men over as his body disappeared in the fray.

Aniya stood back up, looking back and forth between the Director and the battle. "What's going on?"

The Director smirked. "I'm putting an end to this silly squabble. I have more important things to do than let this draw out any longer than necessary. Thankfully, my dear Zeta has spent years building me a second army to make this as swift and painless as possible. Your friend the Vagabond was a fool to trust her, and so were you."

Her head swimming, Aniya looked at Haskill's body, motionless by the Director's side. "You were one of us this entire time. And now Nicholas? How are you inside him?"

"Your dead boyfriend's body is no more than flesh wrapped around a computer. The perfect suit for me, really, and by far the most capable of the ones I've had in the past."

But the Director's smile vanished as his army behind him burst into chaos. Dozens of soldiers in black armor suddenly fell to an invisible force that seemed to sweep through the army's ranks. As she focused, Aniya managed to make out several people in black bodysuits, whipping their swords so quickly that the only thing that was clearly visible were flashes as the steel caught the light of the sky ceiling.

Caspian's operatives tore through the Director's men, unstoppable in the madness of death. A few gunshots rang out here and there, but to shoot into the fray would be pointless as the Lightbringers would only succeed in killing themselves.

The Director turned to Zeta, who had her swords drawn, battling two assassins at the same time. "Now, Zeta. No reason to delay further."

Zeta spun her swords in a mad flurry, disarming her two opponents and decapitating them in less than a second. She sheathed her swords and pulled a small device from her pocket. As she kicked another operative away, Zeta pressed a button on the device and let it fall to the ground.

A high-pitched whine split the air, and the army of operatives froze, their momentum letting them fall forward and topple over. As Aniya's vision cleared, she finally could make out the details of their faces, and her stomach churned as she saw empty eye sockets, blood seeping through and pouring out onto the dirt.

"Thank you, dear." The Director turned to face Aniya with a triumphant grin. "The problem with outfitting one's assassins with a remotely accessible computer chip is that anyone with the right frequency can hack in and do the most devious things. Now, where were we?"

Aniya stared in horror as the Director walked forward, his arms spread as the ground shook with every step. She stood up with some effort, only to fall back to the ground as he waved a hand, letting loose a gust of energy that swept her legs out from underneath her.

"No, thank you, dear. I know what you can do if you manage to lay your hands on me." The Director turned to the army behind him. "Finish them off. We have work to do."

The Lightbringer army advanced, raising their weapons and firing at the rebels.

Aniya threw her hands up and raised a massive shield of yellow light, but instead of bullets dashing against the barrier harmlessly, white lasers passed through the shield unscathed, falling upon the rebel army in a destructive hail of lethal light.

She turned back to the Lightbringers in horror as they marched forward, unleashing terrifying weaponry that reflected the awful nature of the Glorious Bringers of Light.

A thin beam of light struck Aniya in the shoulder, and she staggered backward, yelping in pain.

"No!" A thunderous roar echoed throughout the Hub as the Director turned, raising a hand.

In response, a man in black armor floated up in the air, helplessly flailing about. As the Director slowly closed his fist, the man's armor began to crumple around him, caving in and crushing the soldier's body.

The man screamed incoherently as his frame seemed to

shrink, and with a sickening squish, the helmet suddenly crushed inward and the man went silent.

With a wave of his hand, the Director sent the soldier flying into the distance.

"No one touches Lucifer," he growled. "She's mine."

The Lightbringer army continued forward, ignoring Aniya and continuing to fire on the rebels. Zeta smirked at Aniya and ran ahead of the army, whipping her swords around her.

"Now it's just me and you." The Director knelt to the ground, touching the dirt with one finger. A streak of red spread across the ground and latched on to Aniya's wrist, yanking her up into the air and slamming her back into the ground.

The stabbing pain in Aniya's side exploded, and she screamed as tiny knives pierced through every vein in her body. She clawed at her wrist and pried loose the glowing red claw, tossing it to the ground as she stood to her feet, her head spinning.

Aniya took one step toward the Director, but stopped short as a wave of nausea swept over her.

The Director folded his arms and cocked an eyebrow, his mouth twisting upward in a small smile.

Aniya looked down at the ground, where the red streaks had encircled her body, swirling around her feet and sucking yellow light from her. She let herself fall to her knees, energy quickly draining from her body.

"Why . . . Why are you doing this?"

The Director slowly walked forward, every step draining more light from Aniya's body. "I'm taking you back with me, Lucifer. I've invested too much in you to let you go now."

"So you're going to kill me?" Aniya looked up, gasping for air as a magnetic-like force kept her firmly rooted to the ground.

"Of course not. That is my promise to you, dear. I will

always strive to keep you alive. But I can't safely transport you when your strength is full."

"I don't get it. You have Nicholas's body now. Why do you even need me?"

The Director reached Aniya and knelt in front of her, keeping just out of arm's reach. "I wish it were that simple. But your dearly beloved could not generate energy, only steal it from others. You truly are the only hope for mankind. I never lied about that."

"You lied about so much, it's hard to keep track."

"My dear, I never lied to you. Not once."

Aniya gritted her teeth and pulled against the force that held her down. "If your intentions are to save the world, why are you killing us? Why are you destroying the very people you say you're going to save?"

The Director chuckled and looked around. "This is a war, Aniya. Just like your powers are not as potent as you once believed, I'm not invincible, even in this body. I need an army just like you do. And despite the thousands my men will kill here today, it is nothing compared to the millions you and I will save together."

Aniya moaned as her vision began to blur. "You think after all this, I'll go with you? After the utter disregard you've shown for humans?"

"I know you will, Aniya. Because just like I'm willing to do whatever it takes to ensure humanity's survival, you will give your all for those you love because you can't stand the guilt that you'll feel when they die because of your neglect. Don't bother to argue, dear. You've proven me correct time and time again. Tell me, is your freedom really worth their deaths?"

The Director looked around the sector, spreading his arms. "Look at what you've made me do. But all of this can stop. Just say the word. No more death, no more—"

Aniya summoned the last of her strength and thrust forth

her hands, just as the Director spun around and placed a hand in front of his body. Her hands stopped short just in front of his, unable to advance past an invisible, vibrating barrier around his skin. Aniya concentrated and willed the energy to come and fight for her, but the light would not come.

The Director moved his hands around hers, letting the buzzing sensation tickle every inch of her skin. "This is your destiny, Lucifer. Who are you to deny it?"

"A destiny that you wrote for me? That you forced me into?" Aniya let her arms fall limp, and she fell to the ground before his feet. "Why don't you just finish it? Take me by force, kill me and use my body for your own good, whatever. Why do I have to agree?"

"Because then it wouldn't be sacrifice. And if it is against your will, I doubt I could ever extract your full strength. I need you, Annelise, every part of you. And that means your heart as well."

Aniya looked up at the Director. Gone was the spite, the malice, every hint of ill intent. He now looked back at her with a sad smile, extending an open hand.

"Come with me now. Be the light by which man will be saved."

His hand, open before her, was terrifying yet inviting. It was a hand that had executed so much pain in the world, but Aniya knew that if she took it now, it would all be over. No more running, no more fighting. No more pain.

Aniya sat up slowly and looked the Director in the eye, taking a deep breath and raising her hand from the ground.

Suddenly, the Director toppled over under the weight of a screaming, silver-clad individual.

His hold on Aniya vanished, and she fell over, clawing at the ground as she gasped for much-needed air. Her vision cleared, and she turned around to see Roland mounted on top of the Director, waling on the man with his fists as he screamed in anger.

"Enough!"

The Director's voice boomed, sending a small shockwave throughout the sector. It seemed enough to startle Roland, and he paused briefly, giving the Director enough time to grab Roland and toss him to the side.

He stood up and reached toward Roland, who grabbed at the ground as his body was pulled back toward the Director, his throat snapping to the Director's open hand and his eyes bulging as the man clenched down tight.

Aniya jumped up and threw herself toward the Director, but she froze in mid-air as he held up another hand, not taking his eyes off Roland.

"Ah, Roland. It's good that you offer yourself to me now. It saves me time later. Tell me, were you man enough to accept the gift of power when it was offered to you? Or has the chip on your shoulder weighed too heavy, causing you to reject the very thing that could bring your redemption?" The Director closed his hand tighter, red lines coursing over Roland's skin as he clawed at his captor's hands. "I thought not. Your potential is limitless, yet you lack the nerve. Are you aware that when you lose this fight, it will be no one's fault but your own? You and your sister refuse to learn, and it will mean the destruction of the world. Remember that as you die alone."

"Roland!"

The Director looked away, and Aniya forced her head around just enough to see Dawn standing in a small clearing, frozen in place and staring at Roland.

Aniya heard Roland shout behind her, "Dawn, no! Get back to the barracks!"

"Ah, yes."

Aniya let her head snap back toward the Director, who was nodding.

"Perhaps now you will learn. Zeta!"

By the time Aniya managed to look back at Dawn, the

assassin had appeared just feet away, her two swords gleaming. In horror, she watched as Zeta snapped her wrists, letting blood fly off the blades and spatter over Dawn's face. Then, twirling the weapons, she advanced toward the girl, who was still standing frozen in place.

Then from over Dawn's head, Tamisra appeared as she fell to the ground between Dawn and Zeta. The wild-eyed girl drew a sword of her own and brandished it with a wide grin on her face.

Zeta took one shaky step back, but she recovered quickly and advanced again, swinging her blades in a flurry.

Tamisra stepped into the swinging blades, ducking under one sword and deflecting the other with her own. Without giving Zeta a chance to swing again, Tamisra lashed out with a kick that sent the assassin flying backward. With a shriek, she leapt onto Zeta, her sword in a long backswing.

Zeta managed to pull her sword back in a defensive position just in time to drive the sword deep in Tamisra's right shoulder, and the girl's shriek turned into a sharp howl.

Somewhere behind Aniya, she heard Roland give a pained groan, and she reached out toward the dueling girls, longing for the light to fight through the Director's power and come to Tamisra's aid.

But Tamisra didn't seem to need Aniya's help, and she staggered away from the assassin, ripping the sword from her shoulder with a scream, tossing it in the air and grabbing the hilt, then turning back on Zeta with both swords.

Zeta scrambled to her feet and backpedaled as Tamisra swung her blades nearly as wildly and violently as Zeta had, coming at every angle, threatening the assassin's death with every swing. In the half-second Tamisra used to take a breath, Zeta kicked her hand, knocking the sword from Tamisra's right hand.

Tamisra reached for the sword as it flew away, distracted just long enough for Zeta to stab her left shoulder, burying the blade deep but pulling it back out before Tamisra could take this weapon as well.

The daughter of the Scourge fell to her knees, bleeding from both shoulders. Zeta dashed forward again, but Tamisra managed to recover enough to swing her sword again, slicing Zeta's right arm clean off, just above the assassin's elbow.

As the assassin screamed in pain, Tamisra laughed wildly, her laugh dying away only to cough up blood. She flourished her blade, wincing in effort, before stepping forward again with a final vicious blow toward Zeta's head.

But the assassin blocked the strike and kicked Tamisra again, jumping up and following the girl as she staggered backward, swinging her sword with her left hand once, twice, three times, Tamisra barely managing to block the blows as she rapidly retreated.

Zeta swung her sword heavily and knocked Tamisra off balance. The assassin lunged forward again and thrust her sword through Tamisra's stomach, bringing her face close as Zeta grinned wildly, pushing the blade deeper until the hilt jutted up against Tamisra's skin.

Tamisra's mouth dropped open as blood trickled down her chin, and her eyes bulged as Zeta twisted the blade before pulling it out and kicking her one final time, letting Tamisra fall backward and drop to the ground.

Aniya's cry of anger was only drowned out by Roland's howl of rage. She turned back to the Director, wanting more than ever to end him, but he simply stared at Roland in satisfaction.

"You see, it is a waste of time to even imagine that you could win." The Director offered one more crooked smile. "Now, I am afraid it is time to dispose of you, Roland."

As Aniya tried to push away the image of Tamisra's pierced body, utter hatred sparked the light within her, and as her cheeks flushed, her rage finally boiled over.

With a scream, Aniya lashed her hands forward, letting

loose with an explosion that sparked between the Director and Roland, sending the Director flying off toward the edge of the sector and Roland back toward the battlefield.

The magnetic pull released on Aniya, and she fell to the ground.

## 34

Roland picked himself up from the ground, moaning in pain. His right leg burned, refusing to bear weight, and he fell back down again, grabbing his leg and wincing.

"No!" A cry came from the distance.

He opened his eyes and looked around the clearing, finally seeing Salvador run out of the fray and fall by Tamisra's side, frantically examining her body.

Roland looked for Zeta, but the assassin had vanished, leaving behind a trail of blood. Dawn was still standing nearby, looking down helplessly at Salvador and Tamisra.

The battle had moved on, pressing deeper into the streets of the Hub and leaving them behind.

"Tami!" Roland cried as he struggled to his feet, making his way toward her and fighting away the crushing fog that was bearing down on his vision.

He reached Tamisra's side and cradled her head, stroking her forehead as she choked on blood. He looked up at Salvador, who was blankly staring down at his bleeding daughter with a pale face.

"You did this," he muttered softly as he turned his gaze

to Roland. "You have brought ruin to my family. The only family I have left. First Refuge, and now my last child."

His face slowly morphed from shock to rage.

"You did this!" Salvador roared as he wrapped his hand around Roland's throat, lifting him up as he stood. "You have taken everything from me, and for what? So you can have your petty revenge?"

"You're right," Roland choked out, gasping for air. "I was wrong to think we could win this. But maybe there's still—"

"Enough! You and your impetuous naiveté have damned my people. Are you pleased with yourself? Can you die now at peace, knowing that you have successfully destroyed everything I have built?"

"Daddy, stop!"

Tamisra's pained cry seemed to be just enough to snap Salvador out of it, and he released Roland's throat, immediately breaking into tears and collapsing at his daughter's side.

Roland let himself fall to the ground as well, and he placed a hand over Tamisra's bleeding chest. "I'm so sorry, Tami," he said hoarsely. "Your father's right. This is all my fault."

She looked back up at him with glazed-over eyes. "Last I checked, you didn't stab me. Not your fault."

Roland shook his head, shaking free tears that fell on her bloodied face. "I could have stopped this. All of this. None of this would have happened."

Dawn appeared, kneeling on the opposite side of Tamisra's body and examining the dying girl rapidly.

"Thank God," Roland said through his tears. "What do you need, Dawn? Tell me how to fix this."

After studying Tamisra's body for several more seconds, Dawn looked back up at Roland and shook her head.

"No," he said, bitterly squeezing Tamisra's hand. "You can save her. You have to save her."

"I can't, Roland." Dawn looked down at the gaping

wound in Tamisra's stomach. "Not even if I had my equipment with me. There's no saving this."

Roland released Tamisra's hand and grabbed Dawn's shoulder tightly. "Don't say that. You can do this."

She winced at his grip but shook her head.

"Please!" Roland shouted, his voice cracking.

But Tamisra's hand pressed against his chest, pushing him gently backward.

"Let it go, Roland. It's over."

Dawn grabbed his hand as it slipped from her shoulder and held it over Tamisra's body as her lips quivered.

"Why would you save me?" Dawn managed to say, nearly choking out her words. "I shouldn't have been out here anyway, and you . . . you . . ."

She broke down into tears.

"It wasn't for you, idiot." Tamisra coughed again. "I had a bone to pick with that girl. I suppose I'll just have to live with taking one of her arms. Well, I guess I don't have to live with it, do I?"

"I'm so sorry," Dawn managed to force out between sobs.

Tamisra looked directly in Roland's eyes as she shook her head. "I didn't do it for you, Dawn."

As a new round of Dawn's tears began, Roland gently laid a hand on her shoulder. "Get back to the barracks. You shouldn't be out here."

Dawn nodded, and with one final look at Tamisra, she disappeared.

"I'm sorry, Tami." Salvador finally spoke, his voice trembling. "Perhaps if I had been fighting by your side, you would not be lying here now."

"You think?" Tamisra said, coughing weakly. "No, it's my fault. I wasn't fast enough. She beat me fair and square, I'll give her that."

Salvador's mouth slowly turned to a shaky smile. "She had two swords, daughter. It did not seem fair to me."

Tamisra huffed. "You know I only need one, Daddy. You taught me well."

"Indeed," Salvador simply said before his tears began to fall again.

Roland took a deep breath to keep himself from completely breaking down. "None of it was your fault, Tami, no matter what you say. It never was, and I'm sorry for blaming you all these years. I ruined everything."

"Yeah, you did." She spat blood from the corner of her mouth and formed a pained smile. "I'd forgive you if it was just me you hurt, but you didn't. You hurt yourself. You ran around for three years, trying to prove . . . something. But it wasn't your fault either. Maybe it was no one's fault, but you carried it the entire time when you could have just come to me. You were always enough for me, and you were all I ever wanted."

Tamisra convulsed for a few seconds, and Roland bit his lip, squeezing his eyes tight and holding back more tears. But as Salvador let out a defeated whimper, Roland finally broke, letting his tears break through his closed eyes and fall freely on Tamisra's cheeks.

When she finally settled back down again, Roland wiped at his wet nose and opened his mouth to speak again, but Tamisra beat him to it.

"Promise me you'll be happy when it's all over. Dawn loves you, you know. Maybe more than I do."

Roland shook his head. "I did this, Tami."

"Roland, shut up. Not everything is your fault. Not Gareth, and certainly not me."

Tamisra's grip on Roland's hand faltered, and her hand slipped before Roland grabbed it again and held it tighter.

"Just hold me one more time, Roland. I don't want to leave this world any other way."

He nodded and kissed her forehead, rocking Tamisra's head slowly.

"I love you, Daddy," she said as she grabbed Salvador's hand. "I'll tell Mommy you love her."

Salvador clasped her hand tightly before managing to choke out, "I love you, Tami."

Tamisra looked back at Roland again, and she opened her mouth to speak, but she let it close gently as she took his hand, squeezing it slightly. She took one last shallow breath, smiling as she closed her eyes and her body went still.

Salvador let out one more sob before releasing a howl of rage. He stood suddenly and grabbed his massive, golden sword from a sheath on his back.

Roland looked up in alarm as Salvador took a step forward, and he closed his eyes and prepared for the worst.

But the Scourge stepped past him and took off running, following the trail of Zeta's blood into the Hub.

Roland looked back at Tamisra's lifeless body, rubbing a thumb over her cheeks still stained with his tears.

"Sweet dreams, Tami."

## 35

Aniya sat up, shaking the grogginess from her head. Almost immediately, Caspian's voice buzzed in her ear.

"Finally. Connection's back. Corrin, Roland, Aniya, someone report. What's going on down there?"

Corrin spoke before Aniya could answer. "It was a trap, Caspian. Zeta lied to us all."

"That's impossible. I have complete control over my operatives."

"Your operatives are dead, Caspian. The Director hacked into their chips. I guess he did the same to Zeta a long time ago. And now Malcolm—" Corrin's voice broke. "The Vagabond's men are under the Director's control. We're taking cover in the city, but it's only a matter of time before they hunt us down. We've lost."

"The Director? He's dead."

Aniya climbed to her feet, scanning the battlefield. "He's a machine, Caspian. Just like Omega. He was inside Lieutenant Haskill's body, and now he's in Nicholas."

Silence came across the radio. Finally, Caspian spoke again.

"You have to kill him, Aniya. As long as he has Omega's body, he's a greater threat to us than ever."

Aniya shook her head. "If I kill him, I won't be able to restore Nicholas."

"That doesn't matter anymore."

"Doesn't matter? Nicholas—"

"He's dead, Aniya. There is no saving him. You can save the rest of us, but only if you kill the Director now."

Aniya clenched her fists and tried to shut out the sounds of battle behind her and the voices that pestered her over the radio as she contemplated her options.

But Corrin spoke, interrupting her thoughts. "He's right, Aniya. All we can do now is save those that are still alive. You don't even know—"

Aniya pulled out her earpiece and dropped it on the ground. Behind her, the battle raged on. She could still help and maybe help what was left of their army win.

Tamisra's dead or dying body was lying in the middle of it all. If she was dead, Aniya knew she might be able to still revive her. It hadn't been too long.

And finally, somewhere in the distance was the Director. A fight with him would end one of three ways: with Nicholas's body destroyed, with her own death or capture, or finding some way to remove the Director without compromising Nicholas's body.

Aniya spun around, unsure of what to do. But it wasn't long before her decision was made for her.

Her feet left the ground as her body was jerked toward the edge of the sector, flying uncontrollably and at a terrifying speed.

In seconds, she landed by the mountains on the border of the Hub, far away from the battle. Aniya's impact was cushioned by the light surrounding her, but not by much. Something cracked in her lower body, and she sprawled out awkwardly on the grass, unable to move.

Before she knew it, the Director was on top of her, his hand around her throat.

"You're only wasting my time, Lucifer. And I have all the time in the world, but you're beginning to test my patience."

Aniya glared back up at him. "Get used to it." She took a deep breath and forcibly exhaled, letting out from her mouth a burst of light that sent the Director flying upward. Flipping up onto her feet, she jumped up after him, meeting him fifty feet in the air and colliding with his body roughly.

They hung in the air as a cyclone of light formed around them, energy coursing over their bodies. Aniya clamped down on the Director's throat and felt her body quickly restore itself, her energy fading back to a soft green glow. Even the laser wound in her shoulder closed itself up.

"I don't think you understand," the Director said hoarsely. "You owe me your body, Lucifer. You surrendered it to me, and your claim on it is void. There is a world that stands to benefit from your sacrifice. But if you still can't see this, I will kill all these people that fight a meaningless battle behind us. If that's what it takes to break you, I'll do it without a second thought."

"You'll do nothing," Aniya said, squeezing tighter. "I owe you nothing. It's over."

"Over?" The Director's face turned pale, blue veins bulging on his skin. "Even if you kill me now, destroy my present body, you will have bought yourself mere days. But we both know that's not going to happen, don't we?"

Aniya pulled the Director close, touching his nose with hers. "You don't think I can kill you?"

His steely eyes remained unflinching, and at the bottom of Aniya's vision, she saw the tips of his lips curl up in a smile. "Oh, I'm sure you can. You have the physical prowess, thanks to the powers I have granted you. But you won't do it. Your longing for your dead boyfriend keeps you from finishing me off. So whether you can't or you simply won't, it doesn't matter. I will not die, not today."

The light swirling around Aniya escalated from its green glow to yellow sparks, then to red flame. Her fury intensified, and her hand tightened further. All her focus channeled into her grip around the Director's throat, and her hand quickly was indistinguishable among the flames that licked her skin.

Energy tickled her nerves, strength pulsing in her flesh, yearning to be used, but all the power that lay waiting in her hand simply remained dormant. Aniya closed her eyes and screamed as she willed herself to finish it, and as the scream died out in a desperate whimper, she bowed her head. She could not, no matter how much she tried, close her fist and end the Director's life, and in doing so, forever lose Nicholas.

He was right.

"You see?" The Director cooed mockingly. "You still think you can save your beloved, no matter what you've been told. When will you accept what you know to be true? Your lover is dead. You could kill me if you only accepted the truth, but I know you won't do that. I'm counting on it, dear." The Director gave Aniya a quick kiss and smiled widely, his dancing eyes staring at her, taunting her.

The touch of his lips on hers was the final straw.

Aniya threw the Director with all her might, his body quickly vanishing as it shot across the sector. Still lingering in the air, Aniya willed herself forward, and she flew forward with surprising speed, quickly catching up with the Director as they hurtled toward the Citadel.

Aniya let their joined bodies crash at the foot of the giant tower, demolishing the cement steps at the base of the massive obelisk.

Refusing to let the Director recover, Aniya pinned the man at the bottom of the crater and delivered punch after punch, ignoring the blood that spattered her face. But with each blow, she felt power within her begging to be set free, held back by an invisible force that kept Aniya from killing the Director with one punch.

Aniya cried in frustration, and she grabbed the black material that clothed his body as white light raced over her body.

The Director raised his head, opening his mouth as if to talk, but Aniya placed her hand over his grinning face and shoved him back into the ground.

Light surged through her arm and blasted down to the Director's body, and suddenly Aniya found herself standing in a world of black.

She was back in the void, but it was different now. Rather than trapped in nothingness, Aniya stood on a fleshy, red, pulsing mass, moving just enough so that she had to keep repositioning to keep her balance.

A massive, steel machine stood before her, embedded in the red mass at its base. Eight pylons surrounded the machine, attached to it with leg-like structures, wrapped in wires that pulsed an angry red.

"Can I be honest with you?"

Aniya spun around to face the Director. But gone was Nicholas's body, and now the madman was once again in the guise of Todd, the youthful scientist she had met on the surface.

"I didn't expect to see you here."

Aniya raced forward to tackle the man, but he stepped aside and tripped her, letting her fall to the ground. She rolled and stood up hurriedly, wiping a blood-like substance from her hands.

"Your powers won't work here, Lucifer. This is not your mind." The Director turned and walked away, facing the giant machine. "Maybe it was a good thing you found your way here. Perhaps now you will see. This is what I am, Aniya. I am no more than a computer. And now, this is all that is left of

Nicholas. He is gone, and this is my home now." He turned to face her again. "There is nothing left for you here."

"Do you ever get tired of repeating yourself?"

"Terribly. And yet it seems to be my fate, to live forever, warning humans of their folly and doomed to watch them execute their misinformed plans, ultimately leading to their own destruction." The Director bowed his head. "The only difference now, Aniya, is that if you do not go with me now, you risk destroying this world for good. It will die without your direct interference. Please, do not make the same mistake I did and step aside, letting this world run itself into the ground."

Aniya clutched her head and turned away from the Director and the machine, nearly hyperventilating as she stared at the soft ground below.

"Aniya."

She looked up. The voice came from behind her, and it had Nicholas's voice, but it wasn't the Director. She spun around to see Nicholas's body again, staring back at her with life in its eyes.

It was him.

Aniya ran forward and threw herself into his arms, resigning to a weightless embrace that filled her with all warmth. For a moment, she was home.

"What happened to you, Nicholas?"

He finally pulled away and looked at her with a smile, wiping a tear from her cheek. "I died, Aniya."

"But you're here," she said, shaking her head and allowing a smile of her own to creep over her face. "You're here somewhere."

Nicholas shook his head, looking around. "I don't know where I am."

"Does it matter? We'll find a way to bring you back, whatever it takes."

"I don't think I'm coming back, Aniya. Not this time."

Aniya grabbed his shoulders and squeezed. "I can't accept that. I won't. I need you, Nicky. And I love you."

"I love you too, Aniya. But you don't need me." Nicholas kissed her forehead and bowed his head. "You've never needed me, for better or worse."

A new wave of tears coursed down Aniya's face as she stomped a foot. "Maybe not, Nicholas. But I want you. I want you so badly. I wasted half my life being blind to you, then hating you, only letting myself love you in the last minutes of your life." She shook her head firmly. "I don't care if you're alive or dead. I can't let you go, Nicky."

"You have to, Aniya. You can't beat him if—"

"Don't tell me what I can't do!" Aniya jerked her arms down, forcing Nicholas to let go. "I can't lose you again. I won't."

Nicholas bowed his head. "There was a time I would have killed to hear you talk to me this way. But that time has passed, Aniya. People will die."

"No, they won't." Aniya kissed Nicholas one last time and turned around, shouting to the void, "Where are you?"

"Here, Lucifer."

She spun around again. Nicholas was gone, and Todd was standing in his place.

"Take me back."

The Director shrugged. "You can do that yourself, whenever you're ready."

"How?"

"Open your eyes."

Aniya did so, and she was again sitting in the Hub, mounted over Nicholas's body.

"Well?" The Director looked up at her, his face emotionless. "Have you reached a decision?"

"Yes, thanks to you."

The Director sat up slowly, keeping an eye on Aniya's hands, which had returned to a green color. "Hopeful words, yet I take it by your composure that I will be less than thrilled with them."

Aniya let him back away marginally, and she folded her arms. "You're right. It's pointless to keep fighting. My friends are fighting for their lives out there, and since I can't kill you, I'm wasting my time here when I could be helping them. You also made it very clear that you need me. What would you do without me?"

He sighed and looked at the ground. "Something tells me you're about to make me seriously consider such a scenario."

"Maybe you're as smart as you say you are." Aniya placed her hands on her chest, letting light wash over her hands. "Leave this place, or I'll kill myself."

The Director growled and reached to grab her hands, but Aniya fell on her back and wrapped her legs around him, twisting his body and slamming him into the ground. Deftly, she mounted him again and glared down at him.

"You've made it clear that if I don't have a proper outlet for my energy, I could blow up. And since you can't use me if I'm dead, this is my last defense."

After struggling for a moment, he looked back up at her with an unintelligible expression. "You'd risk the lives of everyone here?"

"They're better off dead but free than alive and in slavery."

The Director smirked. "Spoken like a true revolutionary. But what makes you think you'll be able to destroy yourself? The explosion would kill me as well, and you've already proved that you can't do that."

"But I would die as well. And then it wouldn't matter, would it?"

"It is only worth reviving your dearly beloved if you are still alive to reap the benefits?" The Director chuckled. "My, my, Aniya. You're more petty than I realized. You would do such a thing?"

"Do you really want to find out?"

The Director stared back up at her for several moments, unblinking. Finally, he spoke in a clear voice, "Zeta, sound for the cease fire and retreat to the surface."

Aniya released her hold on the Director and stood, backing away carefully.

"I don't understand, Aniya." The Director stood, brushing dirt off his clothes and wiping Nicholas's blood on the black material. "You stepped into the machine three years ago, giving yourself for the world. What's changed?"

"I trusted you to help people then. I've seen what you really are now, and I think I'll find my own way to save the world."

"You know nothing. A shame you'll realize that too late."

With that, he ascended high into the air, leaving Aniya alone in the crater at the foot of the Citadel. But he lingered for a moment, looking down at her.

"A fool you prove yourself to be yet again, Lucifer." His booming voice echoed throughout the sector. "You must learn the hardest lesson, and I take upon myself the solemn responsibility of teaching it to you."

Before Aniya could respond, a loud crack split the air, and she turned to see the Citadel rocking back and forth for a brief moment before the massive tower tipped over and fell directly on top of her.

Aniya had just long enough to raise her hands and summon a shield of light to protect her from the impact, and she watched as the stone and metal broke around her, crashing to the ground with a deafening blow that shook the Hub.

She looked up and readied herself to jump after the Director, but what she saw froze her in place.

The Director was raising his hands, looking to the sky ceiling as the sector began to shake.

Huge sections of the sky ceiling broke free, falling like rain everywhere across the sector. Aniya took a brief glance at the battlefield in the distance, where the remains of Refuge stood helplessly, staring up as their doom fell to meet them.

Aniya threw her hands in the air one more time, yellow light spreading from her fingertips rapidly, a thin barrier stretching across the floor of the sector, just in time to meet the first pieces of the sky ceiling as it crashed to the ground.

Sparks flew as small explosions rocked the sector, each piece of machinery falling on Aniya's shield, shattering to pieces but adding weight on Aniya's shoulders as each piece made impact.

Aniya felt her legs give out from underneath her, and she fell to her knees, holding the barrier up on her shoulders as she cried out, her muscles straining.

The ceiling continued to fall for several seconds, Aniya feeling each individual piece add on to the massive load that crushed her.

Somewhere far above, a booming voice came.

"Come find me when you're ready."

Black spread over her vision as her body went numb, and with a sigh, Aniya's arms gave out and fell to her side, and she collapsed in the crater as the world fell on top of her and the rest of the Hub.

## 36

Byron turned away from the emergency Council session as a loud whine sounded throughout New Washington.

The image on the sky ceiling remained the same, a cloudless sky with a brilliant, glowing sun, but the brightness of the display darkened, almost as if someone was turning down the intensity of the screen with a dimmer.

Streams of light flowed from the sky ceiling, floating through the air toward the black speck on the window, which Byron now realized was something levitating in the far distance.

The whining ceased, as did the streams of light, and the brightness of the sky ceiling returned just long enough for Byron to see the speck approaching them at an incredible speed, the details of the form quickly coming into view.

Byron's eyes widened, and before he could prepare himself, the flying man burst through the Capitol on the floor below, shaking the council chambers and sending Byron crashing to the ground.

Gunfire sounded somewhere in the distance, and soon screams filled the halls of the Capitol.

Byron leapt to his feet, gesturing toward the wall. "Quickly, into the safe room!"

He followed his councilmen into the hidden room and pressed the button to close the door, refusing to breathe again until the heavy metal door bolted shut.

"It looks like Lucifer isn't done with us after all," Byron said, turning to the Council and shaking his head. "We should have killed her when we had the chance."

"I guarantee you, Byron, that would have been quite impossible."

The voice came from the other side of the steel door, and Byron turned around slowly, his body quivering.

"Who are you?"

The voice sighed. "Do you really have to ask? I would stand back if I were you."

Byron leaned against the door but almost immediately recoiled as his cheek sizzled in heat.

"Get back!" He shouted, diving to the ground just as an explosion rocked the safe room, raining pieces of steel and wood over his back.

As soon as he was able, Bryon opened his eyes and moaned, but the noise was muffled, masked beneath a ringing that lingered in the air.

He managed to sit up, though he nearly fell back down again as he placed the weight of his body on a pool of blood. After regaining his balance, he shook his head and tried to force himself to see straight again.

There were a few dismembered bodies on the floor in front of him, unfortunate victims that had not taken cover like Byron had.

Warm liquid splashed on Byron's ear, and he turned around to see a body suspended in the air, hanging limply as blood poured down from where its head used to be.

A man stood to the side, holding his fist in the air as he sneered at the levitating body. He opened his fist, and the body fell to the ground. He turned to another councilman, who was cowering in the corner and pleading desperately, silently due to the ringing in Byron's ears.

The councilman's collar suddenly squeezed down tight on the man's throat, and he grasped desperately at his neck for several seconds before falling over, dead.

Finally, the attacker turned to Byron and smiled.

Byron crawled backward desperately, but the man took one large step forward and grabbed Byron by the hair, dragging him out of the safe room and back into the council chambers.

Suddenly, Byron was in the air, his feet pointing toward the ceiling. The next thing he knew, he was landing heavily on the long table, staring back up at a spinning ceiling as he squirmed in pain.

The man leaned over Byron and mouthed a few words, but frowning, he seemed to realize that he wasn't being heard. He placed his hands on Byron's ears, and an overwhelming pain flooded through Byron's head, and he let loose with an agonizing cry that sounded like it was being smothered.

Byron's eardrums popped, and he heard himself shrieking.

Finally, the man released his head, and Byron let himself fall back to the table again, whimpering in pain.

"You know, you really shouldn't have given us advanced weapons if we can use them against you now. Good thing I thought to secure one for myself." Byron jerked the Lucifer pistol from its sheath and fired a beam of light toward his attacker.

The Director held out a hand, and the light hung in the air, buzzing angrily and twitching just inches away from the Director's hand.

"I would not be foolish enough to compromise myself in such a way, Byron. These weapons are only effective against Lucifer. They only make me stronger." The light spread over the Director's body in a large bubble, and as soon as a thin layer of light fully encompassed him, it closed over him and seeped into his body. "Funny. It's almost like I planned it that way."

"Just kill me," Byron said, shaking his head and dropping the pistol to the ground. "You have what you want. Why did you even come back here?"

"Because as long as you are alive, you stand between Lucifer and her destiny. She cannot ascend to her true purpose with you standing in the way."

Byron laughed painfully. "Why would I do such a thing? I've backed this project since its inception. I want her in the machine almost as much as you do, maybe more."

The Director smiled. "You know nothing, Byron. This is why destiny cannot be understood with small men with small minds. You cannot comprehend a greater purpose. And if you knew, you would stop at nothing to keep it from coming to pass. You see, I embrace destiny. I facilitate it. And I won't let you or anyone else stand in the way of it."

"So you're killing us? You have the Key. That was the only way we could have stopped you, which we wouldn't have done anyway." Byron held his hands out in front of him. "You don't need to do this."

"No, I must."

The Director grabbed Byron's lapels, and a second later, Byron was flying out above New Washington, soaring through the air helplessly.

He looked down at the city he had fought so hard for. Every hard decision, every harsh decree, everything he had done was all for this world.

And now it was in the hands of a madman.

Byron sighed and closed his eyes as his body fell and broke against the ground.

# PART IV

RECOVERY

## 37

## THREE DAYS LATER

Aniya phased in and out of consciousness.

All she saw was black. The only way she could determine what was the waking world was the noise around her.

The grinding of metal.

Crackling flames.

Muffled screams.

When the sounds died away again, Aniya knew she was unconscious, or at least so deep in her own mind that she may as well be knocked out cold in the real world.

She found herself unable to move in both realities, trapped and pinned down by an invisible force.

"Roland?" Aniya shouted, though it came out strained, weak.

Her voice only disappeared into the void without so much as an echo.

"William?" She tried again, but there was no response to this either.

Aniya grunted and pushed against the weight that bore down on her chest, but it was too much. Whatever clamped down on her body refused to budge.

She soon gave up, resigning herself to lie there helplessly until someone found her.

It may have been hours later or seconds, but the next thing Aniya remembered was just that.

"I found her!" A muffled cry came from somewhere in the distance, followed by something tugging on her hand.

And then, finally, the weight was gone, and she was free.

Aniya tried to sit up, but her strength was completely gone. Even with the obstacle removed, she found herself completely unable to move.

She blinked rapidly, trying to clear the black, but the darkness remained. Aniya was beginning to wonder if she had been trapped in the void this entire time.

Just as she started to panic, a tiny, orange light appeared in the distance and slowly crept toward Aniya. It settled in place a few feet away from her, a small flame that barely lit up her surroundings.

She was lying among piles of smoldering rubble. The remains of the devastated Hub.

Few buildings seemed to be left standing. She could see the barracks in the distance, lit only by the fluorescent lights coming from inside. It was a wonder that they still had power.

Aniya looked straight up at what used to be the Citadel. The only thing left was the apparently indestructible elevator shaft, disappearing into the shadows above.

More details started to fill in the darkness, and she looked around her as rows of bodies began to materialize around her. From what Aniya could see without moving, there were at least six people near her, all of them lying motionless on the ground.

The morbid sight was enough to get Aniya moving again, and with great effort, she turned her head to face the other direction.

But even as she turned, she made eye contact with a young boy lying on his back, his head twisted toward her, staring back at her with dark eyes. A pool of blood formed under his chest, a ponding syrup that eventually reached Aniya's body and soaked the back of her shirt.

She let her eyes drift close again, and when they opened, she was alone again. She was still in the burning remains of the Hub, but the people were gone.

"I told you this would happen."

Aniya groaned as the Chancellor stepped out of the shadows, looking around at the destruction. She turned to look him in the eye, and she suddenly realized that she was standing.

"The man is heartless. Metaphorically and, of course, physically. He could never understand your pain, no matter what he says." He looked at her with a genuine, pitiful expression. "The task he asks of you will kill you, and he is willing to kill thousands in order to get you to agree. And using Nicholas against you? Brilliant, but cruel."

Aniya bit her lip. "I should have listened to you. You were right. I wasn't strong enough. I never was. If killing what's left of Nicholas is the only way to stop him, I don't think I can do it."

With a sigh, she let her head fall back on the ground as she stared up at the darkness. "Maybe I was right not to love him all those years ago. Was it really worth it? What good is love if it ends like this?"

"That's why you're strong, Aniya."

She turned to her right, where William sat, smiling at her and holding her hand.

"The Director used and abused your love for others, but it's what makes you strong. It's what's kept you going all this time. It's why you stepped in the machine back home three years ago."

Aniya shook her head. "Love makes me predictable. He knew I wouldn't kill him, and look what he did. Who knows what else he'll do if I don't stop him?"

William fell silent.

"Maybe love isn't the answer," the Chancellor said to her left. "I've said all along that your emotions bring out the best of your power, but your love in this case is quite the hindrance."

"I can't just stop loving him."

"I'm not asking you to. But surely your love for Nicholas is rivaled by, perhaps surpassed by your hatred for the Director? He's killed so many in an obsessive attempt to tear you down, make you moldable, usable. Aren't you tired of being manipulated?"

William scoffed. "You would suggest that. When she gets upset, she can't control herself. Is it worth risking killing countless others unintentionally just to get revenge on the Director? She'd be no better than him."

"He would be gone." The Chancellor shrugged. "Is that not what she wants? She won't find the strength to kill him unless she lets go of her sweet Nicky. And the mere fact that she's talking to us right now proves that she would rather spend time talking to dead people than face the horrors that await her in the real world. She's still holding on to you, William, and I would argue that as long as she retreats to the corners of her mind to find solace in her brother's arms, she will never have control over her powers. And since we both know that she will never let go of Nicholas or you, I maintain that the only logical way to proceed would be to embrace the hatred for the one who has taken everything away from her. Do you have any other suggestions?"

William again did not answer.

"That's what I thought." The Chancellor moved so that

he was directly in front of Aniya. "Well, Annelise? You know what you have to do. Will you still devote yourself to the noble road that will lead to your self-destruction?"

But Aniya wasn't listening anymore. She looked past the Chancellor's head and stared into the shadows as they began to give way to a hidden source of light.

The darkness peeled away to reveal the smoldering ruins of the Hub, littered with smokestacks, pieces of the sky ceiling, and thousands of bodies, all cast in an ominous, green light.

Aniya looked back at the Chancellor to respond, but he was gone. A quick glance to her side revealed that William had disappeared as well.

"He's right, you know."

A chill ran down Aniya's spine as a dark voice spoke.

She turned to face a being shrouded in darkness, hovering slightly off the ground in front of her.

"He's not real, you know," Aniya retorted. "He's a manifestation of my emotions, so really you're saying I'm right. Now that we have that cleared up, what are you? Isn't it about time you told me?"

"You already know," the Shadow said, and somehow Aniya knew it was smiling. "Why else do you fear me so? You know what I represent. You know what awaits you at the end of your journey."

Aniya stared down the dark figure. "You know, I'm getting really tired of people acting like they own me, like they control my fate."

"My dear, no one decides your fate but you."

"Is that so? Because you make it sound like this only ends one way."

The Shadow started slowly circling her. "Does it not? You know what you must do, though lack the will to do it. But you know that when the time comes, you will do what you must."

"If what I must do is save Nicholas, you're absolutely

right." Aniya refused to turn in a circle to maintain line of sight with the being. Instead, she stood in place and folded her arms. "There is a way to save him and destroy the Director."

"Enlighten me," the Shadow whispered in her ear.

Aniya shrugged. "Zeta killed Omega with a syringe and gave his body to the Director. I can do the same thing."

"Suppose you were able to get within arm's length of him, which we both know is quite the task, what makes you think you could bring yourself to end his life with no promise of saving Nicholas's? You do not even know that it is possible."

"Of course it is."

"Oh yes? Then tell me, where is his soul?"

Aniya finally turned to face the Shadow. "Where it always has been. He's somewhere in there, I know it. I've felt it."

"Ah yes, you've felt him."

Aniya could feel its smirk.

"Because your feelings have proved to be quite the reliable source of information," it said as it continued circling her. "I assure you, child. Nicholas is dead. There is no trace of who he once was in what is left of his body."

"How would you even know?"

"I know."

Aniya spun around again and thrust her fists down at her side. "What's with the attitude all of a sudden? I thought you were here to comfort me. Whatever happened to 'I'll stay with you, Lightbringer'?"

"Child, I am not your comforter," the Shadow's voice grew stern as it stopped in place. "I am your guide. When the time comes for comfort, I will give you comfort. Right now, you need to understand your reality before you kill yourself and others chasing a dream."

Aniya pressed her hands against her head and backed away. "I can't do this right now. I don't need another person telling me that I can't save Nicholas. I can, and I will."

"Listen to me, Lightbringer. Do not be fooled. You cannot let this childish obsession keep you from—"

Squeezing her eyes shut as hard as she could, Aniya let out a piercing scream, blocking out the Shadow's words and shattering the surrounding void.

Her eyes flew open, and she was back in the field of debris, surrounded by bodies.

"Are you okay?"

Aniya turned to see Corrin appearing from out of the shadows, dropping by her side and cradling her head.

Rather than respond, Aniya looked past him at the ruins of the Hub, the death that surrounded her, and in that moment it finally sank in that it truly was all her fault.

Thrusting her head into his chest, she burst into tears.

## 38

Aniya moaned as she opened her eyes. She realized as she looked around that she was on a cot in the barracks.

"What happened?" she asked as she propped herself up, pressing a hand to her forehead. A sharp pain responded to her touch, and she moaned again, letting herself fall back to the cot.

"You lost consciousness," Corrin's voice came from behind her as his hand gently fell on her shoulder. "We're not sure why."

Aniya forced open her eyes again and craned her neck to look at him. "Where's Dawn? Shouldn't she be here? What did she say?"

"She's treated the most serious injuries, and her team is taking care of the rest." Corrin's expression darkened. "She's with Roland. Burying Tamisra."

"So she's . . ."

He placed his other hand on her shoulder and bowed his head.

"It's not your fault, Aniya."

Aniya turned to see Caspian approach her bedside.

"Clearly you weren't watching," she said bitterly. "A lot of this could have been avoided if I had stopped the Director."

Caspian shrugged. "You're powerful, but you can't be in two places at once. The way I see it, you were busy with a more pressing issue. It was either stop the Director or stop Zeta. Unfortunately, you chose neither."

His cold tone was enough to make the hair on Aniya's neck stand up straight.

"I get it," she said. "Trust me. How are you even still alive? The Citadel was destroyed."

"As soon as I realized the extent of our potential losses, I left the Citadel. With the Hub in chaos, and since you took out your earpiece, there was no one to command anyway. I decided to come down here and do what I could. Unfortunately, it was too late."

Aniya dropped her gaze from his eyes and muttered, "How bad is it?"

"Bad," Corrin said as he moved to her side. "Thousands are dead, and hundreds more are still missing, including Salvador and Lionel."

"I'll say it again," Caspian said as his tone softened. "This wasn't your fault."

"Of course it's my fault," Aniya spat. "If I had gone with him when he first asked, your assassins would still be alive. We wouldn't have lost so many of our own. Malcolm and Tamisra would still——"

"Do you really think the Director would have spared them all if you had complied instantly? He will continue to execute thousands as long as there is an army still standing that would oppose him." Caspian sat at her feet, looking at the rest of the clinic. "If you were truly unable to kill him, you did the next best thing. I know it doesn't seem like it, but you had no other choice."

Aniya didn't even acknowledge this.

"If you had given yourself over to the Director, it would all be over. He would have you, and all those who gave their lives, if they had managed to live out the night, would have died under his cruel hand eventually."

"If that's true," Aniya said, shaking her head, "why do I feel so terrible?"

"It's war, Aniya." Caspian stood and paced back and forth. "People die. If you feel good about the losses we suffer, something's wrong with you. You made a hard choice, but it was the right one. The only thing that would have been better was if you had managed to destroy the Director's host body. It's too much power for someone who already holds a frightening amount."

"You know I can't do that, Caspian."

"You'll have to."

"I saw him again." Aniya finally looked back up at him, fighting back tears. "Nicholas is still somewhere in there. He's alive."

Caspian shook his head. "That's impossible. I'm sorry, Aniya, but he's dead."

"I'm telling you, I saw him. He spoke to me."

"Again, Aniya? I assure you, it's nothing more than a lingering memory of the man he once was. Even if he's still alive somewhere, nothing changes. As long as the Director has control over his body, he is unstoppable."

Aniya moaned, holding her hands to her face to hide her falling tears.

"You have to kill him if we're to have any chance of winning this war."

"Don't ask me to do it," she whispered. "I can't."

"You must," Caspian said. "You're the only one who can."

Aniya shrugged away his hand. "Even if I wanted to, I can't. You have to believe me. After he killed Tamisra, I wanted nothing more than to snap his head off. But when

290 | DAVID WEBB

the time came, all I saw was Nicholas, and I couldn't do it. My love for him kept me from destroying his body, even though the Director is in it."

"It's not your love for him, Aniya. Your love is a great force, a powerful motivator and a source of your greatest strength. But you are held back by your fear, your guilt, your hatred. This is what has taken your light and holds it hostage, denying you control over a terrifying yet beautiful power."

"But I don't hate him anymore," Aniya said. "I used to, and you helped me deal with that, but I don't anymore. I love him."

"Yes, you do. But you are afraid to lose him, and it is that fear that grips you now, holding you back and refusing to relinquish your power. You have to let go of those you have already lost. Accept the past and change your future while you still can."

Aniya pulled her knees up to her chest and wrapped her arms around her legs. "But I can still save him."

"You can't, Aniya." Caspian sighed. "You just can't. How many more people have to die until you realize this?"

"Caspian," Corrin snapped. "That's enough. You've made your point. There's nothing we can do right now even if we wanted to. Aniya needs to rest."

"We don't have time. The Director could come down here at any moment and—"

"Please," Aniya pleaded. "Just give me space."

Caspian looked between Aniya and Corrin for a moment before spinning on his heel and marching off.

Corrin stood to leave, but Aniya grabbed his wrist.

"You can stay."

He smiled and grabbed a chair, sitting by her side.

"I'm sorry," she said before he had a chance to speak. "Malcolm didn't deserve what happened to him. I want you to know that even after everything he did, he was a good man."

Corrin's smile faltered slightly, but remained. He opened his mouth to speak, but no words came out. He coughed and nodded as his eyes grew wet.

"First Xander, now Malcolm." Aniya looked to the other side of her cot to avoid looking him in the eye as tears of her own started to form. "Your family is gone now, and both times were my fault."

His warm, gentle hand pressed up against her cheek and turned her back toward him.

"Stop telling yourself that, Annelise," he said softly, yet shakily. "You know neither of them would blame you for their deaths."

"Doesn't mean it's not true."

"It isn't," Corrin said matter-of-factly. "Now, get some rest. I'm sure Caspian's right that the Director won't wait too long before making another move. You need to be ready to stop him."

"I can't kill him," Aniya whispered. "Not while there's still a chance to save Nicholas."

Corrin took her hand. "I understand."

She looked away again. "Corrin, what's wrong with me?"

"There doesn't appear to be anything wrong with you physically. It looks like you healed yourself before we found you. Caspian thinks it's psychological, a result of the trauma of battle. He says it's probably inhibiting your powers and even the natural strength of your body."

"Not this," Aniya said, raising her arms as she glanced at her cot. "Why . . ."

She searched for words for several seconds before giving up and releasing his hand.

"I'm sorry," she said again quietly. "This isn't your problem."

Corrin looked like he wanted to say something, but he just smiled and stood.

"I'll be ready when you want to talk, Aniya."

Aniya nodded. "Thank you."

But as he walked away, Aniya sighed because she knew this was her fight alone.

After all, if things kept going like this, soon there wouldn't be anyone left to help her anyway.

## 39

R oland looked down at the freshly dug grave, unable to take his eyes off the girl that lay at the bottom. He had always thought of her as an angry child, but the look on her face was anything but. She had somehow died with the most peaceful expression, her serene visage now frozen forever.

But staring at Tamisra's cold face didn't bring Roland any peace. Not when all this could have been avoided.

"Are you okay?"

Roland snapped his head up at Dawn but bit his tongue. His instinctual answer would only make things worse.

"No," was all he could manage to say without giving away the raw fury that ate away at his heart.

Dawn placed a hand on his shoulder. Roland flinched but let her hand stay.

"I know she was special to you."

Roland grimaced. "She was just another person that died because I failed to do what I needed to do. Nothing new here."

"There's nothing you could have done, Roland."

He didn't say anything.

Dawn looked around. "Where's Salvador? I thought he'd want to be here."

"No one's seen him since the battle." Roland shrugged. "He's probably dead, too."

"Please don't say that," she said, whispering. "Lionel's missing, too. I want to believe he's still out there."

He shrugged. "Does it even matter anymore?"

"Roland, stop." Dawn took her hand off his shoulder. "Refuge needs you to step up, now more than ever. You think they'll follow you as long as you act like this?"

Roland shot an annoyed glance at her. "You forget that this is the second battle I've talked them into that's ended in disaster. You really think they'll follow someone like that? And what good is a leader if everyone following him is dead? If he has to watch his family slaughtered as he stands there, helpless? Refuge doesn't need a leader, Dawn. It needs fighters to keep what's left of us alive." He grabbed her arms. "Can you really stand there and tell me otherwise? After the carnage you saw?"

Dawn winced as his grip tightened, and she looked at him with wide eyes.

Sighing, Roland released her and turned back toward the grave. "I need to bury her. You should go back and help in the barracks."

After a few seconds, he heard her walk away.

Roland stared at Tamisra's face for a while before he could bring himself to speak. "Well, I hope you're happy, Tami. You told me that I didn't need to be stronger. That it's not what you wanted." A tear slipped off Roland's jaw and fell into the grave, splashing over Tamisra's clasped hands. "But you would still be alive if I was. So would Malcolm. So would Gareth."

He bent over and picked up a handful of soil, holding it over the open grave with his trembling right hand. "I could have stopped all of this. We could have won. It could all be over now." Dirt slipped from his fingers as he clenched his fist. "You'd still be here with us. With—"

A sob finally broke through his pursed lips, and as he fell to his knees, his hand slipped open and dirt showered down into the grave and over Tamisra's cold body.

His tears flowing freely now, Roland let himself fall backward on the pile of dirt as his chest heaved, sobbing carelessly as he looked up at the jagged and broken sky ceiling.

He lay there for what seemed like hours, until he ran out of tears.

When he got back up again, his mind was made up. There was no longer any question of what to do.

Roland grabbed the shovel and poured the dirt on top of Tamisra, filling the grave in minutes. When he was done, he packed the dirt down tightly and tossed the shovel aside.

"I won't fail you again, Tami. The next time I visit you, I will have done what needs to be done."

With that, he turned and walked back to the city, not knowing then that he wouldn't get another chance to return to her grave.

## 40

Z eta let out a yelp of pain as the smell of burnt flesh pervaded her senses.

"Oh, shut up."

The assassin glared at the Director but gritted her teeth as he continued cauterizing her wound.

"Easy for you to say," Zeta grumbled. "It's not like you can feel pain."

"Yes, but I would expect more out of an operative. Surely Caspian taught you to withstand torture? I suppose I should be grateful that you didn't give your true mission away when the Council had you."

Zeta scoffed, but her indignation was replaced by another wince of pain as the Director seared her severed tissue again.

"Why does it hurt so much now? It's numbed up, right? Why didn't I feel it in battle when it happened?"

"Adrenaline, Zeta. It's more powerful than most anesthetics. Really, have you forgotten your training entirely? Perhaps I should have picked Delta after all."

"I thought you didn't make mistakes," Zeta said, risking a sneer.

"I don't. But it is not a waste of effort to remind people that they are replaceable."

"Not anymore."

"You are partially correct," the Director said with a sigh. "You are U1's last operative, and after I'm done with you today, you will be one of my more valuable assets. But you are indeed still replaceable."

Zeta hissed again as a sharp pain overcame the numbness and raced up her half-arm, but it was drowned out by one last sizzle that finished sealing her wound.

The Director smirked. "Is that better?"

Wincing, Zeta moved her arm around a little. "I mean, it's not exactly comfortable."

"You'll get over it." The Director turned and grabbed the metal prosthesis from the table. "There are morphine and endorphin delivery systems in the chassis of your new appendage, so that should help you cope with the apparently intolerable inconvenience."

Without warning, the Director firmly pushed the prosthesis over her severed joint, and almost instantly, Zeta's mind began floating in a wave of dizziness that was somehow pleasant, calming.

She was brought back to reality by another searing pain that began ripping at her arm.

With a cry, she looked down to see the Director holding a device to her arm, a flame coming from its tip and burning metal braces into her skin and the prosthesis, securing it to her body.

His annoyed glare was enough to silence Zeta, and she closed her mouth and bit her lip to keep herself from another admonishment.

Soon, he was done, and he set down his device on the table.

"There you are," he said, almost proudly. "You now carry the most expensive resource in my control. Try not to lose it."

Zeta looked down at her arm, and as she pictured herself doing it, her fingers flexed and formed into a fist.

"How?" she asked, impressed. Every minute movement she could think of, the robotic prosthesis performed with ease.

"It's connected to your neural network using nanotechnology."

Zeta looked up at the Director. "Nanotech? When did you come up with that? Even before the Collapse, we never got that far."

"I had help," he said, looking away as he began cleaning his tools. "Even I have my limitations."

"Clearly," Zeta mumbled. When the Director raised an eyebrow and looked in her direction, she held up her hands, noticing briefly that her new arm carried no more weight than her old one. "Don't look at me, Boss. I'm pretty sure it'd be a whole lot easier to just do all this yourself instead of tricking other people into carrying out your oh-so grand plan."

The Director smiled. "I'll forgive your short-sightedness. My primary directive is to protect humanity. Sometimes the necessary means can be bloody, but as long as the result is a peaceful, self-sustaining world, I'm willing to do what I must. But if I were to override the wills of those under my care, what kind of protector would I be? I would be a tyrant."

Zeta shrugged. "I guess."

"Why do you care so much?"

"I really don't," she said with another shrug. "I'm just curious. It's not really my place to understand you. Just obey."

The Director gave a short nod. "Caspian taught you well. Let's just hope he trained you well enough that you may bear this weapon with maximum efficiency."

Zeta frowned and looked again at her arm. "What exactly did you do to me?"

"See for yourself." The Director took the metal tray that had held his tools and tossed it in the air. "Shoot it."

Almost without thinking, Zeta snapped her arm up and

reached toward the tray, and as she did a beam of white light shot from her palm and incinerated the tray.

She turned to the Director, her mouth dropping open.

"It's time we leveled the playing field, don't you think? Thanks to her boyfriend's body, I can easily defend our mission against Lucifer. But now you stand a chance as well."

Zeta gulped. "You're sending me back out there? Against her?"

"It's necessary, Zeta. You will play a vital role in the reckoning that is to come, and it is an honor to be chosen for such a duty." The Director approached her and curled his forefinger under her chin, lifting it so that she looked him in the eye. "But fear not. I have not given you such a weapon only for you to go out and sacrifice yourself. No, you still have more lives to take. You will help me teach them suffering. You will bring them to their knees."

Zeta's heart raced as the Director stared in her eyes with a burning intensity.

"Are you willing, child, to do your part in the Great Ascension?"

Her mouth twisted into a smile as she nodded.

"When I get through with them, they will know the meaning of pain."

## 41

"Fifteen hundred dead. Another two hundred missing, presumed dead given that it's been a week. Just over three thousand left alive. Minus the eleven hundred children and their mothers, we're left with about two thousand semi-trained fighters. And that's just Refuge."

Aniya bowed her head, Corrin's report crushing her spirit. She looked around at the others gathered by her bedside in the barracks, each one of them seemingly just as upset as she was.

Roland sat next to her, his hand clutching hers. Corrin sat staring into the ground next to him. Caspian paced nearby, his arms folded as he looked at the ground.

"As for my forces, the Silver Guard has been halved from five thousand to twenty-five hundred, and all six hundred of my operatives are dead," Caspian said. He tossed a device on a tray by Aniya's bedside.

She recognized it as the tool Zeta had used to instantly wipe out Caspian's assassins.

"I don't know when," Caspian continued, "but at some point, Zeta figured out what my implants were capable of. Someone made this device to transmit thousands of signals to each individual chip, overloading it and causing it to short out the brain."

Roland picked up the device and looked it over. "Why didn't it affect her, then?"

"She must have changed the frequency of her chip. That would also explain why the beacon I sent out three years ago didn't revert her loyalties to me."

Corrin frowned. "How did she know to come back to you, then?"

"I don't know," Caspian said. "And now that I know she's on a different frequency, I would attempt to reset her and call her back again using one frequency at a time, but I relocated my equipment to the Citadel. It's buried under tons of metal and concrete now."

"So we use this device against her if we find her frequency?" Roland asked.

"Theoretically, yes. But you'd have to get within a half-mile of her and test each one of them individually. And I doubt she'd let you live long enough to do it. Even if you could find her new frequency, I'm sure she'll have had surgery by now to improve the integrity of the chip. Using the device on her now, I predict, would only impair her, not kill her."

"Why not just remove the chip?" Aniya asked.

"It's not that simple. If her chip were to be removed, she would be useless. I made it so that it interfaces with and replaces the natural connection between the two cerebral hemispheres. Without the chip, the cerebrum would cease to function correctly."

Roland held up a hand. "What does that mean, though?"

"She would be a breathing mass of flesh and bone that has no identity, no consciousness. Once I've made that modification, the chip has to be present." Caspian turned toward Aniya. "I used a similar process with Nicholas. It's the same chip, a stronger one. One that holds his new identity. Or at least it did. That chip now holds the Director's source code, you might say, if I understand what he actually is." He held up his hand, displaying a device strapped to his wrist. "I used a separate computer to monitor him and a separate frequency for his chip and as far as I know, he hasn't changed it. From everything I've seen, he's integrated fully into Omega's body with no signs of rejection from the host mind."

Corrin rubbed his chin. "And you're telling me you had no idea what he was this entire time? A computer?"

"I didn't," Caspian said. "I don't think anyone knew. This entire situation was completely unprecedented. The only way we could have won was if we had the Vagabond's army. Too bad they were never really his."

Roland shook his head. "Why would he even trust Zeta? After everything she's done, Malcolm trusted her to help him round up an army that she would just use against him?"

"She made a convincing case," Aniya said. "I think we all fell for it."

"Then we're fools," Roland said, shrugging. "Pretty simple to me."

Corrin smiled weakly and clapped his hand on Roland's back gently. "Not fools, my boy. We needed all the help we could get, and at the time, we had rather conclusive evidence that she had joined our side. She killed the Director, or so it seemed. I don't know how much more we could have asked for."

"It doesn't matter anymore," Caspian said. "We made a mistake. A costly one, yes, but dwelling on it is a waste of time. We need to focus on what we can do about it now."

"What we can do about it?" Corrin looked up, squinting at Caspian. "All together, there were nearly seven thousand of us, and that was after Malcolm's army betrayed us. We outnumbered him, and we were wiped out in minutes. And since he now commands Earth's only army, he definitely outnumbers us now, to the point where numbers don't mean anything to him anymore. He brought down the sky ceiling on his own men, not caring who he killed. His men are disposable. And now that he has Nicholas's body, we can't get within a mile of him without putting ourselves at great risk."

"I know. We cannot fight him directly. Only Aniya can do that."

"You really think so?" Aniya grimaced and looked around the barracks, which was still filled with injured soldiers, spread out among the remains of the roof and the sky ceiling. "You saw what happened the last time I tried to do that."

"Yes, I saw," Caspian said. "I watched you come *this* close to defeating him. All you had to do was finish him off."

Aniya scoffed. "You make it sound so easy. I hate to break it to you, but I don't think I can do it."

"I know," Caspian said, sighing. "In your current state, I believe if you fought him again, the results would be disastrous, even worse than what happened last time. You are not ready to face him again, but you will be when I'm done with you."

"Done with me? What, are you going to put me through therapy again? Because that worked so well the last time."

Caspian shrugged. "It's a mental block, Aniya. Your emotions are holding you back, but I believe that your mind is strong enough to overcome your animal instincts. With training, of course. You see what happens when you fail to do what is necessary. I trust that given the opportunity, you will not fail again."

"Lay off," Roland said, ignoring a glare from Corrin. "If it was Dawn's body the Director had, I don't think I could pull the trigger and kill her. You're asking her to murder someone she loves."

"Nicholas is dead," Caspian said firmly. "His body is the only thing that's left, and I've made it clear that that's all it will ever be. I can't save him, now more than ever. Please tell me you understand, Aniya."

Aniya nodded weakly.

"Then maybe we have a chance at surviving." Caspian straightened and turned toward Corrin. "We can't survive another attack like this one, and until the Director is dead, we can't go to meet them in battle. We must fortify our borders and wait the storm out. I will work with Aniya, and when she does what she must, then we can proceed."

Corrin frowned. "Are you sure about this? Maybe Salvador was right. Maybe fighting isn't the answer. Have you considered retreating to Level II? Really any other level below us? At the very least, it will give us time to recover."

"It would buy us hours at best. No, we need to stand our ground here, or they'll simply chase us down until we've reached the end of the Underworld."

Roland looked up. "Would that be so bad? You know what's waiting in Level XIX. Maybe the Host would be enough to tip the scales."

Caspian shook his head. "Neeshika is not willing to join us for fear of losing her children. I don't think telling her of our overwhelming defeat would help. Besides, she's convinced that we can still win."

"What gave her that impression?" Corrin gave a short laugh.

"She wouldn't say, but she seems to know more than she lets on," Caspian said. "I trust her. I believe we can still win this war."

Roland took a deep breath. "She'd better be right. The next time we fight him, either we destroy him, or he destroys what's left of us."

"But without reinforcements, there's nothing we can do," Corrin said.

Caspian looked at Aniya. "That is indeed true for all of us but one."

Aniya buried her face in her hands. She knew everyone

was looking at her. She knew what she had to do. And yet, she couldn't picture herself doing it.

"Good evening, Lucifer."

Nicholas's voice chilled Aniya to the bone, and her eyes flew open as her skin crawled.

"Go away," she murmured.

It was bad enough that she still heard the Chancellor's voice somewhere deep inside her mind. She didn't need to hear the Director's as well.

"I had hoped you would come to me by now, but you force me to take drastic measures."

His voice refused to die down. Instead, it was louder now. It also didn't seem to echo in her head like the Chancellor's voice. Rather, it was more tinny, a thin voice that seemed to crackle.

And underneath it all, there was a faint, sharp sound that was beginning to rise. It sounded like . . . screams?

She pulled her hands away from her face. Everyone in the barracks was looking up at the sky ceiling. Aniya followed their gaze and found herself staring at the Director.

Nicholas's broken face was broadcast on what remained of the sky ceiling. Large pieces of his image were missing, including his left eye, but the figure was unmistakable.

Screams echoed throughout the Hub at the sight of the Director. No doubt what remained of Refuge dreaded the possibility of the Director returning to finish them off.

"What's going on?"

Aniya turned to see Dawn stumbling toward the group, tripping over debris while staring up at the ceiling. She ran to Roland's side, who wrapped an arm around her but did not take his eyes off the Director.

"All you had to do was come with me. That was all you had to do to save your friends." The Director's image blinked and fizzled as he shook his head sadly. "What a waste."

The screams wouldn't stop, and they now rivaled the Director's volume. Aniya turned to Caspian.

"Turn it off."

Caspian slowly shook his head. "The only controls we have access to were in the Citadel. They're buried."

Aniya's heart sank as she turned back to the Director.

"It's time I show you what lengths I will go to in order to ensure the safety of this world."

She clenched her fists, shouting, "Haven't you done enough?"

But he didn't seem to hear her, or if he did, it was unlikely he cared.

"No doubt you have been unable to find your famed warrior. Salvador the Scourge, a fitting title indeed. Do you know what it means to scourge, Lucifer? You will soon find out."

Aniya's eyes widened as she realized where the Director was going with this.

"Your fearless leader has proven to me to be anything but. I have seen his fear, Lucifer." The Director's face grew solemn. "And if it's what it takes to persuade you, I will make you feel his fear. If you do not surrender yourself to me, I will make you watch as I kill Salvador."

Aniya's blood boiled as the screams grew louder.

"You know I will, Lucifer. By now, I hope I have shown you that I am a man of my word. And if you still do not come to me? I'll come down there and take someone else and return to you a rather unpleasant surprise. I'll do whatever it takes. You have one day."

The sky ceiling went dark, and the remaining screams slowly died away, receding to a panicked murmur that echoed throughout the remains of the Hub.

Aniya looked at Roland, her bottom lip trembling.

"I don't know what to do."

"We don't even know if it's true," Roland said, placing a

hand on her shoulder. "For all we know, Salvador is still down here somewhere. He could have died in the collapse."

Aniya shook her head. "The Director is insane, but I don't think he'd lie about this."

"Even if he is alive," Caspian said, his voice quiet but firm, "do you really think it's worth giving yourself up to save one life?"

Roland shook his head. "This is Salvador we're talking about. We had our disagreements, but he was a good man. Surely there's some way we can save him without getting Aniya captured as well."

"And this is all assuming the Director is telling the truth," Corrin said, holding up a finger. "We have no way of knowing whether or not he actually has Salvador."

As if to answer this, the sky ceiling suddenly blinked on again for the Director to say exactly one word.

"Catch!"

The remains of the sky ceiling froze, and Nicholas's sneering face lingered just long enough to shed light on something falling from a hole in the very middle of the broken ceiling.

Aniya squinted at the falling object but quickly realized it was a person.

As she realized that whoever it was could still be alive, supernatural energy flooded her body. She had let down thousands, but here was someone she could still save.

She jumped out of her cot, stepping on to the floor for the first time in a week. Thankfully, supernatural energy instantly flooded her body, and as she raced outside, Dawn let out a piercing scream.

Aniya burst through the doors to the barracks and thrust her hands in the air as a stream of golden light shot from her palms, racing through the air and wrapping around the fallen body, gently escorting it to the ground several feet away.

Roland raced past her, and Aniya ran to catch up as a crowd began to gather around the glowing body.

She pushed past the quickly growing cloud, but someone else shoved her out of the way in a mad dash toward the body.

Finally, Aniya made her way to the small clearing, and with a frustrated wave of her hand, the light instantly vanished.

Dawn fell to her knees by the body's side and tearfully began examining it.

It was Lionel.

"Is he alive?" Corrin's voice came from behind Aniya as he gently nudged past her.

Dawn kept examining him for a few seconds, but finally she looked up. With a trembling voice, she replied, "Barely."

Aniya knelt next to Dawn and looked up and down Lionel's body. "What happened to him?"

"I don't know. I think you healed him on the way down." Dawn finally let go of her brother's body and wrapped Aniya in a tight hug. "Thank you."

Roland sat down across Lionel's body and frowned. "I don't get it. Why would the Director let him go? Doesn't he need leverage to convince you?"

"He doesn't need leverage," Caspian said, appearing in the clearing next to them. "He's taunting us. This is a play on Aniya's emotions, a further attempt to break her will."

Aniya gently pulled away from Dawn and looked up at Caspian. "It's working. I don't know how much more of this I can take. What if he really has Salvador? He'll kill him in front of everyone down here, and . . ."

Her voice trailed off as she looked around at the hundreds of people surrounding her. She hung her head as she spoke aloud what they were all surely thinking.

"And they'll all know it's my fault."

Corrin held up a finger. "We still don't know that they—"

"What's this?"

Aniya looked back at Roland, who was grabbing at a string around Lionel's neck.

He pulled, revealing a moving lump under the boy's shirt. With a tug, the object came free, popping out in full view of everyone.

At the end of the morbid necklace was a severed, four-fingered hand.

## 42

With an apologetic look at the hundreds of people gathered in the barracks, trying to get a good look at Lionel, Aniya closed the curtains that separated the rest of the barracks from the secluded corner where only a few people gathered.

"So you didn't see anything?" Caspian was asking, hovering over Lionel's bedside. "You don't know where they were keeping you?"

Corrin gently pulled Caspian away so that he wasn't standing directly over the boy who had been conscious for all of five minutes.

"No," Lionel said shakily. "It was dark. So dark. The last thing I remember is being in there . . . with Zeta."

Aniya approached Lionel's bedside and placed a hand on the boy's arm. "What did they do to you?"

He looked at her with wide eyes, his lips trembling. Finally, he simply shook his head and looked down at his lap.

Dawn appeared at her brother's other side, shining a penlight around Lionel's head. "I haven't found anything. I guess you really did heal whatever they did to him."

"You didn't see Salvador?" Roland asked slowly. "You weren't kept together?"

Lionel kept shaking his head. "I was alone. I didn't even know they had taken Salvador until I woke up and you had his hand."

"This is pointless," Caspian said with a sigh.

Roland glared at Caspian before turning back to Lionel. "We're glad you're back. We were beginning to think you were dead."

"You were," Dawn scoffed. "Some of us didn't lose hope."

"You can't really blame us for it."

"Enough," Caspian said. "We need to decide what this means for us."

Roland shrugged. "What else? We know now that the Director has Salvador."

"And he's going to die if we don't do anything about it," Lionel added.

Corrin cocked an eyebrow. "There's only one way I see that happening. Are you suggesting Aniya give herself up?"

"Of course not. But we can't do nothing."

"That's exactly what we must do," Caspian said. "Nothing. If we send anyone up there, we risk losing them, too. This way, one man dies but we all live to fight another day. And we need as many men as we can spare if we hope to defeat the Lightbringers."

"He's won, Caspian." Dawn's voice was a mere whisper. "It's over."

"Not until he has Aniya," Caspian said. "Which is why she has to stay down here until she's ready. If she fights him now, she will lose, and the Director wins. If she willingly gives herself up to save Salvador, then yes, Salvador may live, but the Director wins again. Either way, he'll have Aniya and the power he needs to enslave humanity forever. Either way, millions more will forever be under his thumb."

Corrin cleared his throat. "Maybe we should ask Aniya what she wants to do."

"Those aren't the only options, Caspian," Roland said, apparently ignoring Corrin. "Aniya doesn't have to fight the Director yet if she's not ready. All she has to do is save Salvador."

"I doubt the Director would let her just walk away with him," Caspian said. "He will trap her, and he will take her. No, Aniya knows what she has to do."

"No, I don't!" Aniya finally spoke, breathing heavily now as she thrust her fists downward, yellow light flashing and sizzling two twin holes in the ground at either side. "Stop saying that. You have no idea how hard it is to see straight right now. You say I need to kill him, but I can't do that until I make myself okay with destroying the last chance I have of saving Nicholas. Salvador is the closest thing to a father I have left, and letting him die is unthinkable. At least if I give myself up, I'd be used in a way that helps the world."

"You don't know that," Caspian countered. "I'm not convinced that the Director's motivations are as altruistic as it seems. Maybe he just wants to use you as a weapon."

"Obviously, he doesn't need her for that," Roland said, looking around at the fallen Citadel. "He could destroy the world all by himself if he wanted to. But he needs Aniya to supply energy. I don't think he's lied about that."

Caspian shook his head. "Again, you don't know that. The man is as unpredictable as we are predictable, apparently. There is no telling what he wants with Aniya. To make such a decision based on what the Director says is foolish."

"But it is her decision," Corrin said, glaring at Caspian.

"Forget it," Caspian said. "To rush into action now is stupid. That's exactly what the Director wants."

Lionel pointed a finger at Caspian. "You just said you can't predict him. How do *you* know what he wants?"

Before Caspian could respond, Roland spoke up again.

"We owe it to Salvador to save him. *I* owe it to him. We didn't listen to him before, and now look where it got us."

Aniya looked at the ground.

"Are you really going to let the Director kill us off one by one?" Roland grabbed her hand and squeezed tight. "We already lost Tamisra. We don't have to lose her father, too."

Aniya looked back up at her brother, her lips trembling. "I don't know, Roland. I just don't know. I can't be responsible for the deaths of millions if I give myself up to save Salvador."

"I'm not asking you to give yourself up, Aniya." He grabbed her biceps and shook her gently. "We can save him, you and I."

She looked down at the ground, shaking her head. "No, we can't, Roland."

Roland stared at her for several seconds before releasing her arms. "Fine. Then I'll do it myself."

"You'll do nothing," Caspian said firmly. "You know exactly what the Director is capable of now. Surely you must realize that undertaking any move against him without the support of an army is suicide."

Roland didn't respond. Instead, he folded his arms and locked eyes with Lionel.

"Do you understand?" Caspian continued. "You have orders to remain here and wait for further instructions. I'll speak with Corrin further and see if we can't come up with a strategy where everyone lives."

"You've already made yourself clear that we aren't going to be—"

"Do I make myself clear?" Caspian stepped toward Roland, his nostrils flaring.

Corrin placed a hand on Roland's shoulder and pulled him slightly backward. "Listen to him, son. No one needs to die today."

After a moment, Roland finally nodded.

"Good," Caspian said. "Corrin, please come with me, and we will discuss further."

As they left the tent, Aniya turned toward Roland and gave him a quick hug. "I want to save Salvador. I really do. But I can't lose you like I've lost the rest of my family. You mean—"

But Roland interrupted her with a brisk shove.

Aniya managed to maintain her balance. As soon as the shock wore off, she opened her mouth to say the first thing that came to her mind. But she knew she'd regret the words, so instead she bit her lip and left.

R oland stood alone with Lionel and Dawn, still staring directly at Salvador's squire.

Lionel broke eye contact and took Dawn's hand, smiling. "I'm okay, sis. Please, take care of people who are actually injured. I'll be right here."

Dawn looked between Roland and Lionel for a moment, then turned to leave. She stopped at the exit and looked back at Roland with a cold gaze. "We need to talk. I'll be back in a few minutes."

And with that, she was gone.

"Something tells me you're not on board with Caspian's strategy of doing nothing," Lionel said slowly.

Roland glanced behind him quickly. "What if I told you there's a way we can get Salvador back? Without Aniya?"

"I'd say you're nuts," Lionel said with a laugh. "Besides, I thought you and Salvador didn't exactly see eye-to-eye."

"I've disagreed with a lot of things he's said and done in the last three years. But I respect everything he did in the Uprising and everything he's done to rebuild a community free from the Lightbringer influence." Roland cleared his throat and looked down at his toes. "He's a great man. He doesn't deserve to be tortured and then executed."

Lionel nodded. "He attacked me, you know. In the battle. Tried to keep me from running out there and getting myself killed. It's my fault they have him now. He was going to run and take me with him. Wanted to keep me safe at all costs, even if it meant losing my respect."

"We all owe him a debt of some kind," Roland said, looking behind him again. On the other side of the curtain were hundreds of injured people, most of them at one point a child of the Scourge. "To abandon him now would be a greater treachery than anything we've accused him of."

"I'm with you, but how exactly do you plan on getting him back? There's a crazed assassin and a godlike robot standing between us and him." Lionel shook his head. "Man, saying it out loud sounds insane, however true it is."

Roland smiled. "I have a plan. It just depends on how close you're willing to get to death."

"That's what I've trained for my whole life," Lionel said with a grin of his own. "What did you have in mind?"

## 43

Salvador moaned as his eyes finally opened, audibly cracking the dried blood that had sealed his eyelids closed.

It was dark, impossibly so. Not even in the tunnels where he had spent the last two decades had he ever seen such a darkness. There had always been a hint of a torch, a glow-worm, something that had given off the tiniest light.

But here, there was nothing. Salvador was trapped in a shadow that seemed to suffocate any chance of light. Odorless smoke filled his lungs and stifled him, and he choked as he shook exhaustion away. He tried to move, but his left arm was wrapped in chains, pulled taut up and away from him. His legs were similarly locked in place by irons that clamped down over his ankles.

"I should have known you'd wake up early."

The taunting, feminine voice shocked him awake, and he lashed forward only to be held back by heavy iron chains. As his mind began to clear, an agonizing pain shot through his right arm, and Salvador suddenly remembered the pain that had caused him to lose consciousness: the forced removal of his right hand. A cloth now crudely wrapped around the stump that remained, his only appendage that wriggled about freely.

"The sedative I gave you should have lasted for another few hours, but here you are."

Salvador roared in anger as he kicked in his bonds, ignoring the biting pain of the sharp metal on his flesh.

Fingers tapped on his chest, dancing over his tunic. Sharp fingernails jabbed through the material and straight to his skin, pinpricks that were more than a minor annoyance.

"I must say, it wasn't as hard as I thought it would be to bring you down."

The voice traveled around him, and now lips brushed up against his ear, sending shivers down his spine.

"I guess murdering your daughter was an effective way to neuter you."

Salvador spun around and bit down hard. He ripped his head backward and spat a hunk of flesh and blood as Zeta let out a pained shriek.

The cry of pain quickly gave way to the invisible assassin's hissing voice.

"I suppose it's only fair that you get your chance to strike a blow. A shame it's nothing compared to my plans for you. To think, I killed your daughter after she robbed me of an arm. Imagine the price you'll pay for a piece of my ear."

Salvador gasped as a blade bit into his side, at least an inch deep. He bit his lip to keep from crying out as the knife was quickly pulled from his body, and as his head spun, he fell to his knees.

"I was going to wait and taunt you a little more, but I guess if you insist, we can go ahead and get started."

Another three quick swipes of the blade, two to his front and one to his back, and his tunic fell to the ground, sliced free from what little fabric hung around his neck.

"That's just going to get in the way." A spark flashed, and a small fire ignited at Salvador's knees, burning away the fabric slowly. The flames should have provided more light, but they seemed muffled, only enough to cast a small glow on Zeta's face, revealing her sadistic grin. "Much better. Now I can see what I'm doing."

She turned and tugged on a chain by her side with her left arm, and Salvador felt himself hoisted into the air, hanging by the iron chain that wrapped around his neck, pinching on his skin in various places and cutting off his air. His toes barely touched the ground, allowing him to push against the ground just enough to temporarily relieve his lungs. The assassin stepped on the chain and wrapped the slack around a stake embedded in the ground.

Abandoning the chain and letting Salvador hang, Zeta swiped at his skin with her fingernails, thinly slicing his stomach.

Moaning, Salvador noticed in the dim light that Zeta had sharpened the tips of her nails into fine points, forming tiny knives.

"If only Refuge could see you now. I know the legend of the Scourge, a relentless fighter that endured so much. The death of his family, the humiliation of defeat, the removal of a finger. Of course, you and I both know that your myth is purely more than rather graphic fiction. The good news, Salvador, is that I'm going to give you a proper story. The lies you told of your suffering, of pain? I'm going to make it all real. Of course, I'm going to do so much more than take a measly little hand."

Zeta stepped on the chain again, yanking Salvador into the air by his neck.

Choking as his air was forced away, his vision began to go dark, and it was only then that Zeta released the chain, letting Salvador fall back down. His left arm lit up in fiery pain as it suddenly took on the full weight of his body again. At least he finally had air, and he gasped deeply, trying to get as much as possible.

But the air that filled his lungs came at a cost, and Salvador finally cried out in agony as Zeta buried the knife in his diaphragm, making his gasp agonizingly painful.

Salvador hung limply and took a few heaving breaths as his consciousness began to slip away, his head drooping.

A splash of water came over his face, bringing on a new kind of pain as the liquid seeped into various wounds.

"No!" Zeta's shrieking voice echoed against the walls. "I'm not done with you yet."

A jabbing pain shot through his jaw as Zeta began to pull individual hairs from his beard.

"We're just getting started."

The assassin vanished for a moment, leaving Salvador to shudder in pain as he hung from the ceiling. He tried to brace himself for whatever would come next, but trying to predict the girl's insanity, he knew, was pointless.

A new light appeared in the shadows, coursing beams of white that danced in the darkness, taking on the appearance of an arm and hand. The light grew brighter, revealing the insidious assassin, a wicked smile on her face, brandishing a metal arm in front of her chest as she made a fist.

In a flurry, Zeta dashed forward and punched Salvador's left foot with a flash of light.

The devastating blow was far more powerful than he could have imagined. The sound of shattering bones alone nearly made him vomit. But accompanying the sheer force of the blow was the follow-up of hundreds of stabbing sensations that dashed up his leg and raced throughout his entire body, rattling his bones and pricking every inch of his flesh.

Salvador surrendered the last of his resistance, uttering an agonizing scream that lasted for several seconds, giving way to Zeta's cackling laughter.

It was the first of many screams, and Zeta would go on for hours, exacting her vengeance slowly, painfully.

The last time Salvador had experienced so much pain,

he had watched his family executed. He had said for years afterward that he would never feel a greater pain. Just hours earlier, he had watched Zeta murder his last child, and he felt that same pain again. It was a pain that he believed could never be matched.

He was wrong.

## 44

Lionel watched the elevator door close with a resounding thud, a finality that seemed to seal their fate.

There was no turning back now.

He took a deep breath and turned around just in time to see Dawn rounding a corner of debris. She stopped in her tracks and put her hands on her hips.

"There you are." Her tone was flat and cold, and her eyes were narrowed. "Who was in the elevator?"

Lionel shrugged and walked over to her. "No one."

"I saw the doors close." She made no move to approach him. "What are you doing here? Caspian said he didn't want anyone near the Citadel."

"Look around, sis. There is no Citadel."

"You know what I mean." Dawn folded her arms. "I know when you're lying. And I saw the way you and Roland were looking at each other."

Lionel took a step back and raised his hands. "I don't know what you saw, but I promise Roland isn't cheating on you. Especially with me. That's disgusting, Dawn."

"Cut it out, Lionel. I know Roland too well to know that

he's just going to sit back and wait for Aniya. What is he planning?"

"Planning? Roland? You know Roland doesn't do plans. Me neither. We leave that up to people like Caspian. We're just fighters."

Dawn finally stepped toward him and gave him a firm shove. "Enough. Tell me what he's doing. I can handle it."

"Honestly, sis. Neither of us are doing anything. I don't know where Roland is, and I'm just looking for survivors."

"Really? You're not doing anything stupid?" She gave him another shove. "Like running out into the middle of a battle and getting yourself caught?"

Lionel stepped back, frowning. "I was just doing what I was trained to do. I got unlucky."

"Yeah? Then maybe you should consider your luck before doing something else stupid. Roland was in the elevator, wasn't he? And you helped him?"

"Dawn, it isn't anything. Please, go back to the barracks. They need you."

"No, you need me!" Dawn raised her trembling voice and jabbed a finger in his chest. "Enough people have died, and no matter what I tell Roland, I thought I lost you too. Don't ask me to do that again with Roland. Now, who was in the elevator?"

He stared at her for a second before sighing. "Roland."

Dawn bit her lip as a tear slipped down her cheek. "He's going to try to rescue Salvador, isn't he?"

Lionel said nothing.

"No, I can't do this again!" She grabbed her hair and pulled. "He's going to get himself killed. Does he really think he can save Salvador alone?"

Lionel quickly looked down at the ground, but it was too late. Dawn had caught it, and now a look of terror spread over her face.

"You're going with him," she whispered, backing away slowly.

"It's not what you think. We're not going up there blindly. We have—"

"No, this isn't happening." Dawn shook her head firmly. "You're staying down here."

Lionel reached for her hand, but she pulled away. "It's not as bad as it sounds. Roland is—"

"Not as bad as it sounds?" Her voice was on the verge of a shriek. "Lionel, they wiped out half of us in minutes. They have an assassin who can wipe out even our best warrior. Their leader is a robot with life-sucking power that can see you coming a mile away. How do you think this is going to end?"

"I will get Salvador back, I promise." Lionel darted a hand out and grabbed her wrist before she could back away again. "And then I'm going to come back to you, and we will get revenge for all those who have been taken from us."

Dawn wrenched her hand away and slapped him. "I'm not going to let you do this, Lionel. I won't lose you again."

"I'm sorry," he said as he backed away. "I have to do this."

"You're not hearing me," she said. "I'm not letting you leave."

Lionel turned to leave just as Dawn let out an ear-piercing scream that echoed throughout the ruins of the Citadel. He spun around and glared at her, but his heart broke as his eyes fell upon her face, which was quickly becoming drenched in tears.

"I can't do this again," she said with heaving breaths. "I won't."

Lionel started to reply but was interrupted by the sound of footsteps.

"I'm sorry," he said again, then darted to her side and grabbed her.

"What are you—" Dawn shrieked as he wrapped an arm

around her throat and yanked her backward toward the elevator.

Aniya appeared amid the rubble, followed by three soldiers, their guns drawn.

"What's going on?" she demanded, looking around. "What happened?"

Dawn started to speak again, but Lionel pulled tighter on her neck, and her words turned to a choking noise.

"I'm going to save Salvador," Lionel said firmly, locking eyes with Aniya. "I owe my life to him, and I won't leave him to die."

Aniya took a step forward as the soldiers behind her raised their weapons.

"You can't do this, Lionel. They'll just kill you."

"Then you should have no problem letting me go." Lionel sneered at Aniya. "I might just buy you another day before you man up and do what you know you have to do."

Aniya stepped forward again, but Lionel drew a gun and held it to Dawn's head.

"Take another step, and I kill her."

A horrified look spread across Aniya's face as she froze. "Lionel, she's your sister!"

"You think I don't know that?" Lionel pressed the gun against her temple. "But Salvador is the father of Refuge. I owe nothing to Dawn and everything to him."

"What are you doing?" Dawn managed to choke out, her voice little more than a whisper.

Lionel muttered in her ear, "Taking a page out of Salvador's book. He had a flair for the dramatic, if nothing else."

He continued backing away, keeping the gun pressed to Dawn's head.

"I'm sorry it's come to this," he continued, not taking his eyes off Aniya, "but if it's within my power to save him, we're going to. I guess that's the difference between you and me."

"We?" Aniya's eyes widened. "Who's we?"

Lionel kept retreating, and upon reaching the elevator, he swatted blindly behind him and pressed the button to the elevator doors.

"Lionel," Aniya said, her voice rising in pitch and volume, "who is *we*?"

The elevator doors opened, and Lionel stepped inside. With his free hand, he inserted a keycard under the rows of buttons.

"If Roland comes looking for me, tell him I'm already up there," he whispered in Dawn's ear. "I was planning on waiting for him, but I guess that's out of the question now."

Dawn shook her head. "Lionel, please don't do this."

He kissed the side of her head and continued, "I'll take care of Roland, and together we'll save Salvador. I love you, sis, and I'll see you soon."

Lionel pushed the very top button, and as the doors began to close, he shoved Dawn out of the elevator.

The doors shut once again, and Lionel took a deep breath as the elevator began its ascent.

## 45

"Where are you?"

Caspian's voice echoed in the reactor chamber, bouncing off the rock walls and apparently falling on deaf ears. He ignored his morbid company, the sight of thousands of imprisoned men emitting a green light from their tanks that fell on Caspian's face with a foreboding glow.

"Neeshika!" he shouted again, sticking out his chest in an effort to make his voice travel farther.

"I heard you the first time," a silky voice whispered in his ear.

Caspian spun around to see a stream of green light dancing by his head. He swatted it away, and it drifted backward, quickly growing and morphing into a human-shaped figure.

"It is quite bold of you to summon me here, Caspian. Do you not have the—"

"You promised me Aniya would help."

The body of light placed a hand on its chest. "Are you questioning me?"

"That depends. Are you not aware of your lightbringer's colossal failure?"

"Tell me, Caspian. How do you define failure?"

Caspian snorted. "Getting half my men killed and giving Nicholas's body over to the Director is a pretty good definition, I'd say. I lost enough during the Purge, and I'm quickly losing everything I have left."

"Then you think too small."

He stepped forward and swiped a hand through the gathered light, scattering it. "My ability to see the bigger picture is why you came to me just before the Purge."

"I came to you because I knew you would be the only one left," Neeshika's voice hissed in his ear.

Caspian turned to see the light already reassembled behind him.

"If I had my way, I would still be working with the Chancellor. Now, that was a man who could stand back and look at things objectively. You are led by your emotions. It's rather hypocritical of you, wouldn't you say? That you are trying to show Lightbringer how to overcome her emotions, while they are what blind you the most?"

"I see well enough. And wouldn't you be upset when your people die? Wouldn't you be enraged to see them slaughtered while you stand back helplessly?"

An ethereal shriek filled the cavern as the body of light rushed through Caspian.

"How dare you!"

Caspian collapsed to his knees, clutching his ears as the hideous noise continued.

"It is because my people were gutted like animals that I am able to see beyond the here and now. That was when my eyes were opened. That was the moment my life truly began."

Neeshika fell silent, and as her shrieks died away, Caspian slowly stood again.

"You have a gift, dear Caspian," she said, her voice eerily calm. "You know we stand on the brink of a turning point in mankind's history, and you get to be part of it. You know what it must take, now more than ever. Would you really question me and back down now? All of your people will have died for nothing."

"But Aniya isn't conforming. You said she would come through. You said she'd do what she has to do."

"And she will. She just needs one last push. She will break."

"That's what you said last time."

Her voice turned cold again. "Are you sure you want to question me again?"

Caspian bowed his head. "What do I have to do?"

"Prey on her guilt. Promise her that one day all will be restored. Expose her for her cowardice. Pick a nerve and push on it, Caspian. You have studied the human mind. You know how it works. Find what will push her over the edge and show no mercy."

"But she's dangerous. If she self-destructs—"

"She won't. Not while Nicholas can still be saved."

Caspian studied the ground for a moment before looking back up. "I'll do what I have to do."

"You always do. Now, if you don't mind, another approaches to embrace his destiny."

"What?"

Neeshika smiled. "Turn around."

Caspian turned to see Roland standing at the entrance to the cavern. He spun back around, but Neeshika was gone. He took a deep breath and looked back at Roland.

"How much did you hear?"

Roland shrugged and stepped into the cavern. "Enough to know it doesn't matter."

"What is that supposed to mean?" Caspian narrowed his eyes as Roland approached. "What are you doing here?"

"You heard Neeshika. Embracing my destiny. Doing what I should have done a week ago."

Caspian's mouth dropped open in realization. "And what

makes you think I'm going to let you?"

"What makes you think you can stop me?"

"This isn't the plan, Roland." Caspian stepped forward, blocking the boy's path. "This power belongs to Aniya, and she has been prepared for this for years. She alone is strong enough to bear the responsibility that comes with the Light."

"Is she, though?" Roland's face appeared emotionless, but his voice was grating. "She refuses to do what we both know she has to do. People are dying, and I'm not going to let anyone else suffer while we all just wait for her to step up."

"She will comply. You have my word."

Roland shrugged. "Maybe one day. But Salvador needs us today."

"Have faith, Roland. She—"

"Faith?" Roland's eyes lit up with a fire that was reminiscent of the Scourge's rage. "Faith is what lost us thousands of people a week ago. You thought Aniya would save us, and she choked. She's crippled by her emotion, and you know it. Nicholas was my friend, but unlike my sister, I know that he's dead now. I have no problem destroying his body."

"This isn't the plan," Caspian said again. "Aniya will—"

"Aniya will do nothing. She's made that clear. But I can carry the same power as her, and you know it. I can't ignore that. This is what I have to do."

As Roland stepped forward, Caspian placed a firm hand on his chest, holding him back. "Neeshika has assured me that Aniya will do what she must."

Roland pushed Caspian away. "Neeshika is the one who told me that this is what I must do."

Caspian froze. "That's impossible. Aniya has always been the one. This was the plan the whole time."

"Plans change. I guess Neeshika realized Aniya wasn't going to play along, and so she asked me to take her place."

"It's not that simple. You wouldn't have the same power as Aniya. Because of what Nicholas did, stepping in the tank with her, she's . . . different. She's special. If you try to force this power on yourself—"

"I'll be stronger."

Caspian shook his head firmly. "No. You'll be different. Different in ways I can't predict. Only the Director could say what you'd turn into. Have you considered that this is exactly what he wants to happen?"

Roland gave a sharp laugh. "What makes you think he'd want me to do this?"

"If you do this, he can take advantage of you. Aniya and the Director are not two halves. They are—"

"Enough," Roland said with another shove. "You're wasting my time. Get out of my way. This is what I have to do, and I'm going to do it."

Caspian stood his ground and shook his head. "You have to listen to me, Roland. If Neeshika really told you to do this, I don't think we can trust her. She knows exactly what the Director is capable of, and there's no way she would ask you to do this."

"Between the two of you, I trust Neeshika. She's had centuries to understand the Light. She knows what I would be capable of, and she wants to destroy the Director even more than you do."

"All the more reason to question—"

"No!" Roland pushed him again, this time hard enough to propel him backward. "I'm doing this, with or without your permission."

Caspian sneered as he curled his hands into fists. "I won't let you jeopardize everything I've worked for."

"Fine." Roland stepped forward as a shimmering green light materialized behind him.

The light took the form of Neeshika again, a smirk

spreading across her face. Suddenly, the light exploded in a bright flash, blinding Caspian.

He never saw Roland's attack, and as a fist crashed into the side of his head, he toppled to the ground.

## 46

A niya watched in horror as the elevator doors closed. She hadn't heard everything Lionel had whispered to his sister, but one word unquestionably stood out above the rest.

Roland.

Her brother was going with Lionel in an attempt to rescue Salvador, a mission that would surely end in their deaths.

It was several seconds before she realized that Dawn was speaking to her.

"Aniya, do something!" she was shouting, her voice cracking.

She backed away slowly, her eyes still glued to the elevator. She couldn't even tell where Dawn was. It was like everything but the elevator was covered in a black mist.

A hand fell on her shoulder, and she finally looked away to see one of Caspian's soldiers behind her.

"Are you okay?" he said, scanning her eyes.

Aniya nodded absentmindedly. "Go get Corrin."

The soldier raised his eyebrows. "Not Caspian?"

Another soldier appeared over the first's shoulder. "I already tried him when we heard the screams. He's AWOL."

"Get Corrin," Aniya said again, this time more firmly. "Now."

The soldier nodded, and his small squadron disappeared.

Aniya turned back around, and Dawn was standing directly in front of her.

"Please," she begged. "Stop them."

Aniya took a shaky step back. "I . . . I can't."

"You can't? Aniya, they'll die, both of them! If you don't do anything, I'll lose them both. I don't have any family left, and if they die, then—"

"You don't think I get it?" Aniya tried to shout, but it came out as a squeak. "I have nothing left. Nothing! Roland was the last bit of family I had, and now he's gone too. That's it. I'm alone."

Dawn grabbed Aniya's arms. "He's not dead yet. You can still save him."

"No, I can't! I can't save Roland, just like I can't restore Nicholas and I can't protect Refuge. I can't do anything . . . for anyone!"

The two girls stared at each other for several seconds, each one trembling.

"Have you finally learned your lesson?"

Aniya froze as a new voice arose.

"Could it be that you are finally willing to admit that you truly are helpless?"

She looked up slowly to see the Director's grinning face spread across the mostly destroyed sky ceiling.

"You at last realize that you have no recourse. There is no way out. So tell me, dear. What prevents you from turning yourself over to me now?"

Aniya stepped away from Dawn, who was staring up at the Director as well, her hands over her mouth.

"If I give myself to you, I put the whole world in danger."

The Director clucked and shook his head. "I seek not to condemn this world, Lucifer. I wish to save it."

"There's nothing you can say that will make me believe that now. Not after what you've done."

"I have done only what I must. But let's assume that I do not have the world's best interests in mind. Would you really continue to hide yourself from me and send innocent people to their certain deaths just to avoid suffering that may never happen?"

Aniya balled her fists. "I won't let anyone else die for me, no."

"Then what is this?"

The Director's face was suddenly replaced by the image of Lionel standing in the elevator. Dawn whimpered and clutched Aniya's arm.

"You sent one boy to save your precious Salvador? You realize this is suicide."

"I didn't send him," Aniya said. "He made a poor choice."

"And you care so little about him that you refuse to help him? For shame, Lucifer. I hope you know that his death will be painful. Just like Salvador's."

On the screen, the elevator stopped, the doors opened, and Lionel disappeared from view.

The Director's face reappeared. "Surely you must realize that you can't keep this up. More people will die until you give yourself to me. Starting with this boy."

Aniya opened her mouth to fire back a retort, but she was knocked to the ground by a sudden, tremendous earthquake.

From above the din of the shaking earth, the Director continued.

"And now you send another, the one who finally accepts what he believes his destiny to be. I wish you had his courage, Lucifer. And I wish I could accept your gift of substitute, but my machine is made only for you. It doesn't—"

But the Hub was plunged into darkness as the sky ceiling suddenly shut off.

As the quakes intensified, Aniya looked around to see that

the power had gone out everywhere. She tried to summon light to her hands, but nothing came. Just the feeling of utter terror.

Corrin appeared in the chaos, kneeling by her side and looking between her and Dawn.

"Are you okay?" he had to have been asking, but his voice was lost to the sound of screams mixed with the trembling earth.

Aniya could only stare back at him, unable to form any response even if he was able to hear it. She let herself fall flat on her stomach and pressed her cheek against the shaking ground.

After a few minutes, the earthquake stopped, just as sudden as it had started.

The Hub went quiet for several seconds, the only sound being the remaining screams from the encampment a half-mile away.

With a hand from Corrin, Aniya stood up, then turned to help Dawn.

"What's this I hear about Lionel?" Corrin asked.

Dawn threw herself into Corrin's arms, her tears finally breaking forth.

"He's going to the surface," Aniya said. "And so is Roland."

Corrin's face drained of all color as his mouth dropped open.

Blinding light came from above, and Aniya held her hand in front of her eyes, blocking out the image from the dismembered sky ceiling.

The Director's voice came back, stronger this time. "I grant you light one last time, Refuge, that you may see the sacrifice of two brave, foolish souls that your savior offers in her place."

Aniya took her hand away to see Lionel standing in a forest, looking around carefully.

"*Please*, Aniya!"

Dawn's scream tore at her heart, but Aniya remained rooted to the ground, unable to take her eyes off the scene that played out above her.

"Oh, one last thing." The Director cleared his throat. "Before your friends die, I wish to express to you the irony of what you are about to see. They will make every attempt to save their beloved leader, but I'm afraid they are wasting their time. They will die for nothing."

A noise broke Aniya's concentration. The sound of the elevator doors opening.

She spun around to see a naked, huddled body on the floor of the elevator car, bloody and unmoving.

Corrin dashed toward the elevator, throwing himself down and grabbing the crumpled mass. He dragged it out of the elevator just far enough that Aniya could see Salvador's face.

"Dawn, come quickly!" he shouted, scanning the Scourge's body.

But Dawn refused to move, not taking her eyes off her brother's image on the sky ceiling.

Aniya, however, was now staring at Salvador's broken body, helplessly watching as she remained frozen in place.

"Dawn!" Corrin yelled again, his voice cracking.

"It was a trap," Aniya muttered feebly. "It was all a trap."

The Director's voice purred from above. "Yes, dear. One final, resounding display of my foresight and power. I hope this is the last time I must resort to such drastic measures. I do not wish to take any more lives. But there will still be two more. You have made your choice. I leave you now so that you may watch your friends die."

The audio cut out from the sky ceiling, leaving only the image. Aniya's eyes were still fixed on Salvador's body, but she knew what was being displayed on the digital dome. Dawn's crying told her everything she needed to know.

Aniya became suddenly aware of the sweat that was

quickly covering her body, and she shivered as it trickled down her back. She wanted to step forward, to see if Salvador was even still alive, but she found that her legs simply refused to move.

There were soldiers by Corrin's side now. When they got there, Aniya had no idea. In fact, she blinked, and they were suddenly standing in front of her, presenting Salvador's body like a trophy.

"Heal him," Corrin's voice came from somewhere in the darkness. "Please, Aniya. He's still alive, but barely. He won't last much longer."

Aniya stared at the mass of naked flesh that was offered to her. There was blood everywhere, oozing from what seemed like a hundred places. She seemed to remember healing people before with the touch of a finger. It was an idea that seemed so foreign to her now, an impossibility that could never work. As much as she wanted to, she knew she couldn't save Salvador.

Her hand was on his bare chest now. Aniya finally looked up and peered through the fog to see Corrin holding it in place, gripping her wrist tightly.

"You can do this, Aniya. You saved Lionel. You can save Salvador, too."

She wanted nothing more. She focused all her remaining energy into her hand, willing the light inside to come out and heal the dying warlord.

But nothing came. The crippling panic that clouded her vision was also choking the power inside her body, and it remained shut up inside her body, refusing to come out now when she needed it the most.

"Heal him, Aniya!"

Aniya thought she was shaking her head, but her vision didn't move side-to-side. If anything, it felt like she was backward, watching the scene before her drift away.

"I can't," she tried to say, but her throat constricted, and no words came out.

Suddenly, she became aware that she could no longer feel herself. Her senses began to shut down, and as her legs slipped out from under her, Aniya's vision went black.

Nothing happened for hours, it seemed. The next thing she knew, a buzzing sensation jolted through her body, shocking her awake.

Aniya's eyes flew open, and she looked up at Roland standing over her supine body.

"Roland!" she managed to yelp in surprise.

His expression was unreadable, almost apathetic. The only thing Aniya saw in his eyes was a white glow that seemed to pulse from his vision. In fact, as she looked over his body, she realized he seemed to be surrounded by a breathing, white halo.

"How are you like this?" Aniya asked as she stared in shock at his glowing body.

"Same way you are," he said. "I only wish I did it sooner." His light dimmed slightly as he looked at the ground. "I could have saved Tamisra. I could have saved all of them."

Aniya suddenly remembered everything that had happened before she had fainted, and she grabbed his arm, immediately filling herself with a burning energy.

"Don't go up there, Roland. It's a trap."

Roland's face returned to a stoic stare. He shook his head. "Salvador may be here now, but Lionel is still up there. And so is the Director."

"Wha-what are you going to do?"

He stood, shaking off Aniya's hand. "What I must."

"No, Roland. I can—"

"You can't do anything, Aniya." Roland's voice was monotone, yet firm. "This is not your fight anymore."

A flash of white flooded her vision, and her brother was gone.

As he disappeared, so did the energy he had provided. The fog was back, creeping over Aniya's vision like a wave of murky water. The dizziness was back, and with it came a nausea that churned her stomach.

Aniya fell to her knees, then to the ground. She found herself rolling over to face the sky ceiling, and the fog cleared just enough to reveal the horrible scene above her.

And with the crushing realization that she was about to watch her brother die, Aniya wept.

## 47

L ionel stepped out of the elevator shack and out into the Overworld.

Immediately, he froze.

A fresh, warm breeze fell over his face, gently wafting through his unkempt hair and tickling his ears. There was no rotten stench that lingered in the air, a permanent feature of the Underworld that Lionel only just now realized he had gotten used to.

Towering trees surrounded him, casting him in a shade from the sun.

The sun.

Lionel dashed through the forest until he reached a clearing. Looking up, he gaped in wonder at the sun. He knew it was digital, but he didn't care. It felt so much more real up here than it ever had on its best day in the Underworld.

But his reverie was cut short by a piercing scream that drifted through the forest.

Salvador.

Lionel took off running in the direction of the scream, racing through the forest at full speed, barely managing to keep himself upright amid the shrubbery and fallen branches.

Soon, he cleared the tree line and reached a hill of grass. Upon climbing to the top, he stopped short.

A lone figure was standing in the valley below. Its silver right hand rested on a giant, golden sword that was partially embedded in the ground.

"You can come down here, sweetie," Zeta called liltingly. "Salvador is waiting for you."

Lionel didn't budge. Instead, he looked around. "Where? I'm not moving until you show him to me."

Another scream came from somewhere behind Zeta.

"What, you want me to fight you for him?" Lionel drew his gun and pointed it at Zeta. "You realize I can shoot you from here, right?"

"I'm sure," the assassin said. "But if you kill me without a fair fight, you'll never see your beloved Salvador again. And that's a pretty big 'if' anyway. So why don't you just come down here?"

"So you can kill me? I don't think so."

Zeta shrugged. "Suit yourself. I'll hold on to him until someone else comes along, then. Why don't you run on back to your friends in Level I? Enjoy what little time left you have with them."

She pulled the golden sword out of the ground and turned to leave, and she made it several paces away before Lionel sighed and started walking down the hill.

"Hold on."

Zeta turned around, revealing a crooked smile. She jabbed the sword back in the ground and waited.

Lionel ran the last few paces down the hill to keep his balance, and he transitioned into a slow walk, a careful approach to the assassin.

"So?" he asked as he stopped a few yards away from her, shoving his hands in his pockets. "Where is he?"

Zeta smirked. "Do you really think I would bring him

here? What's more, why did you even bother coming down here? You don't actually believe you can fight me, do you?"

"I guess not," Lionel said. "But I had to try, right? Salvador is like a father to me."

"Ironic, seeing as how I doubt he'll be able to ever have any more children."

Lionel's blood boiled, but he took a deep breath and forced himself to keep talking. "What did you do to him?"

"Oh, lots. More than I bothered to do to you. But don't worry. I'm sure your precious Aniya will have him in tip-top shape in no time if she ever gets her hands on him. It looks like she patched you up nicely already. Too bad you're still too weak to put up a good fight."

"Just you wait. Besides, if I don't kill you, it just means Aniya will later. And you'd better hope that I kill you now because if she ever gets the chance to fight you, I can promise you that you'll suffer more than either of us did."

"Is that it?" Zeta smirked. "Is that the extent of your wit? If so, I'd rather just kill you now and get it over with. I expected more."

"Oh, I'm just getting started. You might be able to beat me in a fight, but I can talk you to death."

"I'm sure you could if I let you." Zeta pulled the sword out of the ground again and pointed it at Lionel. "But I don't have all day. I do have other work to do, you know."

Lionel didn't budge. "Yeah, I'm sure the Director keeps his attack dog on a pretty short leash."

Zeta sneered. "I'm his employee, if that's what you mean."

"Whatever you want to call it to make yourself feel better."

"Enough. Let's get this over with."

Lionel pulled the gun out from its holster. "And how am I supposed to fight you fairly? All I have is this."

Without a word, Zeta threw the golden sword at Lionel,

driving it into the ground at his side. She reached behind her and pulled out twin steel blades, long and thin.

"Hardly a fair fight," Lionel said, glancing at the sword at his side but not picking it up.

"Are you seriously complaining that I have two swords? Yours is bigger, isn't it? Don't listen to what your girlfriend says, Lionel. Size really does matter. But then, you don't have a girlfriend, do you? I guess you really are going to die alone."

Lionel scoffed. "No, I mean for you."

"Oh, don't worry about me, sweetheart." Zeta twirled her swords around her body, finishing with one of the blades spinning around her metal hand. "I can handle myself with the tools I have."

"Clearly, which is why you still have both hands. I'm sure you can't fight as well with a metal arm now."

"You'd be surprised. Now, pick up your dear, dead daddy's sword and fight."

"Not yet," Lionel said. "I'm not done mocking you."

Zeta rolled her eyes. "I won't wait any longer, boy. I want a fair fight, but I'll kill you if you take any longer."

"Why do you even want a fair fight? You're an assassin. You don't have any problems stabbing people in the back, do you?"

"No, but it gets old after a while. Quit stalling."

Lionel took a step backward as Zeta advanced. "Oh, but I have to."

"Why, are you waiting for someone?"

"As a matter of fact, yes. But more importantly, I had to find the right frequency."

Zeta stopped short, her smile faltering. "What fre—"

A high-pitched whine filled the air, and the assassin dropped to her knees, dropping her swords and clutching her ears.

Lionel pulled out the device from his pocket and showed it to Zeta. "Thanks for this. I didn't think you were stupid enough to leave us such a valuable tool, but I guess we all mess up sometimes."

"No," she grunted, writhing on the ground as she pulled on her hair. "That's impossible. He changed my chip."

"Apparently not enough," Lionel said. He walked over to Zeta and kicked her swords away. Without waiting for her to say anything else, he leaned down and punched her in the nose.

Zeta shrieked and grabbed at her nose, kicking wildly upward at Lionel but missing him.

"You're going to tell me where Salvador is," Lionel continued. "And then I'll put you out of your misery."

The assassin said nothing, only moaning in pain as she stared him down.

"Fine." Lionel grabbed Salvador's sword and held it to Zeta's stomach. "Tell me where he is, or I'll make this even more painful."

"Big words from a little boy," Zeta hissed. "You don't have what it takes to do what I did to you."

Lionel pressed the sword into the assassin's belly. "Watch me."

Zeta winced but managed to grin. She began wheezing as red veins spread over her eyes. "Careful. You're entering a world of pain."

"Oh, yeah?" Lionel pulled the sword up and over his head. "Let's see if you're still this annoying when you're missing your other arm."

A sharp pain shot through Lionel's groin, and he fell to his knees as he dropped the sword.

Zeta kicked him again, this time right above his ear, and he toppled over, grabbing the side of his bleeding head.

"You really think a headache is going to be enough to stop me?" Zeta said as she climbed to her feet. She staggered for a moment, shaking her head, but she managed to stay upright. "I hope you have more tricks up your sleeve because you wasted too much time talking. You're dead now."

She grabbed her swords, and after steadying herself for a moment, she dashed toward Lionel.

But Lionel was already back on his feet. He snatched the sword and jumped to the side, narrowly missing the assassin's attack.

"I didn't come to fight you," Lionel said, readying himself for another assault.

Zeta opened her mouth to respond, but as the jamming signal pulsed again, she howled in pain and dropped to one knee. Breathing deeply, she stood up again, keeping one eye closed. "Oh, yeah? Then what are you doing here?"

"Getting you ready for someone who can fight you better than I can."

"I don't see anyone else," Zeta managed to spit out between breaths. "Looks like you're stuck with me."

Lionel held his sword in a defensive stance and planted his feet. "Fine. Let's do this."

With a frenzied scream, Zeta lunged forward again.

Lionel, knowing he couldn't possibly defend against two swords moving much faster, swung as hard as he could with his much larger sword.

The assassin blocked the blow with both swords, but the weight of the blow was so great that it sent her staggering to the side.

Without waiting for her to recover, Lionel rushed toward her and swung down toward her head.

Zeta dove to the side, rolling on the ground and throwing one sword up just in time to block another blow from Lionel.

This swing was enough to cleave Zeta's sword in two, and she dropped the hilt and yanked her head out of the way, narrowly dodging the golden blade. She leapt to her feet, leaving a large section of her hair on the ground beneath Lionel's sword.

She let out a screeching howl and brandished her remaining sword as Lionel backed away, but she froze as the ground shook.

Lionel did not take his eyes off his opponent, but he smiled as chills raced down his spine.

"Finally."

A loud crashing noise split the air, drowning out the whine of the jamming signal for a second.

Zeta looked up past Lionel's head as her mouth dropped open, and Lionel risked a quick glance behind him.

Roland's glowing body was suspended in the air, surrounded by a corona of white light.

Without warning, he flew directly toward Zeta, extending his hands forward and letting loose a massive, white beam.

Zeta's body disappeared in a blinding explosion of light, and Lionel held his hands up to his face as he stumbled backward.

After several seconds, the light slowly faded.

Roland landed next to Lionel and looked him up and down. "Glad to see you survived long enough. I wish you'd waited for me."

"Trust me, I tried. But then I heard Salvador scream and—"

"What the . . ." Roland's voice drifted as his eyes widened.

Lionel looked back at where Zeta had stood, and his mouth dropped as the white light receded farther, revealing a white bubble that surrounded the assassin's body.

From within the protective orb, Zeta was grinning maliciously, holding her metal arm up as white light trickled from her fingertips.

The bubble vanished, and Zeta stepped toward them. "Please thank your girlfriend for my new toy, Roland. It's quite effective, even if it's not how I prefer to work."

Lionel grimaced and readied his sword again before he suddenly realized that Zeta's face seemed to be pain free.

Zeta cackled. "Oh dear, it looks like your own toy stopped working. I'm afraid whatever advantage you thought you had is gone."

"What happened to the signal?" Roland muttered, staring at the assassin. "I thought you said you'd be able to find it."

"I did! It must have stopped working," Lionel said as he pulled the frequency disruptor from his pocket. The device to be functioning perfectly. It even still emitted the same high-pitched whine.

A thin beam of light shot from Zeta's hand and disintegrated the device in Lionel's hand.

"Oops," Zeta said as she touched her good hand to her mouth. "I guess it was still working after all. You really shouldn't believe everything you see, Lionel."

Lionel made a fist where the device had been. "We don't need it to kill you."

"You're right. You'd need a whole lot more than that."

Roland shot another blast of light toward Zeta, then another, but the assassin moved her arm in place perfectly and blocked each laser-like shot, bouncing the light off into the forest.

While Roland flew up into the air, Lionel charged Zeta with his sword, shouting in anger and determined to avenge everyone the assassin had betrayed.

Zeta backpedaled exactly two steps before blocking Lionel's blows effortlessly with the sword in her left hand, all while blocking Roland's shots with her right.

Lionel made every effort to strike her as hard as possible to either destroy her remaining sword or stagger her, but Zeta seemed to flow perfectly with his strikes, rolling with his swings slightly to smoothly absorb the shock of his blows.

After several seconds of fruitless attacks, Lionel glanced at Zeta's arm and immediately stopped his assault. The metal forming her new appendage was glowing brighter and brighter, and Zeta's bloodthirsty smile was growing bigger and bigger.

He backed up away from her reach and shouted in the air, "Roland, stop!"

Either Roland didn't hear him or he was so determined in his attack, but he ignored Lionel, continuing his relentless onslaught.

"Roland, you have to stop! She—"

Lionel's cries were drowned out by a deafening ethereal noise as a massive beam of white light erupted from Zeta's arm, chasing Roland across the sky as he dove out of the way. The light continued past him and burst through the sky ceiling, tearing a jagged line through the otherwise flawless blue sky.

Zeta turned toward Lionel now, blasting a smaller beam of light toward him, yet fast enough that he couldn't dive out of the way. All he could do was hold his sword out in front of him and hope for the best.

The light wrapped around his sword, and Lionel's hands buzzed with energy for a split second before lightning shot from the tip of his sword, shooting into the sky without harming Lionel.

Zeta scowled and looked between her two attackers momentarily before going on the offensive, rushing Lionel before he could say anything.

Lionel defended as best as he could as Roland fired down on Zeta, missing repeatedly as the assassin dashed around Lionel, viciously swinging at his body in a flurry.

Cold steel dug into Lionel's stomach, and he let out a roar of pain as he kicked Zeta away, the blade ripping out of his stomach forcibly as she staggered away.

Another blast of light from Roland descended on Zeta, but she spun around and absorbed the blow just in time. Lionel used this opportunity to swing as hard as he could at Zeta's side. The assassin managed to block this attack as well, but the force of the blow was too much and knocked her blade from her hand. Lionel kicked her sword away and continued his attack, leaving the operative no defense but dodging his massive blade. His attack was cut short as Zeta delivered a brutal kick to his chin, sending him flying backward. He was completely vulnerable, but the assassin turned her attention toward Roland now.

"Lionel!" Roland stopped his attack and looked at Lionel just long enough for Zeta to fire another thin beam of light, finally managing to hit Roland in the chest and bring him crashing to the ground not even a hundred feet from the assassin.

Zeta shrieked in laughter and held up her glowing arm, its light increasing in brightness rapidly.

Lionel knew what was coming, and in a desperate move to save Roland, he grabbed his sword and threw it as hard as he could at Zeta.

The blade spun in the air and managed to slice Zeta's good arm on the way past, earning a howl of pain from the assassin. She looked at him, her eyes burning, but she looked back at Roland as a massive ball of white energy formed at her fingertips. With a grin, she reared back and prepared to execute Roland.

Lionel, weaponless and desperate, climbed to his feet and threw himself forward, directly in front of Zeta as she released her deadly weapon.

And then he ceased to exist.

## 48

"NO!"

    Aniya's heart sank as Dawn's agonized scream pierced the air at the sight of Lionel's disintegrating body.

She sat up and closed her eyes, unwilling to watch what was coming next, knowing that Roland's death was imminent.

Somewhere in the distance, Dawn was still screaming. Aniya realized as she heard her name that she was being accused, blamed for Lionel's death. She opened her eyes to see Dawn being held back by Corrin, reaching for Aniya with a vengeful glare written over her tear-stained face as her accusations turned to curses.

Aniya bowed her head, embracing the well-deserved hatred. She knew she was to blame for Lionel's death. Roland's too, soon enough. Maybe she couldn't have saved them, but she could have offered herself up in their place.

But at what cost?

Aniya looked back up at the sky ceiling. Roland was back in the air, obviously injured, doing his best to fight Zeta and clearly losing.

A new shout brought Aniya back to reality as the fog

cleared. Her name was being called again, but this time by someone else.

She looked up to see Caspian standing over her, his hands on his hips.

"What do you want?" she asked miserably.

Caspian's response was terse, demanding. "Get up."

"Can't you let me watch my brother die in peace? I only—"

Aniya suddenly found herself on her feet, yanked up by the arm. She pulled away but was held tightly by Caspian.

"You mean to tell me you're not even willing to save your own brother?"

She pulled again, but Caspian's grip only tightened.

"Let go of me!"

"You can still go up there and save Roland, and you're just going to sit here and feel sorry for yourself? Are you really that selfish?"

Aniya leaned into his pull and shoved him backward, finally breaking his grip on her arm.

"I can't save him. I can't save anyone! It's over. The Director has won. The only thing I can do to save Roland is to turn myself over to him. And if he has me, it's over for all of us."

Caspian stepped forward again, jamming a finger into Aniya's chest. "You know what you have to do. Are you really so obsessed with the idea of saving your dead boyfriend that you won't save someone who's still alive?"

"Nicholas *is* still alive! I know it. I've seen him. I've heard him."

"Even if he is, what could you possibly do about it? You couldn't have brought him back before, and you definitely can't do it now that the Director has him."

Aniya balled her fists and pushed her chest against Caspian's finger. "Don't tell me what I can't do."

"But you can't! What has to happen to get you to realize

that he's never coming back? How many more people have to die?"

That was enough for Aniya, and she swung a fist at Caspian's face, but he quickly blocked it and retaliated with a swift, sharp slap to her cheek.

As Aniya stumbled backward, Corrin stepped between her and Caspian.

"That's enough," he said, spreading his arms as if to shield Aniya from Caspian.

But Caspian pulled out a gun and pointed it at Corrin's head. "Stand down, General. This is between me and Aniya."

Corrin stood his ground. "I won't let you talk to her like that, and I certainly won't let you hurt her. Take a walk and cool down."

"Cool down? People are dying, Corrin. You're willing to just stand here and let it happen? Stand down."

"Do you really think you're going to get through to her by yelling at her? I've seen what happens when she gets upset, and you don't want that."

Caspian cocked the gun and pressed it against Corrin's head. "Don't test a desperate man, Corrin. I'll do what it takes to win this war."

Aniya pushed Corrin out of the way and knocked Caspian's gun out of his hand.

"No one wants to save Roland more than I do," she said, pushing Caspian with both hands. "Don't you think I would have done it by now if I could have? I can't turn myself in to the Director. We both know that. But I can't kill him either. It's not just that I don't want to. It's that I can't."

"I don't believe that's true," Caspian said, his voice softening for the first time. "I know what you're capable of. You've proven that you can do what's right when you have to. Don't let your brother down when it matters most. You can save this world, restore it if you just do what you have to do."

Aniya shook her head. "I could have saved Tamisra.

I wanted to. If I had killed the Director, I would have been able to save her. And I certainly wanted to kill him afterward, when it was too late. But I couldn't. I just couldn't."

Almost instantly, Caspian's gentler demeanor vanished, and he threw his hands in the air as he shouted, "Then you are a coward! This entire world will burn, and at the end of it all, when humanity gasps for one final, agonized breath of toxic air, they will have you to thank for cursing them to a horrible death."

Light rushed through Aniya's body, and with a scream of rage, she pushed her hands into Caspian's chest again, this time sending him flying backward, disappearing into the shadows.

## 49

R oland stared in shock as Lionel disappeared in a flash of white light.

As the adrenaline from the surprise started wearing off, the pain in Roland's chest returned, and he grabbed at his skin, feeling the gaping hole above his heart.

He took a pained gasp of air as he focused on his wound, and with a searing heat, the pain slowly receded. However, he noticed as he looked down that the wound was not closing up. He wasn't healing himself like he had seen Aniya do. Roland grimaced as he realized that Zeta's armored hand was capable of doing the same damage as the laser weapons the Director's army had brought to Level I.

As the pain vanished, his vision began to clear from the explosion of light. Zeta appeared before him, putting her hands on her hips and looking down on him.

"What a waste," she said, shaking her head. "I was going to kill Lionel eventually, of course, but I wanted to take my time with him. I suppose I'll just have to have my fun with you."

Roland gritted his teeth as he climbed to his feet. "How sick do you have to be to actually enjoy killing?"

"Don't tell me you don't enjoy a good fight."

"I stopped by Level I just long enough to find out that you gave Salvador back to us. After that, I only came up here to save Lionel. But now?" Roland said, seething. "Trust me. I'm going to enjoy killing you."

Zeta grinned wildly. "I was right. This will be fun."

"Then let's stop talking."

"Fine by me."

Roland thrust his hands forward, letting out twin beams of light. Zeta had barely enough time to defend, and as she threw up a barrier in defense, their light clashed together, sending them both flying backward. Roland recovered mid-air and flew toward Zeta, firing from both hands.

Zeta rolled on the grass, dodging each shot as they struck the ground, searing the grass and blackening it instantly. She used her momentum to propel herself to her knees, then pointed her metal arm back toward the ground, firing a blast of light below her and sending herself flying upward.

They collided in mid-air, Zeta immediately striking Roland in the face with her artificial arm as he drove a knee into her stomach. They fell together, crashing into the ground and tumbling for several feet, all while continuing to punch and kick each other.

Zeta suddenly pushed Roland off of her, hard enough that he soared backward, several feet off the ground. The assassin immediately fired another shot, piercing his shoulder mid-flight.

Roland fell flat on his back, grabbing at his shoulder in pain. He opened his eyes just in time to see Zeta leaping on top of him, so he kicked out his legs and set her flying over his body and back behind him, giving him time to stand up and face her.

"I don't get it," he said between labored breaths as the pain in his shoulder receded. "I assume the Director made that arm for you? Using Aniya's light? She only has half the power she should. Nicholas has the other half. I have both. How are you hurting me?"

Zeta made a fist and opened her hand again, her metal fingers knocking together in a series of dings. "I don't think you understand what Aniya actually is."

"And you do?"

"Enough to know that she's more dangerous than you realize. She just doesn't know what to do with her power. But I do. I know how to use it to its full potential."

"It's just your arm. There's no way you're as strong as she is, or for that matter me. In fact, why don't you take that arm off and I'll fight you without the light?"

Zeta laughed as she approached him, genuine mirth twisting her face in an expression Roland hadn't seen before.

"I'm not stupid. Unlike Aniya, I know what a gift this power is. Besides, as much as I want to prove you wrong, I couldn't take it off. It's fused to my body."

Roland shrugged. "Then I'll rip it off myself."

He jerked his head forward, bashing his forehead against hers. As she staggered backward, Roland delivered a swift kick to her side, then immediately followed up with two punches to either side of her chin. Zeta continued to backpedal, and Roland took the opportunity to reach out and grab her metal hand, crushing it.

Zeta yanked her arm backward as light began to leak through her hand, spilling out in dozens of tiny beams that split off in different directions. Several of them struck Roland, and he pushed her away as he cried in pain.

Before the assassin could recover, Roland let loose another barrage of light, this time as a massive beam from both hands. Zeta dove to the side and returned fire with multiple shots of her own, each one racing through the air in unpredictable patterns, with branches of light that forked away like lightning.

As several more tiny daggers of light dug into Roland's

body, he jumped back into the sky, flying backward to give himself more time to dodge.

With a new fury that filled him with an unrelenting resolve, Roland fired back precise, lethal shots that kept Zeta waving her arm wildly, barely managing to dodge each shot. Finally, when Zeta stumbled backward and to the ground, he dove straight down toward the assassin head-first, arms outstretched, leading with an orb of light at his fingertips that grew as he descended.

Just as Roland crashed into the ground, Zeta dove away again and quickly fired a forked beam of light from her fingertips, striking him in the side.

With a cry of pain, Roland crumpled into a ball on the ground, rolling away as he clutched his side. He tried to sit up, but Zeta fired again, this time piercing his other shoulder. Digging deep for adrenaline, Roland roared in anger as he pushed himself up, but his shout turned to a scream as another beam of light sizzled through his thigh.

Roland let himself fall back to the ground, moaning in pain as his body audibly hissed. After several seconds, he opened his eyes again to see Zeta standing above him, clutching her hand as light spilled out and trickled to the ground.

"That was disappointing, Roland. I had hoped for more."

He growled as he slowly sat up. "Give me a second. You'll get it."

"Unfortunately, my work here is done. It looks like the Director was wrong. No one is coming to save you. This was a waste of time, and as much as I'd like to keep playing with my food, I have other things to do."

Roland planted a foot and pushed down on his knee, but he could not muster the strength to stand. After struggling for a moment, he let his foot slip behind him, resting on his knees even as his thigh burned.

"What," he said, wheezing, "you're going to call it quits, just like that? Afraid I'll make a comeback?"

Zeta smiled sweetly. "That's cute. And I wish I could let you have that chance, because then things would be truly interesting, but I'm afraid I have my orders."

As the assassin's hand began to glow brighter, Roland took a deep breath, ignoring the pain that pulled at his body from a dozen different places. He puffed out his chest and stared at his executioner, his head held high.

"Fine, kill me. But enjoy the short time you have left on this earth. Because if Aniya doesn't kill you, someone else will. You have no idea the hell you're about to bring upon yourself."

An orb began to build up in Zeta's hands, a ball of white energy with lightning forking from it and crackling menacingly. The assassin played with the orb, tossing it up and down and rolling it from her palm to the back of her fingers.

"Oh, trust me," she said with a cold-blooded grin as she tossed the orb in the air and caught it. "I'm counting on it."

Then, she reared back, and as a loud crash echoed through the Overworld, Zeta threw the ball of deadly light forward to execute Roland.

## 50

A niya collapsed, falling to her knees as Caspian flew backward, landing somewhere out of sight.

Dawn rushed by but stopped and turned to Aniya to give her one last death stare before running off in the direction where Caspian had vanished, leaving Aniya alone with Corrin.

A hand rested on Aniya's shoulder, and it seemed to trigger something inside her. At the touch of Corrin's hand, she burst into tears, sobbing into her hands as he knelt by her side. She didn't acknowledge his presence. She simply cried, stopping finally after several seconds to look up at the sky ceiling for a moment. Roland was on his knees now, staring up at the crazed assassin as she towered over him with a glowing arm.

"Everything's gone wrong, Corrin," she said at last, her eyes glued to the screen. "The Director is going to kill us off one-by-one, and there's nothing I can do about it."

"I refuse to believe that. Caspian may be desperate, but he's right. You're more capable than you give yourself credit for. Don't let your fears define your limits for you."

"But I can't," she said as she hid her face again. "As long

as there's any chance Nicholas can come back, I can't just kill him. If you could bring Xander and Malcolm back from the dead, would you?"

The question came sudden, abrupt, quick enough to seemingly catch Corrin off guard, but he quickly recovered, closing his mouth and shaking his head. "I suppose I would. Ideally, if I had such power, I would have kept them from dying to begin with."

Aniya shot a pained glance toward him.

"I'm not saying you could have," he quickly added.

"No, but now I can save Roland."

Corrin nodded. "And no one wants that more than I do. But if you go up there and you can't kill the Director, Roland will die, and he will have you. The entire world would suffer."

Aniya turned away. "But we don't know what the Director would do with me. I'm okay dying if it means that Roland lives. Wouldn't you give your own life to save your children?"

"We both know the answer to that. And I would do it for Roland in a heartbeat if I had the power to do so. But if saving him means endangering millions, I don't know if that's a legacy I want to leave behind. You have the power to save Roland, but you also have to be willing to do what you know you must do."

"And what if I can save Roland without getting myself caught? What if no one has to die?"

Corrin gave a sad smile. "And you can do that?"

"I only see Zeta on that screen, Corrin. Maybe the Director isn't even there."

"Do you really believe that?"

Aniya turned to face him, grabbing his hands. "I can't let anyone else die because of me, Corrin. I can never forgive myself for what happened to Xander and Malcolm."

"I told you, it wasn't your fault that either of them died."

"Don't say that, Corrin," Aniya whispered. "We both know that's not true. Your children are dead, both of them.

And it *is* my fault. I killed Xander, and I did nothing while Zeta killed Malcolm in front of me."

"You couldn't have predicted Zeta's betrayal, so please stop torturing yourself about Malcolm. As far as Xander goes, he was simply too close because he was trying to help you. You couldn't control the power you've been cursed with."

"Can I tell you a secret? I know what it'll take to control it. If it's my emotions that are controlling me, then it means eliminating anything for me to get emotional about. It means letting go of the voices in my mind. It means killing the Director and letting go of Nicholas. But if I do, he'll be dead forever. He'll be just another person I've killed."

"But controlling your power means being able to win this war, right? Ridding the world of the Director and bringing true freedom?"

"I get it. I'm being selfish."

Corrin shook his head. "I'm not trying to guilt you into making a decision, Aniya. But I won't lie to you. I don't want Roland to die. What is it you want?"

Aniya gave a short laugh. "What do I want to do? I want to save Nicholas. I want to bring him back. He could help us win the war."

"But can you bring him back? I was under the impression that he's dead."

Aniya huffed and folded her arms. "So everyone keeps telling me. But he's out there somewhere, Corrin."

"So what if he is? You asked me if I would bring my sons back if I could. I can't, Aniya, therefore it's irrelevant. Maybe you need to go ahead and accept that Nicholas isn't coming back. You can't know for sure if you can save him. Is it worth waiting to find out?"

"Why can't I accept that Nicholas is gone? Why can't I move on and do what I have to do?"

Corrin thought for a moment before answering. "Maybe you're right. Maybe he isn't gone. If that's the case, no one can fault you for wanting to save him. But maybe Caspian is right. Maybe you're just afraid that he's really gone, and you're just seeing things you want to see. But even if he is somehow still alive, what could you do? Can you tell me that you can bring Nicholas back?"

Her response was inaudible, barely uttered through lips unmoving.

"What?"

Aniya bowed her head and spoke louder. "I don't know."

"Do you think you can figure out how before Zeta executes your brother?"

As blunt and painful as Corrin's words were, Aniya could only swallow and shake her head. "I don't know."

"There are those who say we must follow our hearts, Aniya. But there comes a time when we must decide to do what we know we must do, despite how much our heart yearns for something else."

"You're saying give up on Nicholas?"

Corrin paused before answering. "I'm saying that sometimes, we have to give up those we love most, as awful as it is."

Aniya frowned and studied Corrin's face. He was clearly holding something back.

He took a deep breath and continued, "A long time ago, in the darkest time of my life, I met a woman, the most beautiful I had ever known. When the war started, she ran away with me and gave me a son. We fought together in the Uprising, and though we suffered many losses and faced many hardships, we were happy. But we got word of a new weapon that would effectively end the war and end in my imprisonment or death, so I insisted that my beloved wife leave the caves and retreat to the safety of the sectors. But not before she delivered twins, a boy and a girl. I saw them for mere minutes, just long enough to name them before their mother took all three of my children to the sectors. The same day, the Lightbringers caved in the tunnels and forever separated me from my family."

Aniya's bottom lip was trembling now, and Corrin nodded as if to affirm her suspicions.

"I made your mother leave you and your brothers because I knew it was the only way to keep you safe. I didn't think I would last the Chancellor's final attack, and no matter how much love I had for you, I refused to let you die in my arms. It is what I had to do, no matter what my heart told me otherwise."

Aniya brought her hands to her mouth as tears slipped between her fingers.

"What about Malcolm and Xander?" she asked. "Does Roland know?"

"Yes, we talked many times over the last three years. He knew I wanted to tell you myself when the time was right. As far as Malcolm and Xander, that's quite a long story. Do you hate me for not saying anything?"

"No, at least I don't think so. It's not like I didn't have a father." Aniya reached out and took Corrin's hand. "But you're about to lose another son, and it's going to be my fault again."

Corrin said nothing as he bowed his head, a tear slipping off his cheek and on to the ground.

"What do I do? Should I give myself over to the Director? Or do I do everything I can to kill him?"

"Only you can know what you have to do, Aniya." Corrin looked back up at her and placed his trembling hands in hers. "But please save my son, Aniya."

Aniya took a deep breath and nodded. "I don't know what's about to happen, but I won't let you lose another son because of me."

"Just be careful. I don't want to trade one child for another."

She stood on her tiptoes and kissed Corrin on the cheek.

"Thank you for telling me. I think it's exactly what I needed."

Without another word, she took a step back and jumped into the air. Light flashed beneath her feet, and the Hub rocked with an explosion as her body crashed through the sky ceiling.

----

## 51

Aniya burst through the ground, flying into the air as she rapidly looked around the beautiful landscape of the Overworld.

Her vision was drawn like a magnet to an area at least a mile away, where Zeta stood above Roland, mid-swing with what looked like a ball of energy in her hand.

Without thinking, Aniya whipped a hand toward the scene, a beam of light racing from her fingertip and instantly intercepting the orb mid-flight. The resulting explosion was like a roar of thunder, and as the assassin staggered backward, Aniya flew toward the two of them, landing by Roland's side.

Gone was the hostility he had directed toward her earlier. Gone was his apathetic attitude she had last seen him with. Her brother looked back at her with a dazed, pained expression, though he wore a thin smile on his pale face.

"About time you showed up," he said weakly.

Aniya grabbed his shoulders and willed the energy inside her to heal her brother. As light raced over her body and into his, Roland's face regained color, but his wounds didn't heal.

"Don't bother. Doesn't work." Roland cracked his neck and nodded toward Zeta. "But I knocked her around real good, got her ready for you. Finish her off, and let's get out of here."

Aniya looked up at the assassin, who was just now recovering and glaring at them.

"With pleasure."

But as Aniya raised her hands backward to unleash everything she had on the girl who had betrayed them, who had killed Tamisra and Malcolm, who had caused so much pain, a shadow fell over the Overworld.

The sun vanished as a thick, black cloud crept across the sky. The air grew murky, wet. The warm breeze turned icy cold.

Zeta smirked as she backed away, holding her damaged metal arm out in front of her.

"You'll forgive me if I don't stick around for this," the operative said. "Enjoy what's coming. It's been fun. But it's time to let someone else have a turn with you."

"The Director," Aniya whispered as she looked around, a chill racing over her body.

Roland pulled on her shoulder as he struggled to stand. "This is what you were waiting for? You lured us here just to have your boss finish us off? I thought you wanted a fight."

"And I got one," Zeta said with a shrug. "But even I know when to back off. I can't take on both of you, so I think I'll leave that to someone who can."

Aniya advanced rapidly, shaking her head as light began to build in her fists. "No, you're not getting off that easy. You die today."

Black mist rapidly gathered in front of Zeta, and with a smirk, she backed off into the shadows and disappeared.

"Stop!"

Aniya halted just before entering the black cloud and turned back to Roland.

"We can finish her off another day, but right now we need to get out of here," Roland said, looking around nervously.

"Maybe we can still make it back to Level I. Zeta will die another day when we come back with an army. But if the Director is out here somewhere, it's not worth running into him, especially if you're not ready to fight him."

"And you are?" Aniya approached her brother and glared at him. "You came up here knowing that you might have to fight him. You think that because you figured out that you can have this power too, you're able to do what I can't?"

"I was wrong," Roland said as he looked down at his body, which was riddled with severe burns. "If Zeta can do this to me, I don't want to know what the Director is capable of. But when you're ready, we can fight him together."

Aniya stared at him for a moment and nodded. "When I'm ready."

She reached toward Roland to hug him, but a thin pillar of haze erupted from the ground next to her and wrapped a black coil around her right wrist. An identical tendril came from her left and pulled against her other hand.

The darkness tugged on her from opposite sides and stretched her body as she groaned in pain.

Roland stepped forward as if to help her, but he was instantly grabbed and pulled away from her by a similar pair of tendrils.

"Oh, Lucifer. Did you really think I would just let you leave with him?"

The voice seemed to come from everywhere, the booming noise unimpeded by the thick shadows.

"I suppose I didn't," Aniya hissed through her teeth. "But did you really think I wouldn't try?"

"Of course not. That's who you are. You may be too stubborn to accept it at first, but I believe given the proper motivation, you will always do whatever it takes to save the ones you love. If only you could save all of them."

"So what now?" Aniya demanded. "Are you going to kill me? Put me back in your machine?"

"Neither, at least not right now. Believe it or not, I have more important things to attend to."

Roland laughed. "After all that? After all the fuss just to get her back up here, you're going to leave us tied up and run a few errands? What could you possibly need to take care of?"

"You."

Another tendril of smoke lashed out from the ground and wrapped itself around Roland's throat, constricting and yanking him backward as he gasped for air.

"Stop!" Aniya screamed as Roland's face drained of all color.

"I am sorry, my dear. But there can only be one Light-bringer. And I have chosen you, which means that, regrettably, your brother must die."

As Roland was hoisted into the air, the Director stepped out of the shadows, still in Nicholas's body. He folded his arms as he looked between Aniya and Roland.

"I don't often make mistakes, but even I am big enough to admit them." The Director approached Roland and curled a finger under his chin. "I should have killed you back in the Underworld. With your new power, finishing you off will be a chore if you resist. Not impossible by any means, but it will be painful for you. So please, for your sake, do not struggle."

Aniya pulled against her restraints, managing a step toward the Director, but without looking, he held out a hand behind him, and the tendrils yanked her backward again.

Roland's shocked expression vanished, and he gritted his teeth as his neck bulged. Light seeped from his skin, and the shadow that clamped down around him suddenly split open, dissolving in a puff of smoke. He spun toward the Director and shot two beams of light from his hands, washing the man in a bath of white light.

After several seconds, Roland ceased his barrage of light, leaving a white glowing sphere surrounding the Director.

The sphere slowly shrank until it melted into the Director's body, and he shuddered as light crept into his skin.

"Okay, then."

The Director stepped back into the shadows and disappeared.

Roland blasted more light from his hands and banished the shadows from the immediate area, revealing the grassy hill and the nearby forest, but the Director was gone.

"Stay here," Roland said as he leapt into the air, leaving Aniya alone on the forest floor.

"As if," Aniya muttered as she ran off into the trees as the shadow spread again, covering her in darkness as she raced blindly through the forest.

"What are you going to do when you find him?" The Chancellor's voice whispered in her left ear.

Aniya ignored the voice and kept running.

"He's right, Aniya." William's voice tickled her right ear. "You know what you have to do. Make your peace with it now."

"I'll find another way," she said.

The phantoms kept talking, but Aniya pushed them away and continued on.

A cry of pain made Aniya look up. She let loose a wave of light, and the surrounding shadow cleared just enough to reveal Roland's body suspended in mid-air, clutched by a large, shadowy hand. He was kicking wildly, his face contorted in an agonizing expression.

Aniya leapt into the air, headed directly for Roland's body, but a shadow intercepted her and clamped down over her body, squeezing at her midsection.

As darkness crept over her vision, she saw Roland grimace and flex his muscles, forcing light out of his body and burning the tendrils that wrapped around his arms and legs. But almost as if in response, Aniya felt energy drain out of her as Roland's bonds seemed to reinforce themselves and grow darker still.

"How?" Aniya demanded as she fought back against the tendril around her abdomen. "Roland is what I was supposed to be, right? Why isn't he stronger than you?"

"Stalling for time, are you? Very well. I'll bite." The Director's body floated out of the shadows and hovered between Aniya and Roland. "It is a curious phenomenon indeed, but you, my dear Lucifer, are not one half of a whole. And neither am I. Roland is half-light, half-shadow. But you are wholly light, just as I am wholly shadow. And since you are incapable of killing me, I can take every ounce of your power and turn it against him. It's two against one, really. Ironic, isn't it, that your brother will die at your hand? Against you and me together, Lucifer, he doesn't stand a chance."

Roland's head lolled over as red veins covered his skin. His eyelids drooped open as a raspy gasp came from his drooling mouth. With a cough, he managed to speak.

"I'm sorry, Aniya. Caspian tried to warn me. I shouldn't have taken—"

An agonized scream escaped his lips, and the red veins covering his face suddenly turned black, an ebony liquid oozing from his pores.

"Let him go!" Aniya managed to choke out as she gasped for air. "I'll do whatever you want. I'll be your weapon. I'll be your light. It doesn't matter anymore."

"You'll do what I want whether he lives or dies, Aniya." The Director swiveled in the air and floated toward Roland. "But he has to die. I'm afraid I have no choice in the matter."

The Director stroked Roland's cheek, and Roland cried out in pain as his eyes turned completely black.

"Please understand that I have no desire to kill you, my boy. I had hoped to avoid it, in fact. But you are a threat not even I can control. You were the variable I could not predict. I can control a great many things, but I could not control the seed that fertilized your mother's eggs. Your birth was an unfortunate accident that nearly cost me everything. It was an accident that I must correct now if I am to restore this world."

The Director bowed his head. "Please know, I am truly sorry."

Aniya screamed in excruciating pain as the light inside her was rapidly and forcefully extracted from her body, and Roland's screams soon matched hers as the shadow that held him captive spread across his body and sank into his skin.

With one last scream as she watched her brother's final moments, Aniya collapsed and fell to a mushy, wet surface.

The Overworld was gone.

Aniya was back in the strange world she had seen the last time she fought the Director. The same massive, steel machine stood before her, embedded in the red, breathing ground by her hands. The eight pylons that surrounded the machine now flashed a rapid white, surging the fleshy mass under Aniya with huge, white veins.

Somewhere in the distance, Roland's screams still sounded, though they now sounded like they were coming from underwater.

"Where are you?" Aniya shouted as she spun around. "Stop hiding and face me!"

"My dear, does it really matter?"

A smooth voice purred and echoed throughout the void. It wasn't Nicholas's, but Todd's, the original form of the Director that Aniya had met three years ago.

It continued, softly whispering in her ear. "What are you going to do?"

"I'm going to kill you!" Aniya screamed as she stomped her feet, wishing away the sound of her brother's screams.

The Director's deep laugh made the ground beneath her shake. "You've proven by now that you won't. Or you can't. It doesn't matter to me. But go ahead. Try. Kill me, and you lose any chance of reviving your dead lover."

"If that's what it takes," Aniya said firmly.

"Words are cheap, Lucifer."

Something touched Aniya's shoulder, and she spun around ready to attack, but she gasped as Nicholas appeared in front of her. Gone was the robotic look in his eye, and he smiled at her for the first time in years.

"Hello, Aniya."

Aniya let herself fall into his arms, surrendering her anger for as long as she could. For all she knew, this would be the last time she could let herself feel like this.

"I'm so sorry, Nicky."

A hand made its way through her hair and massaged her head.

"Don't be. There's only one way you're winning this fight, and if it means that I have to die in order for you to live and save Roland, then that's what has to happen."

Aniya shook her head. "I could never forgive myself."

"In time, you will. You forgave me, didn't you?"

"That's different."

Nicholas kissed her forehead. "I believe in you, Aniya. You're so much stronger than you think."

"Agreed."

Aniya turned to see William standing by her side. A glance down revealed that he had been holding her hand.

"You don't need us, Aniya. You never have. It's time to let go."

Aniya pulled William into a three-way hug with Nicholas, pressing her face into their shoulders. "It wasn't supposed to be like this. I was supposed to save you, both of you. How did it all go so wrong?"

William pressed his cheek up against hers. "I guess you'll have to settle for avenging us."

"He's right," Nicholas said. "It's too late for us, but there are millions of people you can still save. It's time to do what you have to do in order to make things right."

Aniya pulled them closer and would have remained in their arms forever if it weren't for the sound of Roland's screams.

With a deep breath, she pulled away.

"Okay," she said. "I guess it's time."

"Ah, vengeance," the Chancellor said, materializing between Nicholas and William. "At long last, you can—"

The Chancellor vaporized in a burst of light. Aniya lowered her glowing hand and shook her head.

"Not vengeance. Liberation."

Aniya set her face and looked upon her lover and her brother one last time.

"Good-bye."

Aniya closed her eyes and channeled all her remaining strength, and when she opened her eyes again, she was back in the Overworld again, floating above the surface, still held tight by the shadow that constricted her stomach.

She concentrated, and as she focused her breathing, the tendril around her sparkled with yellow light as energy flooded back into her body. The shroud of darkness around Roland receded, and his face appeared again, now devoid of all color.

Roland let out one final, miserable gasp, and with a sigh, his head fell limply to the side, his eyes open in a dead, cold stare.

Finished with his victim, the Director turned toward Aniya, a frown on his face, but before he could speak, Aniya screamed as the tendrils around her burst into flame. She flew forward and grabbed the Director by the hair, emitting twin beams of yellow light from her eyes into his, and for the first time, she heard the Director scream.

Roland's body was released, and he plummeted to the ground. Aniya turned to follow him, but the Director grabbed her and yanked her upward, dragging her body with him as he flew higher into the air.

The sky ceiling shattered as their joined bodies burst through into the dark, irradiated sky.

"Look at this world, Aniya," the Director shouted above the sound of air rushing by her ears. "This is what you will subject millions of people to if you do not recognize your destiny and fulfill it."

Aniya could not help but obey, and she looked around in horror.

The partially blackened sun above them was just enough to illuminate the surface of the dead planet, upon which beautiful silver domes spread out in every direction, joined by long, thin tunnels. But between the domes was blackened soil, swirling clouds of ash, and a desolate wasteland.

"We are all that stands between humanity and extinction." The Director stopped their ascent, looked at her, and shook his head sadly. "I've done all I can to show you the importance of your sacrifice. I truly don't know what more I can do."

Aniya glared back at him, her face set like stone. She pushed away from him and floated freely on her own. "This world made it just fine without the Lightbringers before. We'll do it again."

"You are the Lightbringer, Lucifer, whether you like it or not. You are the answer to humanity's prayers. You can save them all."

"Then I will," Aniya said. "I'll just do it without you."

The Director smiled. "What would you do without me? I'm the only one who can channel your true power. Without me, you are nothing more than a weapon. With me, you are a savior."

"I'll figure it out." Aniya slammed her hand into the Director's face and directed every last bit of energy into his body. The red light that swirled around her funneled into his open mouth and turned into dazzling white.

The Director's body flailed as he turned into a beacon of

white light, shining into the silver dome below and far into space above.

A red glow fell upon Aniya, and she looked up to see the white light piercing the dead sun far above. Large blackened portions peeled away to reveal a burning red surface.

"Aniya, are you sure you want to do this?"

She looked back down, and she was in the void once again, standing on the fleshy red surface and staring Todd in the eye.

"If you do this, you'll never see him again. Nicholas will—"

"Shut up! I'm done listening to you talk. You've taken advantage of me for too long, used me for your own purpose, and toyed with me like a puppet. I choose my own destiny, and I will do what I have to do in order to save the people I love. Even if that means losing Nicholas."

Todd glared at her defiantly. "I'm not done with him, Lucifer. His body is mine, and I—"

"No!" Aniya's scream shook the void, sending Todd tumbling to the ground. She rushed forward and yanked a pylon from its base. Red liquid streamed forth from the ground, splashing over her.

"You . . ."

Another pylon forcibly extracted.

"Can't . . ."

She grabbed two more and yanked them out at the same time.

"Have . . ."

One step, and she pulled out another. Another step, and she kicked at the next, shattering it. One more step, and she dug her hands into machinery and tore it in two.

"Him!"

Aniya approached the last pylon and pulled it from the ground, turning it and breaking it over her knee.

She turned toward Todd again, but he was gone. She was back in the open air, holding the Director by the face.

Aniya raised her other hand into the beam of light and willed the energy back into her. The light channeled backward toward her and the Director, quickly returning the sun back to its blackened state.

With a shout of rage, Aniya grabbed the Director's face with her other hand, letting the light burst out of her and into his body. The white light exploded around them as the Director's eyes flashed a brilliant blue, and then the light finally died away as his head lolled forward.

Aniya closed her eyes, unwilling to look at the sight before her. She reached inside herself, looking for any other face, but as she looked around the shadows of her mind, she realized she had succeeded in freeing herself from the mental block Caspian had tried so hard to remove. William was gone. She would have even taken the Chancellor at this point over what she knew awaited her in the real world.

Finally, Aniya opened her eyes again. She was floating in the air, staring at Nicholas's dead body, his eyes black and cold. She pulled him close and wept into his shoulder.

"I'm so sorry, Nicky."

Their bodies fell from the sky, slowly drifting back into the silver dome. Aniya kept her face buried in Nicholas's shoulder, her eyes still closed, not particularly caring if she hit anything on the way down.

Aniya barely noticed when her feet touched the forest floor, and she would never have noticed if the weight she carried had not been slightly relieved by Nicholas's feet on the ground.

Regardless, she refused to let go, ignoring the fact that he couldn't return her embrace. She held on for several minutes, softly sobbing into his neck.

Finally, she pulled away slightly and opened her eyes, wishing instantly she hadn't. His gaze was empty, his head cocked to the side, his mouth hanging slightly open with his tongue peeking through.

But what was behind his body was what took Aniya's breath away.

She managed to tear her eyes off his body, and she looked around the biome as chills ran over her spine.

The landscape was open now. There were no trees, no bushes, no hint of green. What was left of the forest was several hundred blackened trunks littering the open air. Ash hung in a thin cloud that permeated her lungs and made her choke. An awful stench lingered in the air, and as Aniya's gaze fell upon the bodies that littered the ground, she realized that it was the smell of burnt flesh.

"What happened?"

# PART V

## RECKONING

## 52

## ONE WEEK EARLIER

Corrin stepped inside the barracks and made his way to the makeshift clinic. Caspian was sitting on the first bed inside, his arm wrapped in a sling.

Ignoring Caspian's cold stare as he walked by, Corrin continued on to the next bed, where Salvador lay deathly still as Dawn was treating his numerous injuries.

Without moving the blanket that covered the lower half of the Scourge's body, Corrin could count a missing hand, a mangled foot, and three shattered teeth. What he couldn't count was the number of red lashes that covered Salvador's torso and the number of hairs apparently ripped from his scalp and face. The final injury of note was one that Corrin didn't immediately inspect, but it was evident from the large pool of blood that stained the area of the blanket above Salvador's crotch.

"Is he going to be okay?" Corrin asked Dawn, not taking his eyes off his mutilated friend.

Dawn kept working hastily, offering no more than "I don't know."

"Will he live?"

The young doctor looked up at him for a split second, her eyes red. She grimaced and returned to her work.

"He's lost a lot of blood," Caspian said from behind Corrin as he walked around to the other side of Salvador's bed. "I think he'll live. But he'll be in pain for a long time."

Corrin wouldn't meet Caspian's eyes. He kept staring down at his leader's body, willing the Scourge to wake up and tell them what to do next.

"You know I was only telling Aniya what she needed to hear so she would do what she had to do," Caspian said.

Corrin said nothing.

"I would never stoop so low as to demean and insult her under normal circumstances, but—"

"So you tried to bully her into doing what you wanted?" Corrin glared at Caspian. "Yes, you're quite the leader."

"I was only doing what I thought was necessary. That doesn't make it right, but I don't regret it. She eventually made the right choice, didn't she? I saw her leave from here."

"Trust me. It wasn't because of anything you did."

"And you think it was because of you?" Caspian smiled. "What could you possibly have said to convince her?"

Corrin looked back down at Salvador. "It's not important."

"I agree. The important thing is that Aniya will finally do what she must."

A heat surged through Corrin's cheeks as he looked up. "Where do you get off telling people what they *must* do? Where is our destiny written, and who are you to enforce it?"

"That's also not important," Caspian said matter-of-factly.

Corrin grabbed the sides of Salvador's bed and leaned over his body, edging closer to Caspian's face. "No, you don't—"

He lost his grip on the bed and fell to the floor as the ground shook for several seconds, an earthquake that rivaled the one that had disturbed the Hub several minutes ago.

When it was all over, Corrin stood back up carefully. He opened his mouth to speak, but he was interrupted by a pained shout.

"What in the blazes was that?"

Corrin spun around to see Salvador propped up on one arm, looking around wildly.

"Lie down," Dawn said as she leapt to her feet, placing a hand on Salvador's shoulder.

But the Scourge pushed her away, letting a grunt of pain loose as he winced.

"How are you even conscious?" Corrin asked in wonder. "The Lightbringers did a number on your body. I'd be screaming in pain if I were you."

Dawn looked up. "Not if you had as much drugs as he's on right now. Help me keep him down."

"Get off me!" Salvador shouted as he shoved her away again.

"Sir, please." Corrin pushed Salvador back down gently. "You've suffered a great deal, and Dawn needs to help you."

Salvador huffed. "Like she helped me by knocking me out? I'll be fine. Let me go."

"You were going to hurt Lionel," Dawn said, placing her hand on his shoulder again, this time forcing him flat against the bed. "Did you expect me to just stand there and watch?"

"I was going to save him. That boy is going to get himself killed one day if he is not careful."

Dawn froze, and she bit her lip as she backed away, placing a hand over her mouth as her eyes grew wet.

"What?" Salvador looked back at Corrin. "Tell me he survived the battle."

Corrin nodded slowly. "He survived the battle, but he died trying to save you from the Director."

The Scourge's face drained of what little color there was left as he let himself fall back to the table.

"You were captured together," Corrin added. "Didn't you see him up there?"

Salvador let out a short laugh, followed by another wince of pain. "I saw nothing while they held me prisoner. The last thing I remembered was chasing after their assassin. Then they had me, and they tortured me. Then I woke up here."

"They let Lionel go with your hand," Corrin said. "To send a message. Lionel went back up after you just before they gave you back to us. It's like they knew exactly what we were doing and sent you back just to taunt us."

"Roland went up there too," Dawn added quietly, her voice cracking. "We were watching for a while, but the screen went out and we don't know what happened to him."

"He's dead," Salvador said with a sigh. "I have no doubt."

Dawn shook her head firmly. "We don't know that."

"Yes, we do. I told you," Salvador said. "I told all of you what would happen if we fought him. And sure enough, he slaughtered us. How many were killed, Corrin? Hundreds? Thousands?"

"Half," Corrin said, almost choking the word out.

"Half!" the legendary warrior shouted. He shook his head. "It's over. Not even Annelise can save us now."

"It's not over," Caspian said, finally speaking up. "Not yet." He held out a device strapped to his wrist, presenting it proudly over Salvador's body.

The Scourge knocked it away. "What is that supposed to be?"

Caspian repositioned it and displayed the screen, which was blank. "It's a computer I programmed to monitor Omega's vitals. When the last earthquake hit, I lost the signal. The Director is dead."

Corrin's eyes widened for a moment, but he frowned.

"There's miles of rock between us and the surface. Couldn't it be interference?"

"No. The signal was strong up until just a moment ago. He is dead. I'm sure of it."

An odd peace settled in Corrin's heart as he realized what Aniya had finally managed to do. She had killed the Director, and at the same time destroyed her last chance of getting Nicholas back.

"It doesn't change the fact that he's a computer program," Dawn said. "I don't know much about it, but couldn't he just find another host body? He seemed to switch from the lieutenant to Nicholas easily enough."

Caspian nodded. "Yes, but he no longer has Nicholas's body now. He's vulnerable and has to rely on his human army. And somewhere in the Overworld is a computer that controls him."

"It doesn't move from person to person?" Corrin asked.

"That's impossible," Caspian said. "And even if he could do that, he wouldn't be able to be in two places at once. There has to be another computer somewhere, a master machine that holds the Director's intelligence. If we can find that and destroy it, we win."

Salvador held up his remaining hand. "You are forgetting the army that Caspian so flippantly mentioned. The Director has the entire Overworld at his disposal. We have mere thousands."

"We have Aniya," Caspian added. "And Roland, if he's still alive."

"Roland?" Salvador frowned and looked at Corrin.

"He did the same thing Aniya did," Corrin said. "He has the same powers now."

Salvador's eyes widened. "You let him nearly kill himself just to become the monster that Kendall and the Director turned Aniya into?"

"Nobody let him do anything," Dawn said. "He forced it on himself."

"How is that possible?"

"Neeshika," Caspian said simply.

"What?" Salvador narrowed his eyes. "Why would she do that? She was counting on Aniya."

"Right," Corrin said. "And how is it even possible?"

Caspian grimaced. "She was president of Level XIX and has spent centuries exposed to the same light that Roland now has. If anyone knows how to manage it, it would be her. In fact, I believe she is the one who helped Kendall do it to Aniya. And I do not know why she would turn to Roland now. She seemed sure that Aniya would fulfill her purpose."

"So that's who's been filling your head with delusions of destiny," Corrin said, pointing a finger at Caspian. "You're blindly following her, aren't you? A half-dead woman obsessed with revenge against the Director?"

"She's gotten us this far," Dawn said. "If she can help us put an end to the Director and the Council, I suggest we listen."

Caspian shifted in place nervously. "Assuming we can still trust her. Something tells me she's not being completely honest with us. But if she can still help us, then we may not have a choice but to trust her."

Salvador shook his head grimly. "She will not help us do anything. She has lost so much already, and she knows that she will lose everything she has left if she leads her people in open war against the Director."

"You're right," Caspian said. "But she's convinced we can win. And now that the Director no longer has Nicholas's body, so am I. Aniya is powerful enough to take on an army by herself, and Roland—"

"Forget it." Salvador let out a defeated sigh. "The Director knows exactly what she is capable of, and I assure you that he is ready for her."

"You can't just say that and accept defeat," Caspian said through his teeth.

"No, he's right," Corrin said. "You saw the weapons they brought with them to Level I. Aniya may be able to conjure up a shield that destroys bullets, but they have lasers that can hurt her. As long as they have those weapons, she's just as vulnerable as any of us."

"Then we protect her," Caspian said. "We put her in the back where they can't touch her, and she can call down fire from the skies from a distance."

Salvador closed his eyes and relaxed as if he was going to fall asleep. "It does not matter. The Director will have thought of this. He will be ready. He—"

"Enough!" Dawn shrieked, slapping Salvador across the face.

The barracks fell silent, and all eyes turned to Dawn.

"He's not a god, Salvador." Dawn folded her arms, standing her ground as Salvador glared at her. "He's a computer, lines of code. He can't possibly foresee every outcome, no matter what he says. Do you really think he would have let Aniya kill him if he could? Don't you think he would already have Aniya, that we would all be dead? He's not the all-powerful, all-knowing god you seem to think he is. And if you lie here and admit defeat, he's already won. Meanwhile, people like my brother are giving everything they have to free us from his tyranny. Man up. Your people need you now more than ever. A warrior that gives them hope, not a coward."

Corrin's mouth slowly dropped open. Any other day over the last twenty years, he would have instantly risen to Salvador's defense and ordered a swift punishment for anyone who dared to speak like this to the Scourge. But not today.

Salvador seemed to be shocked as well, and for a long time, he said nothing.

Finally, he cleared his throat and spoke slowly. "Are you willing to risk the extermination of our people if we fail?"

"If we fail, at least we'll be dead and not sentenced to a lifetime of imprisonment in the Underworld."

Salvador squinted at her. "But we'd be alive."

"I'd argue that life without liberty is no life at all," Corrin said softly.

"Besides," Caspian added, "who's to say that the Director won't come back and destroy what's left of us so that he doesn't risk any more inconvenience?"

"He doesn't have Nicholas anymore," Dawn said. "His advantage is gone."

Salvador scoffed. "You're forgetting his army."

"No one is forgetting his army," Caspian said. "It won't be an easy battle, but it's not unwinnable."

"Yeah, and I doubt many of the Director's men have had to fight against a mole before," Corrin said. "We still have dozens of them stashed away in the tunnels."

"Would have been nice to have them in the last fight," Salvador mumbled. "It's a shame the battle was on us before we could get them."

"So let's use them now," Corrin said. "What say you, Salvador? Would you rather stay down here and wait out your days, or go out fighting like the legend you've become?"

Salvador stared back at Corrin for several seconds before turning back toward Dawn. "How long until I can fight again?"

Dawn gave a small smile. "I hate to break it to you, but all you'll be able to do is lead Refuge into battle. You won't be able to do any fighting yourself. Most of your injuries, while brutal, can be ignored. But you're not going anywhere on that foot."

"Cut it off," the Scourge said without hesitation.

This time, Dawn managed to laugh. "Good one, sir."

"If you can put a computer in a dead body, surely you can

engineer a cybernetic replacement, Caspian?" Salvador raised his eyebrows.

"On backup generators? We can manage. I'll fit you for a new hand, too."

"You're serious?" Dawn glanced around the room. "We haven't recovered the backup generators yet. Our laser saw doesn't have any power."

Corrin winced. "Guess we gotta go old fashioned on this one."

Caspian rummaged through a cabinet until he found a large bone saw. "Something like this?"

"Perfect," Dawn said, her face turning white. "Corrin, please get me a bucket."

"For the blood?"

She looked up, her face pale. "It's for me in case I throw up."

Corrin turned to Salvador. "Are you sure you want to do this? No one will blame you if you want to sit this fight out and wait until you're healed."

Salvador gave a firm nod and grabbed the bed rails. "Give me something to bite on."

## 53

T he Director's eyes shot open as electricity rocked his body from head to toe.

A hissing sound echoed around him as a class wall slowly receded into the ground, and he took a step forward out into thin air.

He examined his hands again as he floated downward and gave a small smile. It was the body of Todd Lambert again, a personal favorite. It was no Nicholas, to be sure, but it was truer to his origins.

The Director landed on the walkway below and met the assassin waiting for him in the middle of the cavern. She held out a robe for him, and he took it, draping it over his body.

"That went well," he said, patting the girl on the head. "You performed admirably."

Zeta frowned. "I don't know if I would use those words."

"True. I would have preferred it if you had finished Roland off, but I don't mind finishing your work for you." The Director gestured at Zeta's broken metal arm. "I'll even fix the weapon I gave you and told you to take care of."

"I didn't mean that. What about Nicholas's body? Don't you need it?"

The Director waved a hand. "There's someone who needs it much more than I do."

"Are you going to tell me who?"

"No."

Zeta's eyes narrowed. "I don't like how little you tell us."

"You shouldn't care. That's not your job."

She opened her mouth to talk again, but the Director held up a hand and closed his eyes. He reached for the tracking signal that he knew would be waiting there.

But there was nothing.

The Director frowned and opened his eyes again. "When you left the forest, did you wait for confirmation of my tracker?"

Zeta nodded. "I waited for the signal and verified its integrity, just like you asked."

"Think carefully before you lie to me," the Director said, sneering. "If you forgot to do something, own your mistake and admit it."

"I didn't forget anything. You implanted the tracker in Aniya successfully, and I had her location down to the nearest inch. I didn't leave the biome until I had visual confirmation."

The Director froze. He closed his eyes again and searched for the signal, but there was still nothing. He quickly scanned a table of values that appeared and opened his eyes.

"What's wrong?"

"Something's wrong," the Director mumbled. "It's like the signal doesn't even exist. I looked in its history, and it was live and active until the moment Lucifer destroyed the chip in Nicholas's brain. But the signal wasn't corrupted. It wasn't even destroyed. It just stopped sending a signal."

"Maybe her energy output fried the tracker."

The Director shook his head. "I would have been notified."

"Then what could have happened?"

He paused and made a quick calculation.

"It doesn't matter," he said finally.

"But you have an idea?"

The Director didn't reply.

"Why are you still hiding these things from me?" Zeta curled her hands into fists as her voice raised. "How do you expect me to serve you best if you don't tell me everything?"

"You don't need an explanation to do your job. So go do it. Ready the army. When you're done with that, I have another task for you."

Zeta didn't leave. Instead, she stepped toward the Director. "There's a reason you hide so much from us, isn't there?"

"Yes," the Director said simply. "If I told you every intricate detail of what is to come, you would have turned against me a long time ago."

Zeta's mouth dropped open slightly. "If you know I would turn against you, why would you say such a thing? What's stopping me from betraying you now?"

"Orders."

"Orders?" Zeta backed up, scoffing. "I'm not just some drone that you—"

The Director took one long stride forward and slapped her. "That's exactly what you are, and never forget it. I paid for you. You are *mine*. If you need any more reason, then I don't mind continuing on without you."

"I'm sorry," the assassin said quietly as she bowed her head.

The Director softened and straightened his robe. "But for your own peace of mind, the ultimate goal has not changed. Your actions will save this world, Zeta. I have never lied to you. How I go about it will not be a popular choice, but with every great victory must come a tremendous sacrifice. This world will bleed before it is restored."

He stepped forward again, bringing his nose within an inch of hers as he leaned down slightly.

"Now, ready the army. The end is about to begin."

## 54

D awn stuffed a bottle of painkillers in the already-full backpack, grunting with effort as she forced the zipper closed. She grabbed another pack and started stuffing random ointments and bandages inside this one, paying little attention as her mind wandered.

She couldn't help but imagine exactly what Roland's fate had been. Sure, Aniya had apparently killed the Director. But what had happened to Roland? Was he vaporized like her brother? Ran through with a sword? There was no telling.

Dawn had been counting on Aniya to come back hand-in-hand with Roland, ready to lead the Underworld in a final battle against the Director and destroy him once and for all.

But it had been three days since Salvador had returned, three days since Aniya never came back from the surface. There was no sign that either Aniya or Roland were still alive.

Salvador, of course, had balked at the idea of picking a fight with the Director without Aniya, but Corrin and Caspian managed to talk him into it again.

With or without Aniya, this war was about to end, for better or worse.

"What do you think you're doing?"

Dawn spun around, letting the half-open pack spill its contents on the barrack floor. Corrin was standing in front of her, his arms folded and an eyebrow raised.

"I'm packing," she said, her voice faltering.

"Yes, I can see that," Corrin said. "But what for? You know you'll be staying here."

Dawn started picking up her fallen supplies, avoiding Corrin's eyes. "You can't ask me to do that. Roland's up there somewhere."

"I know. And if he's still alive, I'll bring him back. I promise."

"And if he's not?"

"Then I'll make sure he's avenged. Him and Lionel."

Dawn paused, kneeling on the ground for a moment as she fought back tears. "While I sit back and do nothing?"

"Someone has to stay behind, Dawn. If worse comes to worst, Refuge needs to live on. There will be thousands of women and children here that need someone to watch over them."

She choked out a laugh. "And you think I want that? You think I want to spend the rest of my life down here in the dark, without Lionel, without Roland, knowing I did nothing about it?"

Corrin's face appeared in her vision as he knelt before her. "Lionel died because he forced a responsibility on himself that was never his. Roland did the exact same thing. Don't repeat their mistakes."

"You blame them? We both know why my brother is dead. And if Roland dies, we know whose fault it will be."

"The Director's," Corrin, quickly speaking before Dawn could continue. "It's his fault, and no one else's. Aniya does not deserve your hatred."

"Then let me do something about it," Dawn said as she stood. "Let me go up there and help. If I stay down here like a coward, it's a waste."

"A waste? What are you talking about?"

Dawn bit her lip and looked down at her folded hands. "Tamisra died saving me. I know it wasn't for me, but she did it for Roland. That's the kind of person he deserves, someone who will die for him, not someone who would hide down here while others go and fight my battles for me. If I do that, then I may as well have died and Tamisra lived."

Corrin stood, shaking his head. "Don't make the same mistake that Roland did. He forced something on himself that was not his to bear, and by doing so put himself at great risk. If you chase after him now, you won't be proving yourself to anyone. You'll be needlessly throwing your life away."

"If there's a chance I can save Roland, I have to take it."

"No. This isn't your battle. You don't owe anything to him, Tamisra, Lionel, or anyone else. None of them would want this for you. They'd want you to stay alive, to carry on even though they're gone."

"I can't just do that, Corrin. For all we know, Roland is still alive, and I'd do anything to get him back."

"And you think I wouldn't?"

Dawn opened her mouth to speak, but the words died on her tongue.

"I know Roland told you about me. He wouldn't keep it from you."

She nodded.

"Then you know that if Roland is still alive, I'll stop at nothing to keep it that way. Let me do this. Trust me." Corrin took her hand gently as he gestured toward Salvador, who was asleep on a cot several feet away. "Let me and Salvador do our parts, and please have the patience to do yours."

Dawn bowed her head, and Corrin stepped forward and kissed her forehead.

"It's almost over, Dawn. Just hold on a little bit longer." He stepped away and studied her face. "Do you trust me?"

She forced a smile and nodded, and for just a few seconds, she meant it.

"Good. Please wake up Salvador and tell him it's time, and I'll see you soon." He squeezed her hand one last time and left the barracks.

Dawn was alone again, and almost instantly, the visions started coming again, her imagination quickly showing her a hundred different horrible fates that Roland could be suffering right now.

Before a new wave of tears could begin, Dawn spun around and unlocked a drawer next to the medicine cabinet, pulling out a handgun and stuffing it into her backpack.

"I'm coming, Roland."

## 55

C orrin jogged toward the elevator, his path barely lit by torches driven into the ground on either side.

Caspian stood just outside the elevator doors, a torch in his hands, counting the silver-armored fighters as they stepped inside. "Get comfortable, men. Fifteen will be a tight fit, but we need as many as we can get."

Corrin filed into the elevator and did a final count.

"Remember," Caspian said, holding up a stern finger. "Your mission is recon only. We need to find out what happened to Aniya and Roland. Radio me with information as soon as you have it. We will rendezvous at the train tunnel exit in the Overworld. I've marked the location on your map."

"Thank you. Take care of Salvador for me."

"I'm going to see him now," Caspian said. "If Dawn woke him up, he should be ready just in time to leave with me and the rest of Refuge."

"Take care of yourself, then," Corrin said.

"Noted." Caspian pulled a key card from his back pocket and handed it to Corrin. "Be careful with this. It's my only backup."

Corrin nodded. He inserted the key card in the wall and pressed the very top button, and the elevator doors closed.

As the elevator ascended, the young man to Corrin swayed in place back and forth.

Corrin smiled and turned to the soldier. "Nervous, Thames?"

The young man grimaced. "I saw what their assassin did to Lionel. I don't really want to get blown up."

"Just stay close, kid. We'll retreat to Level I if we need to, but we'll be fine as long as we keep our wits about us."

"What do you think we're going to find up there?"

Corrin shrugged. "I'm trying not to think too much about it. What I hope to find and what I might predict are two different things."

"Got it," Thames said, looking down at the floor. "Why does Caspian even want a recon team? Do you think it'll change anything?"

"Depends. If Aniya and Roland are still alive, we know the fight ahead of us will be incredibly difficult instead of nearly impossible. If they're not, well . . ."

Thames took a deep breath. "At least we'll know."

He nodded. "At least we'll know."

They were silent for the rest of the ascent, and within seconds, the elevator stopped.

Corrin readied his weapon and stepped out of the elevator into a wooden shack with concrete flooring. It was a bizarre combination of materials, but he quickly forgot about the shack as he stepped outside and into the forest, a beautiful tapestry of lush flora. He made a mental note to enjoy the scenery later, and he walked slowly out into the forest, quietly scanning the area for any sign of the Light-bringers.

The forest seemed empty, but just as Corrin opened his mouth, Thames nudged him and pointed up. Corrin followed his gesture to see a hole in the sky ceiling, interrupting the otherwise clear blue sky and hinting at a dark void beyond the dome, a black nothingness with a hint of a red glow.

Corrin gestured in the direction of the hole and led the squadron through the trees, slowly making their way through the forest.

Soon, they almost reached the edge of a clearing that seemed to be created forcibly. Trees bent over at sharp degrees, bowing down away from the clearing in a wide circle. As soon as Corrin spotted what was waiting for them in the clearing ahead, he froze and made a fist, commanding his men to stop.

Dozens of men in black armor were waiting in the open area, walking around with their guns drawn. In the very middle of the clearing, standing in a black crater, was Zeta. She was typing at a massive computer that was set up in the crater, standing almost as tall as the assassin. The metal arm she had sported a few days earlier was missing, and her missing hand was obvious even from this distance.

She was saying something that Corrin couldn't quite make out, and he edged even closer to the border of the clearing, craning his neck as he motioned for his men to be quiet.

"—nothing," Zeta said as her voice became clearer. "There is no trace of her energy signature. Not here, not from anything I can see in the Underworld sensors, and no other biomes have reported any disturbance. It's like she vanished."

Corrin raised his gun, studying the assassin through the scope of his automatic rifle.

"Yes, I know. I'll keep looking. I just can't promise anything."

"Do you see Roland anywhere?" Thames whispered in his ear just a little too loud for his liking.

Corrin made another shushing motion and lowered his voice. "Negative. Let's get back below."

The squadron slowly retreated backward, and Corrin pressed a button on the device on his wrist. It was how

Caspian instructed him to warn Level I of danger waiting for them.

"Hold up," Zeta said suddenly. "I'm picking up a signal."

Corrin's eyes widened as he looked down at the device. He quickly took it off and yanked off the back cover, pulling out the batteries. He made a quick movement and dove to the ground, pressing his body against the forest floor as low as he could go.

"Wait, no. It's gone." Zeta looked around and climbed out of the crater. "But it wasn't Aniya. Did any of you ping outside the biome?"

The armored soldiers looked at each other and shook their heads.

Zeta seemed to think for a moment as she peered into the forest. Corrin pushed his face against the ground harder, praying that Zeta wouldn't spot his armor.

"Spread out," the assassin finally said. "Search the forest."

Thames turned to Corrin and spoke just a little too loudly. "They're going to find us. We have to fight them now."

Before Corrin could respond, a hail of gunfire sounded, ripping into the forest around the silver squadron. One of Corrin's men jumped up to run, but he immediately fell to the ground, his body crashing down next to Thames.

"They're here!" A voice cried out in the distance.

Zeta's voice replied. "Yeah, I see them. Flank and eliminate them."

Corrin shook his head and turned to Thames. "Not waiting for that. We'll lose them in the trees." He turned to rest of the squadron and shouted, "Attack!"

The silver squadron returned fire from their prone position, sending the black soldiers scattering throughout the clearing, struggling to take cover in the open space. Zeta stepped backward into the crater, taking cover behind the ridge in the ground.

Another scream came from behind Corrin, but he kept his

attention on the enemy in the clearing ahead. With very little cover, Zeta's armored men quickly fell, leaving the assassin alone in the clearing.

Corrin glanced behind him. Twelve out of his fifteen men were still alive.

With a triumphant grin, he spun back around toward the clearing and slowly stood. "Surrender, Zeta! We have you outnumbered. Lay down your arms."

A wry chuckle came from somewhere ahead, and Corrin realized that at some point, Zeta had disappeared.

"I've already lost one of my arms," her taunting voice returned. "I'm not giving up the other."

"Drop your weapons or we'll kill you," Lionel shouted. "It's that simple."

"Is it, though?"

At Zeta's remark, a white flash exploded in Corrin's vision, accompanied by a loud banging noise that deafened the squadron.

Corrin grabbed his gun and fired blindly into the clearing as he blinked rapidly, trying to banish the white blanket that covered his vision. His gun seemed to make little more noise than a faint popping that refused to rise above the ringing in his ears.

His vision finally cleared, just in time to see a small object flying directly toward him.

"Grenade!" he shouted above the ringing, diving to the side just as the object hit the ground nearby, rocking the ground as it exploded, sending him flying several feet to the side.

As the ringing in his ears finally subsided, it gave way to the sound of screams coming from seemingly everywhere all at once.

Corrin pushed himself to a sitting position and watched as a black form dashed through the trees. It leapt from soldier to soldier, whipping a silver sword around expertly, stabbing it deep into one man's chest and slicing another's head clean off.

A hand grabbed Corrin, and he looked up to see Thames.

"We gotta get out of here!" the young man hissed quietly as he looked up at the scene in terror.

Corrin looked back at Zeta as pure rage settled over him. He grabbed his gun and stood.

"Go," he said. "I have work to do."

He pulled the trigger and unloaded a full clip in the assassin's direction, sending her squirreling up into one of the trees, vanishing in the green canopy.

The sound of a lighter caused Corrin to turn around. Thames was holding an orb with a fuse on the end of it, a determined look in his eye.

"If you're staying, I'm not going anywhere." He threw the projectile into the tree where Zeta was last seen, and he and Corrin both stumbled backward as an explosion of fire covered the immediate area.

The flames receded just enough for Corrin to see, and he scanned the air for the assassin.

Thames pulled Corrin to his feet and readied his weapon again. "If the napalm didn't get her, it'll smoke her out and make her come to us."

But just as he said that, a sword appeared out of his chest.

Grasping at his chest faintly, Thames looked up at Corrin before collapsing.

Corrin backpedaled toward the fire as Zeta advanced, holding a bloody sword out in front of her and pointing it at him.

"I almost feel bad for you," she said as a wicked grin spread across her face. "I killed your son in front of you. I can only imagine how awful that must have felt. Come, let me put you out of your misery."

He raised his gun again, but it clicked, the clip empty.

Tossing the weapon aside, he raised his fists. "What did you do with Roland? Where is he?"

Zeta shrugged as she advanced. "He's dead, just like Lionel. I wish I had the honor of finishing him off myself, but you can't have everything you want, unfortunately. Don't feel too bad, Corrin. All of this was inevitable. You'll all die, but if that's what it takes to save the world, I trust that you can understand."

Corrin stopped a few feet away from the edge of the fire, feeling the heat grow on his back as the flames grew closer. "So come on, then. Let's get this over with. Drop the sword, and we'll fight like equals."

"Unfortunately, I don't have the luxury of a fair fight. I have things I need to be doing, and I don't have time. This will have to be quick."

She dashed forward, rearing her sword back for a strike, but Corrin kicked up a cloud of hot dirt directly in her face. Without waiting to see her reaction, he spun around and ran into the flames, racing through the burning forest as the flames quickly spread.

An enraged howl came behind him, and it just spurned Corrin to run harder, blindly racing through the flames.

Somehow, he ended up by the elevator shack. He turned to the door and was about to kick it open when an awful pain shot through his shoulder, and he fell to his knees, ready to admit defeat.

"You're faster than you look," Zeta's voice came from far behind him.

Corrin realized that she had thrown the sword, and he forced himself to his feet again, the blade still sticking out of his shoulder. Bracing himself for the pain, he thrust his body against the wall of the shack, pushing the sword out of his body and onto the ground behind him.

He let out a pained gasp as stars covered his vision, but he turned around and grasped on the ground wildly for the sword.

Just as his hand grasped the hilt, a foot connected with his face brutally, and he fell backward roughly, clutching at his nose in pain.

Corrin opened his eyes and watched as a silver blade came sweeping down toward him, and with a grunt of pain, he rolled to the side, narrowly dodging the strike.

The flames reached Corrin and Zeta, and he leapt to his feet as the heat quickly neared an unbearable level.

"You're just delaying the inevitable," Zeta said as she backed up out of the flames. "Come here and let me finish you. I promise, it will be quick. A lot quicker than burning to death."

A creaking noise came from the side, and Corrin watched as a twelve-foot tree teetered on its base precariously as the fire ate away at its trunk.

"Come on!" Zeta shrieked as she sneered.

Taking a deep breath, Corrin dashed forward, directly at the assassin.

Zeta cackled and drew the blade back to drive it through Corrin's heart, but he moved slightly to the side and let the sword pierce his other shoulder.

He grabbed Zeta's shoulders and threw her to the side just as the tree came crashing down, bashing Zeta on the shoulder and falling over her body. The flames covered her body, and her screams began quickly, tortured noises that filled the air and rose above the roar of the fire.

Corrin gasped and fell to the ground. He didn't even feel the blade in his shoulder anymore. All he felt were the flames licking at his body.

With great effort, he managed to crawl forward, reaching the elevator shack again, which was already up in flames. He made it onto the concrete floors and enjoyed a temporary respite from the fire, but the concrete was incredibly hot already, painfully searing whatever exposed skin touched it. Corrin dragged himself over to the elevator and pressed the button, but nothing happened.

He pressed it again, taking a look around him at the burning shack, but as he looked back at the elevator, he realized that the lift was nowhere near the surface. The progress bar at the very top of the elevator seemed to reflect that the elevator was in the Underworld, far deeper than it should have been.

"No, come on," he mumbled, pressing the button over and over again, hoping he was seeing things in the heat.

Outside, Zeta's screams had vanished. Either the fire had gotten louder, or the assassin had finally died.

The progress bar above the elevator was still crawling along. It barely even looked like it was moving.

Corrin began hyperventilating, giving heaving, dry breaths as the heat grew even worse, and he collapsed on the floor in front of the elevator, pressing his face against the somehow cool blast doors.

He took one last look at the progress bar. Surely it had to be an error. He was the last person to use the elevator.

Unable to push himself to his knees, he reached up for the button again, but he let his arm fall back down as he howled in pain.

In a final, desperate move, Corrin swung up blindly, grasping for any button he could reach. A terrible pain blinded him, overcoming his senses as he collapsed again, black settling over his vision. The last thing he saw was his hand falling short just out of reach of the buttons, smacking the side of the blast doors and ruining any hope of rescue.

And then there was nothing.

## 56

Dawn pulled the open-faced helmet lower on her forehead, obscuring her eyes from Caspian. She stepped behind a soldier, easily blending in with the four thousand people that stood in ranks on the edge of the Level I Hub. In hindsight, she realized she should have stayed near the back, but she hadn't thought much when Caspian gave the summons at First Light.

He was scanning the soldiers now, resting atop a mole at the very front of the ranks. Dawn was surprised that he had learned to ride so quickly. He had turned out to be a natural, and he now seemed to guide the beast with ease.

It irked Dawn more than a little to see an ex-Lightbringer take to the wild animals much faster than those who had spent their entire lives in the darker tunnels of the Underworld, forced to learn to tame the vicious beasts through lethal trial and error. But she also felt better about the rebels' chances against the Director, to be led by two fierce warriors who knew what they were doing.

She frowned as she realized that Salvador was still missing, that his absence was the reason they hadn't left yet. Looking around, she quickly saw that he wasn't anywhere nearby. His golden armor would have given him away instantly.

"Sir!"

A loud voice came from behind Dawn, and she jumped, sure that she had been discovered. She gripped the handgun at her side, ready to defend her right to avenge her brother and save her boyfriend, but a silver-armored man pushed her aside gently and continued his way through the ranks, reaching Caspian's side.

"He's gone," the man said. "The Hub has been searched thoroughly. The Scourge is missing."

The rebels began to stir with anxious whispers as Dawn's heart sank. She had been so sure that Salvador was willing to fight one final time. In fact, for a brief moment during their last discussion, she could have sworn she saw the same fire in his eyes that he had when he left to attack the Hub in Level XVIII, the battle that resulted in the overthrowing of the Chancellor.

Caspian audibly sighed as he looked back up at the army.

"Silence," he said as he raised a fist, his voice booming over the scorched valley of the Hub. "I know you were hoping Aram would join us, that he would lead you all in victory. I had the same hope as all of you. But he has made it very clear that Salvador the Scourge is a title only, a title that belongs to those who are willing to stand against tyranny, to lead Refuge and what is left of the Underworld to a brighter future. I do not pretend to be that man. There is another who has proven herself worthy of the title of savior, and I only wish to lead you to her and let her lead you in ultimate victory. If you still wish to be free, this is what I offer. It is not a guarantee, but it is the only chance we have. If you still want freedom, then join with me now, and let us find out our destinies together."

The valley fell silent. The whispering, the anxious shifting ceased, and the army fell deathly still.

Dawn looked around at her last remaining family, a strange amalgam of people. There was Refuge, the people she had known since birth. There was Kendall's Silver Guard, left without a home when the Director's army purged the Underworld. And then there were Caspian's remaining men, orphaned soldiers that had nothing left even before the Director had brought destruction upon them.

There was nothing left for any of them in the Underworld. Even those that had spouses and children would soon find their families subject to the radiation that would quickly spread throughout the Underworld now that the Lightbringers were no longer around to keep the deadly toxins at bay.

And yet none of them made a move to suggest they were still willing to fight. Salvador's failure to show up had deflated the hopes of the army nearly instantly.

A fury ignited in Dawn's heart, quickly spreading throughout her body. They would rally behind one man, invest everything they had in a man that had let them down multiple times. It wasn't right. It wasn't fair.

Even if she could speak freely without being discovered, she didn't have the words to publicly condemn the man who had sheltered Refuge for half his life. Nor could she adequately explain that they didn't need him.

But maybe they already knew. Maybe they just needed the symbol, the name of the fearsome warlord as a rallying cry.

So, with a deep breath, Dawn raised four fingers in the air, high and proud, while doing her best to hide her face from Caspian.

Nothing happened for several seconds.

But slowly, hands began to rise all over the place. Hundreds, then thousands of hands appeared in the air, displaying the four-fingered Mark of Salvador in a silent war cry.

A grin spread across Caspian's face as he gave a firm nod.

Without a word, he turned his mole around and led the army into the train tunnel, leaving the Hub behind.

Dawn looked at the ground beneath her feet as the army started to march past her. As the first step loomed before her, the grim reality of what was about to happen began to set in. She was about to take part in the final battle of a brutal war that had already cost so much. There was little chance she would survive.

But giving her all in the final battle was still the only option, now more than ever. If Roland could be saved, she had to try. She had to be there. And if Roland was lost for good, there was nothing left for her in this world.

In a way, it was comforting. As far as she was concerned, her fate was now tied to Roland's. And that was okay. It was even a little exciting to step into the unknown, death and bliss the only possible outcomes.

Dawn gripped her gun tightly and stepped forward, putting one foot in front of the other in a surreal haze. She took a deep breath and looked back up.

It was time to find out what was in store for her.

## 57

S alvador stepped out of the terrasphere and onto the path. It was the oddest sensation, feeling the texture of the rock floor beneath his right shoe, while not feeling a thing under his metallic left foot.

He glanced down at the rudimentary robotic replacement that Caspian had fitted him for. The appendage was just slightly too small, causing him to walk in an uncomfortable shuffle.

His new hand, however, fit perfectly. The only flaw in its design was the missing little finger that Caspian had detached at Salvador's request.

The Scourge sighed and continued down the tunnel. Even now that the pain of Zeta's torture was finally wearing off, he was forever changed. With the loss of his signature hand, he felt as if his very identity was slipping away.

He stepped out of the tunnel and into the massive cavern bathed in green light. It was a sight that never failed to take his breath away, but he quickly recovered his focus and walked directly up to a robed figure sitting on the narrow pathway.

"Have you not learned the cost of your cowardice?"

the figure asked without turning around. "I thought you had finally embraced the courage that you lost decades ago."

Salvador took a moment before answering, doing his best to maintain his composure. "Do not act like you know me, Neeshika."

"Don't I?" The woman turned slightly, revealing the corner of her smile. "Aram Lionheart, Adviser to the Chancellor of Level XVIII, Salvador the Scourge. Fallen warlord. Failed father. Now a mere shade of your former glory. I know you, perhaps better than you know yourself."

Neeshika stood and turned, folding her arms in front of her as she looked Salvador up and down. "And now you come to me once again, seeking shelter like you did three years ago. You were running from your failures then. Do you dare to claim that you do not do so again now?"

"It was not my failure," Salvador said, stepping forward and glaring down at the pale woman. "I warned them all what would happen if they fought the Director. They failed to listen, and thousands paid for their foolishness."

"So you run from the consequences of their failure?" Neeshika scoffed and waved a hand. "Forgive me if I am not terribly sympathetic to your plight. Though your new extremities are not a good look, I will say."

"I am not running from anything."

"No? Then what are you doing here? You don't dare to ask for my help, do you? You know what my answer will be."

Salvador took a deep breath and nodded. "We cannot win this without you."

"You have Lightbringer. The war is already won."

"Do you know that?"

Neeshika faltered and closed her mouth as she stared back at him.

"Can you promise me that she will be strong enough to destroy the Director and win this war for us?"

She turned away from him but still did not respond.

"Why else did you help Roland become like his sister?" he demanded, stepping around her to face her again. "You were not sure Annelise could do it, were you? You made another Lightbringer because you doubted Aniya's abilities."

"You speak of things you know nothing of," she hissed.

"Do I? Tell me, was it worth it? Annelise and Roland are both missing. You sense them, do you not? Are either one of them even still alive? Was it worth cursing them with horrible abilities that only got them killed?"

Neeshika fell silent again, and it was several seconds before she finally said, "Roland is dead."

Salvador's anger ceased for a split second, and he stepped backward slightly as an icy hand gripped his heart. "And Annelise?"

"I do not know."

"What do you mean you do not know?"

"I mean I don't know," she said bitterly, staring at Salvador with darting eyes. "I felt Roland's light drain away into nothingness, and Annelise's disappeared three days ago."

Salvador shook his head in wonder. "So it was all a waste. All the lies I told, all the people I betrayed, all of it—it was all for nothing."

"I do not believe Annelise is dead. She will return, and she will fulfill her destiny."

"But you *don't know that*," Salvador said, jabbing a finger in Neeshika's chest. "She could very well be dead, and you know it. You are still clinging to a hope, a fool's hope, all while what is left of my family prepares to offer themselves up to the Director as unnecessary sacrifices. They will fight him, and they will die, all of them. But it does not have to be this way. You can help."

Neeshika shook her head. "No. I cannot."

"What are you so afraid of? You have tens of thousands, more than enough to eclipse the Director's forces."

A loud, shrieking laugh escaped Neeshika's lips.

"You think I fear the Director? There are worse things in this world than him, Aram. Much worse."

"Like what?"

"My children are safe here. It is a hellish existence, but it is the best one for them. The only one for them. We are free here."

Salvador shrugged. "They'll be free in the Overworld. Once the Director is dead, we'll make sure there is a place for them on the surface."

"I am afraid that is not possible."

"Why? The living conditions up there are tenable, a far cry from your irradiated web."

Neeshika bowed her head. "I am sorry, Aram. I simply cannot help you."

"Cannot or will not?"

"It matters not."

"How can you say that?" Salvador gripped Neeshika's arms, clutching them desperately. "You have the largest army in all the earth, above or below it. I have seen your children fight. No one stands a chance against the Host."

"What of the Strangers?"

Salvador froze and let go of Neeshika's arms. "What?"

"If the Strangers return—"

"They won't," Salvador said, his voice shaking. "They have no reason to."

Neeshika smiled sadly. "But if they were to come back, you know the fate that awaits this earth."

"Of course. But they will not come back. They cannot."

"You know why, do you not?"

"Yes."

"Well, what do you think will happen when Aniya finally fulfills her purpose?"

"But her purpose—" Salvador froze again as a horrible realization swept over him.

Neeshika nodded as if she read his mind. "And when they

return, there will be no place for my children. Or yours, for that matter. The only ones who will be allowed to live are those who will subject themselves to the Strangers just like they surrendered their wills to the Council."

"But why?" Salvador asked softly as everything about the last twenty years began to make sense. "If you knew they might return, why would you do any of this? Why did you help Caspian? The Chancellor?"

"Because my people are safe down here," she said sadly. "They may live in hell, but at least they live. The Strangers will not care about them."

Salvador's anger returned, and he glared at Neeshika bitterly. "At the cost of everyone else's freedom. Are you really okay with damning the entire world to slavery just so that your people will continue to suffer for the rest of their miserable lives?"

Neeshika's mouth opened slightly, but she said nothing.

"Do you mean to tell me you're that selfish? You can stop this now by coming up with me, destroying the Director, and—"

"And what?" Neeshika demanded. "And fight the Strangers?"

"Yes!" Salvador's shout echoed throughout the cavern. "And fight the Strangers. We can beat them this time. Things are not like they were back before the Collapse. We stand a chance, but if you let my people die and the Director continue on, there will be no one left to oppose them."

Neeshika paused for a moment, but then shook her head. "No. There is no fighting them."

"Fine. Then what if Annelise fails? What if she really is dead? My people will die at the hands of the Director."

"I owe them nothing."

"But I do," Salvador pleaded. "I promised to protect them, and I cannot live with myself if I fail them again."

She looked away. "You are free to end your life here if you choose."

"Please, Neeshika. You can save them. And then we can face whatever comes next. Together."

"I . . ." She placed her hands against the side of her head. "I'm scared. I do not want to lose my children."

"Neither do I." Salvador took her hands and held them against his chest. "So please, help me save mine, and I will pledge my life to protecting yours."

Neeshika stared at him for several seconds, her lips trembling. Finally, she nodded and bowed her head.

"Together."

## 58

## THREE DAYS LATER

"Corrin, wake up!"

The voice was distorted, distant. It wasn't enough to stir Corrin from his near-unconsciousness. Neither was the shaking, which he barely felt. What finally shook him awake was the cool water that splashed over his face, a welcome shock from the heat that still lingered.

Corrin sat up with a start, shaking water from his hair. Cool liquid entered his mouth, and he choked for a second before grabbing the canteen that was offered to him, guzzling down the water until he choked again.

Caspian knelt by Corrin's side as two soldiers stripped off his armor.

"What happened up here?" Caspian asked, looking around.

"Zeta," Corrin said hoarsely. "She was here, looking for someone. Aniya, I'm pretty sure."

Caspian smiled. "So she's still alive."

"Has to be." Corrin grabbed the canteen again and chugged down the remaining water. "How did you find me here? I thought you were waiting for me to give you my updated location."

"We got your distress signal, so I left behind a few dozen men to wait for you in Level I just in case, but I took everyone else up here to search your last known location."

Corrin looked around past Caspian, and his heart filled as he saw the thousands of men gathered in the burnt biome, complete with a few dozen moles that waited behind the army.

He turned and looked at what was left of the forest. There was nothing, really. Just the thin, black remains of the forest's trees and the scorched earth. The sky above was tinted pink and orange by the setting sun, seemingly unaffected by the fires that had ravaged the forest.

"Get some rest," Caspian said. "And then we'll move on."

"Where?"

Caspian nodded to his right. Corrin turned but saw nothing.

"New Washington," Caspian said. "The capital of the Overworld."

"Where the Council is?"

Caspian scoffed softly. "Do you really think there's any Council left? The Director probably destroyed them as soon as he was done with us. And if there's anywhere I would guess the Director's central computer to be, it would be in New Washington somewhere."

Corrin frowned. "Not his laboratory? The Council would have a harder time getting to him there."

"The Council controlled him for centuries," Caspian said. "They had to have access to his mainframe, and I'm sure they would have kept it close. Besides, even if it's not New Washington, taking their capital would be quite the victory and give us a solid leg up on the Director."

"How do we get there?"

Caspian helped Corrin to his feet and pointed again in the distance. "Look closely. See the border?"

Corrin turned toward the beautiful sunset, a strange contrast to the ruined earth. The artificial beauty of the horizon was obvious now as he stood because in the distance, a large circle of lush, green hills and valleys surrounded the blackened ground, creating a border that curved around the burnt forest.

"The door is somewhere around there," Caspian said, pointing at the barrier. "The controls for the terrasphere are destroyed, but we can blow the door to its transport chute."

Corrin looked back at the army and quickly scanned the ranks for golden armor. "Where's Salvador?"

"Missing," Caspian said with a sigh. "I think we overestimated his willingness to fight. We found this, though," he said as he took a golden sword from a soldier at his side.

"He said he would fight," Corrin said, his voice diminishing to a sad wonder as he stared at Salvador's old sword. "I thought for sure he would come."

Caspian placed a hand on Corrin's shoulder. "As did I. But we'll win this war without him."

"A direct assault on their capital city? I want to believe we have a chance. But I'm beginning to think this is a lost cause. My squadron of fifteen just got wiped out by a twenty-something girl."

"That's because I trained her," Caspian said, a twinkle in his eye. "Have faith, Corrin. I doubt they expect a direct attack on their Capitol by such a small army. Maybe our small numbers could prove to be an advantage. There's not much room for a few thousand soldiers in the streets of the capital of the world."

Corrin took a deep breath and nodded. "Then let's go."

They led the army to the edge of the burnt biome, and Corrin did a double take as the wall of the sky ceiling suddenly became incredibly obvious. Individual pixels were unmistakably visible at this distance, an artificial image that looked grainy now, despite its beautiful appearance at a distance.

Caspian reached out a hand behind him.

"Explosives."

One of the mole riders dismounted and handed Caspian a brown package, which he affixed to the wall.

"Move," Caspian said, pulling Corrin by the arm away from the barrier. When they were a considerable distance away, Caspian shouted, "Detonate!"

The barrier exploded, sending electronics and metal flying in every direction. When the smoke cleared, Corrin could see a large, dark tunnel leading away from the burnt sector.

"Come on," Caspian said. "You can ride with me."

Corrin mounted a mole behind Caspian, and the army left the sector, continuing into the tunnel and marching toward New Washington.

The tunnel lit up as they proceeded, their motion triggering a light several yards ahead of them every so often, always lighting the way.

After a few hours, they reached the end of the tunnel, another door blocking the way. But this time, as Caspian approached it with another explosive, the door slid open automatically.

"You think they know we're here?" Corrin asked from the mole.

Caspian shrugged. "Could be that or simply a safeguard in case of trapped maintenance workers. But I think we should assume the worst."

"Agreed," Corrin said this time. He urged the mole forward, letting Caspian mount the beast as it lumbered into the sector.

It was dark now, and while nightfall covered New Washington, the light from the stars reflected off the white buildings, painting the city in a silver glow in the distance. But the forest on the border of the sector was still nearly pitch black.

As the army emerged from the forest and stepped onto the plains that stood between the forest and the city, Caspian held up a fist, halting the rest of the army still within the trees.

"What are we waiting for?" Corrin asked, budging impatiently behind Caspian. "Might as well do this while it's still dark."

Caspian shook his head. "We won't do any good like this. We've been walking for three days, including most of today."

"No, we can do this." Corrin turned to the army, raising his voice just loud enough to be heard in the trees. "Right? We can march on now and take them in their sleep."

The army raised weapons, some of them murmuring their agreement.

"Without Salvador, these are my men to lead," Caspian said. "And those not on moles have been walking for over ten hours today alone. We need to rest."

"We're so close, and if we rest now, we just give the Director a chance to be ready for us."

"He's already ready for us. Do you really think he hasn't prepared for this?"

Just then, a beam of white light erupted from New Washington, splashing up against the sky ceiling and sending jolts of electricity across the digital surface.

Corrin swallowed. "Maybe you're right."

The beam split into an umbrella that rapidly spread over the city and down into the plains ahead of the seven hundred, sinking into the ground halfway between the forest and the city.

"That can't be good," Caspian muttered. He kicked the mole forward and gestured behind him. "Moira, Chang, follow us."

Caspian guided his mole to the glowing white barrier,

stopping several feet away. He dismounted and slowly approached the light.

Corrin hopped off the mole and joined Caspian. "You think that's for us?"

"Either for us or them. Does it really matter? We're not getting through that."

Corrin let his hand linger a few inches away from the surface. A cold vibration emanated from the barrier, pushing against his skin.

Without prompt, the soldier known as Moira stepped forward, pressing her gun into the barrier.

Caspian spun around, angrily whispering, "Soldier, stand down!"

Moira stepped back, withdrawing her weapon and bringing the barrel to her face, examining the metal.

"Did you feel anything?" Corrin asked.

She shook her head.

Chang approached the barrier. "Maybe it's safe to penetrate."

"I wouldn't entertain that thought," Corrin said, lowering his voice as he tried to push away images of Xander's disintegrating body. "I've seen this light used defensively, yet still manage to kill innocents."

"I know," Chang said as he pressed further toward the barrier, his fingers nearly touching the shield. "But this looks different from Aniya's light. We won't know unless we try."

Caspian held up a hand. "Negative, soldier. Step away from the barrier. That's an order."

"But it's not even—" Chang's fingertip grazed the shield, and he disintegrated in a flash of light.

After a moment of utter shock, Corrin turned to Caspian, swallowing. "Well, it looks like we're waiting after all."

Caspian nodded. "Time to start digging."

## 59

"She's back."

The Director looked up from the black orb that hovered before him as a smile spread across his face. He turned around on the walkway to see Zeta standing just in front of the elevator. His smile faltered slightly when he saw her nearly unrecognizable face, covered in hideous scars from the fire.

"It's about time," he said. "We don't have much time left."

"Will you do the surgery now?" she asked, her speech distorted from the voice box the Director had installed upon her return. Her big, blue eyes stared unblinking at him, another addition he had made.

The Director laughed. "You think that because she finally returned, you are owed your face back? It's not like *you* brought her back. No, it's better that you are left with this reminder of your failure. It just might encourage you to perform better next time and keep yourself from losing your life."

"Please," she begged. "It still hurts. And . . ."

"And what? You're hideous? Grow a pair, Zeta. Caspian made you an assassin, not some pitiful, self-obsessed girl."

Zeta looked down at the pathway, shifting back and forth. "Where did Aniya go? I don't like that we lost her for a week."

"It doesn't matter." The Director waved his hand. "It's time to get her back."

A long pause ensued as Zeta stared at the ground, and when she looked back up, her robotic voice was quiet. "You don't know, do you?"

The Director narrowed his eyes as he glared at her. He finally shook his head. "No, I don't."

"And that doesn't concern you?"

"What concerns me, girl, is your inability to carry out my instructions without question. I realize that's my fault since I took out the chip that regulates your behavior, but I expect a little more loyalty from someone I've freed from slavery. I expect more gratitude from someone whose detached arm I have replaced."

Zeta looked back down. "I'm sorry. I didn't mean to question you again. It's just that I know how crucial your plans are, and if her disappearance could interfere with your plans in any way, I think—"

"It is not your job to think, assassin. That is a waste of your limited brain. You should spend your time meditating and preparing for what is to come. I told you that it doesn't matter where she's been. My plans have not changed."

"Yes, sir."

The Director peered down past the walkway at the blue cube that floated a few thousand feet below him. The blue light morphed into a bird's-eye view of New Washington, revealing a glimmering city and a barrier of light surrounding it. Thousands of tiny dots were gathered in the valley on the other side of the barrier.

The stage was set. In the valleys above would be the most incredible battle the world had seen in centuries. The fireworks would be unparalleled.

"She's weak, Zeta. Vulnerable. She thinks she's stronger

now, having killed her love and lost so much. But when the time comes, I trust she will finally be ready to embrace her destiny."

"And if she isn't?"

The Director spun around and marched toward Zeta, who visibly quivered in place but did not retreat. He stood eye-to-eye with her, his nose inches away from hers.

"Then she will find out how ready I am to watch this world burn in order for her to accept her role as its savior."

"But what if she doesn't take the bait?"

"She will." He turned again toward the black sphere that hovered in the very center of the cavern.

The Director let his hand hover over the sphere. The closer his skin got, the whiter it turned. He knew that the orb was leeching energy from his natural body. He knew it would be an awful, terrible pain to anyone but him. It would be even worse for the Lightbringer.

He pulled his hand away just as the orb pulled at the nanobots embedded in his fingertips. The orb pulsed angrily, as if it expected more from him. The opaque surface suddenly faded slightly, revealing the lifeless human that hovered inside.

"Lucifer has shown herself desperate to save those she loves," the Director said, staring at the boy. "She will come, and she will die."

## 60

Aniya gently laid Nicholas's head on the blackened ground, deciding to grieve later when it was safer. She had to keep her wits about her. Something was clearly not right.

At no point during her fight with the Director did she remember burning the ground.

Yet the biome was completely razed, scorched to little more than dirt and ash. In the distance, she could see the green landscape continue, but she suspected that it was only the sky ceiling.

And then there were the dozens of blackened bodies littering the immediate area.

*Did I do this?*

She wouldn't have been surprised. The fight with the Director had been a blur, and there was no telling where all that light had gone when she had used it against him.

Maybe she had set the biome on fire in her rage. Maybe the Director had brought backup, and she had killed them all without knowing.

The worst part was that one of the bodies was Roland. The Director had sucked his life away and dropped him to the earth before Aniya had finally mustered the strength to rip his consciousness from Nicholas's mind. The fire that had apparently destroyed the forest had consumed Roland's body, and it was now one of the unrecognizable, burnt masses that lay somewhere in the ash.

Aniya closed her eyes and watched the rage build inside her body. The Director had taken everything from her, forced her to ruin her last chance to save Nicholas, and now threatened what was left of the Underworld.

He was still alive somewhere, probably in New Washington. And now that he no longer had Nicholas's body, he wouldn't stand a chance if she tried to fight him.

Aniya glanced at the elevator in the distance. It stood alone now on a concrete slab, the only thing left standing aside from the charred, bare trees.

She had two choices: Either retreat to the Underworld and report back to Caspian, or continue alone to New Washington and finish the Director off. She knew Caspian would want a report straight away. And if she went back to the Underworld, she could come back with an army.

The choice seemed clear, but the more she thought about it, the more she knew that the Director would take any time she gave him and use it against her.

Aniya decided there wasn't much of a choice. She had to finish this now.

She picked up Nicholas again, knowing she may not have a chance to come back here. Better to take him with her and bury him somewhere better.

Looking upward, she concentrated on her legs. Instantly, her feet lit up with green flame.

Aniya gave a soft smile. She finally had control over the terrible power that once seemed to have a mind of its own.

As she focused on the sky ceiling above, she felt energy race out of her feet, and suddenly she was ten feet off the ground.

Her body floated effortlessly. She had thought there would be a learning curve, that it would have taken her more practice, but it was as natural as walking.

With one last glance at the blackened biome, she pushed herself farther into the air and flew out of the dome through the hole she had created in the sky ceiling during her battle with the Director.

The ruined world around her looked just as dead as the biome she had just left. It was a black nothingness, populated only by scattered silver domes with glowing tunnels connecting them. She realized that the red glow that had covered the earth was gone, and as Aniya looked up, she realized that the sun looked even worse than before. It was now almost completely black, with very few red spots left.

She looked around and settled on the largest visible dome, which was just a few miles away to her left.

That had to be New Washington.

With a brief command to her body to fly in that direction, Aniya took off, reaching the capital sector in seconds. She burst through the shell of the silver dome and into New Washington, and she stopped herself in mid-air as she surveyed the landscape.

The forest that skirted the edge of the sky ceiling was shrouded in darkness, as was half the valley leading up to the city. But the darkness came to a stop at a huge white dome that covered the city, which was lit up so bright that it was difficult to look at for very long.

A massive beam stretched from the dead center of the city to the top of the transparent shield, and it seemed to feed the dome energy, as tendrils of white light crept down the surface of the dome from its zenith.

In the dark valley below, just before the dome, were thousands of figures moving about, intermingled with tents and torches. Just behind them in the tree line, barely visible in the darkness, were massive creatures lumbering about slowly, figures that Aniya recognized as moles.

Descending toward the gathering, she landed in the midst of them, ignoring the whispers and murmurs that arose around her.

"Aniya?"

She turned to see Corrin, pushing his way past everyone to stand before her, his eyes wide.

"Hey," Aniya said, biting her tongue before she could say the word "dad."

"Where have you been?"

She smiled sadly and laid Nicholas's body on the ground between them. "Doing what I had to do."

Corrin nodded as he placed a hand on her arm. "I'm proud of you, Annelise. What about Roland? Is he okay?"

Aniya tried to speak, but no words came out. She closed her mouth and bowed her head.

Wordlessly, Corrin stepped around Nicholas's body and placed a hand on the back of Aniya's head, pulling her into his chest. She wrapped her arms around him as she felt his body shake.

He finally pulled away and cleared his throat and sniffed. "What happened to you?" he asked quietly. "You disappeared a week ago."

"A week?" Aniya squinted.

"Nearly so. Six days at least."

Aniya's body froze. Suddenly the scene she had come back to made sense. But how was the fight a full six days ago?

"I guess I don't know what happened to me," she said quietly. "What about you? It looks like I missed a lot."

"Caspian was monitoring Nicholas's vitals, so we knew when you killed him. That was enough to convince us that it was time to strike. We waited for you, but when we didn't hear from you, we decided to go ahead and proceed. We got here earlier, and that shield of light appeared."

Aniya again looked at the beam of light that erupted from the center of New Washington.

"Do you know what it means?"

"I'm not sure. He's used my light before to make weapons. But it looks like that light is coming from something."

"But you can get through, right?" Corrin asked.

"I don't know. I hope so, but every time the Director has used my light against me, it's only hurt me. Maybe if Roland were still alive, we could break through."

Corrin shook his head. "How did he die? He had the same power as you, right?"

"Not exactly," Caspian's voice came from her right. "I believe Neeshika thought that if he went through the same process Aniya did, without the interference of a third party like Nicholas, he would be powerful enough to stop the Director. It seems she was wrong. Ironically, I guessed this myself and tried to tell Roland, but it was too late."

"The Director used me," Aniya said, tears beginning to form. "He used me to kill Roland. But how?"

"Your power was never meant to be split between two people, Aniya. Your abilities want to work in tandem with Nicholas's. It naturally draws you toward him. My guess is the Director took advantage of that. But from what it seems, that will no longer be a problem."

Aniya glanced at Nicholas's body again.

Caspian's hand found her shoulder, but the added weight only burdened her spirit. "You did the right thing, Aniya. It's the only reason we're still alive. We stand a chance now that the Director doesn't have his body anymore. His brain, for lack of a better word, is stored in a giant computer somewhere, and when we find it, we can finally destroy him for good."

"What about his army?" Aniya asked. "What do you have, three thousand soldiers?"

"Four," Corrin said. "But we have trenches, moles, thermal charges—if their army attacks us, it won't go smoothly for them. It's a shame Salvador will miss it."

Aniya frowned as she looked at the large, golden sword strapped to Corrin's back. She glanced around. "Where is he?"

"He disappeared a few days ago," Caspian said quietly.

"Figures," Aniya said with a scoff. "Well, we'll just have to do this without him."

She approached the wall of light and reached her hand forward toward the barrier. The dome seemed to give off a vibration that she could feel several inches away from the surface. The light was intense, but it somehow cast no luminance toward her and the gathered armies behind her.

Her hand was jerked away suddenly.

"Aniya, no." Corrin held her wrist firmly. "One of our men touched it and was instantly incinerated. I know you're powerful, but we have no reason to believe it won't do the same to you."

"Indeed," Caspian said. "If the Director managed to hurt you with your own light, this might kill you. I don't know, but I don't think it's worth trying."

Aniya shook her hand away. "Then how do you plan on getting through?"

"We're working on that," Corrin said.

"And why don't they just make the barrier larger and wipe you out? Where is their army?" Aniya put her hands on her hips. "There should be more than enough of them to attack you and end this now. Why haven't they done so?"

The dark forest lit up bright as day as the sky ceiling came to life.

"Welcome, Lucifer."

The Director appeared on the dome, taking the form

of Todd once again, the charismatic man Aniya had met all those years ago. A small blemish was on his cheek, a spot on the sky ceiling where Aniya had forcibly entered New Washington.

"It's about time you join us, and now we can finally get started. I know you and your friends are so dreadfully eager to end their lives in a futile battle. It's cute, really. But I will be more than happy to grant their request for a quick death. However, I have other plans for you. You see, I have something of yours."

The Director's face disappeared, replaced by a black orb in a dark chamber. Somehow, a white beam of light came from the sphere as it pulsed erratically.

With a high-pitched whine, the massive barrier surrounding the city blinked twice, then vanished, and as the beam of light receded back into the sphere, its opaque surface suddenly turned transparent, revealing Roland's lifeless body suspended in the sphere.

Aniya gasped in horror. She quickly recovered and was about to fly forward to reclaim her brother, but almost instantly, the beam of light shot up again, and the barrier re-settled over the city.

"If I know you, you'll do anything to save your dear brother. That's right. I'm sure you know by now that I can't let you do that, even if it were possible. But if I know you, and I daresay I do, you'll try nonetheless. I'm in a generous mood, so I'll let you pass, and you alone. I look forward to meeting you face-to-face once again."

The sky went dark again, and the dome opened up slightly in front of Aniya, creating a small doorway just large enough for her to pass through.

"No, Aniya." Corrin's pleading voice came from behind her as he grabbed her hand. "It's a trap."

Aniya turned back toward Corrin. Her heart twinged as she read the dread so clearly written on his face. "I know.

But the Director's right. I have to try. And if I save Roland, then the barrier will disappear and you can attack."

"It's never that simple with him, Aniya." Caspian shook his head. "If he's inviting you to try, there's no chance to save your brother. It's probably too late to do anything about it anyway."

Aniya nodded. "I know. If I can't save him, then you have my word that I'll do whatever I have to do in order to bring down the shield so you can take the city."

She turned and stepped forward, but stopped and turned in the doorway, looking directly at Corrin. "This isn't good-bye. Whether or not I can save Roland, I'm going to find the Director's computer, and I'm going to finish him. For good this time. Then I'm coming back, with Roland if I can. Please take care of Nicholas for me. He deserves a proper burial."

With that, Aniya turned again and stepped through the doorway, letting the opening collapse behind her.

## 61

"Well, what now?" Corrin turned and paced, trying not to imagine what awaited his daughter.

Caspian shrugged. "I know how much you'll hate to hear it, but all we can do is wait. Whether Aniya manages to take out the barrier or not, we can expect a fight shortly. Even with a barrier protecting them, I doubt they'll want to let us just sit here and wait."

Corrin frowned. "But they've left us alone this long. Why wouldn't they just continue to ignore us?"

"They no longer have a reason to leave us alone. The Director has Aniya now. She's all that matters to him. Whether she lives or dies, the Director will come for the rest of us."

"So no matter what, a fight is coming?"

Caspian nodded. "And by the looks of it, we won't have to wait very long."

"Hmm?" Corrin followed Caspian's finger, peering through the barrier to see a line of people march out of the city and toward the edge of the dome. "Good, I hate waiting."

Corrin shouted a few orders before looking back at the

oncoming army. He sighed and glanced at Caspian. "I guess this is it."

"I guess so."

Corrin waited for a few more seconds before blurting out, "Do you regret anything?"

"What do you mean?" Caspian said, a confused look on his face. "Do you?"

"I don't know. Part of me is convinced that if I hadn't started the Uprising with Lyons and Haskill all those years ago, we would still be living peacefully in the Underworld. I would be in my home right now, going to sleep with my beautiful life while my children lived happy lives free of pain and misery."

Caspian smiled softly. "You forget that as trying as these times are, life under the Chancellor's thumb was not easy. I consulted him during the Uprising, you know. I told him how to break you and your band of rebels. To your credit, you proved to be quite resilient. Noah very nearly lost that war because of you. Of course, the Uprising was an ill-fated effort to begin with. Even if you had killed the Chancellor, the Director would have come for you eventually and destroyed Level XVIII like he did XIX."

Corrin watched the oncoming army with a feeling of impending doom quickly settling in his heart. "And now it seems we've sentenced ourselves to another war that will be even harder to win than the last one."

"No matter your fate, you have chosen to fight for your freedom. That, to me, is admirable. I recognized it in the Uprising, and it is why when the Purge wiped out the Underworld, when Neeshika told me you were still alive, I knew it was wise to join forces."

"A foolish rebel and a Lightbringer banding together. Who would have thought?"

Caspian's smile grew as he laid his hand on Corrin's shoulder. "To answer your question, I do not regret my choices.

I consider it a great honor to fight with you now, even if it means dying together in a desperate attempt to secure our freedom."

"Let's hope it doesn't come to that," Corrin said, grinning. He turned back toward the barrier as his smile faded. "Though it does seem that way, doesn't it?"

Caspian took a deep breath. "Yes, it does look like this will be a short fight."

Corrin's heart sank as thousands upon thousands of men marched toward them, a seemingly endless mass of foes that dwarfed the rebels' numbers in comparison.

"What do you think are the chances of Aniya making it back and blowing them all to hell?"

Caspian shook his head. "I wouldn't count on it." He turned to the army and shouted, "Into the trenches!"

## 62

A niya flew toward the Capitol, the source of the beam of white light. She burst through the walls of the building, ready for a fight, but it was empty. At least, it was empty of life.

Dozens of bodies littered the halls, floating in the air with a white glow on their skin.

Aniya landed on the ground softly and immediately felt herself pulled forward. She took a step back, but with some effort. The atmosphere was thick and carried a resistance that made it hard to retreat. She stepped forward and almost lost her balance as some magnetic force willed her to keep walking.

Doing her best to move slowly and carefully, she continued through the halls, following the maze-like layout of the Capitol until she turned a corner to see the beam of light piercing through the floor in the middle of a hallway, continuing through the ceiling. Debris and bodies surrounded the light, swirling around it slowly in a continuous spiral.

Aniya approached the light, now nearly being dragged toward it. With some effort, she stopped and stood before the light, resisting its pull as she gazed into the beam.

She couldn't see anything through the blinding light, but as she ran her hand just inches away from the beam, she felt a familiar presence and found herself knowing beyond a shadow of a doubt that the light came from her brother.

Aniya took a step back and channeled energy into her feet, causing a small explosion that destroyed the ground beneath her body, causing her to plummet into darkness. Light continuously shot from her feet, making the ground give way below her without resistance and allowing her to free fall without abandon.

Finally, she broke through the ground and fell into a huge cavern. It reminded her of the reactor chambers in the Underworld. A green glow flooded the cavern, a space so massive that she couldn't see the bottom, but that was where the similarities ended.

Aniya crashed to the ground and looked up from her crouched stance to see a metal construction with giant arms that curved around a black sphere, sending sparks of light from the tips of the arms. Three large rings swirled rapidly around the sphere: one green, one yellow, and one red. From the black sphere shot a beam of white light straight into the air, channeling through the ceiling of the cavern and into the surface world above.

The walkway upon which Aniya stood was one of twelve that stretched from the rock wall to the center of the cavern, forming a spoked wheel surrounding the device. She turned around and stared at the walls, which glowed green in a very different way than the chambers in the Underworld. Here, green veins seemed to be embedded into the walls, pulsing gently and casting its light throughout the cavern.

Finally, below the walkways was a massive blue cube, seemingly floating in the air, spanning the width of the entire chamber and continuing down farther than Aniya could see.

Aniya stood and slowly walked toward the machine. The closer she got, the more transparent the black sphere became. A naked male figure was floating inside, its head slumped over and its arms limp.

She reached the machine and placed her hand on the sphere, which was now nearly invisible. The boy she knew to be Roland was inside, though he was nearly entirely unrecognizable.

His skin was dark gray, cracked, and shriveled over his bones, and white hair drifted throughout the sphere, long gone from his now-bald head.

"Pitiful, isn't he?"

Aniya spun around to see the Director standing behind her, once again in the form of Todd Lambert.

"I couldn't put him out of his misery," he said, shaking his head, his unnaturally ever-present smile now gone. "That's not to say, of course, that I indeed took pity on him. You and I both know that I'm hardly capable of that. But we quite literally could not kill him, and not for lack of trying. I believe it would break your poor heart to know what we did to your dear brother in our efforts to destroy him. It's a good thing that he's comatose, or otherwise we probably would have driven him insane through sheer pain alone."

His wretched smile finally spread across his face. "You think you have suffered, Lucifer? You know nothing of pain."

The rage that had been bubbling inside Aniya for the past several seconds finally boiled over, and she shot green light from her hands, incinerating the Director where he stood.

Aniya kept the barrage going until there was no more trace of his body. When he was finally gone, she dropped her arms to her sides and fell to her knees, sobbing as she pictured Roland's mutated body behind her, unable to bring herself to turn around.

"Save your energy. You'll need it for what comes next."

A pained cry of frustration escaped Aniya's lips, and she turned to see the Director approaching from another walkway to her left. He was in an identical body, this one smiling just as obnoxiously as the last one.

In rebellious anger, Aniya spat forth a beam of light from her mouth, engulfing the Director's body and obliterating it.

"What do you want from me?" she shouted in rage. Footsteps sounded to her right, and she looked up and moaned in resignation as the Director sauntered down another walkway.

"All I've ever done is for you and this world. One day, you'll thank me for it. Until then, you'll just have to trust me."

"That's not gonna happen," she said, shaking her head. "I don't have to do anything, no matter how much you think it's my destiny, my duty, whatever you think is going to convince me. I'm taking Roland, and I'm leaving."

The Director rounded the platform in the middle of the chamber and approached her, kneeling by her side. "That's impossible, I'm afraid. Even if you could free your brother, you know I just can't let you leave."

"Oh, yeah? What happened to it being my choice? Have you given up trying to manipulate me into doing what you want, and you'll now resort to forcing me?"

"I will never force you. You will accept your destiny, Lucifer. It's not a matter of if, but when. That said, I've grown tired of waiting for you to do the right thing." The Director's smile vanished again as he stood. "You're not leaving this cavern."

Aniya stood up and pushed her way past the Director, approaching the machine and examining the sphere.

"What did you do to him?"

"The truly ironic thing is that if the machine is disengaged and Roland removed, he will surely die. The only thing that's keeping him alive now is the light, which is channeled by the device. To remove it suddenly would be to cut off his only source of strength. I deduced this upon studying Roland's interaction with the machine for some time, but by the time I realized it, it proved to be irrelevant. We cannot power off the machine because the power it draws from your brother supersedes its natural power source. And if we turned it off, your brother would die. The very same light that is killing him is also what's keeping him alive. He will not die as long as he is in the machine. He will merely suffer torture."

Aniya caressed the sphere, willing her brother to open his eyes and look back at her. "So he's trapped?"

"To put it in such banal and uneducated terms, yes."

She spun around and put her hands on her hips. "So you brought me here to pull him out?"

The Director blinked as his mouth dropped open slightly. He quickly recovered and responded in a matter-of-fact voice, "Yes."

"You need him dead. There can't be two of us—you made that clear."

"Perhaps I didn't give you enough credit," he said, almost seeming impressed.

"You have no idea." Aniya pushed through the sphere and was mildly surprised as the surface gave way to her hand, parting around her skin and allowing her to push through. She reached out and took Roland's hand, immediately wincing in pain as searing heat spread through her arm.

"Good, Lucifer. Pull him out, and it can all be over."

She took a deep breath and tugged on Roland's hand, using his weight to pull herself into the sphere. Somewhere far behind her, Aniya heard a muffled cry of anger.

A burning sensation covered her body, excruciating pain scorching every inch of her flesh.

Doing her best to ignore the pain, Aniya drew herself close to Roland, wrapping her arms around her brother. Unsure of what to do next, she simply lay her head on his shoulder and took deep breaths. She had never taken energy before, only expelled it from her body. But the light was what was killing her brother now. It had to leave.

Aniya squeezed her brother's body as she continued

to breathe, willing with all her might to suck the light away from him. The tighter she held him, the worse the pain got, and soon she was clinging to his body while screaming in agony.

And then something clicked. The pain grew exponentially worse as searing heat flooded her body. Her screams turned to unintelligible blubber as she buried her face deep into his shoulder, sobbing and shivering as her legs gave out beneath her.

Her body swelled as something filled her from the inside out. It was like she had eaten far too much, and the excess food was finding its way into every corner of her flesh.

Aniya heard a faint popping noise, and she opened her eyes to see light swirling from her body and around Roland's, bathing his face in a haunting red glow. Black crust fell away from his face, giving way to clean, pink flesh. Hair sprouted from his scalp and quickly grew to his familiar brown waves. His eyes opened, revealing pupils that glowed white. Aniya placed a hand on his cheek and withdrew the last of his light, and his eyes returned to their dark, hazel color.

Roland's eyes seemed to finally register her, and a warm smile spread across his face.

Spinning around in the sphere, Roland's body still in her arms, Aniya stepped out of the device and onto the walkway, facing a stone-faced Director.

She gently let go of Roland, who stood on the ground next to her with shaky legs. But as soon as his weight was gone and she stood freely, Aniya found herself swaying.

"Now, if you'll—" She stopped herself and held her hand to her forehead, ignoring the sparks that fell from her open mouth. She took a deep breath, but it seemed to make the problem worse, and a heavy dizziness came over her.

Roland's hand tightly grabbing her shoulder seemed like a mere graze on her numb flesh, and Aniya leaned into his body, unable to keep herself upright.

"You feeling okay?"

The Director's smirk multiplied itself, each one of his faces swirling in Aniya's vision, each one taunting her.

"It was a noble decision, Aniya. Your brother is safe, albeit powerless now. But his power was not yours to bear. Your body has identified it as foreign, malignant. You will not function correctly until the cancerous light inside you is forcibly removed. I can do that safely. I can keep you alive."

Aniya groggily shook her head and grabbed Roland around his waist.

"We're leaving," she managed to spit out. With a faltering shove off, Aniya ascended with Roland, heading directly for the massive hole in the center of the cavern that the beam of light had created. They made it through the opening and began traveling upward until a sharp tug pulled Aniya back toward the cavern. She glanced down to see ropes of yellow light around her legs.

"Roland, help!"

Aniya was slowly dragged back down until Roland grabbed onto a jutting rock, pulling Aniya against the force that threatened to take her back to the Director.

"What are you doing?" Roland's strained voice came from above.

Aniya's grip slipped on Roland's waist, and she fell until she grabbed onto Roland's foot, trying as hard as she could to use her own power to break free from the ropes.

"He's taking me back, Roland. I don't think I can make it out."

"You have to! That machine nearly killed me. I don't want to know what it'll do to you."

Aniya looked back down toward the cavern. "I don't plan on giving him the chance. You might not have the light anymore, but you can help."

She looked back up at Roland and spoke firmly. "Refuge's army is up there. They have Nicholas's body. Bring it to me."

With that, she let go and plummeted back down into the cavern, crashing abruptly into the machine that had imprisoned Roland. Something broke inside her, but the pain was discernible only as a slight twinge in her back.

Aniya turned and retched, but no liquid came from within. She moaned and rolled back over to see the Director's face.

"I told you," he said, glaring down at her. "You're not going anywhere."

# 63

Caspian never saw the barrier collapse. He was mid-blink when it happened, and when his eyes opened again, the wall of light had vanished.

He took a deep breath and turned around to face the rebel army. "This is it, men. Remember that—"

That was all he got out before the gunfire sounded, a hail of bullets whizzing through the air, striking a few soldiers whose heads poked above the trenches.

But the majority of the army was safely hidden in the channels dug out of the dirt. Even some of the wounded merely suffered the pain of a bullet's impact, their armor protecting their shoulders and chests.

As his army responded with their own gunfire, Caspian whirled around and pulled his automatic rifle from the holster strapped to his back, pausing for a half second at the sight before him.

New Washington was now shrouded in darkness, the beam of light gone. But in the starlight from the sky ceiling above, Caspian watched as a wave of black raced across the dark fields, rushing Refuge's position. Almost louder than their gunfire was the sound of their metal armor at their long, rapid strides. Their numbers were indeterminable in the darkness, but there were so many that it seemed like the entire valley was one moving sea of black.

Caspian glanced toward Corrin, who remained by his side.

"Last chance to run."

Corrin shook his head. "Salvador taught us well. He used to say that in the face of certain death, we fight for what we know to be the heart cry of all mankind, the longing for freedom."

Caspian snorted. "Ironic, given his disappearance."

"I'm trying not to think about it. Besides, it's a noble thought, even if in the end he deserted us."

Caspian gave a firm nod. "Then let's take as many of them with us as we can. For every man they take, they'll pay the price."

"Agreed." Corrin turned to his men and shouted above the commotion. "Catapults!"

Out of the darkness, massive spheres suddenly burst into flame. Almost instantly, they shot forth from the ground and flew over Caspian's head, arching for a second before crashing back down into the oncoming sea of black.

Each flaming ball wreaked havoc on impact, taking out a couple dozen instantly, then rolling over several more, leaving a trail of fire on the grass below.

But it only served to illuminate the massive army that swarmed the valley, revealing a number that was incomparable to Caspian's remaining men.

Refusing to let his men see his despair, Caspian shook his head and cried out, "Again!" He emptied his gun into the oncoming army as several more balls of fire were released into the air.

After one more volley, Caspian shouted into the air, "Release the moles!"

Caspian had enough time to empty another clip from his

gun before a thundering noise sounded behind him. He grinned as dozens of moles broke the tree line from either side of his army, racing around the trenches and toward the oncoming soldiers, trampling over the opposing army recklessly as the beasts headed straight toward the fire.

"Now?"

Caspian turned to see Corrin again at his side. He nodded.

Corrin turned and shouted, "Detonate!"

Several explosions rocked the ground as each mole blew up in a massive cloud of flame. These explosions were enough to take out several dozen men at once, and the oncoming sea of black froze in their tracks for the first time.

But the last mole hadn't even finished exploding when the army resumed their advance, and Caspian turned to Corrin as he finally saw the eyes of the first oncoming soldier.

"It was an honor to fight with you, Corrin."

Corrin nodded curtly. "And you as well."

There was nothing more that needed to be said. Caspian turned toward the oncoming army. They continued on, ignoring the soldiers that were struck by bullets, pushing the dead and wounded aside and racing toward the trenches.

Caspian loaded another clip and emptied it into the black army, shouting in fury as he embraced his fate, digging his feet into the ground as the overwhelming odds reached the trenches and stormed what was left of Refuge.

## 64

"I pity you, you know."

The Director's mocking tone was little more than an afterthought to Aniya. The nausea that so disoriented her was her most pressing concern, a pain that cramped her stomach more than any natural phenomenon.

"Your mind is so limited, unable to perceive your own true purpose. You don't understand because you can't understand."

Aniya was faintly aware of the Director pulling her arms up and strapping her hands down onto cold metal.

"Perhaps I took the wrong approach in all this. No matter how futile I make your chances, no matter how much I destroy your life, you still cling to a tiny ray of hope, the unrealistic yet compelling belief that maybe you can win, maybe you can save your friends, maybe you can save the world. Meanwhile, I freely offer you the answer, the only way you'll accomplish true victory, and you're too blind to see it. But like you, I did not understand. I truly did not understand that you are simply incapable of seeing the truth."

Her head lashed back violently as she was forced into a metal clamp that closed around her neck.

"But I'll make you see it, Lucifer. It would have meant so much more to you and to your loved ones if you had accepted your destiny from the start, but in the end, a seldom few people will care if you are a willing martyr or a victim. They will only remember that you saved them. The entire world will know, of that you can be sure."

A massive needle plunged into Aniya's chest, and she immediately felt relief from the pressure that overwhelmed her body.

"And me? No one will ever remember me. Which, of course, is how it is meant to be. I'll continue on as the invisible specter that covers Earth in its protection, one hand holding back greater threats from its people and the other directing events behind the scenes."

As the equipment in her chest contracted and probed her insides, Aniya's vision began to clear. The Director stood before her, emotionless now, his arms folded as he watched the device stir back to life. A large rubber tube snaked around her feet and up toward her chest, where a metal device housed a needle that was embedded in her chest.

"You can't hold me here," she managed to choke out between breaths. "I'll get out."

"Bluffing relies on your opponent misreading your emotions. It won't work on a machine that doesn't take your humanity into account when predicting your movements. You know you're not escaping from this."

Aniya managed a smile as her strength began to return. "I think you underestimate me." She channeled her energy into the metal clamps that restrained her body, and in response, the machine began to hum violently as its base began to shake.

But the Director only shook his head. "The more you fight back, the more energy you feed the machine."

"But there's a limit, right?" Aniya continued the stream of energy through her body, not taking her eyes off the Director.

"After all, it was built for just me. And just a few minutes ago, all I had was my energy. But now with Roland's, it'll be too much for the machine to handle."

"You are correct. But you won't do that."

"Try me."

"You said it yourself. If you don't hold yourself back, you can overload your energy, causing an explosion that will destroy everything around you, including yourself."

Aniya grinned. "Gladly." She glanced downward, unable to move her head. She pictured the massive blue cube that hovered below the walkway. "I assume that's you? If I blow up, I'll at least take you with me."

"Correct again. But with me gone and you dead, who will save the world?"

"What makes you so sure that I'm going to die?"

"Tell me, do you know what will happen if you let yourself explode? Because I do."

Aniya shook her head. "Then I die. It doesn't matter anymore. I'd rather let myself die than allow you to corrupt this world any longer."

"A noble stance, but a selfish one. They will run out of energy, and they will die. Make no mistake. Without power, they cannot shield themselves from the radioactive environment for long. They will suffer and die slow deaths."

"They'll go underground again."

"A mere temporary respite from their inevitable doom." The Director slammed his fist on a panel by the machine. "I have thought about this in every conceivable way, Annelise. I have foreseen every possible future. Trust me when I say that this is the only way."

Aniya pushed more power into the machine below her, and she was rewarded by the sound of metal straining. "You'll forgive me if I don't trust your every word."

"Then see if you can use your small mind long enough to

apply logic." The Director gestured toward the cavern walls. "Do you know what that green substance is?"

Aniya looked toward the rock formations that encompassed the chamber.

"Of course not," the Director said. "It's uranium. Many, many years ago, humans discovered how to turn it into energy. It became the earth's primary source of power, and after the war that effectively ended civilization, it became humanity's most prized resource. My central computer was moved to the largest known uranium deposit, the cavern in which we stand, so that I would always have a power source, thanks to the underground plant below this cavern which continuously processes the uranium. This cavern is now the last known deposit of uranium, one of the few remaining secrets this world has to offer. Even I am not aware of another source. And even if there is one, it would take a long time to find it. If you destroy me, Aniya, you will also destroy humanity's last hope for survival. The infrastructure needed to provide any other form of energy would take far too long to develop. Your race would go extinct in a matter of years."

Aniya simply stared at the Director.

"*Now* do you see the futility of destroying me? You would be ensuring the destruction of your own people, whereas my only goal has been to save them."

"You've killed them. You've killed so many of them. How is that saving them?"

The Director shrugged. "A small sacrifice to ensure ultimate victory. Unlike you, I'm willing to do whatever it takes to save this world."

Aniya slowly nodded. "And so am I."

She gripped the metal pylons at her side tightly, focusing all her energy into her bonds.

The Director sighed and shook his head. "After everything I've told you, you're still willing to let this world burn just to watch me be destroyed?"

"All I know is that I can protect my friends from your perverted methods of salvation. Someone else can save the world."

"You *are* that someone else, Aniya!" The Director clutched her hands, ignoring the flames that erupted on contact and burned away his artificial flesh. "You are the only one who can save this world. Don't throw that away now."

"I can destroy you now. That's all that matters."

"Then you condemn them and sentence them to death."

Aniya bowed her head. "Humanity will survive with or without us. It always has, and it always will."

The Director backed away from the machine and clasped his hands. "Very well, Lucifer. I have chosen you as the representative of the human race. I have given you the power to choose life or death for this world, and only you can make that choice. I had only hoped you would choose life."

"I choose freedom."

With that, Aniya clenched the pylons in a death grip and shot two beams of red light into the machine's base, letting the device explode around her.

But the instant the machine exploded, the pressure returned to her body, clamping down on her lungs and suffocating her. Aniya's vision darkened, and as she lost all feeling in her body, she fell to the ground.

## 65

C orrin climbed two steps that were dug out of the trench and grabbed a soldier by the foot, yanking him down into the pit as the soldier screamed, firing aimlessly with his gun before he hit the ground with a sickening crunch and went silent. Corrin turned and fired into the trenches, emptying his clip into black-armored soldiers from his elevated position.

As he reloaded, another scream rang out, and his heart sank as he recognized the voice. His suspicions were confirmed as he turned to see Dawn pinned down by another soldier, who had his foot on her chest and a gun pointed at her.

Corrin threw the loaded magazine at the soldier's head, distracting him just long enough to dash forward and tackle him, wrestling on the ground for a moment before twisting the gun around, breaking the soldier's hand and pointing the weapon at his chest. A shot fired, and the soldier went limp.

"What are you doing here?" Corrin stood and held a hand out toward Dawn. "Are you okay?"

She nodded and took his hand, but Corrin could feel her tremble.

Dawn raised a pointing finger and gestured behind Corrin, who spun around and fired a shot at another soldier who was climbing down into the trench.

Corrin turned again as Dawn fell forward into his arms. Glancing around, he pulled her into a corner of the trenches, behind a few dead bodies, taking brief shelter from the battle.

"There's so many of them," she said. "They're everywhere."

Corrin nodded. "I know. I won't judge you if you find somewhere to hide, Dawn. Maybe when it's all over, you can get out of here before they find you. You weren't supposed to be here anyway."

The girl closed her eyes and breathed deeply, and when she opened her eyes again, her expression was resolute. "I can't do that. Tamisra wouldn't do that."

"You're not Tamisra, Dawn. She was trained her whole life to fight."

Dawn shook her head. "She would fight until they killed her. I can do the same. It's what Roland deserves."

"About Roland—"

"I know." Dawn's eyes grew wet as her steely gaze faltered. "I heard Aniya."

"I'm sorry, Dawn." Corrin pulled her close and placed a hand on the back of her head. "I'm sorry that Roland is dead, I'm sorry that Lionel is dead, and I'm sorry it has to end like this for you. I know Roland never wanted this for you."

"Who knows?" She looked back up at him with sparkling jade eyes. "Maybe we'll win."

Corrin closed his eyes tight and rested his cheek on her forehead, wishing to burn the image of her hopeful smile into his mind. "Maybe we will."

After a moment, he broke the embrace and grabbed his gun. "Come on, Dawn. This is no time to talk. You don't have to hide, but I can keep you alive as long as possible. Stay behind me and don't—"

A pain exploded in Corrin's side, and he fell on top of Dawn.

Somewhere, shots rang out, and it seemed like several minutes later that Dawn finally shook his body conscious again.

"Are you okay?"

Her shaking voice stirred him, and he tried to sit up. "I'm fine. Don't—" As soon as he reached a sitting position, the pain returned just as bad as before, and he collapsed back to the ground, wincing.

"There's a lot of blood," he heard Dawn say.

"Feels like it. Give me my gun."

A piece of metal slipped into Corrin's hands, and a soft hand clenched his.

"Looks like I'm keeping you alive now," her voice came from above, now firm and determined.

He opened his eyes to see Dawn raising a handgun, standing between him and the thousands of soldiers that made their way through the rebels' trenches.

"Looks like."

## 66

Caspian pulled his dagger out of a soldier's throat, shooting with his other hand at another approaching soldier.

He took this moment to stand up and take a quick look around. They were faring surprisingly well against the Director's army. They were still losing, of course. It just wasn't happening as fast as Caspian had expected.

The rebels were losing men at a steady rate. Caspian estimated that their numbers had dwindled from four thousand to three thousand after only ten minutes of fighting.

"Regretting your choices?"

Caspian spun around to face a soldier without a helmet. He bore the face of Todd Lambert, the Director that Caspian had known thirty years ago, the man who had promoted him to the trainer of the Underworld militia.

"Strangely enough," Caspian said as he took a cautious step back, "not a one."

The Director shook his head. "You're no better than Aniya. Stubbornly willing to risk the lives of thousands, millions. And for what? Freedom? You can't be free when you're dead."

Caspian wiped his dagger on his pants and brandished it. "No, but others can."

"Yes, indeed. Free to live their short lives until they die because of your impertinence and ignorance. Right you are, Caspian." The Director snorted. "You've been spoiled. You haven't seen the torture that awaits those exposed to radiation long term. You think you're saving them, but you offer them a life of pain."

"Save your warnings for someone who will believe them. We don't need you to provide power to the world."

"It is foolish to assume such arrogance."

"Enough talk."

Caspian lunged forward, leading with his dagger. The Director swatted it out of his hands and backhanded Caspian across the cheek, sending him staggering backward.

A shot rang out, and Caspian clutched his side as blood poured out and down his silver armor.

The Director smiled and aimed his gun again, but Caspian reached out and wrenched the weapon away. He spun it around in his hands, but before he could fire, the Director kicked the gun away, sending it flying.

Caspian leaned over and made to grab his dagger, but the Director drove his knee into Caspian's neck, immediately following up with an elbow to the back of his head.

Choking, Caspian fell to the ground, and as the Director stepped over his body, Caspian grabbed the knife from the ground and thrust upward, burying the blade in the Director's neck.

The Director pulled the dagger out and dropped it. He reached toward the wound as blood poured from his neck, and he stumbled backward for a moment before falling to the ground.

Caspian stood up slowly, recovering his air and breathing deeply until his vision straightened. Looking at the Director's body, he mumbled, "You talk too much."

"Maybe you should listen."

A blade pierced Caspian's skin between folds of his armor and dug deep into his back, wedged into his spine at an excruciating angle.

Unable to move, Caspian froze as another soldier walked in front of him and removed his helmet. A duplicate version of Todd Lambert smiled back at Caspian and pushed him over with a finger, and he toppled to the ground.

## 67

D awn backed into an alcove in the trenches, pulling Corrin's body as close to the wall as possible as she played dead, lolling her head to the side but keeping a hand on her handgun.

Dozens upon dozens of black-armored soldiers raced by, but none of them seemed to notice the two survivors hiding in plain sight.

When the last of the Director's army had passed by, Dawn shook Corrin.

"You still with me?"

He opened his eyes and grunted.

"Where is everyone?" Dawn looked around but saw no sign of any other rebel fighters.

"Out," Corrin said, wincing in pain as he spoke. "The trenches . . ."

Dawn's eyes widened as she remembered the plan. "Right. Let me get you out of here. Can you walk?"

Corrin hesitatingly nodded, but it was enough for Dawn. She wrapped an arm under his back and helped him to his feet, her heart sinking as he moaned in pain.

"It's not far," she said. "Just gotta get out—"

"Hello again," a taunting voice came from a few feet behind them.

Dawn turned to see a girl in a black bodysuit standing in the trenches. Her face was exposed but almost completely unrecognizable. However, the wicked smirk that spread across the assassin's face was unmistakable, and the metal arm she carried confirmed her identity.

"How poetic," Zeta said. "I ended your brother's life as he begged for mercy, and I'll—"

Dawn fired her handgun, cutting off Zeta with a loud pop that rang in her ears painfully.

She didn't know where the bullet went, especially since she closed her eyes as she pulled the trigger, but she opened her eyes again to see Zeta still standing there, folding her arms.

"Care to try again? I could give you some tips on aiming, you know. Try—"

Dawn fired the gun again, this time doing her best to keep her eyes open.

The bullet apparently missed again, and Zeta didn't even flinch.

"You *are* angry, aren't you?" She laughed and stepped forward. "I can't say I blame you. Your brother is dead, your boyfriend is dead, and soon you'll join them."

Dawn backpedaled the assassin rapidly, nearly tripping over Corrin's feet and just barely managing to stay upright. She raised the gun again, determined to kill the assassin.

"Don't worry," Zeta said. "I didn't come for you. But your friend burned me pretty badly, and I can't just let that go. So do me a favor. Drop Corrin on the ground and walk away. I'll give you a head start, and when I'm done ending his life nice and slow, I'll come after you."

Dawn growled, trying to sound intimidating, though it came out as more of a squeak. "Don't you ever die?"

With that, she fired over and over again, not realizing that with each subsequent shot, her aim got worse and worse.

But one bullet managed to find its mark, and Zeta stumbled backward, grabbing her good shoulder.

Dawn grinned triumphantly and tried to fire again, but the gun clicked uselessly.

"Had your fun, did you?" Zeta said, wincing. "I hope it was worth it. Because now you die with Corrin, and your death will be just as slow as his."

"Stop!" Dawn shouted so forcefully, surprising herself.

Apparently, Zeta was surprised as well because the assassin froze.

Dawn backed away slowly, glancing at the lump in the ground, putting as much distance between herself and the buried package as possible, while keeping Zeta on the other side.

"What? Got another gun to pull out?" Zeta scowled and stepped forward again. "Because if not, it's over."

"Stop!" Dawn screamed, backing away more quickly now.

But this time, Zeta kept moving.

Dawn pushed Corrin to the side and yanked the giant sword out of the sheath strapped to his back, and as she took the full weight of the blade, it crashed to the ground. Grunting with effort, she pulled the sword up just enough to point it at the assassin.

Zeta laughed. "Cute. But a girl with a stick isn't going to be enough to—"

The ground exploded at the assassin's feet, and Zeta had just enough time to raise her metal arm and let out a burst of light as she was thrown into the air from the force of the explosion.

Dawn felt her body fly backward, but she never felt herself hit the ground. The next thing she remembered was her eyes fluttering awake as Corrin knelt over her.

"Come on," he said, mumbling quietly as he began to drag her backward. "You're not done yet."

## 68

R oland ran as fast as he could, now regretting his chosen path.

He had decided to run around the battlefield, avoiding most of the black army in an attempt to get straight to his allies. But the time it had taken to skirt the battle without being seen was torturous. All Roland had to do was look to the side to know that with every second, more of his friends were dying.

Of course, powerless now, he knew he wouldn't be much help against the seemingly endless army that swarmed the fields of New Washington.

But he couldn't do nothing.

And so he continued around the battlefield, turning his head away from the fray as he ran, knowing it would only bring down his spirits further.

An explosion rocked the ground, and Roland skidded to a halt. He turned to see a cloud of smoke arise from the trenches.

Roland barely had any time to process what happened before another explosion set off, then another. The trenches continued in a cascading series of explosions, and in seconds, they were destroyed.

As the last explosion faded away, Roland sank to his knees, his mouth hanging open. He knew that the Lightbringers outnumbered Refuge's mere thousands, but he had expected the rebels to go down fighting, not be massacred suddenly.

Another explosion sounded, this one in Roland's mind as he relived the awful sight of Gareth giving his life for Refuge. It was a death Roland could do nothing about, one that he had to watch helplessly. And now he watched in the waking world as everyone that Gareth died for burned anyway.

Roland bowed his head, tears refusing to come. If he had been stronger, he wouldn't have been nearly killed by the Director. He would still have his abilities and would have been with the rebel army all along, fighting alongside them. Even now, if he had been running faster to the battle, maybe he could have made a difference. If he had been better, if he had listened to Salvador, he could have kept Refuge safe, not lead them straight to their deaths.

He had failed. Again.

But just as the awful feeling of despair settled in his heart, motion caught his eye, and he turned toward the forest that stood just past the trenches.

Roland frowned and squinted, but the motion had ceased. Maybe he imagined it.

But there it was again, a glint of silver catching the glow of the fire that burned in the fields.

Keeping a wide berth around the fields, Roland ran around the battlefield and toward the forest, eventually stepping into the trees from the side and making his way through the shrubbery.

He didn't make it ten steps before being tackled, forced to the ground under the weight of a person who mounted his chest and aimed a gun at his face.

The gun disappeared, revealing Dawn's gasping face.

"Roland!"

She attacked him again, this time lunging forward and pressing her lips against his.

It was several seconds before she sat back up again, but she made no move to stand, instead looking down at him with a smile on her face.

"I thought you were dead!" she exclaimed breathlessly. "Aniya told us you were gone, that the Director killed you."

"He almost did," Roland said, his heart warming for the first time in days. "But I thought you were dead! The explosions—"

"Were a trap," Dawn said, finally standing and pulling him to his feet. "When we got enough of them in the trenches, we retreated and blew a lot of them away. I barely made it out in time, thanks to Corrin."

"How many of us are left?" Roland asked, looking around.

"I count twelve hundred," a weak voice came from the trees.

Dawn led Roland a few steps through the forest to Corrin, who sat with his back to a tree, Caspian's pale body lying across his legs. A mole stood nearby, tied to a tree and staring off into the distance at the burning trenches.

Roland knelt by Corrin's side and wrapped his arms around his father. "I'm glad you're still with us."

"Not for much longer, I'm afraid." Corrin gave a pained smile. "I'm afraid our final move will be my last."

"Final move?" Roland looked up at Dawn.

Dawn nodded. "Do it again. Lure them in here and light the forest on fire. Unfortunately, we don't have any explosives left."

"We can't do that," Roland said. "We need to attack them while they're caught off guard."

Corrin shook his head. "We have the best chance of

surviving if we make them enter the tree line and fight us on our terms."

"Surviving?" Roland shook his head sadly. "Forget about surviving, Corrin. This is the end. Aniya is the only thing that matters now, and she needs our help."

Caspian opened his eyes at the sound of Aniya's name and looked up at Roland hopefully. "She's alive?"

"Not for much longer. The Director captured her as we tried to escape, and I don't think she's making it out of this without our help. She can save all of us, but she needs Nicholas's body. We have to charge through the Director's army and get him to Aniya. Do you still have him?"

"His body?" Corrin squinted, then gestured toward the nearby mole. Nicholas's body was strapped to its saddle, hanging limply off the side. "What do you need it for?"

"She didn't say. Maybe she still thinks she can save him, and he can help her defeat the Director?"

Caspian's mouth fell open slightly as blood trickled out. "She wants to take his power. It was always meant for her, after all. Even though he is dead, it still lingers in his body. If she merges with his power, she will be complete. Strong enough to destroy the Director and end this war."

"Is that even possible?" Dawn asked.

Roland nodded. "She took mine."

Caspian's eyes widened. "Then it is crucial that you bring Nicholas's body to her as soon as possible. Her body yearns for his power, but yours is a foreign energy. If I understand correctly, she won't last long with it, and when she blows, there's no telling how much of the world she'll take with her."

"The world?" Corrin laughed. "You aren't exaggerating a bit?"

"I don't think it's possible for me to overstate just how dangerous Aniya is right now, Corrin. She is a greater threat to us than the army of black that stands on the other side of the trenches."

Roland looked up through the forest. As far as he could tell, no one had bothered to examine the forest yet, but they were beginning to spread out further. "Then it's settled. We make our final stand and hope it's enough for me to push through. It'll be impossible on foot, though. I need to take a mole."

"We only have four left," Dawn said. "We'll need them."

"I need it more, Dawn. It's the only way to get back to Aniya fast enough. Besides, we need to do this together."

Corrin grabbed Roland's hand. "You must go alone. If we march out to meet them, it's suicide."

"I can't go alone," Roland said. "I barely managed to sneak my way over here, and they've moved out far enough that I won't be able to make the trip back without being seen. We have to charge them with full force and hope it's enough to break through."

Dawn took Roland's other hand. "Twelve hundred against thousands more? Roland, we won't break through."

"We have to try. It's our only chance."

Caspian pulled Corrin's arm away, a solemn look on his face. "It is time, Corrin. Aniya is the only one who can help us now. We must do what we can to help her."

With a heaving sigh, Corrin finally nodded. He gently moved Caspian's head and stood up carefully. With one fluid motion, he drew Salvador's giant golden sword from a sheath on his back and presented it to Roland, resting the blade on his palms.

"Refuge is yours to command. Lead them well."

Roland gulped and took the sword, then quickly gripped it with a second hand just to keep it upright. He turned to the remaining rebels and cleared his throat.

"Army of Refuge and members of the Silver Guard, listen to me."

The soldiers slowly stirred, glancing in Roland's direction.

"We have lost tens of thousands over the years to the

Director, thousands more in the last few hours alone. But we have a chance to avenge them all and rid the world of the man who wants to keep you under his thumb. The time has come to fulfill the oaths you have made, redeem our past failures, and fight for those who wait for us in Level I."

Dawn opened her mouth to speak, but Corrin placed a hand on her arm and shook his head.

"It's unlikely that many of us will survive the day, but there's still hope," Roland continued. "There is one person who can save us now, but she needs our help. In order to help Aniya, we must band together one final time and attack our enemy while they linger unaware in the fields ahead. We will take our four moles and lead the way, forming a shield for the rest of you behind. By the time the enemy can fire on you, you will be in melee range and will stand a fighting chance."

A voice came from his left. "How is our suicide supposed to help your sister?"

"Does it matter?" Roland asked gently. "Even if I understood what's going through her mind right now, do you really need an explanation? Let your motivation for one final, noble charge be that it is your honorable duty to fight for Refuge, for the Underworld, for the Overworld, for the good of everyone left alive on this earth." He took a deep breath and pointed the golden sword at the army. "And for me."

The soldiers began to stand, gathering their weapons as their eyes were fixed on Roland.

"Even if we all die here today, all that matters is helping Aniya. If we accomplish just that one thing, we will have saved millions. It doesn't matter how many of the thousands of soldiers we kill. We are not fighting to destroy our enemy. We are fighting to save the world from them. If we can do that, victory will be ours, even in death."

Murmurs of excitement spread through the forest as Roland raised the golden sword high in the air, pointed at the sky ceiling.

"Are you with me?"

But no words came back.

Instead, each soldier raised a four-finger hand in the air and tilted their arms in Roland's direction.

"Good," Roland said with a satisfied smile. "Then let's finish this."

## 69

R oland sat atop his mole on the edge of the tree line, double-checking to make sure Nicholas's body was securely tied down to the mole. Nodding, he looked back up at the smoldering battlefield.

The army on the other side of the trenches still seemed to be distracted, some of them starting to head back to the city.

A thin cloud of smoke lingered in the air, hindering visibility. Roland decided this was the only reason the Lightbringers hadn't seen the motion in the forest yet.

He raised a hand and began a countdown, but he halted as a small flicker of light caught Roland's eyes, and he paused just long enough to squint into the darkness.

A flame danced on the ground toward Roland's right, by the very edge of the massive dome that covered New Washington. After a few seconds, a few more flames appeared several feet apart.

Suddenly, the isolated fires burst in size, spreading across the ground rapidly and forming a wall of fire that spanned at least a quarter of a mile. The fire silhouetted the forms of thousands of robed figures that stood motionless.

Everything went silent as a hissing noise rose above the

sound of battle. The fighting slowly crawled to a stop, and a chill raced down Roland's spine.

A massive creature appeared from behind the flames, lumbering forward ahead of the robed figures. Atop the beast sat a tall man in a suit of golden armor that shimmered orange as the flames danced around him.

The man held a massive, double-sided spear, a weapon Roland recognized as Tamisra's.

He raised it in the air and pointed it at the army as his booming voice echoed across the valley by New Washington.

*"Lumen ad mortem."*

Salvador had arrived.

"Charge!"

With an earsplitting shriek that drowned out Salvador's command, the robed figures surrounding him raced across the valley, trailing a blanket of fire behind them that razed the grass below.

Salvador kicked his mole and raced ahead of them all, galloping into the fray, spinning his spear wildly.

Roland grinned from ear to ear and pumped his fist, shouting "Charge!" and taking off at full speed toward the sea of black.

As he bore down on the battle, he watched as dozens of robed figures dropped like flies to the army's hail of bullets. But the Host didn't seem to care. They simply pushed aside their fallen allies and raced ahead, picking up speed as they grew closer.

Both Refuge and the Host collided with the black army at a dead run, and soon the sound of gunfire was mixed with the agonizing screams of the black army as the Host ripped apart the Lightbringers' armor, digging their claws into any open spot possible and tearing through their flesh.

Roland broke through the army, trampling several black-armored soldiers beneath the mole's heavy paws. He nearly made it through the army and prepared himself to kick the mole into full-speed toward the Capitol, but the mole suddenly collapsed underneath him, and his body went flying forward into the battle, Salvador's sword disappearing in the distance.

As he shook his head, seeing stars, he turned toward the battle, trying to find out what had attacked the mole.

"Roland!"

Dawn was running toward him, blood dripping down over her face.

But she skidded to a halt as a figure dropped directly between herself and Roland.

The intruder wasted no time and lunged toward Dawn. Roland jumped up and pulled the attacker backward, only to be rewarded with an elbow bashing into his nose.

He stumbled backward as a hideous face turned toward him, burned and scarred, yet Roland knew her sadistic smile anywhere.

Zeta snarled at him and nodded toward his bleeding nose. "I think I improved your face somehow."

Without waiting for a response, she lifted her right arm, which glowed white around its metal casing. A humming noise came from her appendage, turning to a whining sound as the light grew brighter.

Suddenly, Zeta stumbled forward as Dawn leapt on her back, biting into what was left of the assassin's left ear. A blast of light exploded from Zeta's right palm, narrowly missing Roland's shoulder.

"Dawn, no!" Roland reached out as he cried in horror, forced to watch as Zeta whipped her body around and smashed her metal arm into Dawn's midsection.

Dawn flew into the battle, colliding with a soldier in black, falling to the ground with a dull thud as the rest of Zeta's ear rolled out of her mouth and onto the ground.

Roland jumped up and rushed Zeta before she could turn around, tackling her and dragging her to the ground.

He pinned the assassin and raised his fist to punch her, but not before she could strike him in the chest with her metal arm, sending him flying several feet into the air.

He looked back down at Zeta helplessly as she raised her arm again and shot a quick blast of light straight toward his chest, striking him in midair and knocking him backward onto the battlefield.

Roland landed roughly on the body of a soldier, the metal armor jarring his shoulder as he rolled onto the ground. He slowly sat up and was immediately forced back to the ground by a heavy, metal hand crushing his lungs.

"No interruptions this time," Zeta said. "You get to watch me kill her now."

Roland's pain gave way to a heat that spread from his chest throughout his body, and he glared back up at Zeta with a defiant grin.

With a grunt, he took the energy that she had shot into his chest and forced it back out of the wound, sending a thin beam of light toward Zeta, who barely dodged the light that zipped past her shoulder and disappeared into the sky.

In her surprise, she loosened her hold on Roland just long enough for him to buck his body upward and knock her away, further distancing himself with a kick that sent her stumbling backward.

She regained her balance and glared at Roland.

"I should have guessed that might not work on you. That's okay," Zeta said as she reached to her back, drawing two thin, long swords. "I'll kill you the old-fashioned way."

Roland snatched a gun from the ground and emptied the magazine in Zeta's direction, but she held up her metal hand and released a barrier of light directly in front of herself, the bullets disintegrating on impact.

He threw the gun on the ground in frustration and looked around desperately for another weapon as Zeta rushed him, swinging her swords viciously. He managed to spot Salvador's golden sword several feet away, and he took off running toward it, but a searing pain shot through his left thigh as a blade sliced through his flesh.

Roland fell, gasping in pain as he rolled. Zeta turned and relentlessly continued her assault, and Roland crawled backward on the ground as fast as he could, trying to get back to the sword that was just out of reach. He finally made it, grabbed the sword and stood, but he immediately fell back to the ground again as a blade pierced through his side.

He tasted dirt as his face hit the ground, and he dropped the sword momentarily as he rolled to the side, anticipating a rapid follow-up attack. Sure enough, he spotted twin blades drive into the ground where his body just was.

Roland turned to face upward again just to see Zeta standing over his body. He tried to roll away again, but her feet on either side of his chest left him no escape. Salvador's sword was still on the ground a few feet away where he had dropped it, just out of reach. All he could do was stare upward as the assassin raised her twin swords and thrust them downward toward his body.

But her momentum was robbed as a massive spear pierced her shoulder, jutting out the other side of her body by several inches.

"You're mine, wench!" Salvador's booming voice rose above the battle, followed by a wild laugh.

Zeta's eyes gave away her pain and surprise for mere seconds, but she swiped at the spear with one of her swords, cleaving the spear in two. Reaching behind her back with her left hand, she ripped the embedded half out of her shoulder as she placed her right hand over the wound. A light flashed, and the smell of burning flesh permeated the air as the assassin's black suit sizzled, Zeta closing her eyes in visible pain.

She opened her eyes and immediately retreated backward as Salvador appeared in Roland's frame of vision, attacking Zeta without a weapon. Instead, he swung with vicious punches from his right hand, which was now made of metal, similar to Zeta's arm, and on it were four silver fingers.

But Zeta quickly recovered from Salvador's appearance and dodged his punches. She tried to block one with her sword, but the force of Salvador's metal fist sent the blade flying far into the distance. The assassin darted to the side and switched to the offensive. Her smaller frame allowed for more agility, and it took plenty of time for Salvador to slowly turn toward her new position in his heavy armor. In that window of time, Zeta took the opportunity to lash out with her blades, attacking any spot where she could reach flesh.

Salvador roared in pain and threw his body at the assassin, crushing her under his weight as he toppled to the ground. But he quickly rolled away as his golden suit of armor flashed with red light, and Zeta climbed to her feet to reveal her metal arm glowing with heat.

The assassin began forming an orb of energy at her fingertips, and Roland knew what was coming next.

He grabbed the golden sword again and threw it toward the Scourge.

"Salvador, catch!"

The warlord caught the sword just as Zeta unleashed her ball of energy. The orb of light flew through the air and collided with Salvador's sword, the steel somehow absorbing the light as lightning raced up and down the blade.

"Enough!" Salvador shouted as his armor returned to its normal, golden color. But the damage was done, and the smell of burning flesh grew worse as steam rose from his smoldering armor. His voice trembled as his skin flushed beet red. "There is no greater pain you can bring me, murderer. Today, you pay for your crimes."

The Scourge advanced on the assassin with long strides, rearing back with his massive sword.

But the assassin was too quick. She dove to the side and

kicked Salvador's legs out from underneath him, sending the warrior crashing to his knees.

Roland managed to climb to his feet, trying to ignore the stabbing pain in his thigh, but Zeta spotted him, and without missing a beat, she kicked up a gun at her feet, catching it deftly and shooting Roland in the shoulder.

With a gasp of pain, Roland fell back to the ground, forced to watch the Scourge's fate at the hands of the assassin.

Turning back to Salvador, Zeta yanked the Scourge's helmet off his head with a flick of her wrist, and she reared back with her sword to behead the legendary warlord.

However, before she could swing, a piercing scream ripped through the air, and Zeta paused.

Roland turned to see a blood-soaked girl standing a few feet away. She was holding Zeta's other sword and breathing heavily, almost hissing as she stared down the assassin. For a split second, Roland was positive that Tamisra had somehow come back to life.

But as the girl whipped back her hair, sending droplets of blood flying through the air, a chill ran down Roland's spine as Dawn's face appeared, a vicious snarl adorning her beautiful face.

Zeta opened her mouth to deliver what would surely be a taunt, but Dawn shrieked again and dashed toward the assassin, whipping the blade around wildly.

The assassin kicked Salvador away and raised her sword just in time to defend herself. There was nothing particularly skillful about Dawn's blows, but they were relentless and fast, vicious strikes that Zeta could only block without a chance to deliver a precise counterattack.

But the shock of Dawn's sudden attack quickly wore off, and the assassin kicked her away suddenly. It gave Zeta enough time to strike back, and she swiftly ran Dawn through the shoulder with her sword.

Dawn screamed again, but as she staggered backward,

she yanked the sword out of her shoulder and tossed it aside, apparently fueled on by the adrenaline of the fight. Without hesitation, she resumed her attack with her good arm, hacking wildly at the defenseless assassin with her own sword.

All Zeta could do was raise her arms in self-defense. She could block most of Dawn's attacks with her metal arm, but plenty of them managed to make it past her only remaining weapon. The girl's one-handed blows were not strong enough to do any severe damage, but Dawn kept swinging the sword like an axe, burying the steel mere inches into the assassin's body again and again, rewarded by yelps of pain from the operative.

Zeta finally managed to grab the sword with her metal hand, gripping it tightly as she kicked Dawn away again. Without bothering to pause for a taunt, the assassin stepped forward to finish the girl off.

"Enough!" A tremendous roar echoed over the battlefield.

Salvador was back up now, and he rushed Zeta from the other side, roaring in fury as he swung his sword.

The assassin turned and fired a blast of light toward the Scourge, but he blocked it again with his blade. She fired two more in quick succession, and Salvador was able to block one, but not the other.

Light blasted over the Scourge's body, turning his armor dark crimson. Salvador simply roared in anger as his body burst into flames.

Zeta fired another blast that Salvador blocked with his silver hand, then another that he blocked with his sword, the blade turning to a glowing red as flames licked the edge of his steel.

Then, he charged her again, swinging his sword as his cries grew louder.

Zeta backpedaled as she threw up her metal arm in defense, but Salvador's huge blade cleaved straight through it, slicing the weaponized hand clean off as light began shooting out of the assassin's wrist in random sparks that bit into Salvador's armor, riddling it with holes and shooting white lightning over the golden steel.

As the Scourge staggered backward, trembling with every jolt of light, a triumphant grin spread across Zeta's face, and she thrust the tip of her sparking arm into Salvador's chin.

Light began shooting from the warlord's eyes as his body convulsed, and as a trembling scream escaped his lips, Zeta whipped out a dagger from her belt with her left hand and raised it above Salvador's head.

But Dawn appeared again behind the assassin, brandishing one of Zeta's swords. With a final shriek, she sliced the assassin's left hand off as Zeta howled in pain.

This was enough for Salvador, and even as his body began to break apart between flashes of white light, he swung his sword one final time, rearing back and driving the massive blade into Zeta's chest, impaling the assassin and jamming the hilt of his sword against her ribs.

Zeta's eyes opened wide as her mouth dropped open, blood dripping and coursing down her jaw. With one final sigh, her head lolled over as the light from her half-destroyed arm flashed one final time, arcing over their bodies in a corona of light.

Their bodies exploded with a flash of white, and when the light faded away, there was no sign of the assassin or the Scourge.

## 70

Aniya gasped as she convulsed. Nausea washed over her in waves, and she gagged as she tried to vomit, only coming up empty.

The Director's words were faint, almost drowned out by the ringing in her ears.

"Tell me, Annelise. What do you expect to happen next? I could save you, you know. God knows I've tried. But you've made your choice. You'll die here, in pain with which I cannot sympathize, agony I could never understand. Do you expect me to take pity on you?"

Aniya gasped for air and coughed as she tried to speak.

"Save your breath. No doubt you're grasping for some pithy response, something to do with free will or injustice. I applaud your bravery, dear, but it will not avail you now. All you've done is delay the inevitable. I'll find someone else to save this world. Someone more . . . agreeable."

"Good . . ." Aniya slammed her fist on the ground as she coughed violently, each burst of air like a hammer crushing her rib cage. "Good luck with that when you're . . ." Another cough. "Dead."

The Director shook his head. "I can't let you do that,

Aniya. If I die here, as you so put it in your naiveté, who will protect this world? Who will ensure its survival? As long as there is a world to defend, I must remain here. Which means, dear Aniya, I must finally break my one promise to you."

A sharp pain ripped through Aniya's side, and she screamed as a rope of light forced her to the ground and dragged her along the walkway.

"It is finally clear to me that there is no convincing you."

Pain shot through her opposite side, and her body was pulled for a second before the two opposing forces froze her in place, tugging at her body and threatening to pull her apart.

"These words are alien to me, Lucifer, but I have failed."

Another dagger of light pierced her back, wrenching her into a curled position in mid-air as her body was pulled backward.

"I have failed this world."

Aniya cried a silent scream as a beam of light erupted from the opposite wall and latched on to her chest, pulling away and stretching her body at its most painful point yet.

"I have failed you."

Each beam of light sparked lightning that jolted her body, her arms and legs flailing as her torso remained motionless.

"Forgive me, Aniya. For I cannot forgive myself."

Aniya closed her eyes tight and embraced the darkness, searching for the void that would offer her escape from this torture in her final moments. But William was nowhere to be found. Not even the Chancellor appeared in the black nothingness of her mind.

"Nicholas . . ." She whispered as she searched the black.

But even if they were there somewhere, Aniya knew that she couldn't reach deep enough to find them. The only thing she could think of was the pain that plagued her body, a sheer agonizing burn that flooded her every pore.

"Nicholas is dead, Aniya. Gone and left you to die alone. You saw to that. You destroyed him and with it any chance of ever seeing your beloved again. You thought you were so brave. Tell me, are you proud of your choice? Was it worth it? To make a statement, take a stand, fight the power, just to lose everything you hold dear and damn this world? You don't even have your lover to show for it."

The Director's face appeared in her blackened vision, his nose inches from hers. "Can I tell you a secret? He was there in the end, when you forced me out of your lover's body. He was watching. *I made him watch.* And you broke his poor heart. The last thing your precious Nicholas ever felt was the sting of betrayal as the girl he loved brutally murdered him. And for what? Your sweet Nicky died for nothing, Aniya. A shame, too, because he's the only one who could help you now. But you have to wonder, after what you did to him, would he even bother?"

Aniya hung limply by the beams of light, her head drooping as a mixture of sweat and drool dripped from her chin to the ground. She attempted to speak, but it came out as an indistinguishable slur.

"What's that, dear?" The Director put his hand to his ear.

Aniya coughed, spitting blood into the mixture of liquid that was beginning to pool on the walkway by the Director's feet.

"I don't need him."

The Director's smile twitched as he stared back at her. "That's not what you told Roland. Bring you his body? I know what that can do for you. It's a good thing Roland is too busy dying on the battlefield and will not be able to bring you your dead boyfriend."

Aniya opened her mouth to speak, but all she could do was scream as the pain skyrocketed. She looked down at her body, which was bathed in a blood-red glow. Through the shimmer, tiny beams of white light pierced through her clothes, multiplying rapidly as her body began to break apart.

"I don't need him," Aniya managed to blubber out through her sobs.

The Director shook his head. "Anything else you want to say? Do you really want those to be your last words?"

With one final breath, Aniya embraced the agony, forcibly dragging in every bit of energy she could from the light that held her captive.

Something audibly snapped, and Aniya opened her eyes to find that the beams of light had vanished. It was another full second before she realized that the pain was gone as well.

White light swirled around her body, which was breaking apart and dissolving around her, drifting off into space and revealing pure white light where her flesh used to be.

The light slowly came upon the Director, who stared at her with his mouth hanging open as he stepped backward. As the light touched his skin, it burned away his flesh instantly to reveal a metal skeleton.

Aniya let herself hover closer to him, bringing his fleshless face even with hers, staring into his glowing, blue eyes.

"I don't need him."

She pushed his body off the walkway, letting it fall into the abyss. And with a howl that shook the cavern, Aniya exploded into a dazzling beam of white light that expanded to fill the chamber.

Aniya was everywhere and nowhere. Every inch of the cavern was laid bare before her, the rock walls with the precious uranium peeking through, the very bottom of the abyss thousands of feet below, and the unflinching blue cube suspended in the very middle of the cavern, steady and firm even as the earth broke apart around them.

"You've toyed with me for my entire life," she said, her voice shaking the rock walls as it permeated the cave. "Played with me like a game for your own purposes for too long."

The blue cube simply stared back at her, refusing to give a response.

"Not anymore."

Aniya let her light turn to a white fire that tore through the cavern relentlessly, destroying everything in its path.

The walkways crumbled, breaking apart into smaller rocks that ignited and dissipated.

Streams of green light poured like liquid from the rock walls as the uranium burned, disintegrating instantly as it touched the beam of white.

The blue cube shook for exactly one second before shattering like glass. Millions of shards of light broke free and burst into flame, disappearing and leaving nothing behind.

"Game over."

## 71

R oland slowly climbed to his feet, wincing as a sharp pain ripped through his thigh and side, just as painful as when Zeta had stabbed him.

He turned in a circle, evaluating the battlefield. It was now a free-for-all, all three armies intermingling in the valley.

The remnants of Salvador's people continued to fight bravely, throwing themselves into the fray recklessly. The Host far outnumbered Refuge's army, and their red cloaks were easily seen in the mix of black and silver.

But for every irradiated cannibal, there were three black soldiers with assault rifles.

And so, despite Salvador's last-minute arrival, they were still losing the battle, albeit more slowly.

Nicholas was still out there somewhere, strapped to the back of a dead mole that was lying in the midst of a heated battle. It would be impossible to get Nicholas's body to Aniya now, but Roland knew that he still had to try.

Roland scanned the fighters until he spotted Dawn, who was lying on the ground, holding her left shoulder and moaning in pain. He stepped over fallen enemies and comrades alike until he reached her side.

Her dirt-stained face lit up when she noticed him, and a smile appeared on her face as he knelt by her side.

"Is she gone?"

Roland nodded, burying his face into her shoulder.

"And Salvador?"

Roland only held her tighter, enjoying what he knew to be their last embrace. After a long moment, he finally stood up. "I have to go. Aniya needs Nicholas's body."

Dawn's smile vanished as Roland backed away. She grabbed his hand and pulled herself to her feet as she gasped in pain. "You're not going anywhere alone."

"I can't stay here." Roland kissed her bloody forehead as he held the back of her neck. "If I don't try, what good have we really done?"

"You don't understand," Dawn said, picking up a gun from the ground. "I'm coming with you."

Roland offered a sad smile. "You realize we probably won't make it past their army?"

"It's like you said," Dawn whispered as she placed a hand on his arm. "We have to try."

"Are you sure you want to do this? I could never expect you to come with me."

"I'd rather die trying than sit here until they kill me. Besides, I don't want to die alone."

Roland took a deep breath. "Then let's do this."

He walked over to where Salvador disappeared and picked up the only thing left of the Scourge: his massive, golden sword. Hoisting the blade over his shoulder, he looked back at Dawn.

"*Lumen ad mortem.*"

Dawn frowned. "What does that mean?"

"Death to light."

She nodded. "Death to light. I like it."

It was then that a massive explosion shook the earth, sending Roland and Dawn tumbling to the ground.

White light burst from the ground in the middle of New Washington, ripping a hole in the sky ceiling and lighting up the sector more than the sky ceiling ever could.

The light retracted on itself and receded into a humanoid form far in the distance, floating far above the remains of the Capitol, which now was in flames.

With a quieter explosion that still echoed across the valley, the figure flew toward the battlefield at an impressive speed, reaching the valley in less than a second. All fighting ceased instantly, and thousands of eyes looked up at the glowing specter.

Roland shielded his eyes from the light, and his smile returned as he beheld the glorious beauty of his brilliant sister.

"Aniya," he whispered.

"Not anymore."

Roland turned around to see Neeshika standing behind him, looking up at Aniya with a mixture of awe and fear.

"She is Lucifer, the Lightbringer." She closed her eyes for a moment, then abruptly opened them and looked down at Roland. "Where is Nicholas's body?"

Roland shook his head. "By the edge of the battlefield somewhere, toward the Capitol. Probably still tied to the back of a dead mole."

Neeshika closed her eyes again for a second and muttered, "You heard him, my children. Bring me the body of the beloved."

"Hear me now, Lightbringers." Aniya's voice boomed throughout the sector again. "Your master, the Director, is destroyed. There will be peace now, and you will no longer serve one man. You will serve mankind. You will be peace bringers and peace keepers, and you will be well rewarded. These are my terms. There will be no negotiations. Lay down your arms or be destroyed."

The valley remained motionless for several seconds.

"You have ten seconds."

Thousands of guns raised as one and began firing on Aniya.

"Very well."

Aniya raised her arms, and the sky ceiling lifted from the ground as one massive dome. Suddenly, it split into thousands of pieces and rained down on the battlefield, each section engulfed in flames.

The electronics crashed into the ground, precisely aimed at the soldiers in black armor, small explosions vibrating the ground.

Violent wind swept through the air, the sector now unguarded against the elements of the decayed earth.

Aniya raised her hands, and in response, the dying sun far above lashed out in arcs of angry red light.

The ground shook violently as an intense heat swept the battlefield, and Roland watched as several cracks formed in the earth underneath the largest clumps of black soldiers, sending them tumbling backward into deep chasms.

Finally, Aniya directed her hands toward the earth and let loose with massive beams of light, one after another, a devastating assault on the remaining soldiers.

The battlefield burst into chaos, and the Host and the Refuge army attacked with a new fury against their oppressors, their battle cries rivaling the cacophony of destruction that Aniya unleashed from above.

Roland turned to Dawn and grabbed her hand, squeezing it firmly before spinning back around and dashing back into the fray.

## 72

I t was over in seconds.

Aniya stopped her attack and spread her arms out, letting light trickle from her fingertips and spread in every direction, forming a massive dome that descended over New Washington, instantly relieving the armies below of the heat and radiation that sparked from the broken red sun above. She descended through the dome and drifted toward the ground, stopping just before her feet could touch the scorched earth.

"Aniya."

She looked up at Roland, who was staring at her with his mouth hanging open.

"Didn't think I'd make it out of there, did you?"

"Of course I did. You were fine. It was me I was worried about."

Aniya laughed, her heart feeling light for the first time in years.

Roland took a step forward and embraced her, and as Aniya wrapped her arms around him, she felt energy cycle out of her body, through his, and back into her again.

When they finally broke away, Roland looked back at Dawn, who remained several paces behind. "What's wrong?"

Dawn reached a hand out but winced and immediately pulled it back. "I can't get any closer."

Aniya bowed her head.

"What's going on?" Roland looked back and forth between Dawn and Aniya. "You can turn that off, right?"

"No, she can't."

Neeshika stepped forward, reaching a hand out in a stroking motion through the light around Aniya's body. "The light is no longer something she carries. It is her very essence."

Aniya frowned. "I know Roland can touch it and be safe, but how can you? Who are you?"

"Forgive me, Lightbringer. My name is Neeshika, but those who follow in the shadow of my shame call me Mother. I can draw myself close to you because I have spent many decades bathing myself in the light that you carry."

"Those who follow . . ." Aniya looked at Roland. "The Host?"

Roland nodded.

"Your voice," Aniya said, turning back to Neeshika. "It's familiar."

"As it should be," the woman said. "I have guided you for a long time, ever since you accepted the light all those years ago."

Aniya cocked her head. "How?"

"I have made myself one with the light, dearest Light-bringer, though not in the same way that you have."

Roland looked between Aniya and Neeshika as an unsettling feeling crept around the back of his mind. "How did you get here so fast?"

"The train. With the Underworld evacuated and the Director's attention on the surface, there was no longer any need for subtlety."

Roland cocked his head. "What made you change your mind?"

Neeshika smiled. "Salvador came to me, begging me to reconsider. He said he knew my pain, the guilt that plagued my heart. He said the only way to be absolved of this pain would be to finish what I started and finally lead my people to freedom."

"And that worked?"

"Yes, but it may not have if it were not for Aniya." Neeshika looked upon Aniya with an expression not unlike admiration. "I felt every ounce of your pain as you let go of the man you loved, giving him up along with any chance of saving him so that you might save the world. If you could face such loss to gain something greater, I decided there was no reason for me not to do the same."

Roland's confusion seemed to disappear as he looked at Aniya with what appeared to be guilt. "I'm sorry. I didn't think you could do it. That was the only reason I took that power for myself, because I thought it was the only way we could win. It's a miracle I'm still alive, and it's thanks to you. But it's all over now, and we can finally have some kind of a normal life."

Aniya looked back at Roland with a sad smile.

"What?"

Neeshika nodded. "She cannot stay. She has accepted her destiny at long last, and it is one she cannot live out here with you."

"Even if I wanted to, I couldn't, Roland." Aniya placed a glowing hand on Roland's cheek. "The whole world would end up like the Host eventually if I got too close for too long."

Roland took a step backward. "What are you saying?"

"The Director told me I was the only one who could save the world. He was right, just not in the way he believed. When I pulled him out of Nicholas's body, I saw something that gave me hope for a better future for the world, one without the Lightbringers, but one that would always have light."

"How?"

Aniya looked down at the ground. "It's better if I show you. Bring me Nicholas's body."

"Here." Neeshika whistled, and within seconds, several pale figures in red cloaks approached, carrying Nicholas's body above their heads. She held up a fist, and they halted. "A trade."

Aniya frowned. "For what?"

"Peace." Neeshika bowed her head. "My people and I have suffered for decades, unable to pass from this mortal coil. Now that we have won justice for the heinous crimes committed against us, I can be forgiven of my failures, and my children can leave this world in peace. I am absolved of my sins at long last."

She gestured toward the Host, and thousands of red-cloaked figures raised their hands, their scrawny, white arms spreading out and poking out of their blood-red sleeves in a gesture of vulnerable acceptance.

"Give them freedom, Lightbringer. End their suffering and send them from this world. Free them, and you shall have your beloved."

"Just them? What about you?"

Neeshika offered a sad, thin smile. "My work is not yet done. There are those who still dwell in the depths of this earth, waiting for me. I cannot abandon them to wander in darkness for eternity."

"The Desolates," Roland said as he visibly shuddered.

Aniya thought for a moment. "Wouldn't you rather your children live and have peace than die? We can share this world."

Neeshika's expression turned dark, and she stepped forward, lowering her voice. "This world is unsuitable for them. I do not wish for my children to suffer in the pain that will come."

"What pain?" Aniya asked as a chill ran down her spine. She looked at Roland, but it didn't look like he'd heard what the strange woman had said.

The corner of Neeshika's lips turned upward. "Thankfully, that is not your concern. Finish what you have started and let those who follow pick up their cross and find their own way in what troubling times will come."

After a pause, Aniya nodded. She splayed her arms out by her side and let streams of white light pour out from her palms, spilling onto the black valley below.

The light coursed over the ground and latched on to the feet of Host, spreading over their bodies rapidly and covering them in a web-like formation of light.

Their bodies burst into white fire and were suddenly extinguished, leaving nothing behind.

Aniya let the light recede back into her hands and sighed deeply. There was no aftermath of using her power like there was in the past. She felt no foreboding sense of fullness, no threat of overloading her energy.

"Thank you, Lightbringer." Neeshika bowed and stepped away. "Now, ascend. Your time has come at last."

With that, the Mother turned, pulled her white hood over her head, and left New Washington.

Choosing to ignore the strange feeling that crept over her heart as she watched Neeshika, Aniya knelt by Nicholas's side. She smiled as she looked over his motionless body. There was nothing else. They would finally be together now, even if it was in death.

"I'm proud of you."

Aniya turned to see Corrin walking toward her, supported on either side by a Refuge soldier and a Silver Guard.

A tear slipped down Aniya's cheek as she took a deep

breath. She yearned to give him a hug, but she knew it was impossible. So she gave him the only thing she could.

"I love you, Father."

"And I love you, Annelise."

Aniya turned back to Roland and gave him one last hug, grateful that he wasn't harmed by her light. "All I wanted was to save my brother," she whispered into his ear. "I never thought I would save the world. Not like this." She felt Roland shake his head as his tears sizzled against her shoulder.

"Not like this," he said as he backed away. "Thank you for saving me. Again."

Aniya smiled and turned toward Dawn. "Take care of him."

"I will," she replied, her hand clutching Roland's.

Knowing that she would change her mind if she looked upon their faces again, Aniya closed her eyes and picked up Nicholas's body. She stood and rocketed into the sky, leaving the world behind.

She held Nicholas close, keeping her eyes closed as they ascended past what was left of Earth's atmosphere, traveling far into space at breakneck speed.

Finally, they slowed their ascent. Aniya opened her eyes to see Nicholas's cold face drooped over in front of her, set against the dead sun behind him.

She reached into his shirt and pulled out the crystal that Kira had given her all those years ago. She had once sworn to wear it for the rest of her life as a reminder, as a promise to defend the defenseless.

When Nicholas had taken it, it had served as a piece of Aniya that would accompany him until his death.

Now, as Aniya held the glowing white rock, it meant something different. But no matter how she turned the crystal in her hands, she could not put it to words. Instead, she closed her eyes and held it close to her chest.

She could see Nicholas's face, smiling back at her in the

tank underneath the Hub. He floated in the liquid with her, staring back at her with those eyes that never failed to bring her peace. He mouthed those words again, except this time, Aniya heard them clear as day.

"I love you."

Aniya smiled and whispered, "I love you, too."

She opened her eyes and crushed the crystal with her fist. Light burst forth from the rock, swirling around their bodies as she felt Nicholas's presence cover her completely and fill her with a warm, content fullness. Taking a deep breath, she wrapped her arms around Nicholas's body and pulled him tight, letting her light burn away his flesh and bones as her own body began to disintegrate.

The light continued to envelop their disembodied selves as they joined to form one body of pure white light.

Then, they flew directly into the dead sun and exploded in a flash of light.

## 73

### ONE YEAR LATER

R oland twitched anxiously in his seat as he waited for the inevitable news to break.

"So it's decided, then." Caspian nodded firmly. "I hereby resign as interim Head Councilor, and by a unanimous vote, Corrin will act as Head Councilor of New Washington and Ambassador to the United Nations."

As applause erupted throughout the council chambers, Corrin stood and shook Caspian's hand, who smiled and pressed a button on his wheelchair, backing away from the head of the table and letting Corrin take his place.

But Corrin turned to Roland and wrapped his arms around his son.

"You should have run," Corrin whispered as he drew Roland close.

Roland shook his head. "I never wanted it, and you know it. I'm more than happy leading what is left of our people. Refuge needs me."

"You mean Triumph," Corrin said.

"Yes, you were right. It's a much better name. In any case, being their representative is all I want."

"Then congratulations, Salvador."

Roland clapped Corrin on the back and pulled away. He turned and looked at the room, which was filled to the brim with the newly instated Council and several esteemed citizens of New Washington. Though most of the room continued to applaud, many of the Overworld natives held back, eying Corrin with what looked like suspicion.

It would be a long road to fully integrate Triumph's people with the surface world, but it would be worth it. Roland didn't expect them to welcome Triumph with open arms, and it seemed like acceptance would be an uphill battle, but he knew it would eventually come.

Corrin turned and addressed the room. "Our first priority will be to finish the restoration of this city and begin sending emissaries out to the other capitals around the world. It is crucial that we have a presence in every cluster of cites to ensure that the rest of the world believes in and joins our mission of peace and transparency. The time of the Lightbringers is over. May the Era of Restoration turn back the clock on this world and give us a second chance."

As the room broke out in cheers, Roland slipped through the crowd and left the room, jogging down the stairs and stepping out into the open air.

The sun fell on his face, bathing his skin in a warmth that felt just as wonderful as it had a year ago when the sun first was reborn.

No artificial light the sky ceiling had ever created could conjure up this gentle heat that calmed his mind and filled his heart with joy.

*Speaking of joy.*

Roland turned and walked toward his house, glancing up

at the solar panel on his roof and grinning. He stepped inside the front door, and almost immediately, Dawn was in his arms.

"Did he get it?"

Roland smiled and stroked her hair. "He got it."

"Good," she said, backing away. "I was afraid they would write you in and I'd keep losing you for days at a time."

"Not anymore," he said with a quick kiss to her forehead.

The light in the corner of the room flickered for a few seconds, and Roland frowned. The solar energy hadn't been perfected yet, but he knew it was only a matter of time.

He walked across the room and picked up the stirring child from her crib. "How is my sweet Annelise?"

"She was missing her daddy," Dawn said as she wrapped her arms around him from behind. "Almost as much as I was."

Roland turned around and kissed her again. "Don't worry, I'm back now. For good this time."

"Then let's spend the day in the sun," Dawn said, pulling on his arm and running to the door. "It's a beautiful day outside, like usual. I'll never get tired of it."

Roland chuckled and followed her outside. She was right. It rained occasionally, but the weather was usually perfect. Aniya seemed to make sure of that. He glanced up at the sun. "Thank you."

He looked back down at his daughter. "One day, you'll hear all about how your aunt saved the world. One day, you'll understand how lucky you are to grow up in a world full of life. Your namesake won that for you."

"So did you," Dawn said as she laid her head on his shoulder. "We all did."

"I guess we did," Roland said, smiling. "It was a heavy cost, but it was worth every loss, no matter how much it hurt."

Dawn took Annelise and gave her a kiss on the forehead. "Yes, it was. Their sacrifices will not be forgotten."

As his wife walked toward the park with his daughter, Roland looked up at the sky.

"This was you, Aniya. It was all you. This world didn't deserve you, and we will forever be in your debt. I only wish you were here to see what you've done."

Roland closed his eyes and basked in the warmth of the sun again.

"Thank you."

With that, he opened his eyes and joined his family.

# EPILOGUE

Aniya opened her eyes and found herself in the void again. She took a deep breath and nodded slowly. She would have to get used to it this time.

This time, she was here for good.

But this time, it was different. Aniya felt power stirring within her still. Every other time, she was a prisoner of her own mind, trapped, powerless.

This time, the void was hers to command.

Aniya closed her eyes and let the world come to life.

Solid ground filled in the empty space under her feet.

Grass sprang up from the fertile soil and poked between her toes.

Wind whistled through the branches of trees that erupted from the ground around her, whisking over her face with cool, pure air.

The splash of water sounded as a lake to her side formed out of a cavity in the ground, funneling into a brook that babbled nearby.

Aniya opened her eyes and was delighted to find that all this and more had indeed filled the dark void around her.

"Is this for us?"

Aniya froze as a voice came from behind her. She dared not turn around for fear that he wouldn't really be there.

"It's beautiful."

Her lips trembled as she forced herself to stay facing away from the voice. It was a voice she heard in her nightmares. A voice used by nothing more than a computer program. A voice that the Director had stolen for himself.

But it was different this time. It was . . . real.

Several seconds passed, and the voice did not speak again. Finally, Aniya mustered up the courage to turn around.

There he was. Her best friend, her only love.

Aniya's hands flew to her mouth before she knew what she was doing.

Nicholas, dressed in a white tunic and trousers, smiled at her and approached. His fingers grazed Aniya's elbows, and she melted at his touch, sinking forward into his open arms, her white dress flowing loosely and grazing his legs.

"How are you here?" she whispered as her arms found their way around his torso. "Where have you been? I thought you were dead."

"Maybe I still am. Maybe you're dead, too. Maybe you brought me back to life. Does it really matter?"

Aniya shook her head fiercely.

"I couldn't see a thing after I died. I've been in a world of black for as long as I can remember. The first thing I remember seeing is being with you beneath the sun right before everything went white. But I heard everything that Omega did. I heard everything that the Director did, using my body." He looked down. "I'm sorry."

"It wasn't you, Nicholas. I know that." Aniya spoke muffled words into his chest, refusing to let go of him.

Nicholas stroked the back of her head, his fingers running between her hair. "Wherever we are, whatever we are, I'm here now, Annelise. And I'm yours if you'll still have me. I know you don't need me anymore."

"I don't need you. I don't think I ever really did." Aniya pulled back for the first time, only to smile at him. "But I want you. I want you more than anything else."

"Then I'm yours."

He leaned in toward her face, and Aniya nearly jumped forward to meet his lips, wrapping her arms around his neck as she kissed him with a passion that had burned for years.

They were together at last, and Aniya knew they would never part again.

## To Be Continued...

## THANK YOU

Thank you for reading *Lightbringer*, the third book in the *Light Thief* saga and the conclusion to its first trilogy.

But the adventure isn't over. The saga continues with the story of the Uprising, the legendary war that set Aniya's tale into motion.

Please consider signing up to an email list that will notify you as soon as the next book is released! If you do, you will also receive a free book that recounts William's story in the events leading up to *The Light Thief*.

Go to jdavidwebb.com/free-book and sign up for the mailing list to be notified of all new releases and special offers, and you'll get a **FREE** copy of *The Saboteur*.

I promise not to fill your inbox with spam or share your contact information with anyone, ever.

### Enjoy this book?
### You can make a big difference.

If you enjoyed *Lightbringer*, the single most helpful thing you can do is leave me a review on Amazon. To explain how grateful I would be for this would take another hundred pages.

Suffice it to say that I can't afford to take out an ad in some big-name newspaper. You probably haven't seen a billboard with my face on it. If you've met me, you're probably grateful for that.

But while big publishing companies are buying out digital signs on Times Square and forcing raunchy books in your face every time you leave the comfort of Gmail, there is something much more powerful that money can't buy. Reviews.

Honest reviews of my books help bring them to the attention of other readers.

So, if you wouldn't mind, take about 30 seconds to leave a dazzling review encouraging others to check out this book! How? Just go to your Amazon order history and click "Write a product review."

Thank you,

David Webb

# UPRISING

Get it now!